The Q

Book 4

Peter Meredith

Fictional works by Peter Meredith:

A Perfect America
Infinite Reality: Daggerland Online Novel 1
Infinite Assassins: Daggerland Online Novel 2
Generation Z
Generation Z: The Queen of the Dead
Generation Z: The Queen of War
Generation Z: The Queen Unthroned
The Sacrificial Daughter
The Apocalypse Crusade War of the Undead: Day One
The Apocalypse Crusade War of the Undead: Day Two
The Apocalypse Crusade War of the Undead Day Three
The Apocalypse Crusade War of the Undead Day Four
The Horror of the Shade: Trilogy of the Void 1
An Illusion of Hell: Trilogy of the Void 2
Hell Blade: Trilogy of the Void 3
The Punished
Sprite
The Blood Lure The Hidden Land Novel 1
The King's Trap The Hidden Land Novel 2
To Ensnare a Queen The Hidden Land Novel 3
The Apocalypse: The Undead World Novel 1
The Apocalypse Survivors: The Undead World Novel 2
The Apocalypse Outcasts: The Undead World Novel 3
The Apocalypse Fugitives: The Undead World Novel 4
The Apocalypse Renegades: The Undead World Novel 5
The Apocalypse Exile: The Undead World Novel 6
The Apocalypse War: The Undead World Novel 7
The Apocalypse Executioner: The Undead World Novel 8
The Apocalypse Revenge: The Undead World Novel 9
The Apocalypse Sacrifice: The Undead World 10
The Edge of Hell: Gods of the Undead Book One
The Edge of Temptation: Gods of the Undead Book Two
The Witch: Jillybean in the Undead World
Jillybean's First Adventure: An Undead World Expansion
Tales from the Butcher's Block

Chapter 1
The Day Before

The day that Eddie Sanders had been dreading for the last four years dawned just as he imagined it: cold and grey with a cutting wind that stole past his robe and rippled down the back of his silk pajamas. Still half-asleep, he pulled his robe tighter across his thin chest, yawned without bothering to cover his mouth, and lit his cigarette.

He took no pleasure in the taste. It tasted like sin and betrayal.

Eddie smoked exactly one cigarette a day and he always smoked it first thing in the morning on his front stoop. The habit had started as an excuse fueled by his rabid paranoia. What if someone saw him come out every morning and look directly southeast across the sound? He didn't have a dog to watch as it hunched out a turd onto his lawn, and he couldn't pretend to be fetching the morning paper since there were no more morning papers.

What if they did more than just notice him come out every morning like clockwork? What if they asked him why? The first time he might say it was because he liked the view and the second time he might have gotten away with checking the weather even though their weather always came from the northwest. But how long would these flimsy excuses hold up?

That's why he smoked the cigarettes even though he detested them to no end. And he had to actually smoke them; there could be no pretending because if someone saw, it would lead to more of the same sort of questions.

In those first couple of years he'd been paranoid about everything and had walked around with his heart racing and his blood-pressure at dangerous levels. It got so bad that he could feel his pulse in his eyes. The fear and the paranoia reached a high point after the first year; then it gradually faded. Things looked like they were going to return to normal. Then Gina got pregnant and the fear grew so bad that it kept him up at night and he walked around with hollows under his eyes and a constant sheen of sweat on his forehead.

If he'd been caught before, well that was that. They would kill him and Gina, and it would be deserved. But little Bobby was an innocent and there was no doubt he would suffer as the son of the only traitor in Bainbridge's history. "The sins of the father..." was something he had muttered every morning during the pregnancy as he toked away.

The paranoia gave way to the joys and trials of parenthood and Eddie looked exhausted for another reason for a good six months. Once the baby began sleeping through the night, Eddie had regained some peace. He still wrote his reports concerning the state of Bainbridge's defenses, their food and ammunition stocks, and their political divisions, none of which had changed all that much in four years. And he still picked up the bullets that were left for him; what he called the wages of sin.

So little had changed for so long that Eddie nearly missed the signal. The smoke drifting up from the Alki Point Lighthouse, across the chilly, still waters of Puget Sound formed a wavering grey feather rising against the backdrop of the grim morning. As if in a trance, he stared at it until the cigarette scorched the ginger hair from one of his fingers.

He dropped it and, without caring if it burned down the island, went inside to where Gina was scrambling eggs with Bobby practically glued to her wide hip. She wore one of Eddie's t-shirts and compared to her velvety dark skin, the shirt was a sharp white. "I have to go," he told her. "Now."

"What? But your breakfast."

His stomach was beginning to churn and it would only get worse. If he ate, he would puke...and if he puked, people would ask why. He glanced at the windows, all of which seemed far too open...far too transparent. "It's the signal."

"The sig..." She drew in a sharp breath and went stiff. She too glanced at the windows. "Are you sure?" she asked, yanking shut the drapes that hung over the kitchen window. Forgetting the eggs, she went to the dining room window and shut the drapes there as well. "It could be just a normal fire, you know. It could be some of the bandits making breakfast. We don't know."

Before she could close up the entire house, Eddie grabbed her arm. "Maybe, but I doubt it and we can't just ignore it. We have to, you know, proceed like it's real." He found his breath starting to run in and out faster and faster. He tried to control it by forcing himself to relax; however, the more he fought to control his breathing the more his hands shook. "And that means we have to act as normal as possible. If something, you know, bad happens we can't have anything point towards us. We have to be normal. Got it?"

Suddenly Gina didn't know what normal was. She felt like puking and crying. She felt like hiding or packing a bag and running away— these felt like very normal responses just then. "But what do they want?" Her dark eyes were huge and unblinking. "You-you-you've been giving them the stuff, right? You never missed a single month. They know that, right?"

Eddie began re-opening the drapes. He didn't know what the Corsairs knew beyond the handwritten notes he left in the drop-off spot every month. The reports had so much sameness to them that after the first, he didn't think they were worth one bullet a month, let alone ten. "The papers are never there the next month so that means someone is picking them up."

"Then why do they want to see you now?" she asked in a high, squeaking voice. She began bouncing Bobby on her hip, her agitation making it like a ride on a mechanical bull for the toddler. "Eddie, they may be done with you. Have you thought about that? They may be tying up loose ends."

This had crossed his mind and he hadn't been able to dismiss it. What Gina didn't seem to realize was that she was a loose end as well. She was the reason Eddie had turned traitor in the first place. She had been caught and it had been her screams which had led to the entire six-person scavenging team being captured or killed. Only the fact that they were husband and wife kept them from being butchered like the others. Their love had been used against them and it wasn't long before they were both begging for the chance to turn against the people who had taken them in and protected them.

"They aren't going to kill me. It's something else, trust me." For the first time in his life, he actually wanted one of the nasty smelling cigarettes. He lit one, coughed out blue-grey smoke and then dragged in deeply.

Watching his hands shake and his face turning as red as his hair, Gina wasn't reassured in the least. "They-they-they are going to kill you," she stammered. He shook his head and was about to go on, uselessly trying to make her feel better. She would never feel better about any of it. She snapped her fingers and hissed, "I know they're either going to kill you or make you do something that'll get you killed."

In answer, Eddie took another drag, sucking the glowing embers right down to his knuckles again. "Yeah, well," was all he could reply.

"Yeah, well, nothing! Don't go, Eddie. We're safe here."

He loved her too much to laugh in her face. They weren't safe. His reports, written in his hand and signed by both of them, were all the evidence needed to convict them of treason. They'd be executed and Bobby would grow up and forever be the traitor's son.

"We're not safe; we're stuck, at least for now. But if we can hold it together for a few more years until Bobby is bigger, maybe we can figure a way to get out of this." By that, he meant running away and starting over. It was a scary thought. Nowhere on the planet was safer than Bainbridge and, as far as anyone knew, it was the only place with running water and electricity.

The two had gotten used to the amenities as well as the "free" ammunition. It wasn't a lot, but it made everything that much easier. They had a good life and now...

"I have to go," Eddie said, kissing her and Bobby.

She wanted to say more; she wanted to throw herself at his feet and beg. It would be useless, she knew it. She told him she loved him and then took Bobby into his room and sat on the floor while he waddled about sticking brightly colored hunks of plastic in his mouth.

Eddie left five minutes later, an M16A2 in one hand and his pack over his shoulder. He smiled and waved to the people he considered to be his closest friends, however his throat was so dry and constricted that he couldn't manage a proper hello to any of them.

Danny McGuinness, the night harbormaster, watched him heading towards the dock. McGuinness didn't bother getting up from his chair. He was the fattest man on Bainbridge, and the most bribable. "Boats are gone. You were too slow, Eddie. Early bird and all that."

There were three boats still at the dock: a barnacle-covered rowboat with peeling paint and six mismatched oars that was kept for emergencies, a strangely bloated, twelve-foot sailboat, and finally the *Calypso*, which hadn't been touched for weeks and was scheduled for auction.

"What about the Scamp?" Eddie asked, gesturing at the oddly fat boat.

McGuinness turned stiffly to give it a glance. "Right, the Scamp. Sorry to say, it's reserved. You know how it goes. I'd let you have it, but there'd be arguments and bad feelings. I wouldn't want anyone to get bent out of shape for *nothing*."

His emphasis on the word nothing meant he'd let people get bent out of shape for *something*. He was looking for a bribe. Eddie's eyes flicked to the smoke rising across the sound. It was very faint. Would the Corsairs wait? Likely…for a little while, but frequently the harbor boats were gone for hours.

And yet a bribe would raise the reddest of red flags. If anything big happened, McGuinness wouldn't hesitate to spill the beans about Eddie. *I got to play this cool*, he thought. Aloud, he said, "Maybe I can catch a ride. Who's got it reserved?"

McGuinness leaned as far forward as his gut would allow to whisper, "Mason and that little 'partner' of his. You just know they've beed doing it on the side. It's downright scandalous is what it is, seeing as he's married and all. Oh, he thinks he's fooling people, but he ain't. Not in the least."

Eddie never liked gossip, and just then didn't have time for it, either. Once more his eyes strayed across the Sound; the smoke was only a wisp. Time was running faster and with it went his racing heart. If Mason really was going out with his mistress, there was no way he'd want Eddie tagging along. A bribe was Eddie's only option.

"Sounds very scandalous," Eddie said, shaking his head. "I don't think I want to be a part of any of that."

"Damn skippy," McGuinness replied, scratching the undercarriage of his ponderous belly. "You know, he asked for the Scamp in particular." Eddie didn't need the raised eyebrow to guess why. Bainbridge possessed only a handful of boats, none of them larger than fifteen foot. Because of its deep design, the Scamp was the only one with an actual cabin. It wasn't very large, barely long enough for Eddie to stretch out in and he wasn't the biggest of men. It was big enough for some hanky-panky, however.

"Yeah, it's a sad situation all right," Eddie said, playing up sorrow he didn't feel. "We should do something. You could let me have the boat and say there was an error with the paperwork."

McGuinness looked as though he had expected exactly this reply. "I don't know. Maybe for a couple of Nines I might fudge the reservations a bit." Nines were small silver coins that were in fact, backed by 9mm rounds sitting in the Island's armory.

Two Nines was a lot of money for a bribe of this nature. Eddie threw his hands up. "Half a Nine, and I don't know why I would even pay that since we're trying to do some good here."

This line of reasoning was lost on McGuinness who was only interested in doing good for himself, but Eddie stuck to his guns and got his price. In exactly two minutes and four seconds, he had the Scamp's sail up and was pulling through the harbor gate. He didn't look back as he swung the Scamp south on a heading that would take him three miles south of Alki to the same little church where he dropped off his reports every month.

Like the rest of the city, the little church was in a state of advancing ruin. Its stained-glass windows were now only a litter of multicolored glass on the floor, its roof leaked in seven different spots, and there was mold growing in profusion, climbing up the corners of the walls and making everything look dirty.

"Hello?" he called out in a carrying whisper. The church was tomblike in its coldness. Eddie, his body beginning to tremble, drew his camouflaged coat around him more tightly. "Hello? I came alone and…" He put his M16A2 down on a pew. "I'm unarmed."

He stood with his head cocked waiting on a reply, however the only sound was a steady drip, drip, drip, coming from somewhere behind the altar.

"I came as fast as I could. Hello? Hello?" After a minute, he realized that he was alone. His body stopped trembling immediately; his stomach however began to churn. Did this mean he was too late, and if so, what would they do to him? Would they expose him? He thought about calling out even louder, but knew it would have been foolish. There were too many zombies roaming around Seattle to make himself a target.

With no idea what he should be doing, he picked up his rifle and went to the seventh pew on the right, shuffled sideways along it until he was midway down and stuck his hand beneath the wooden bench. This was where he left his reports and picked up his payment. Instead of bullets he found a small black bag. Inside was a razor blade, a handwritten note, and a glass vial, filled nearly to the top with some sort of black fluid.

The note was nothing more than a set of instructions; a road map that led straight to hell. Once he read them the trembling set in again. "Oh, God," he whispered, clutching his stomach. He was about to vomit. He could feel it happening in slow motion. Swallowing hard, he yelled out, "I can't do this! Do you hear me? I can't and I won't!" The louder he became, the more his fear turned to anger. They wanted him to kill…no, assassinate, Neil Martin. It didn't even say why. If there was a reason, even an iffy reason he might consider it, but Neil seemed like a nice guy.

"I'm not doing it," he muttered as he strode from the church. Almost immediately, the fear settled back into his bones. He tried to fight it by getting stupidly loud, and he raged, "I'm not doing it!"

His voice echoed through the city streets which only brought the fear on stronger. Anything could be listening—and anything had been. He had barely made it up the block before he saw one of the lumbering beasts heading his way. It was eight feet of terrifying death.

Quickly, he slunk down and scampered to the nearest building: an old Mexican restaurant. It was a dim, low-ceilinged place with chairs and tables flung about, some bearing the claw marks of zombies. Seeing them made Eddie hesitate. He squinted around at the shadows just to be on the safe side, though he was almost certain there was no one or nothing in the…

Eddie jumped as one of the shadows moved.

It was a man, half wrapped in a black cloak. The cloak hid most of his face; only a set of hard, dark eyes shone out from the shadows. "What are you not going to do?" the man challenged in a harsh whisper as he limped closer. He was oddly twisted and humped. His right arm bulged with steel muscles, while his left was stunted and withered. Because his left leg was shorter than his right, he walked and stood in a hunch.

These deformities did nothing to make him any less frightening. Eddie tried to summon what bravery he possessed, only just then he saw that the man had his hand wrapped around the shaft of a black axe. It was an executioner's axe. Eddie swallowed loudly, which made the man's dark eyes crinkle.

"Take it from me, friend," he said in that growling hiss. "You'll do what you have to. You do or you die. It's the one constant in our world."

Eddie couldn't feel his body. Ungovernable fear turned him completely numb from head to toe. This had to be the Corsair who had given him the vial and the razor blade. This was the man who could destroy his life. This was the man who could send him and Gina to the gallows and ruin Bobby's life before he was out of diapers.

The twisted man looked like he would enjoy it, too.

"I'm sorry," Eddie said. "I'll do it, I swear. Just don't hurt my family." Eddie fled without waiting for the man to reply. He had his instructions and he would follow them to a T if it meant never having to see the man again.

Chapter 2

Standing in the doorway of his house, Neil Martin bent and picked up the razor blade. The sharp edge was wet and black as oil, the rest of it gleamed in the starlight. He stared at the blade, with slowly blinking sky-blue eyes. His mind was moving at an even slower pace and it took longer than he would later care to admit before it hit him.

"Someone's trying to kill me. Jeeze…lou…ise." His chest was suddenly very tight, like someone much bigger than himself—and most men were—was squeezing the breath out of him.

It was a stunning concept to think there was an assassin somewhere out there in the dark, probably watching him, and more than likely, quietly laughing. Did the assassin have a gun? Was he even then peering through the scope of a sniper rifle? Neil could easily imagine the crosshairs centered on his chest, which only made his lungs constrict even more.

Twitchy as a squirrel, he started casting useless glances into every dark patch surrounding his little bungalow, looking for the killer. As it was night, there were many places an assassin could hide, especially if he was done up in proper ninja-wear, complete with a samurai sword, which was how Neil pictured him.

It was, of course, preposterous, but so was the idea that anyone would want to kill him. It was crazy. He was a nobody. In fact, nobody tried harder at being a nobody than Neil Martin. Ever since coming to Bainbridge a decade earlier, he had purposely faded into the background of life on the island.

Few people knew anything about him and even fewer knew the things he was capable of. Most people thought of him as the weird little guy who controlled Jillybean. She was weird and he was weird—it seemed like a good pairing. But beyond that, he kept to himself and didn't bother anyone.

In other words, he was a harmless, sweater-vest wearing man who wasn't a threat to anyone. So why would someone take the risk of trying to kill him? That was the question that kept him rooted in place, his panicked mind spinning in slow useless circles.

A distant part of him knew he should be flying into action, but that was the nature of panic. It almost always led one to do the wrong thing, the counterproductive thing. Instead of racing inside to clean the wound, he wasted precious time picturing ninjas stalking him in the shadows, at the same time as imagining himself as the most innocent man since Ghandi strapped on a pair of sandals.

"What if they have the wrong guy?" he whispered, grasping at the thinnest of straws. "Or the wrong girl?" That straw was far thicker. What if they were after Jillybean? With the night and being bundled against the cold, Neil guessed that he and his adopted daughter were somewhat similar in appearance. They were roughly the same height and each was blue-eyed and pale.

If someone was after Jillybean, Neil didn't need to strain his panic-stricken mind to guess why. Revenge. The one word was no solace to Neil. Revenge was a form of insidious insanity. From first-hand experience, he knew that someone hell bent on revenge could not be reasoned with. Fear and love meant nothing to them. All that mattered was their unbridled hate. The last time someone plotted revenge against Jillybean, dozens of people were killed in the crossfire.

He could still remember how the nerve gas had contorted their bodies into grotesque twisted shapes, and how their faces were such a dark purple that they looked black. The images were so horrible that his fear was quickly turning into a full blown panic attack.

Pain lanced deep into his chest and he began to struggle to breathe as a new thought struck him: *What if that wasn't zombie blood on the razor blade? What if it had been the liquid form of VX Gas?*

The idea was ridiculously farfetched, but that didn't stop him from standing there uselessly gazing back and forth from the razor blade to his cut hand, his mouth hanging open as he waited for the nerve agent to twist his body into a pretzel. When it didn't, he actually let out a frightened, semi-relieved chuckle. As bad as the zombie virus was, it was nothing compared to the horror of the nerve gas. That moment of relief finally got him moving.

Neil scooted inside and slammed the door behind him—it rattled in its frame. For some reason, the cheap lock and the thin door made him feel even more vulnerable. He ran for the Walther PPK that he kept in his nightstand and with it clutched in his mangled left hand, he went around his house pointing it at every corner and twice nearly shooting the same coat that hung on a hook near the downstairs closet.

Within minutes, he had every light in the house blazing and had locked doors and windows that had never been locked. Only when he had turned his cottage into the world's flimsiest fortress did he look again at his bleeding hand. The cut was small, less than an inch long, but it was deep and bled freely.

"That's a good thing…I hope." *Perhaps the flowing blood would wash out some of the germs,* he thought. He was grasping at straws again. No one knew if cleaning a wound like this did anything to save a person, but it didn't hurt to try. He flung himself down the hall to the kitchen sink, where he held his hand under scalding hot water. When he couldn't take the searing pain any longer, he grabbed the bar of soap and scrubbed the laceration as hard as he could stand it.

After a minute, he rinsed his hand under the same scalding water. "Son of a motherless goat, that's hot!" he cried.

His hand was now a vibrant pink, except where the blood trickled. For the moment it was still red, but would it remain that way? Would it turn sludgy and black, and flow like a stopped-up sewer pipe? "Why the hell did I use soap?" he cried, flinging the bar away. No one had ever trusted soap to stop the zombie disease. Some said bleach might work and others swore by kerosene. Still others thought that the only chance a person had in a situation like this was immediate amputation.

Neil's eyes shot to the knife rack where the largest knife he owned was a serrated bread knife; as bread was rare even on Bainbridge, he'd had precious little opportunity to use it and there was a line of rust along the edge. The knife was out of the question due to the simple fact that he was too much of a wimp to cut off even the tip of his pinky, let alone an entire hand.

He decided to go with the bleach. All he had under the sink was Ajax—and it stung. He wasn't the most physical of men and it showed as he had to hold back another scream and tears leapt into his eyes when he poured the white powder over the wound. "The pain means it's working," he told himself, making up the "fact" on the spot. Despite the tears, he was desperate enough to scrub through the pain.

Five minutes later, his eyes were as red as his hand, and the wound was as clean as he could make it. Now he could do nothing but wait for the fever and the rancid sweats; the mind-numbing pain and the nightmare deterioration of the self.

There was a chance that none of that would occur.

Twelve years before he had been the first-ever recipient of the zombie vaccine. *Guinea-pig* was a much more accurate word than recipient since he had been given a trial version of the vaccine against his will. The "test" that followed: being bitten by a real-life zombie, had also been against his will.

One might assume that a person who'd been vaccinated against the virus wouldn't have anything to fear at all, and Neil had lived for years happily believing that he was immune. Jillybean had ruined his blissful state of ignorance by casually mentioning that vaccinations weren't necessarily foolproof.

"Sometimes viruses mutate," she said in that infuriating way of hers in which she made a smart person feel stupid. "Sometimes a little and sometimes a lot, depending on the pathogen. It's almost a guarantee that you're going to need a booster shot at the very least." She had gone on, as she always did when it came to science, going into what seemed like needless detail, but he hadn't really been listening. Missing those details felt like a big mistake at that moment.

He found himself staring at the small cut, half-expecting the edges to begin turning grey and for it to start bubbling out black pus. It was so disconcerting that he covered it with a band-aide—a Mickey Mouse band-aide. He had found a big box of them under the sink when he had moved in years before.

Now the overly happy face of the mouse was a little disturbing. He tried to put the cut out of his mind, but it nagged at him even as he began worrying over the assassin again.

Was he still out there, lurking? Perhaps ready to finish the job with his sniper rifle? Neil's imagination began to get the best of him as he pictured a black-garbed assassin with deadly eyes, hoisting a long, sleek rifle to his shoulder and peering into a high-tech scope. The imagined scope could easily see Neil's heat signature through the thin walls of the bungalow.

And if it could see through the walls, it made sense that it could shoot through them as well.

Neil wasn't proud of what he did next. With a stifled cry, he dropped to the ground and crawled behind his bed. He didn't crawl under it, which for him was a win. For three minutes he lay there expecting to be shot before it dawned on him that the assassin didn't need to shoot him at all since he had been infected with the razor blade.

"Jeeze louise," he grumbled, getting to his feet. He felt stupid and frightened and sick to his stomach. And embarrassed. He had never been a tough guy or a hero of any sort, but he had lived through his fair share of dangerous situations and had, quite literally, laughed in the face of death.

That had been years before when he was still young. Now, he was forty-six, middle-aged, with a hint of a gut and grey in his hair. His mettle hadn't been tested since Jillybean and he had fought their way out of a bandit chieftain's lair—lucked their way out of it was probably nearer to the mark.

Luck had always been Neil's gift and he'd had need of every ounce of it to get out of that fight alive. Whenever he thought about that night, he cursed his luck. He had lived while another man, a much better man, had died. It had been his best friend, Captain James Grey; the toughest man Neil had ever known.

Sometimes Neil felt as though he sucked the luck from people around him, but now he was alone and for the first time his luck had failed him.

"I'm going to die," he said to the empty house. It was as strange to hear as it was to say; even stranger was the calming effect the realization had on him. Nothing he or anyone could do was going to change the fact that his death was only hours away. "*Maybe* only hours away."

Saying that didn't feel strange, it felt like a lie.

"So, what do I do?"

He knew what he wasn't going to do and that was sit, trapped in his own home. There was an assassin on the island and he had to be dealt with. Neil glanced down at his gun and only just realized that there wasn't a magazine in it; he'd been running around with an empty gun. "No one needs to know about that," he whispered, hurrying up to his nightstand for ammunition.

Once he was properly armed, he slipped out the back door of his house and stood in the dark, gun in hand, waiting for his night vision to kick in, and for his breathing to slow. Although he told himself that getting shot would be a mercy, his body just wasn't buying it. His hands were trembling so badly that the gun would be next to useless if he had to use it.

The emptiness of the night calmed him. The cold and the lateness of the hour were keeping most people inside; Neil was alone as far as he could tell. This was entirely what one would expect *if* one was thinking straight, that is, and Neil finally was. The assassin would have lurked somewhere close by just long enough to make sure Neil cut himself. Then he would have zipped out of there.

But to where?

His mental image of the assassin was of a stranger dressed in black. A stranger wouldn't hang around the island so that meant… "The docks!" he cried. He almost took off at a run, but then remembered how sadly out of shape he was. "A bike is faster, anyway."

Five minutes later, he came huffing up to the small man-made harbor. He threw down his bike and pulled the Walther from his coat pocket. "Who's on duty?" he demanded. There were always two guards and the night harbormaster. Neil knew McGuinness wouldn't come out of his shed unless forced to.

The guards were Todd Karraker, who always wore a splash of vibrant red with every outfit because he thought it made him stand out, and Steve Gordon, whom everyone called "Flash."

"Who is that?" Todd asked, coming forward, his rifle still strapped to his back. "Is that you, Neil? What's wrong?" Even with the dark he could see the gun in Neil's hand and the wild look in his eyes.

"Has anyone picked up a boat in the last twenty minutes?"

Todd shrugged and shook his head at the same time. "No. Why? What's going on? You don't look good." Not that Neil ever looked good, Todd thought. His face was a mass of scars from some long-ago accident. There were plenty of rumors whipping about how he had gotten them, but no one knew for sure.

Neil touched his face with his mangled left hand. He was missing his pinky and had only a nub where his ring finger should have been. "It's um…it's um…I just need to know if anyone's picked up a boat. Anyone strange."

"No, no one strange. It's only been the usual night fishermen and the last one was Renee. She left at like seven or something like that. They'll be trickling back here soon enough. So, um what's going on?"

"I'm not sure except, maybe, someone got on the island. I want you to lock this place down. I don't want anyone to leave no matter what, and I want every boat searched when it comes in. Got it?" Todd, now looking good and nervous, nodded. Neil turned to go but stopped. "You better take that gun off your back."

Todd blanched. They'd had intruders on the island before, almost all of whom were smugglers or immigrants who didn't know the right way of going about things. The smugglers were stripped of their goods and escorted off the island; always without violence. This was the first time the harbor had been locked down and judging by how pale Neil was, something bad had happened.

Neil left the harbor and biked to the Governor's residence. It had been only an hour or so since he'd had dinner there, yet the house was dark and silent. He had his gun out as soon as he stopped the bike. This time he laid the bike carefully on its side, its back wheel turning lazily. It had suddenly occurred to him that maybe he hadn't been the only target of the assassin.

He crept around the mansion, his fear once again ramping up. This time he was able to control it, which was a good thing for the Governor's bushes threw off shadows that resembled crouching, nefarious-minded people. As he went around the perimeter, he very carefully checked the doors for razor blades.

There were none, which was more of a relief than he realized. When he finally came back to the front door, he was sweating through his clothes. "I guess it's just me they were after," he said, just before he rapped on the door. The sound echoed inside the high-vaulted rooms, making the place seem completely deserted. For just a moment, Neil's blood-pressure spiked. Then a light turned on somewhere in the house and the soft, delicate sounds of a girl's bare feet came to him.

It was Emily, the Governor's daughter, and Neil's goddaughter. She was twelve and fatherless. Her dad had been none other than Captain Grey. In many ways, she was her father's daughter. She even moved like him.

"Like a ninja," he said to himself, with a smile. The word ninja made him think of the assassin and the smile faded. He could still be out there with his razor blades and his zombie blood. "How many other people is he targeting?" There was no way to know, but at least Deanna and Emily were safe. Their doors were clear. He hadn't checked the windows, but they would only be a danger if opened from the inside.

And what were the chances they would choose to open a window right then? No. If the assassin had gotten inside, he would have trapped the door...the inside of the door.

Neil suddenly froze with the soft patter of footsteps coming closer. They were right on the other side of the door.

Chapter 3

"Don't touch the door!" Neil shouted.

There was a pause in the pattering steps. "Uncle Neil? What's wrong?" The pause was short-lived. Emily was coming closer, worried about him. He could picture her reaching out and...

Neil did the only thing he could think of, he threw himself at the door, hoping to break it down. Doors were replaceable—not by him, of course. Neil had a good deal of trouble just working a can-opener, and wasn't much better with hammers and screws, and such.

Replacing the door turned out to be unnecessary. It was his shoulder that was in need of service after he slammed into the door, bounced off it, and fell down the steps of the porch.

"Uncle Neil? What was that? What's wrong?" she asked again. He could tell by the timbre of her voice that she had stepped back. He could also hear Deanna hurrying down from the master bedroom.

Jumping up, he went to the door and shouted through the crack, "There's been an...incident and the doors in your house may not be safe. Keep your mother away until I can figure something out." By that he meant something better than dislocating his shoulder. The window was an obvious choice of egress—maybe too obvious. "I'm being stupid," he muttered. The assassin probably wasn't a genius. This thought had his mind straying to Jillybean. If she had been behind this, Deanna and Emily, and maybe half the island would have already been infected. "Now I'm being more stupid...or is it stupider?"

"Neil," Deanna asked from her side of the door. "Tell me what's going on. Why can't we touch the door? Is it, Jillybean?"

"I don't think so. I mean, I really doubt it. Someone glued a razor blade to the bottom of my front doorknob, and it..." He bit off the part about the zombie blood because of Emily. "It might have been a prank but because of, you know, tetanus, it's best to be careful."

Deanna was quiet for a few moments. "The knob looks fine in here. I don't see anything."

"Check for a needle," he said, quickly.

"A needle? Neil, what's really..." She stopped suddenly and then in a slightly higher voice, she said, "There's nothing here. I'm opening the door." She opened it slowly, carefully. Light from the foyer spilled out onto Neil. Although his jaw was resolutely set, he was pale and trembling. The look was even more unsettling than the fear she had heard in his voice. It had been many years since she had seen Neil look like this. It gave her the shivers and she drew the lavender robe around her tighter.

Her gut told her that this was more than just some awful prank with a razor blade. Jillybean's face floated through her mind, and for good reason. She had always been at least slightly crazy and the things she did in that school of hers were downright chilling. But what that had to do with razor blades or needles, Deanna didn't know.

She was about to ask Neil to come inside when Emily darted forward. "A razor? Who would do such a thing? Was it rusty? Aunt Jillybean once told me to be exceptionally careful around rusty metal. Was the razor rusty?" As usual when Emily was excited, she spoke so quickly it was hard to follow. While Neil was still trying to figure out which question to answer first, Emily grabbed his hand.

He yanked it back with a savage: "Don't!"

"Don't be such a baby," she replied, unfazed by his raised voice. Despite his scars, Neil Martin was the least scary person on the island. "I just want to take a look."

Neil kept his hand to himself, clutching it against his thin chest, not so much as protecting his hand as he was trying to protect Emily.

"I think I better talk to Uncle Neil in private," Deanna said. When Emily was gone, Deanna asked, "What's really going on?" He told her everything in such a rush that he was breathless afterwards.

She stared at him, searching for any sign of the zombie virus. "How do you feel?"

He was scared out of his wits, but she wasn't really asking about his mental state. "It's only been a half an hour or so. I feel okay and, and, and I might stay that way. The vaccine might still be good."

"I'm sure you will be," she told him, giving him her best politician's smile. The expression had come out of habit and it was gone again before he could be reassured in the least. She sat down behind her gleaming desk and drummed her manicured fingers on the polished wood. "Who would do this, and why? Jillybean? Is it possible she's back?"

Neil quickly denied the likelihood that Jillybean was involved. "Impossible. For one, she's not like that. She's not a murderer, and if she were, this was too simple, too crude. If she'd had anything to do with it, you could bet it would be elaborate and foolproof. And if it was Eve, she'd be here gloating. She'd want to watch me die slowly."

Deanna agreed. "I suppose that tracks, but it still leaves our questions unanswered. Have you pissed anyone off recently?" It was almost a joke of a question. Neil was small, polite and gentle. He kept to himself and never made waves.

"I don't think so. It's been a long time since I had anything like an enemy, but when I did, they were pretty fierce. I think revenge might be a possible motive."

"Yeah," Deanna said, commingling the word with a sigh. "If it is revenge, we should be able to find the kill…I mean the intruder relatively easy." *He's not going to die*, she told herself. "Ours is a small community and if there is someone haunting us from our past, they will stand out and be caught, quickly." Once again she gave him that practiced politician's smile of hers. This time she put some of her charisma into the smile and Neil was visibly relieved. Not by a great deal, but enough that his pallor looked less pronounced.

She was happy that he felt better because she didn't. A new and terrible idea had crept into her mind: *What if there was an actual killer on the loose?* Not an assassin, but a murderer or a serial killer. Someone like Jack the Ripper or Typhoid Mary.

A psycho could be hiding in plain sight; it could be anyone. And what was there to stop them from killing again? Nothing. The island lacked even the basic investigative tools to catch a killer. They had no polygraph machines, no way to take fingerprints, and they were basically in the dark ages as far as DNA was concerned.

Before the idea was fully cemented in her mind, she was mentally clicking down a spur of the moment checklist of all the "sketchy" characters on Bainbridge. As nice as the island was, it wasn't perfect and neither were the people who lived there. Not that there had ever been anything as bad as this.

"I want you to stay here," she said getting to her feet. "Take the guest bedroom and lie down until…"

"No," he said, cutting her off. "We need to get things moving ASAP. It won't make a difference if I'm lying down or running around. If I'm going to die, it's going to happen either way." He was still weak in the knees and his stomach was twisting as though he had just eaten a gallon of pistachio pudding, but he thought it would be better to be around people than lying in a bed endlessly picturing his skin turning grey and his eyes going black and his brain burning with a fever that would eventually destroy it.

He was so resolute that she gave in. Before they left, the two turned on every light in the mansion, barricaded the doors and made sure that Emily updated and armed. She wanted to go with them to find the assassin but was shot down by a two-to-one vote.

"Do not open the door for anyone," Deanna instructed her. "If someone comes, they can talk through the door."

She and Neil then left, each with their weapons drawn. They headed straight to the little harbor where they found McGuinness huddled in his shack holding a shotgun against his round belly. "Ring the alarm bell," the Governor ordered him.

The bells had never been rung at night, mainly because they had never been rung except for the monthly drills, which were always known about well in advance. "What's going on?" he asked, breathlessly.

"Someone…perhaps an assassin, perhaps even more than one, might have gotten onto the island," she told him.

McGuinness's morbid curiosity drove him to ask, "Did someone die?"

Although Neil's presence next to her seemed to increase until he loomed like a giant in her mind, Deanna forced her eyes to remain fixed on McGuinness. "This is not the time for gossip and rumors. I will make an official statement eventually, but now, please ring the bell." Her warm politician's smile was out of place on that cold, dark night, and McGuinness gave her a queer look as he took up the hammer.

McGuinness was nervous. He didn't like how the focus was on him. He had too many secrets and was running too many illicit side schemes to be comfortable with a midnight inspection or whatever this was. With a glance at the Governor and her little mutilated friend, he rang the brass bell, slowly and without the urgency Neil felt he should.

"Give me that," Neil said, and grabbed the hammer. He pounded frantically on the harbor bell: *Bang! Bang! Bang! Bang!* The harsh sound coming from it was pure fear. For ten long seconds, it was the only bell ringing, then others began to take up the call. Every tower had a bell and soon they were all ringing.

Lights began to blaze in every home and very quickly people were rushing here and there, arming themselves and heading to their battle stations. Most people went to the wall where they asked the universal question: *What's happening?* Others went to the armory, to the clinic, to the communications center, or to the schools where the children were being gathered.

Everyone had a place, including Gina and Eddie. Since the birth of Bobby, Gina's battle station was in one of the childcare facilities. Eddie's was on the Fast Response Team, which was supposed to respond to any point of the wall that was threatened. Just then he was the one who felt threatened. He had not expected the alarm.

The sound sent a shockwave of panic through him. "They're after us," he hissed as he slunk to the living room window and pulled the curtain shut.

Gina was doing the same thing with the other windows. Eddie didn't think a person as dark as Gina could turn pale, but she was now an ashen grey color. "What do we do? Do we try to run away? That's our only choice, isn't it? We should maybe cause a distraction and then steal a boat and go. I'll get our bags." She ran off just as Bobby began to cry. The bells had woken him.

The idea of running away had been with him all day, but instead he had chosen to commit murder for her and the baby's sake. "No, we can't run," he said in such a weak voice that she didn't hear him. She came racing out of the basement with two suitcases.

"What did you…Oh, Lord, Bobby's crying. How are we going to keep him quiet when we…"

Eddie grabbed her arm. "We're not running. If they find out, I'll just say it was me. I'll say you had nothing to do with it. It's the only way, Gina." Her mouth fell open. She had already said this was out of the question, but now that they were at the point where the rubber hit the road, she knew it was the only way.

"You're going to have to denounce me," he went on. "You're going to have to spit on me."

"Never."

A tired laugh escaped him. He knew she would do more than just spit on him if it meant protecting Bobby. She was a good mom. In anguish, she left him, carting Bobby on her hip. She went to the nursery to be with the other moms, while he shouldered his M16 and tromped off to where he met the Fast Response Team. He was the last to arrive.

The fifty men and women formed five lines of ten and were counted off to make it official. The newest recruit was then sent off at a run to report that their headcount was at one hundred percent. Then came an hour-long wait in which everyone sat around speculating why they were there. The theories ran the gamut from over-the-top speculation to one suggestion that made Eddie freeze in place: "Maybe they caught a spy and are looking for more of 'em."

This wasn't the worst jolt he would suffer that night.

The darkness was driven back as the searchlights were turned away from the Sound and pointed inland. They focused their harsh, white beams on one square quarter mile at a time, starting at one end of the island. Hundreds of people, including the Fast Response Team, descended on each small section and searched every inch of it. Houses, sheds, garages, bushes, and businesses were scoured top to bottom before the locust-like searchers moved onto the next area.

Eddie searched as diligently as anyone. He worked both tirelessly and conspicuously so that no one could question his loyalty. For two hours, his team moved north along with the others. The houses looked different under the glare and at one point, Eddie didn't realize where he was or whose house he was searching until he came face to face with Neil Martin.

The two stared at each for nearly half a minute before Neil cracked a tired smile. "Hey Eddie." Guilt hit Eddie so hard that he couldn't respond. He could only stare at Neil, looking for signs that he was turning into a zombie right before his eyes. "You okay?" Neil asked. "You look kind of pale."

You, too. The thought just popped right into his head and was immediately followed by such intense shame that Eddie turned away and was simply going to run out of the house, however he knocked into Governor Grey. "Sorry, sorry," he whispered, unable to raise his voice.

The Governor was as pale as Neil. Grim and pale and angry. She didn't seem to have even noticed Eddie. "Is that it?" She pointed past him.

Eddie suddenly knew where he was. This was the house Neil shared with Jillybean. This was where Eddie had become a murderer. Against his will, he followed her pointing finger and saw the razor.

It sat on the kitchen table, the blood on its edge turning blacker than charcoal. There were half a dozen people in the room and they all stared. That the diseased blade was the opening salvo in a war was the furthest thing from their minds.

Although the Black Captain's lair was only fifty miles away as the crow flies, it was two-hundred miles around the horn by sea, and it was even farther to the desolation of San Francisco Bay where the Queen reigned. The war that had raged there for weeks might as well have been fought on the dark side of the moon for all they knew of it.

The blade filled each of their minds and yet not one of them understood, not even Eddie.

"Yeah," Neil whispered. "That's it. That's the weapon that killed me."

"You don't know that," Deanna insisted.

But Neil did know. The headache had begun twenty minutes before and now he could feel the fever. He could feel sweat trickling down his back. He could feel a blind anger building in him and he had to quash it before he said something inappropriate. "Trust me, I know." He passed a shaking hand over his face and, not wanting to see the pain in Deanna's eyes, he turned and found Eddie staring at him in horror.

"I guess the secret's out," Neil remarked. Eddie jerked in reply, but with his head pounding, Neil didn't think anything of it. He clapped Eddie on the shoulder. "Find me the guy who did this, Eddie. We have to find him and stop him before he kills again."

Eddie wanted to insist that it would never happen again, only that would be a lie. He and his family were still in danger. In fact, they were in more danger than ever. "I-I'll do what I can."

"You're a good man, Eddie."

Neil couldn't have been more wrong.

Chapter 4

The little girl with the scabby knees, the dirty, pale-yellow sundress and the fly-away brown hair took center stage. In her left hand she held a thick manuscript behind her back, while with her right, she made a flourishing gesture and mounted a paint-spattered ladder.

All eyes were upon her. There were hundreds of sets of them, each staring with fixed, unblinking vapidness. *They are spellbound,* she thought to herself, *as well as they should be.*

"Romeo, Romeo, where art you?" she called out, projecting so that her piping voice carried to the furthest member of her hand-picked audience, which happened to be a brown teddy of great age and solemnity. He was so venerable that some of his seams had opened up along the sides of his sagging, slouching belly and she'd had to poke the fluff back in.

I'm down here, her "Romeo" replied. Playing opposite of her was Ipes the Zebra. He was sitting squarely on his script, looking down between his floppy hooves at the words. *I don't really see where we're at,* he whispered. Much to her annoyance, he was sitting on the wrong page.

She kept her smile fixed, flourished again with her right hand and quickly turned to look at her script. Her smile turned into a grimace; just as she suspected, it wasn't even his turn. She still had lines to speak.

Oh, wait. I see something about a sword fight. Are we doing the sword fight?

"Not yet," she hissed out of the corner of her mouth. In her stage voice, she announced, "Yes, you are-est down thither. But maybe you should deny your-est father while you are a-yonder. And also be my sworn-est love and I will no longer be a Capulet."

Jillybean figured this was as fine a bit of improv that had ever graced the stage of Meridian Elementary School, but strangely, the audience remained silent. "They really must be spellbound," she muttered.

That's some spell. Maybe the spell puts them to sleep with their eyes open.

"Zip it," Jillybean warned. "Your line is…" She turned away from the audience, took a quick look at the script and said, "Shall I hear more, or shall I speak at this?"

That's not my line. My line is…where are we? Romeo, blah, blah, blah…What? Mercutio dies! Whoa. I did not see that coming.

Jillybean, a fixed smile in place, cleared her throat, warning the zebra to quiet down. "You want-est to hear more-est? Okay. Tis but thy name that is my enemy; Thou art thyself, though not a Montague. What's Montague? It is nor hand, nor foot, nor arm, nor face, nor any other part belonging to a man. Oh, be some other name! What's in a name? That which we call a rose by any other name would smell as sweet."

She paused, partially because that was one of the best parts and partially because the crowd roared in approval. Half the chairs in the auditorium were filled with stuffed animals she had collected over the course of the evening. There were teddies staring up at her, and giant pandas, which were in a class separate from teddies and thus had a row all to themselves.

There was a row for the bird class: flamingos and parrots and penguins. Another for amphibians: turtles, frogs, and one mislabeled hippo. One row was for dogs, half of whom were beagles, and another for fish, though most of these were smiling dolphins and they weren't even fisheses at all, no matter what Ipes said. The very back row was for the singular sorts that didn't have their own category: a T-Rex sat at one end and a giant, fluffy spider sat at the other.

Neither Ipes nor Jillybean could understand why anyone would want to have a stuffed spider as a toy, but since there were seats to fill, he had been included and had been a perfect gentleman from the very beginning.

The roar from the assembled toys was not the soft, polite clapping that it had been when she had first come on stage. No, this was loud and raucous. It was way too undignified for the theater.

"Do you mind?" she demanded, with a great deal of indignation. She was all set to end the play early when it dawned on her that the sound was coming from outside the school. "What is that?"

Jillybean, hold on, Ipes called to her as she monkeyed down the ladder and leapt lightly from the stage. *I found my spot. Ahem. Juliet is the east where the sun is, and...wait, Jillybean! Come back!*

She wasn't listening. Her once pink Keds were a blur as she hurried up the aisle, past the glassy-eyed stares of the stuffed animals. The sound of the cheering was drawing her on, pulling her faster and faster until she slammed through the double doors of the auditorium and found herself on the wide, flat roof of a building.

All around her were strange, wild men in stained black clothes. Most of the men were tinged blue-green from face tattoos, however those that weren't had shaggy beards and long hair. They were Corsairs...no, they used to be Corsairs. Now they were her men.

Although her heart began to jackhammer and her stomach started to ache, Jillybean did not react outwardly to this sudden change of perspective except to glance down at herself. Gone were the knobby, scabbed knees, and the Keds and the sundress. In their place, she wore thigh-high black leather boots, soft black yoga pants, a button-up black shirt and a three-quarter length black leather coat that she had belted tight against the cold.

Just about the only things about her that resembled her tiny, six-year-old self, were her dead-white skin, her lamp-like blue eyes, and her fly-away hair.

Her hair was being whipped by a fiercely cold wind, but the wind wasn't the reason why she shivered. In front of her, three men were being tortured to death. They were spies and it was necessary.

She was queen and yet she hadn't dared to give any other order than for the most hideous torture, followed by a gruesome butchering of the prisoners. For a dozen years, these men knew only the worst debauchery and deprivation known to humanity. They did terrible things, horrific things and they told themselves that it had been necessary to survive. In their black hearts they knew for a fact that evil was a more powerful force than goodness and kindness.

But they were not completely without laws. The straight-up murder of fellow Corsairs was illegal, stealing was frowned upon, and the usual petty differences between people were almost always settled through savage fights. The Black Captain had allowed no *unnecessary* killing of women and children, though both could be raped almost at will by their owners.

Non-Corsair males were usually tortured and killed in the most heinous fashion imaginable, though this too was subject to strange whims and sometimes they were impressed into the Corsair ranks and made to murder and rape to earn their chance to live.

All of this was abhorrent to Jillybean, despite her reputation for both unbridled insanity and cold ferocity when dealing with her enemies. She hated everything about the scene playing out in front of her. It made her sick and frightened. The mental anguish of having to witness such brutality had sent her away to a happier time when she and Ipes had played and danced and sung songs. She had come back to reality and was hit once again by the horror of her world. With all her might, she wished she could flee back into herself, but that was not something she could control. By definition, if she could control her crazy she wouldn't be crazy.

Not that the spies didn't deserve torture and death. According to all the rules of warfare dating back many thousands of years, it was all they deserved. The three men had information that could conceivably imperil the lives of her people. It was all the reason she needed.

Jillybean remembered giving the order and remembered making the painful decision to watch, knowing that if she hid from the barbarity of it, she would lose face. The next thing she knew, she was back in that elementary school, putting on a play. That first performance had been a bit of a fiasco, but by the third show, she and Ipes had worked out the kinks.

That had been a good time in her life. Sadie was still alive and Estes Park was safe. Deanna was still with Captain Grey and little

Emily was growing inside of her. And the biggest threat to all of them was a thousand miles away playing the lead role in Romeo and Juliet.

She couldn't exactly say this was a good time, not with the screams of the tortured spies ringing in her ears and the smell of their burning flesh in her nostrils. The picture playing out in front of her eyes was horrible and she tried to watch and not watch at the same time. She let her eyes lose focus so that everything was a blur. The other buildings around them became grey and indistinct, while her cavorting soldiers took on a ghostly appearance.

The screams and the acrid stench were still there, but she let them wash over her as if they were part of an old memory. Sadly, she had many memories in which such things dominated and she fully expected her mind to send her back to one of them. It would not have been a relief if it had. In so many of them, she was the cause of the pain.

At least here and now she couldn't blame herself. Spies knew what they were getting themselves into. They knew the risks well ahead of...

It must be nice to absolve yourself so easily.

Jillybean did not flinch, did not stiffen, did not react in any way. Her eyes remained unfocused and everything was still a blur, except one man: Ernest Smith. The bounty hunter's vanilla, overly average face shone clearly through the crowd.

You could stop this if you wished. Even if she wanted to respond, which she didn't, she couldn't, while she was surrounded by her men. Her madness could only be allowed to go so far. *Speaking of being crazy,* Ernest said, *some of us are getting a little cooped up in here. It's always Sadie and Ipes who get to come out and play. When's it going to be my turn, or Eve's?*

Hopefully never, was her first thought, then she realized that he was out now.

This isn't out. This isn't real. I want to be in charge, Jillybean. I deserve it. I created your empire for you. Without me, where would you be? Huh?

"I would be exactly right here, right now. You forget you used my mind. You couldn't have done anything without..."

Just then, her chief lieutenant, Mark Leney glanced back, his smile dying on his lips. "Did you say something, your Highness?" This was his way of reminding her that she was talking to herself. Leney sometimes found himself in a difficult and dangerous position. He knew that Jillybean would be appreciative of the reminders, but there were other "people" inside of her that hated to be reminded of the fact, one of whom had pulled a long-bladed knife from out of nowhere and threatened to open him up on the spot if he mentioned anything like that to her ever again.

"Just thinking out loud," Jillybean answered. "Thank you, however."

Thank you? Ernest began chortling. *Jillybean, he's a pet. You don't thank a pet unless he brings you your slippers.*

She let her mind wander past his words, and she did not ignore Ernest as much as she endured him. Just like with the screams, she let the words coming from his nasty mouth wash over her. The screams and the words mingled together to form meaningless static and once more she let her eyes blur until the carnage in front of her reformed into a curtain of perishable grey.

Time lost meaning as did the static-filled world of grey she had built. A frightened hand touched her. "Your Highness?" It was Leney again, worried who he was going to wake.

She broke from her trance and very slowly cracked her eyes, not certain where or even when she would find herself. The sun was barely up and they were still in the dinky town of Petaluma, where the thirty-seven mile chase had ended. The three spies had fled on foot up the sluggish, mud-slogged Petaluma River, hounded by two platoons of her soldiers. The spies route had been obvious from the beginning since everything to the west of the river was barren ash from the fire Eve had started weeks before, and everything to the east was overrun by zombies.

With their route a near certainty, Jillybean had taken the *Hell Quake* and cut them off after making a landing on the coast west of Petaluma and racing inland. The chase had been exhilarating; the capture less so. Now, she was sitting on a high-backed chair that looked as though it belonged in someone's dining room and not on top of a four-story office building.

"I think we got everything we're gonna get out of them," Leney said. He was down on one knee; the way she had taught him.

"And that is?"

Because of his scars and the many tattoos covering his face, expressions were hard to come by with Leney. For the most part, he looked either angry or very angry, with shades of one or the other thrown in for good measure. Jillybean read this particular shade to mean he was nervous.

"I won't shoot the messenger," she said, trying to calm him.

"Well, it's just the Captain knows you and he knew you were down here before we all got here."

Jillybean remembered the way Phillip Gaida hadn't reacted to her name when she had come aboard the Sea King. He had not been surprised by her presence. "So, there's a spy among us."

"Not among *us*," Leney replied, with the indignation of one bearing the mantle of moral superiority. "It's one of your people. Your other people, I mean. The Hill People or the Islanders or whatever... your Highness." She said nothing to his little faux pas, she only raised an eyebrow and waited for him to go on. They had tortured the three for well over an hour and she hoped for their sakes they had gotten more information than just that.

"Okay, yeah. They also said that we're losing men. They've seen four little groups heading north. One guy says it was twelve men total, the other two said fourteen. The first group has a full day head start. They know everything. Those groups, I mean. The torpedoes, the smoke bombs, how many people we got, everything."

He hissed all of this out, not because it was a secret he was keeping from the other guys, but because he was scared, and he was afraid people would hear it in his voice. The Black Captain was a holy terror. His very name invoked such a feeling of dread that even his captains would piss themselves if it was whispered they were under his scrutiny.

The Queen looked at him blandly. "I don't see why you are so worked up. So far you haven't told me anything that I didn't already know or suspect." She gazed over the top of his head at the others, standing in little knots around the tortured spies. They all looked scared, except the one man who didn't belong. He didn't belong among the living because he was really burning in hell.

You know why I'm not scared? Ernest asked. *Because the Black Captain can't kill me. Like you said, I'm already dead. Ha-ha! But the rest of these guys are crapping themselves because they can see how you've shrunk. When I was running things, I had it all under control. I didn't go off into some fantasy world and leave Sadie in charge. Jeeze, Sadie! She's useless. No, she's worse than…*

Jillybean forced both her mind and gaze away from him. Ernest was right about one thing: her ex-Corsairs were suddenly all nervous. They watched her uncertainly as she strutted forward into their midst. She walked through them until she came to the three tortured spies. There was blood and bits of them everywhere and yet they were still alive, staring at her in frightened misery. Militarily sound or not, the sight of them was sickening and sad in equal measures. The doctor in her saw they had no chance; the burns, the loss of blood, the many, many lacerations would all lead to septicemia which would kill them in three to five days.

"If I actually thought they would live, I would let these fellows go." As expected, her men looked shocked at the idea. A few were comically over the top in their astonishment and a new picture of them formed in her mind: dirty, bearded men wearing brightly colored Easter hats and with large strings of pearls around their necks. *Oh my!* they cried in high falsetto voices as they fanned themselves.

She snorted laughter and said under her breath, "Not now, Ipes." The zebra's chuckles echoed in her mind as if her head was not just vast, but empty as well.

"Yes, I'd let them go. Not out of the goodness of my heart, but because I want them to crawl to the Black Captain and let him know exactly what he's dealing with. Why? Because I want him to fear us. I want him to be afraid of our torpedoes and explosives. I want him to lie awake at night dreading the coming black smoke and I want him afraid of the death he will find in it. I want him afraid of us!"

The men began nodding, their fear dissipated. They were weak men, governed not by principal, properly adjudicated laws, or a higher morality, but by the extremes of the moment. If everyone around them seemed angry, they were angry. If everyone was nervous, then they were nervous. They were followers, perfectly willing to rape, torture and kill as long as they weren't expected to possess and express true independent thought.

She turned back to the chair that had been brought to the rooftop for her. "Tell me, Leney, did you get any useful information from them?" she asked, sitting primly before the half-dead men and her barbarous crew. Leney gave her a look that she read to mean: *Huh?* "Did you ascertain the exact size of the Black Captain's remaining fleet? The strength of his army? His intentions? The names of the spies on Alcatraz? How do they communicate with their handlers? Did you get any of that?"

"No, sorry," Leney said, hanging his head. "We tried, okay? But the Captain doesn't really work that way. He keeps everything in its own separate box. That's how he says it. And only the people who are supposed to know what's going on with each box are allowed to look in. Those guys know more about you than they know about the Black Captain. The only thing we really know is that they were supposed to be heading north to Bodega Bay to check in."

"What do you know of him, Leney?" she asked, catching him off guard. "You were one of his captains, you must know more than the average sailor."

He shrugged. "Well, sure. I know some things. His army is still a lot bigger than your...ours. And his fleet is larger, but they don't have better boats than us. He sent all his best boats to destroy you." Leney saw the Queen's blue eyes turn frosty and he quickly added, "He could've sent them all and you still would have beaten him."

This was a false bit of flattery which she didn't correct, instead she waited for him to go on, but he only shrugged a second time. She tried not to look disappointed; it would have set a bad tone. "Alright. Let's dispose of them and head to Bodega Bay. If we swing around from the north, we'll look like any other Corsair boat."

She was halfway to the stairs leading down when Leney asked, "How do you want it done?" He had a knife out and used it to point at the spies. *Humanely* was the first thought that occurred to her. She knew it wouldn't go over well.

Before she could come up with a response that would satisfy, one of her soldiers said, "Sticky Jim has a good i-dear. Well, ack-sually it was both our i-dears since I brought up the whole apple bid-ness in the first place."

"Apple business?" she asked, her stomach beginning to flutter.

"Oh yeah. You ever seen one of them apple peeling gizmos? You put the apple on it and spin it round and round, and the knife part skins the apple." He grinned showing off a smile that had as many teeth as the average jack-o'-lantern.

What he was suggesting was horrible and yet she had a duty to destroy the Corsairs. They were such a threat that the ends justified the means. A week before, her soldiers and sailors had been Corsairs. They would have gladly killed innocent people to save these very same spies. Jillybean had to find ways to divide her people from the Black Captain's. There had to be "Us" and "Them." Horrible as it was, the sickening deaths would help in the long run.

"Go ahead," she told the man as something inside of her laughed and something else cried. She turned around and headed back to her chair.

She never actually made it. Her vision blurred, only this time the world did not go grey, but instead went a dull brown. When she blinked, the brown solidified into a real physical mass. Confused, Jillybean reached out to touch it. The mass was ridged and formed of thin lines, millions of lines.

"What is it?" she heard her own piping voice ask.

It's crazy is what it is, Ipes replied. He had his bulbous nose pointed way up so he could see as much of the thing as he could.

Jillybean had to agree. *It* was crazy. She looked at the faded plaque once more. *World's Largest Twine Ball!* it read.

Beneath the headline were the facts—Francis A. Johnson spent four hours a day for twenty-nine years wrapping twine into an immense ball that was, according to the sign, forty-feet in circumference.

"Huh." It was pretty much all that could be said. Although words could easily describe the ball, the *idea* of it was immense. A man literally walked in circles for hours every single day for decades with nothing to show for his efforts except the ball and the plaque.

It was the epitome of a wasted life in Jillybean's opinion and right on the spot she vowed that she would do something great with her life. Had she known the terrible things she would have to do to become great, she would have begun rolling her own ball on the spot.

Chapter 5

Sea water as grey and cold as the morning light washed over the decks of the slowly sinking *Captain Jack*. It wouldn't be much longer before she went down. Pockets of air trapped in the cabins were the only things keeping her afloat, but now the wind was picking up and with it came growing waves.

In the east, the sunrise was a baleful red. In the west, it looked as though night would endure far longer than scientifically possible. A storm had built up overnight and now looked ready to fling itself on the stricken boat.

Jenn Lockhart could see the gunwale, the cresting, white-capped waves and the storm, and nothing else. This was a great improvement of what little she had been capable of seeing all through the night: circling stars in an ink-black background. That was when she had been certain she was dead. She had drunk poison, after all and, logically speaking, death generally followed closely on such an action.

All night her soul had been trapped in an unmoving body—her own body she supposed, though she had no way of knowing. She hadn't been able to feel the body and only guessed she was in one by the heart that beat seven or eight times a minute. It had been soft at first, barely noticeable. Now, it was faster, maybe going as fast as thirty times a minute, though to be honest, minutes meant nothing to a dead person.

Then the sun had risen and her perspective had changed. *Maybe I am still alive.* That brought both hope and fear. Dead people had no need of either. When the waves came a few minutes later, she realized, with her fear gaining momentum, that she was on a boat. An abandoned boat she figured, given the fact she hadn't felt a single vibration coming up through the hull that couldn't be attributed to the waves.

I'm alive, but paralyzed from the top of my head on down. Great. Thanks for nothing, Jillybean. This was her doing. It was simply another of her tortures to endure. Jenn was just wondering how long she would live like this, cast adrift and paralyzed, when the first wave splashed over the gunwale. The boat rocked and her head on its limp string of a neck cocked over to see the waves washing over the railing.

Fear grew to panic. The boat wasn't just abandoned, it was sinking! *I'm going to drown*, she thought, the words filling her mind with ghostly echoes. Her vision began to grey until she realized that she was going to faint. The idea was so absurd that just thinking how ridiculous it was staved it off.

Another wave thudded into the boat. Its cold waters rushed across the deck, picked Jenn up and dragged her towards the gunwale.

She thought she was going over the side and she screamed: *No!!!* The sound of the scream never left her head. *I have to do something, but what? I'm paralyzed and that means…*

Just at that moment she realized that if she really were paralyzed she wouldn't be able to feel the water. *It's temporary. Good. I just need to get better before I drown.* But how? She decided to take inventory of her body. She tried to wiggle her toes, bend her knees, flex her thighs, and move her hands.

Her left calf twitched at her command, lifting her heel slightly. That was it. Relief flooded her and with good reason; she was *not* paralyzed and already she was far advanced in her ability to move than just a second before. She tried again to move her different parts, this time straining with all her might.

The leg moved again, which was good, and her left arm unkinked slightly at the elbow. This would have been great if it had not come with a grating pain as if there was a build-up of rust in the joint. There was no time to worry over that, however. Another wave washed over the floundering boat and slid her right to the edge of the deck.

One foot hooked a post of the gunwale and her shoulder hit another, keeping her from flowing overboard like some sort of long dead squid. *Another try!* she demanded of herself and made to move all of her muscles at once. Her back spasmed, her elbow bent and her left foot pointed...all of which was accompanied by a new and torturous pain in her joints.

The pain was so great that it almost made drowning preferable. Almost. A wave brought her to the brink and she saw she was on the edge of the ocean. It stretched away forever. If she went in, she would never be found. A horrible thought. With her entire will she forced her muscles to move. The pain was as immense as the ocean and she heard a cry.

It had come from her own lips.

Another wave and she would have gone over the side and out to sea, but she willed her left arm to crook around a post. The move saved her, for the moment. Her legs were now dangling in the water, dragging her down. Her fear blotted out the pain and she focused everything on her right arm now. The fingers at the end could only bend part-way, however she could crook her elbow almost halfway and with a new cry she hooked it around the same post.

Even with this, she sank lower. The water pulled at her and her lower body was all but useless. She flailed spastically with barely functioning legs; her still limp feet sliding uselessly along the fiberglass hull. Her muscles were weak from the poison and she could feel herself begin to slip. "No," she whispered as a new wave smashed into her back and her right arm fell away.

The boat spun in a slow circle and for Jenn it was like the second hand on a clock and when it reached the twelve o'clock position, the waves would hit her square again and she would slip away forever. Hope left her completely only to be revived a moment later as Mike Guntner suddenly appeared at the rail. The poison had changed him. His face was a wild pink color and seemed to have swollen up; his lips were covered in white foam that bubbled greater with each of his ragged breaths; worst of all were his eyes. There was blood where the whites should have been.

He looked like he was dying.

"Hold…on," he whispered and reached out a knobby, clawed hand. The fingers of the hand were weak as a child's and as stiff and unbending as the branches of a dead tree. Still, he tried to grab her. The pain was immense. It ran from his fingertips, up his arm through his shoulder and radiated down his back.

Mike whimpered as he whispered, "Help me. Kick…or…pull."

With her body still kinked and broken, Jenn could do neither. Mike's hand fell away and now the weight of the water was tremendous. It was like she was trying to haul the entire ocean back onto the boat.

Once more Mike tried to save her. This time he stuck his useless hand under her coat and shirt and up along her arm as far as he could push it. Then he pulled—and screamed. The pain was outrageous and yet he pulled back with all the strength left in his body.

Thankfully, Jenn was small and slim. Even soaking wet, she was light, and had he been at his full capacity, he could have picked her up with ease. Now, it was a struggle. It was one of the hardest things he had ever done in his life and when he finally got her on board, he was shaking and crying unabashedly. No one knew his pain, no one could understand, except Jenn, who was also weeping.

She was trying to curl into a ball. Her body hurt less that way.

"No!" Mike hissed. "Get up. We have…to keep…moving. Or we'll…die."

"It feels like I already died." She hadn't budged from her fetal position and Mike was forced to straighten her by hand…or by claw since his fingers were still hooked. He started with one of her arms, bending it at the elbow. He groaned and she screamed. It hurt them both, equally. It felt like glass had been crushed up and injected into their joints.

Instinctively, Mike knew they had to keep moving and not just because of the poison. They were also on the verge of freezing to death. As he worked her arms and shoulders and legs, he stared about at the *Captain Jack*. She wasn't going to make it. The new fiberglass patches hadn't been given enough time to dry. She was leaking like a sieve and with the storm coming on, she wouldn't last another hour.

"Where the hell is Stu?" he wondered. His first attempt at "looking around" had been an abbreviated twist of his upper body along a very short arc. With the possibility that Stu might be going overboard as well —or already drowning—Mike turned even further. Nothing hurt worse to move than his back and neck, so his resemblance to an old, rusting cyborg was uncanny.

Stu was lying near the bow, his dark eyes open but unmoving. "Get up, Jenn! Stu needs us."

In abject misery, she rolled onto her front and crawled after Mike who had stumped over to Stu and was kneeling next to him, shaking his shoulder. "He's cold," Mike said.

Jenn had touched far too many corpses over the last couple of months and now she was touching another one. Stu wasn't just cold and stiff, his flesh was disagreeably hard. As she was numb, save for the grinding pain, the shock of his death was less than she would have thought. She turned to Mike and laid her head on his lap and found that he was just as cold.

She touched his arm and it too was hard. *Maybe we're all dead*, she thought. *Or all alive.* "Stu!" she screamed as loudly as her feeble lungs would allow. When he didn't budge, she put her ear to her chest and listened. At first it was like listening to the side of a brick wall, but then there came a faint *lub...dub.*

"Stu!" she yelled again. "Mike, he's alive. We gotta move him like you were moving me."

"No, you have to do it. I have to keep us from sinking." Although both Stu and the *Captain Jack* were about to go under, he knew her job was going to be infinitely easier.

The pain in Mike's joints doubled, then tripled as he stood and went to the mast. Slowly, hand over hand, he raised the sail that he had replaced three days before. Tying it off, he went to the wheel and put the sailboat before the wind. Their only chance was to keep the storm on their stern and run before it.

A laugh scraped up out of his throat at the word "run." The *Captain Jack* wallowed in the surf like someone had stabbed a mast into the carcass of a forty-foot whale and he was being asked to pilot it. Still, he had no choice. The sinking boat swung around until it was pointing at the sunrise. A groan escaped the mast as the sail filled.

With luck, Mike thought they had an hour before she went under—unless he could find some way to bail out the water. "I need a bucket," he whispered. A bucket was a laughable idea. Even if he wasn't feeling weaker than he had ever felt in his life, and even if he wasn't shaking with hypothermia and barely able to stand on his own feet, trying to bail out a boat with gaping wounds in its hull in the middle of a storm using only a bucket was preposterous.

Besides, he didn't have a bucket. He had been in charge of towing the *Captain Jack* ashore and getting her hoisted, which had only been possible by emptying it out completely. The cabins and all the cubbies had been emptied.

"Breathe harder, Stu!" Jenn yelled.

Mike gazed dully at them for a moment, noting that Stu wore work boots. Mike pictured himself trying to bail using one of them. It was a terrible idea. A part of him wished Jillybean was there. He knew she could turn the boot into some sort of hydro-magnetic water lifter. She was the genius, not him...so why had she labeled the cubby next to the wheel *EMPTY*? It was her meticulous handwriting. No one alive had handwriting as neat as hers.

And why weren't any of the other cubbies marked in any way? Instead of dissuading him from opening it, the sign prompted him to fling open the door. It wasn't empty. Sitting on top were two tightly coiled garden hoses. Crammed beneath them was a small black plastic drum with two stubby knobs for attaching hoses to and a handle that cranked round and round.

At first Mike thought the drum was for coiling the hoses around, then he saw the label: *Hand-Powered Water Pump.* Excitedly, he read the small print: "Blah, blah, blah. Inlet and outlet can be reduced using standard ABS...blah, blah. Oh, holy crap. Ninety gallons a minute? How is that possible?"

It was possible using an electric drill, which Jillybean hadn't included. "Still, this is something."

What that something was, turned out to be pure torture. Just getting the hoses attached was pain like he couldn't imagine. His hands were brittle from the cold and the poison. He cried out as he threaded the hoses to their couplers.

"Are you okay?" Jenn asked.

"Yes," he said through his tears; he made sure to face away from her. "How's Stu? Is he alive?"

Jenn looked down at Stu and wanted to cry as well. Stu wasn't responding no matter how much she called his name or how diligently she worked his limbs. She guessed that he had been poisoned much more than she or Mike. As the vial of poison had been very small and Jillybean had said that only a few drops were needed, she had made sure to take the smallest sip so that there would be some left for the others. Mike had done the same thing.

Stu had probably finished it off and now he was neither alive or dead. "He hasn't changed," Jenn said.

"Keep going," Mike told her. "We don't have a choice." For the foreseeable future, death was going to be their only available option in pretty much every circumstance. If the boat sank—they would die. If they couldn't get to shore by nightfall—they would die. If they couldn't figure a way to get warm in the next hour, they would die. And so on.

Because of this, Mike gritted his teeth and worked through the pain, getting the hoses connected and turning the wheel. Water came rushing out of the export hose and seeing it, spurred him on. Twenty-two gallons came out in that first minute.

Another two-thousand to go, he thought to himself, just as a wave broke over the stern. At least twenty gallons rushed down into the hold. He cursed with the strength of a hundred-year-old man. It came out in a grumbling, under the breath mutter as he kept the pump handle turning.

On and on he went without looking up, without feeling anything but the pain of each rotation. The shards of broken glass bit into the ball of his shoulder and the joint of his elbow; it ground along his back and his neck. He pumped hundreds of gallons of water over the side of the boat and hundreds poured back in. The storm was picking up and heaving them along. It was hard to tell exactly in what direction. The wind had become chaotic, sometimes hitting them from both front and back simultaneously. As well, the sun was hidden by such heavy clouds that he might have been traveling in circles.

Direction didn't really matter, however. The ocean had become violent, with the waves rising to greater and greater heights. If one of the waves hit them side-on, they would capsize—and if they capsized, they would die. Mike was in the terrible position of having to do two separate things at once. He had to bail or they would die and he had to man the wheel, or they would die.

"Jenn! Is he alive?" A disgusting thought hit him: *If Stu is dead, then Jenn can pump, and we might live.* Ashamed, he cranked the pump harder, groaning as he did. With the storm, he didn't hear her come panting up, dragging Stu behind her.

"I'm alive," Stu said, in a slurred voice. "Unfortunately."

Mike looked up to see the sturdy Hillman, looking like a cast off rag-doll. His eyes were as red as Jenn's, but he was white as snow otherwise and his limbs were limp.

"Toss me over," he whispered. "You know you have to."

"We won't!" Jenn said. She knelt next to him and was already trying to pump his arms at the elbow once more. It made a crunching noise as if there really was glass in them.

With his head back, he grunted. "*She* would have."

Jenn deflated, remembering the slave girl that Jillybean had stabbed through the heart and dumped over the side of the *Saber*. And then there were the children she had murdered in Sacramento, and who knows how many people she had purposely killed on her operating table in Bainbridge. These had all been mercy killings, something Stu looked more than ready for, just then.

"She probably would," Jenn said, agreeing reluctantly. Just then their little group needed every able hand and Stu could barely move, and there was no evidence to suggest he would be able to in the next hour. They were, more than likely, going to be at the bottom of the ocean in an hour unless she could give Mike a hand.

Stu saw all of this as well. "I won't blame you guys," he whispered. "Just slide me over the side. It's that or we all die."

Chapter 6

Mike was suddenly furious. The pain was terrible, their situation was worse and yet it was the ungrateful bellyaching that put him over the top. "You're both being...I don't know what the word is. Petty or something like that. I'm the only one here who never loved Jillybean but I'm starting too. She saved us, okay? Do you guys get that? Those Corsairs were going to throw us off a building, or did you forget?"

"It feels like I *was* thrown off a building," Stu grumbled, without looking up.

"No. You'd be dead," Mike snapped. "We all would. If you ask me, this is better than being dead." He didn't add the proper modifier before the word better, which was *slightly*. Mike could not remember ever being so miserable. "We should be thanking Jillybean. Not only did she save us, she helped us escape."

Jenn nodded and then winced in pain. "He's right. And it was our fault. We forced her away instead of trying to help her."

"Do you mean help her to become Queen of the Corsairs?" Stu demanded. "I would never help her to become that. And if I had known that was what her end game was, I would never have helped her in the first place."

"I don't think that was what she had envisioned at all," Jenn said. "And she was the one who helped you in the first place." She frowned and winced again; everything hurt so badly she wanted to curl back up in her ball. "I think we're making her out to be smarter than she really is. I don't think she came here meaning to be queen at all. We forced her hand."

Mike tried to laugh, but it came out as a whimpering cough. "I say speak for yourself, Jenn. Maybe she did want to become Queen of the Corsairs. We know she wanted to destroy them and what better way? She took over half of them and is going to use them to fight the other half. We all know the Black Captain isn't going to let her get away with this. There's going to be another fight."

"And our people are going to be stuck in the middle," Stu said.

"It was going to happen anyway," Mike said. "I'm like the least smart of all of us and even I can see that."

Stu wouldn't answer that. He only looked out to sea where the storm had turned green-black and was spinning the ugly clouds around alarmingly. "Jenn, help Mike," he said. "Don't worry about me."

"No," Mike said. "Don't listen to him. When we're on a boat, I'm in charge, not Stu. Come take over with the pump. Keep it going as long as you can." Moving like an old woman, Jenn went to the pump and began spinning it. Mike grabbed Stu and heaved him into a sitting position.

"I told you not to worry about me," he said.

"And I told you I'm in charge." Mike lashed him to the mast using the second knot every four-year-old learns: the double-knotted shoelace knot. "When you can get out of that, you can either help us survive or drown yourself, it'll be up to you."

Had his fingers not been hooked like someone crippled by palsy, Stu could have gotten out of the knot in ten seconds. Instead, he pawed feebly at the knot, barely able to hold himself upright. Giving up and just laying down was a seductive choice. It was the easiest, least painful thing he could do. And yet, there was Mike hobbling around doing everything he could to keep the wind and the waves on their stern. And Jenn was cranking the hand pump in circles, tears in her bloodshot eyes.

Their grit shamed Stu. He wasn't ready to forgive Jillybean; she had used his love as a tool and no matter what anyone said, that was just about the nastiest thing a person could do—but that didn't mean he had to give up and die.

He attacked the knot. It was a feeble attack; however, with many breaks and snarled curse words aimed at Jillybean and Mike, and at the sea when heavy waves smashed him into the mast. He was fantastically cold. He was so cold that the frigid ocean water felt warm when it washed over him. They were going to die of exposure, if nothing else killed them first.

It took ages to get the knot undone and by then they were being pelted by a stinging rain that was part ice crystals, part sleet, and part snow. Jenn was whimpering, her arm slowing as she cranked the hand-pump. When he could, Mike went to her and heaved the crank around as fast as he could for half a minute or so, then he would go back to keeping them one step in front of the storm.

Stu's legs weren't working, and he was forced to drag them along until he reached Jenn. "Move over," he told her. "Let me have a go at it." His body was next to useless, all save his right arm. It had been the first to recover and was now at about 40% strength, which meant it was stronger than Jenn's entire body.

He began to crank and crank and crank. As he did, the arm actually got stronger and the pain grew less. The amount of water coming from the hose could have put out a forest fire and yet they continued to sink. The waves were mountains around them and although Mike was the best there was, the *Captain Jack* was dying by degrees.

It groaned when the bigger waves hit and sometimes the deck would stay submerged for long stretches. When that happened, Jenn would drop down and help pump. The two of them would work the pump until their breath was ragged.

"We're not going to make it," Jenn said after one long stint. She was too tired to be afraid.

"Keep us afloat a little longer," Mike yelled over the wind. "The tide probably only took us out ten or eleven miles. We should be coming up on land anytime. Jenn, spell me at the wheel for a few minutes. Keep the wind behind us."

She limped to the wheel, wearing a look of uncertainty. "Why? Where are you going?"

He kissed her on the cheek. Her face was stiff and felt as though he were kissing a smooth cake of ice. They had to get to land soon. "I need to check the compass."

Her eyes grew big around at the idea. The compass was in the boat's navigation room, which was in the middle of the flooded cabin. Under any other circumstances it was a simple swim of twenty or so feet. Jenn didn't think she could make it. Her lung capacity had shrunk and the range of motion in both her arms and legs was a third of what it had been.

She knew Mike was doing better, but not that much better. But she didn't try to stop him. They didn't have much time left.

Mike walked down the stairs to the flooded cabins, took a deep breath, choked and coughed on nothing, then took a smaller breath and went under. He was gone long enough for Jenn's heart to begin to break and when he finally came up again he was grey-faced and barely strong enough to straggle up the stairs.

"We need to make a course change," he said, between gasps. "Just a slight one." He struggled to the mainsail and canted it deeply, making a mockery of the word "slight." The *Captain Jack* heeled over...way over. Almost immediately the waves began hitting side on, making the boat shudder and groan.

Stu could almost feel it coming apart beneath him as he worked the pump faster. A few feet away, Jenn tried to hold the wheel against the strength of the ocean—the ocean won, and she went tumbling to the gunwale and thankfully just managed to hold on. Mike went to help her, however, she cried, "No!" and waved him to the wheel. He hauled it round.

The *Captain Jack* had been going north with the wind; now Mike had to gamble with their lives. "Tie yourselves to something!" he yelled to them after a huge wave had sent Jenn to the edge once again.

In between waves, Mike tried to work out a rough calculation as to where they were. The current would have taken them south and west during the night, while the storm had taken them straight north. There was a good chance they were directly west of San Francisco and that if they could keep the boat from going over for the next two hours, they could conceivably slip right back beneath the Golden Gate Bridge.

They did not make it two hours. They made it less than one before Mike found the *Captain Jack* on the crest of a particularly steep wave. He spun the wheel, frantically trying to turn the boat so it would slip down the face of the wave, but it was too late. The wind heaved the boat around until the rudder was out of the water —they were going down backwards.

"Cut away! Cut yourselves loose!" The scream was meant only for Stu. Mike was already leaping at Jenn. He had tied himself to the wheel post with a mooring hitch and with a simple pull of the loose end he flung himself at Jenn, as the boat was sliding straight down the cliff of water.

Mike collided with her a half-second before the boat hit the trough of the wave. In that blink of time, he took a mental picture of the knot and then held on as the momentum, as well as the weight of the boat, plunged the stern twelve feet deep. The weight of the wave crushed them against the rail. Jenn thought her eyes were going to burst and her chest was going to explode.

But it was only for a second and then up and down changed places as the *Captain Jack* turned a complete twisting somersault. Mike was thrown, cracking hard against the mast and nearly getting caught up in the sail and the lines. With a storm of bubbles all around him, he fought to get clear and when he did he saw that he was trapped under the boat.

Ten feet away, her auburn hair flowing gently around her, Jenn was fighting the knot she had tied like a mad woman. Her nails bent back as she frantically ripped at the rope. She then grabbed it in both hands, planted her feet on the railing and heaved with the result that the knot only became tighter.

With the boat gyrating and making a huge rumbling sound above his head, Mike swam to her and pulled her hands away. He began scraping at the knot just as she had been doing, but quickly realized that it would be like trying to undo a wet shoelace while on a twenty-second timer. She'd be long dead by the time he managed to undo it. Mike gave up on that end of the rope and concentrated on the other, which was looped around her waist.

Because of her fear of being thrown overboard and lost at sea, she had triple-tied the rope into an unforgiving knot that wound around itself in such a complex fashion that Mike couldn't even find a starting point. Still, he did not panic. The ocean was his world, and ideas and solutions that others were slow to grasp came naturally to him there. He saw that she had tied the rope *over* her coat.

Furiously, he yanked the edge of her coat up as he pulled down on the loop around her waist.

She realized what he was doing and began to shimmy the rope off of her like it was the tiniest miniskirt imaginable. Their lungs were bursting when they kicked away and broke the surface in the midst of another crashing wave. They were slammed against the *Captain Jack*, which was upside down.

With its keel broken and jagged, it looked somewhat like a dead shark and yet they clung to it gratefully with frozen, gnarled fingers. Holding on was all Jenn could handle just then; it was all she could think about. Next to her, Mike was looking around, even more fear in his eyes.

"Stu!" he screamed. In his heart, he knew the scream was in vain. Before the boat had gone over, Stu had not even gained the full use of his legs yet and his hands were still halfway hooked. When Mike had yelled: "Cut away!" it had been based on instinct and not logic. None of them had knives. Stu was, more than likely, still under the boat.

Mike took in a lungful of air and was just about to slip back under when he heard a weak, gurgling voice say, "I'm here." It didn't sound anything like Stu.

"Hold on. We're coming for you."

He was on the other side of the boat, which seemed a very great distance just then, at least to Jenn. She didn't want to budge unless it was to somewhere safer and warmer, neither of which were to be found on the other side of the boat. And yet, she didn't want to be left behind.

She followed after Mike around the end of the boat as it went up and down with the rough waves. They found a very wretched Stu Currans, clinging to the battered edge of the hull. "I think a boat fell on me," he croaked.

"It f-fell on us, too," Jenn said in a shaking whisper. She was still in a state of shock; her nerves thrumming from how close to death she had been. "How w-were you able to get your r-r-rope off? Did you have a f-fancy knot like Mike?"

Stunned, exhausted and with thunder rolling continuously in his ears, he shook his head once an inch to the right, and once slightly to the left. Even that bit had him fighting not to whimper; he was one giant bruise. "My knot gave up on its own. It just...I don't think I'm cut out to be a sailor."

"What do we do now?" Jenn asked. "I don't think we can hold on forever." As if to emphasize her point, the water beneath them surged upward and they found themselves on the precipice of another mountainous wave. "Oh, God!" she wailed as the boat began to tumble away from her grip. It rolled down the wave, paused for just a second with its mast stabbing triumphantly straight up in the air, then was plowed over again.

Strangely, in Jenn's eyes, the three of them did not suffer the same rough and tumble fate. The great surging wave passed beneath them without doing any damage. *Like trash*, Jenn thought. This bit of unpleasantness was followed by: *Or corpses. Once you stopped struggling and just died, it almost seemed like the ocean was no longer interested in you.* How many times had she seen corpses floating in the bay? Too many times.

Feeling sick, she fought the pull of the deep and splashed awkwardly through the leaping grey water towards the mostly submerged boat. When she reached it, she clung to it, digging her hands into the ruptured seams in the hull. Jenn's fingers ached; her whole body ached, not just to the bone, but somehow even deeper than that.

She didn't know how she was going to make it through the next ten minutes, let alone the next few hours.

"I'm starting to think this is worse than death," Stu said. He had his face pressed against the slick hull as rain and sleet drummed against it. No one had the strength to reply. The short swim in their heavy water-soaked clothes had exhausted them.

The ocean gave them a breather for the next couple of minutes as the waves failed to break beneath them. Mike recovered first. "Get out of your coats and take your shoes off if you can. They're not going to keep us warm."

Jenn got her coat off just as the next big wave came. Once more the *Captain Jack* fell down the face of it. It rolled with a great cracking sound and when it came around, its mast was gone, and its black sail trailed behind it like a cloak. Another wave hit it and this time she thought it had sunk, but then it breached the surface, again upside down. It seemed so far away.

She was the last one to make it. Instead of taking her boots off, she clung to the hull and shivered. Mike took them off for her.

A new wave came soon after and the swim to the slowly disintegrating *Captain Jack* was easier by the slightest degree. The next time a wave took the boat, she couldn't make it back. She was too weak. It was all she could do to keep her head above water. Mike slipped an arm around her shoulders like a lifeguard might and did the sidestroke through forty yards of freezing chop to reach the boat.

Stu was dragging so badly that Mike got Jenn got to the boat only seconds after him. Mike pushed Jenn up onto the hull and climbed up after her. The *Captain Jack* was down by the head. The bow had been ripped away and there were now gaping holes along it. Only air trapped in the stern kept it from sinking completely, but it wasn't going to last much longer.

"If I don't make it back next time, leave me," Stu said. "Don't try to come after me."

"Me neither," Jenn said.

Mike didn't know what to say. He had never planned on going after Stu; the man was just too big. And if Jenn thought he wasn't going to do everything in his power to save her, she was being ridiculous.

"We gotta figure out what Jillybean would do," he said to change the subject. "We know she'd do something. She wouldn't drown. A little water wouldn't stop her, not when…" A distant roar of water cut him off. *A new wave is forming*, he thought. He was too drained to be afraid. In fact, he had a crazy idea: what if they just surfed the boat down the wave and jumped off at the last second?

If it worked, it would put them that much closer and would mean less of a swim. And if it didn't work…well, Mike didn't have to think about that. The answer was obvious. He stood up as the water began to mount under them. Higher and higher they went until he felt he was a hundred feet in the air. He had a fantastic view of what was making the roaring sound.

They had made it. The land was less than a mile away and yet he didn't jump for joy. He had the perfect vantage to see the waves racing straight at what looked like an endless wall of rock and crashing into it with the power of a two-ton bomb.

"New question. How would Jillybean keep us from hitting that?"

Jenn eased into a crouch, saw the cliff and the suicidal waves, and she hunched back down. Compared to the violent death that awaited them, a nice gentle drowning didn't sound like a bad way to go.

Chapter 7

It wasn't a rhetorical question in Mike's mind. "Really. Someone tell me how Jillybean would keep us from hitting that?"

Jenn was too done in to make plans. With the poison still in her system, and the pain and the cold, it was all she could do just to hold on. Stu's drawn face had soured at the name, but he still managed to summon what energy he had and almost managed to stand. He stared at the rollers as they crashed endlessly into the cliff. "Can you rig an anchor or something like that?"

"We have a real anchor." Mike pointed to the anchor winch, which Jenn was using as a foothold. The actual anchor was flopped over and hanging by its heavy chain three feet under the water. "But I don't see what good it will do us. The first wave that hits us when we're anchored will tear the knees right out of the *Captain Jack*, and that'll be it."

"Sorry Mike, but she's doomed no matter what. I was just thinking that if we can slow her down before she hits it won't be so bad. See how there's like a lull between the waves?"

Jenn and Mike eased up. Between each wave crashing into the cliff there was a ten to fifteen second gap in time when the water churned and frothed as white as beer foam. From this far away, it looked as soft as foam as well. They knew it wasn't. The water was probably convulsing, going in every direction, and more than likely it would suck a person under, and there was no telling what sort of jagged rocks were hidden just beneath the surface. They could be flayed alive if their heads weren't beaten to mush first.

The sight was enough to get Jenn's brains moving at least a little. "Can we steer this thing at all? Maybe if we could get her further up the coast a bit, we might find some sand?"

It sounded like wishful thinking even as she said it. They barely had the strength to hold on, let alone rig a rudder with the bits of nothing they had on hand. Everyone, including Jenn, shook their head at the idea.

"I think we don't have a choice except to go with Stu's idea," Mike said. "It might work." The lie fooled no one. They were doomed, but they had no choice but to keep going.

Mike prayed through numb lips, while next to him Jenn looked for a sign. All she saw were hungry seagulls wheeling in the terrible wind. The birds were not a good omen. They were only there in the hope that everyone on board would die so they could feast on their rotting corpses.

The only good news was that the waves were no longer breaking beneath the *Captain Jack*. This was offset by the fact that as they got closer, they could see the ocean's strength and violence was even more dreadful than they imagined. Even that area of white foam between the waves was more frightening than it had seemed from so far away. The waters there were seething and roiling, sending up chaotic waves as tall as a man. They would come together with explosive force, shooting fountains of water thirty feet into the air. Swimming in such water would be a test for the best swimmers and certain death for the worst.

Mike's hands gripped the hull, fiercely, angrily. He didn't want to die. He wasn't ready for it, but it was going to happen. A sigh and a curse escaped him as he looked at Jenn in the same way he had fifteen or so hours before, right after he had taken the poison. Just like then, her fear had rendered her ghostly white. He hated seeing her so afraid; it made something ache deep in his chest.

"Go ahead and say it," she whispered through quivering lips. She tried to smile, but the corners wouldn't stay upright at the same time. First one would edge up then the other, but never at the same time. "I think now's our only chance."

They had faced death many times, and it seemed to have become a simple ritual to express their love for each other at the last possible moment. Usually, it was stilted and forced, their fear so great as to steal any chance of romance away. Still, it had become a habit and so far, *something* was keeping them alive against the odds. Mike knew their little ritual couldn't work forever and probably wouldn't this time. He was bone-tired and didn't think he'd be able to make the swim. There was no way Jenn could; even when healthy, she was only a mediocre swimmer.

"I love you, Jenn Lockhart," he said, as much because he did love her as because as a sailor, he knew the incalculable value of superstition.

"I love you, Mike Gunter. Should we, uh, say something to Stu?"

As the *Captain Jack* sank lower in the water, the grim Hillman was staring fixedly at the cliff face, the white foam, and the curling breakers. Mike thought Stu had even less of a chance than Jenn. His left arm had been operated on only a few days before, he still walked with something of a limp because of the bullet he had taken a month before, and he had taken the most poison.

But these weren't the main reasons why Jenn had a better chance. Getting to shore safely was Mike's secondary goal, getting Jenn there safely was his first. If that meant he had to walk across the bottom of the ocean holding her out of the water, he would do it. Stu would be on his own.

Mike cleared his throat. "We're going to make it, Stu. That was a good plan. We should make it."

"Sure," Stu answered, matching Mike's lie with one of his own, and smiling as he did. The smile came easily for him since he had been courting death for days, and now it looked like the Grim Reaper was ready to show his bone face. Stu would try to get to shore—the survival instinct was too well ingrained within him to not try—but, like Mike, he knew his chances were slim to none, and no ritual was going to make a difference.

The roar of the crashing waves soon drowned out the possibilities for any more niceties, which was just fine with Stu. He was afraid one of them would bring up Jillybean and that was the last name he wanted to hear.

"Jillybean," he scoffed. "It's the stupidest name I ever heard." Just then a fine spray washed over them. Despite the cold, it was soothing and was a great relief from the stinging sleet which had been pelting them from behind. Stu grinned into the spray, thinking that there was no reason to look back, anyway. If he lived, he didn't think he would ever look back again.

The spray was coming off the looming rocks. Stu gazed up at them and had plenty of time to study their coming deaths. In a strange way, time and space began to compress. It almost seemed as though the waves were stacking up on each other, building higher the nearer they got to shore. The one they were riding in was a beast. It was so huge that Stu felt like the ocean was gearing up to try and kill them one last time—and it was going to put everything it had into it.

The top of the wave began to show white on either side of the *Captain Jack*. It was time. The wave had crossed an immense ocean all the way from the edge of Japan and was about to hurl itself against the rocks just so it could kill Stu Currans. *It's a damned kamikaze*, he thought to himself with a grin. The idea was insane, but it made him laugh.

Grinning, he yelled, "Everyone ready?" Although he was all of seven feet from Mike the yell was necessary. The *THROOM* of the waves was earsplitting.

They were as ready as they were ever going to be and yet there came a dreadfully long pause as the wave heaved up, its crest a pure white mantle over an alien green color. Then they hit the point of no return. The receding water was undercutting the incoming wave and now they were hurtling down at breakneck speed.

Stu screamed for Mike to drop the anchor, but he had already done so, knowing on some level that because the boat was upside down, the anchor wouldn't fall as quickly as they needed it to. The metal links were blurring away, letting out a high shriek that turned to a bubbly whine moments later as the boat went all the way under the water.

It was a strange feeling. They had become part of the wave.

In the span of seconds, the water at the back of the boat went from three inches deep, lapping at their ankles, to waist deep and getting higher as it felt like the boat was sinking to the middle of the enormous wave. Stu sucked in a breath and gripped the torn hull for all he was worth though it really wasn't needed. He was part of the wave. Its momentum was his momentum. He could have let go and he wouldn't have gone anywhere.

Then the wave began to topple as the base of it hit the shore. Suddenly the blunt and broken bow of the *Captain Jack* speared out of the water in mid-curl. All Stu could think was that he was riding a forty-foot surfboard straight to hell. Half a million gallons of water and that one flimsy boat were aimed at what looked like a jagged set of black teeth. All along the base of the cliff were slick spires of rock that would turn the boat to kindling—only just then the anchor bit into rock.

For an endless moment, the *Captain Jack* hung in the air with the huge wave behind it as the chain went taut with a deep *DOOOOOM* sound. The great unstoppable surge slammed through and around them with a tumultuous crash. The rear third of the boat tore away, while the bow and main section landed square on the spires of rock and disintegrated as the wave pounded home in an explosion of noise and white water.

The rear third of the boat was spared that initial explosion, but then the casing holding the anchor winch gave way and the last of the *Captain Jack* was sucked into the maelstrom. Stu was spun and twisted, as he was plunged under the mad, swirling water. Up and down switched places seven or eight times in a matter of seconds before he found himself caught up in the stern railing like a tuna in a net.

Stu and the railing were slammed into the rocky bottom of the shore with such force that the metal bent around his leg, as tight as a vice. Even worse, it was pinned under the rocks almost at the base of one of the spires. He was twenty feet below the raging surface and trapped. No matter how hard he pulled, the railing wouldn't budge. As he was trying to twist his leg, he was suddenly thrown back by a near invisible force. The water from the last wave was rushing back out to sea.

With the tiniest glimmer of hope that the receding water would drop low enough for him to break the surface and be able to get a new breath, he looked back up through the green water and saw rising above him what looked like a looming grey mountain complete with snowy peaks. It was another wave and was just as big as the last.

He ducked down and threw his hands over his head. As utterly useless as this action was, he could do little else. The main weight of the wave hit just past the spires with such force that it felt like Stu's eardrums would burst. Once more he was sent spinning, still with the railing on his leg. For a brief second, he broke the surface, took a half-breath before he was sucked under again and battered. His right arm was smashed, there was a searing pain in his trapped leg and his entire body was bent backwards against what he thought could be nothing else except another body.

As soft as it was, he knew it had to be Jenn's and Stu did everything he could to turn around to get to her. It was not Jenn, it was the long beige cushion from the bench that once sat behind the wheel of the *Captain Jack*. The cushion, which was filled with millions of tiny trapped air bubbles began to wriggle toward the surface.

In desperation, Stu grabbed it with both arms in a bear hug and was pulled upward along with it. It acted like a life preserver—but only barely. He and the long cushion took turns bouncing off unforgiving rocks before they finally broke the surface practically in the shadow of the cliff.

He was being hurtled toward it but now saw that the cliff face was actually set further back than he had expected and that the waves weren't quite reaching it. *It must be low tide*, he thought to himself as he slid through waist-deep water. There was a brief lull and then the water started rushing around him again, pulling him back towards the deadly spires. Still gripping the cushion with all his might, he fought the pull, knowing that the next wave would land squarely on top of him if he got sucked back.

He dug into the rocks and sand with both feet, slowing his momentum so that when the next wave came, it broke well in front of him. A moment of relief was all he had before the surge of water sent him flying back toward thew cliff where he pinballed from rock to rock, the cushion taking the brunt of the damage until he slammed right against the cliff itself. For a few seconds, he was crushed against the rock, unable to move—then the water receded.

He fell back into a few feet of foamy water and gazed blearily around him, certain that he would find himself alone, but Jenn and Mike were about forty yards away clinging to a blue plastic container. Mike's face and head were bleeding and he seemed only partially aware of where he was.

Jenn was a little better off and when the water receded around her, she tried to drag the container along with Mike draped over it.

Stu thought he must have hit his head at least once in all the fury, because his thoughts were coming to him slowly out of a dim haze and when the next wave came, he foolishly placed the cushion between him and it. The water was heavy, but it couldn't hurt him compared to being slammed into the cliff face. It felt like a hundred stubby knives were stabbing into his back at once.

Jenn and Mike, riding the blue container slid close. She had swallowed or breathed in a few gallons of seawater by her reckoning and she fairly sloshed as she struggled to pull Mike behind one of the larger rocks near the cliff. It offered some respite from further battering, but not from the cold wind which was howling along the shore.

She huddled down next to Mike as Stu slogged over still grimacing in pain and still carting the cushion. "We lived," he stated without much enthusiasm.

"For now," she answered with even less.

"Yeah," he agreed. In his view, things had only marginally improved. The cold was so intense that he didn't think they could last another fifteen minutes in it and, as far as he could tell, they still had an impossible cliff to scale. This wasn't like the twenty-foot affair at the north end of Alcatraz with its handholds and soft fall to a sandy beach. This cliff had to be fifty-feet high, it was covered in slime and the wind was like nothing Stu had ever felt. And they were without shoes.

After the next wave swept around the rock, drenching them, Stu chanced a look around and saw that the cliff wasn't as monolithic as he had at first assumed. Not a hundred yards away, a large section of it had been so undercut by the erosion of the waves that the face of it had fallen into the ocean.

"There's a way up," he said to Jenn as he bent and picked up Mike. Every muscle and bone in Stu's body cried out in pain. He ignored it and slung Mike across his shoulder. He waited until after the next wave and then struggled with his burden to the next rock, thirty feet further on. Jenn should have beaten him there, however she was hauling the box along.

He was about to bark at her to leave the thing when he saw there was a placard taped to the clear plastic lid: *Knitting Supplies*. It was written once again in Jillybean's neat hand.

"Where did that come from?" As far as he knew, Jillybean didn't knit and even if she did why would she put a box of knitting supplies on their doomed ship? No, this had to be filled with other sorts of supplies; food and ammo, Stu hoped.

"The boat," Jenn said, gazing down at the box with a glassy stare. "It was somewhere in one of the cabins, I guess. There was at least one more. I saw it just as we went under. It must have sank." She shook her head in disbelief. "I can't believe they were there the entire time."

Neither could Stu. For all he knew, Jillybean might have packed an inflatable raft on board the *Captain Jack* and he had been too caught up in his own pathetic hurt feelings to even look.

Furious at himself, he plunged through the surf, fell twice, but finally made it to where the cliff had fallen. He set Mike down above the water line. "I'll haul the box up. While I'm gone take a look at him."

She gave him only a cursory look over. He was conscious but concussed; bruised and bleeding, but not terribly so. He would not die from these wounds unless there was internal bleeding, something she couldn't check for right there either way. No, what would kill him was the cold—something she wouldn't allow, not while she had any warmth left in her body.

Mike had saved her when they had plunged into the water. He had used his body to shield hers from the many rocks and he had thrust her into the air rather than breathe himself. Keeping him warm was the least she could do. She wrapped herself around him, shielding him from the cold, letting the sleet wash over her.

It sapped her strength and she was nearly as out of it as Mike by the time Stu came back. The Hillman said nothing. He picked up Mike once again, heaved him onto his shoulder and trudged through the maze of rock and sand. Now that they were on land, Stu gained strength with every step. He carried Mike to the top of the cliff and then beyond.

From the heights they could see towns, both north and south of them. Each was a few miles distant and even Stu did not relish carrying Mike that far. Nearer to them was a lone homestead that had a magnificent view of the Pacific. Stu squished along with toes gone so numb that he couldn't bend them by the time they reached the house.

It had been ransacked of course, but there were still clothes and blankets and even a stockpile of firewood. What they didn't have was any way to start the fire. Jenn and Stu both glanced at the plastic box. It was very much like a thirty-gallon Tupperware container. When Stu popped it open they saw, sitting on top, was one of the white and gold flags that first Jillybean, then Jenn had used as their royal banner.

Sitting primly on that, as if it hadn't just been through a harrowing life or death shipwreck, was a note which Jenn read to the others:

"Jenn,

I apologize for the manner of your escape. I'm afraid time was against me and I was unable to formulate a better plan in the spur of the moment. To reduce the effects of the concoction you drank please administer Atropine and Diazepam as soon as possible…"

Jenn didn't wait to finish the note. The pain from the poison had only slightly decreased and the three of them were in silent agony. She pulled out the flag, three large medical books, Jillybean's own Sig Sauer P226, two boxes of ammo, a gold lighter that had once belonged to Matthew Gloom, the now dead leader of the Santas, a few pounds of dried venison, a few more of salted fish and two jars of Jenn's own carrot and beet infused vinegar recipe which went well drizzled on game meat.

Jenn paused, amazed at the jars, wondering how they could have gotten into Jillybean's possession. The wonder was short-lived while the pain in her hands just holding the jars seemed endless. She set the jars aside and plucked out the final box, which was filled with medical supplies. Within it were the Atropine and Diazepam as well as instructions.

The relief from the pain took a few minutes and as they waited, they huddled closer to the fire they had lit; it was some time before the heat of it seeped into their bones. As they shivered, Jenn picked up the note again and finished reading it:

"Remember, you are still a queen. A good queen. It's what the world needs, now more than ever.

Yours,
Jillian

PS The hands of a queen are the hands of a healer—Study!"

"She's given me schoolwork," Jenn snorted.

Mike's head was still pounding—when people spoke it sounded like he was standing in a giant metal bell. He didn't have it in him to laugh. Stu let a forced chuckle slip through his falsely grinning lips, and put his hand out for the note. It had been the only one in the box. He had checked.

Jenn seemed to know what he wanted from the note. He wanted to know if he was mentioned. "You probably had your own note in that other box. We each had one, I bet."

"Yeah, sure." He put more effort into this smile and then sat back with his hands held out to the fire, wondering how pathetic he would look if he snuck out to the cliff to see whether he could find the other boxes. *Very pathetic*, he decided since there was no way the plastic boxes could still be intact with the punishment they were taking.

Very pathetic or not, he hobbled to the cliff two hours later when Jenn and Mike were fast asleep. All that remained of the *Captain Jack* and the blue boxes was some trash, some shards of fiberglass and the shredded remains of her sails, being swept up to the cliff and dragged back down again, endlessly.

He told himself that there had never been a note; it made it easier to turn his back on Jillybean forever.

Chapter 8

Bainbridge Island was divided into sections and then into subsections and each of these was scoured. No building was left untouched, not even Jillybean's school.

It was the scariest, most dangerous place on the island and there was definitely a shortage of volunteers to search it. Zero, in fact. It was why it was left for last.

"I'll do it," Neil said, from his couch by the fire. Emily had heaved the couch within two feet of the flames, which she had fed with enough logs to melt lead. Neil was sweltering. Sweat came from every pore, drenching his t-shirt, his sweater-vest and the heavy pink comforter swaddling him that Emily had dragged down from her own bed.

It was all too much but when he had retreated from the heat to sit near the open window, he had shivered himself into a hunched ball.

"No way are you going anywhere near that school," Emily declared. "You're too weak." She had become his Nurse Ratched and watched over him like an overprotective vulture. Although she insisted he wasn't going to die, she hovered around him, judging his every action and word with a nervous cast to her eyes that he read as: *This is it, he's turning!*

It was hard for Neil to look at his god-daughter. She was so beautiful while he was becoming more revolting by the minute, inside and out. He could feel his mind twisting with hate. "I'm the perfect choice, Governor," he insisted, "since it seems as though I'm your only choice. It'll be fine. I-I have time enough to search the school. And, uh, gather some items we should keep under wraps."

Governor Deanna Grey hated that he was their only volunteer. The ease of life on the island had not bred heroics into her people and after having lived so long in safety, they shied away from danger. She sighed, wishing she had a different choice. Neil wasn't doing well. His eyes had become hollow and there was sweat running in tiny rivers through the crags of his scars. And he was now a stark, unhealthy white, outside the blazing red of his cheeks, that is. He had the disease. There was no second-guessing it now. "Maybe we could just do a quick search of the building and lock it up tighter than ever, afterwards. Her experiments aren't going anywhere, are they?"

"Perhaps now is a good time to just burn that building down," Norris Barnes suggested. He was the Chief of Housing and Infrastructure on the island and had railed for years against what he called the wasted space accorded to Jillybean and her experiments. "If there's a spy or assassin in there, well that'll be just killing two birds with one stone if you ask me."

"You don't want to burn down that lab," Neil advised, using part of the pink blanket to mop his forehead. "Even I don't know everything she has cooking in there. It could be she has…well, let's just say there are some things that even fire won't kill, and you don't want them released into the atmosphere."

Joslyn Reynolds was just bringing a teacup up. It stopped just before her painted red lips. "Are you talking nukes?" She had been one of the Colonel's whores who had escaped at the same time Deanna had and just like her, the years had been kind. She had almost feline features that men found irresistible.

The very notion of nuclear weapons was preposterous, but that didn't stop the six members of the Governor's cabinet from beginning to babble with undertones of hysteria. If Neil hadn't been feeling as though his death was not far off, perhaps just outside the door with its bony knuckles raised and about to knock, he might have laughed. His head hurt too much for that. "No not nukes. Jillybean knows better. But…" He let the word hang in the air, not out of theatrical reasons but because he was reaching his limit and it just took too much energy to run so many words together. After a big breath, he went on, "It doesn't mean there aren't toxins that might be released. We all know her advancements in battery technology have come with a certain level of environmental concern."

"All the more reason to shut that place down," Norris said. He was usually an agreeable man who had the look of an aging lumberjack about him. His paunch had turned to a gut years before and no amount of plaid could camouflage it. "Now may be the perfect time. She's gone and when she comes back, Neil won't be around to control her anymore."

The council members looked sideways at each other as Deanna stared into the fire, knowing Norris was right, but not wanting to admit it. She loved Neil, like a brother and couldn't imagine a world in which he wasn't bumbling about in his sweater vests and ghastly Crocs.

"I could do it, maybe," Joslyn said. "You know, look after Jillybean. I know we don't see eye-to-eye on very much…"

"Very much?" Norris cried. "Is that a joke? Sorry to break the bad news to you, Jos, but she hates you. Don't feel bad, she pretty much hates all of us, and she's going to doubly hate whoever we choose to watch over her."

Deanna balled a fist and looked as though she wanted to leap up and punch Norris. This wasn't something Neil had to deal with as he was dying. Norris was right, of course, but the timing was wrong.

"We could let her pick her own watcher," Emily suggested. Although she was not quite twelve, she had been to cabinet meetings since Deanna had been chosen as the first Chief of Housing and Infrastructure nine years before. Deanna had then moved on to the governor's position partially on her ability to harness Jillybean's genius.

"I don't think so, darling," Deanna said. "Whoever Jillybean picks will be someone she can dominate and then it would be better if there were no watcher at all. We would never know the truth from a lie."

It was strange for Neil to hear them discuss his replacement. Strange but not altogether unpleasant. No matter what people thought of him and his ugly face, he had been needed more than they really knew. He had made Bainbridge what it is and he had protected it; all behind the scenes. *And now I'm dying, and no one will know or care*, he thought, bitterly.

This wasn't true, and he knew it, and yet his head was pounding so miserably that it was hard not to wallow in at least some self-pity. He tried to force a smile onto his face as he asked, "Emily, can you be a lamb and fetch me more medicine?"

"I have some here." She had changed into a white sweater and jeans that were high on the ankle. Her jeans always seemed to be high on the ankle since she never seemed to stop growing. She pulled out a bottle of pills and held them out. Before he could ask, she had a glass of water for him as well.

"Thanks, but could I trouble you for ice? I'm hotter than the sun." The moment she was gone he dry swallowed five of the pills, wondering if it would be bad manners to pour all the pills down his gullet right there. The thought of over-dosing on Jillybean's opiate-based pain meds sounded kind of nice just then. It would have to wait, however. He had sent Emily from the room for a reason. "There is only one person who can take my place."

He was looking steadily at Deanna with his fevered eyes. She mistook the look. "Me? I don't think so, Neil. Jillybean respects me. I know that much, however she still has that teen mindset. It'll only be a matter of time before she begins to resent me."

"I wasn't thinking of you, I was thinking of Emily." Deanna demonstrated how good of a leader she was by not reacting as everyone around her did.

"She's just a kid!" Norris blurted out.

Joslyn was less circumspect than even that. "Who's going to be more dominated than her? Jillybean will be her puppet master."

Neil did not have the strength or really the desire for any of this. He only stared at Deanna as she came to her own conclusion. The Governor thought it through just as she would have with any suggestion from Neil. "Emily is smarter and stronger than her age would suggest. And Jillybean is already teaching her a great deal. It's an interesting idea. My problem is the danger posed to her. I never worried about you, Neil because you have proven to be tougher than anyone gives you credit for."

"That is a sweet lie, Deanna."

"What's a sweet lie?" Emily asked, as she came back into the room with a pitcher of ice water and nine glasses.

Neil sucked down an entire glass greedily before answering, "Your mom said that I was safe from all of Jillybean's strange concoctions and contraptions and weird experiments because I'm tough. The truth is that I'm prudent to the point of cowardice."

"Don't be like that," Emily chided. "A chicken could never have broken *into* the River King's prison. And a chicken would never have led the assault on the Believer's bunker…"

"That was your father. I was just along for the ride."

She was so tall that she could look down her nose at Neil. She looked almost exactly like her mother as she said, "No, that was both of you. And it was you who led the final assault that drove the Azael out of Estes. Don't try to fool me, Uncle Neil. I know better."

"Trust me, the final assault was the easiest thing anyone did that day." It was far easier than seven-year-old Jillybean and fifteen-year-old Sadie battling the King of the Azael and his entire family by themselves, or Deanna attacking two armored personnel carriers and singlehandedly turning the tide of the battle. "Still, you are right, you aren't a fool. It's why I think you should take over my job watching over Jillybean."

He knew that by saying this before it was agreed to, he had crossed the line, stepping over the boundary between mother and daughter. He had also stepped all over the toes of Deanna in her role of Governor. She glared daggers, which he ignored. Emily did not. She saw the look her mother wore and understood the problem.

"I'll have to think on that and get my mom's permission," she said, honoring her mother as a proper daughter should. "But I do think I may be the only one suited for the job. Aunt Jillybean would never hurt me or put me in a position to get hurt. I think it's really sad, but I might be the only person she really trusts, besides you, Uncle Neil."

Deanna drummed her fingers in silence as she sat thinking of all the terrible situations Jillybean could get her daughter into. On the flip side, Jillybean was a genius and, through her teaching, could propel Emily forward. As Jillybean had put it once: "She is my Alexander and I am her Aristotle."

Deanna was torn and, as always when she couldn't make up her mind, she *didn't* make up her mind. Neil thought this ability to put decisions on hold was one of her better qualities as governor. "This is really a moot point at the moment," she said. "Jillybean has been gone far longer than any of us expected. It could be she has found a new home. Or she has managed to find trouble that even she can't get out of. I think this attack on Neil may be a result of what we all feared. She's gotten on the wrong side of the Corsairs and this is their revenge."

From the moment that Jillybean had disappeared with the three people from San Francisco, it had been obvious that she was going to Grays Harbor to steal a boat from the Corsairs. They weren't going to walk the five hundred miles back south, after all.

54

"If it's revenge, let's hope they're done," Joslyn said. "The Corsairs are the last people we want to mess with." Everyone but Neil and Deanna nodded along with this assessment. The reputation of the Black Captain was enough to chill the blood of the hardest of men and the council was made up of two men who were past their prime and five women who hadn't fired a gun in ten years.

"Do you think she set this up on purpose?" Deanna asked. "I don't mean the attack on you, Neil. That was pretty much out of the blue and no one could have seen that coming. I'm talking about stirring up the Corsairs. She knows better than anyone that you don't mess with them and not expect some sort of reprisal."

Jillybean had been warning the Governor and Neil for years about the growing threat that lay just to their south. They had taken the threat seriously, however the people of Bainbridge thought they were unreachable behind their high walls and the mood had been against making trouble. Jillybean had taken a dim view of this.

But would she have stirred the pot on purpose? Neil wondered. "Maybe. Maybe. She would've had a plan of some sort which wouldn't have involved me getting poisoned."

"That brings up a point we haven't discussed," Norris said, absently scratching his belly through its plaid coating. "Why was Neil attacked? Wouldn't it have made more sense to go after you, Deanna?"

Deanna had to fight to hide the shiver that wriggled her back muscles. "Maybe it was a warning."

"They could've sent a letter," Neil grumbled. It was bad enough getting killed, but to be killed like a second-rate character was rubbing salt in his wound. Of all the ways to go out he had never expected to die by cutting himself on a razor. It was officially the least heroic way to die imaginable. "Look, I'm getting tired. I just want to go take a look at the school. I doubt an assassin made it in. It's the most inaccessible building on the island. And if he did get in, there's a good chance he's already dead."

"I don't think you should go," Deanna said, putting a hand on his arm and forcing it to remain, despite the waves of heat coming from it —although he was her closest friend, she couldn't help imagining the waves of disease coming from it as well. "We could draw you a hot bath and I can get some of that chocolate ice cream from…"

Stifling a groan, Neil shook off the arm and stood up. "No. This may be the last thing I do. Killing an assassin would be a good way to go out." Neil was adamant and he strode out into the cold night wrapped in Emily's pink comforter. Shamed by this display of courage, the entire council went with him. A weeping Emily and a stoic Deanna propped him up.

The fifteen-minute walk was an ordeal for him. In the dark, he stumbled and veered left and right. Still, he made it to the last building left to be searched. It had been surrounded by a hundred people, most of whom hung back, smoking cigarettes and whispering to each other.

"Let's check all the windows and doors first." Neil said. With the chill, his voice had grown phlegmy and was not his own. "Maybe no one got in at all."

The Fast Response Team was tasked with the job. In a clump, they went in a circle around the building pointing twenty guns at every window and door. Only Eddie Sanders wasn't afraid of the building. He had his own fear, making him sweat despite the cold—what would everyone do when they realized that there wasn't an actual assassin on the island? He thought he knew. They would begin to look at one another. They would start to ask questions. They would find out that he had gone out alone that morning and they would want to know why.

He stumbled around the building with the others, desperately trying to come up with an adequate excuse.

As Eddie knew it would be, the school was locked up tight. When this was announced, Neil picked himself up from where he'd been sitting on a log, fished out his keys and opened the front door. "Lights," he said with a weak gesture to the bank of switches just to his right. It was all the energy he had left.

Joslyn turned on the lights and then immediately leapt back as the building shook with a fantastic roar. More followed the first until Neil thought his head would split. While Norris, Deanna, Emily and Joslyn were cowering, Neil swallowed four more of the pills. They were the only things keeping him going.

"Give me those," Emily said as the last one got stuck sideways in his throat and he began to gag. He was so weak that he was helpless against even her strength.

"How big are they?" Joslyn asked in a whisper.

At first Neil thought she was talking about the pills—*The size of a horse's balls*, he was about to say before he realized she was referring to the zombies. His answer was only shrugged. He needed to lie down. He needed to close his eyes and let the pain pills wash away his troubles. The next thing he knew Emily was shaking his shoulders and when he cracked his throbbing eyes, she was looking directly into his face. "Hey," she said, softly. "Tell me what you need. Is it time?"

Was it his time to die or was it his time to turn into one of them? The beasts were still thundering, the sound reverberating in his chest, in his head, going to those cancerous lesions eating up his mind and soothing them, lulling Neil into a new stupor.

"I'll do it," he heard Joslyn saying. "Norris, if you'll help him outside. I'll make it quick, Deanna, I promise."

They were going to shoot him! That didn't seem like a good thing…in a vague sort of way. "Not yet," he slurred. He was losing it, or had lost it already, but it didn't matter. He remembered there was an assassin and since he was going to die anyway, he wanted to go out a hero. Even if it killed him.

He stood, wobbled and started walking quickly, afraid that if he didn't walk quickly he would die before he reached the end of the corridor. As he passed locked and bolted doors, he blurted out what was in each room: "In there is where she uses a drying process for nitrocellulose guncotton. This one is where she sterilizes instruments and microfilaments and that sort of thing. This one is where she is trying to replicate the *Super Soldier Serum*. Here is where she condenses synthetic alkaloids. She wanted to grow her own poppies, but I told her no."

As they passed each room, Deanna gave each lock a firm tug while Emily listened or sniffed at the doors. Finally, they made it to the main section of the school where the offices, the cafeteria and the gym were located. It was also where the zombies were housed. The smell from the locker rooms was outrageous even through the triple-barred door.

"You wanted to know how big they were," Neil said and gestured to the door.

Brave as always, Emily started first. Deanna held her back. "I'll go first." The Governor opened the door just a crack and the roars intensified. She went paper-white when she caught sight of the monster. It was ten feet tall with shoulders as wide as a kitchen table. The chains on its neck, arms and legs were as thick as anchor chains and looked like they needed to be upgraded.

Each of them gasped and gaped in turn, hardly able to avert their eyes from what was truly a monster.

At last, they turned back to Neil and found him slumped beside a rusty water fountain. He was unconscious, his face no longer sweating, but bone dry, which meant his fever had reached a point that his body couldn't cope. It would begin to burn down his brain soon.

"I guess it really is time," Norris said. "Back in the day, I must have seen around thirty people who got scratched and the question was always when was right? For once, the time couldn't be more right. I'll just step outside."

"Go with him, Emily," Deanna ordered in a choked voice. She looked like she was about to argue, but changed her mind. Kneeling, she kissed her hand and then touched his forehead with it. Quickly, she drew it back; this was her first and she had never felt a person so hot.

Joslyn had a snub-nosed .38 in her hand. It was the preferred weapon for the situation since exit wounds were rare with the smaller caliber. "I'll do it, Deanna. I know he was your friend."

"That's why I have to." She took a huge breath and held out her hand for the gun. Joslyn handed it over and then stood back. Deanna shook her head. "No, this is something I have to do alone." When Joslyn was gone, Deanna wrapped Neil in the pink blanket and thought to herself that Neil was lucky to the end. Most people would be turning practically feral by then.

"It's better this way," she said, and took another deep breath. "When you see him, tell Grey that I've never stopped loving him. And tell Sadie that we can't get Jillybean to wear any other color..." Her eyes were fountaining tears and she ripped a sleeve across them before continuing, "Tell her that she only wears black. And tell everyone I said hi and that I miss them."

She had lost so many friends she'd be still running down their names when Neil turned if she tried to list them all. "And I'm going to miss you and so will Emily and I...and I..." She broke down again and knew she wouldn't be able to go on. She stuck the gun against his head, closed her eyes and pulled the trigger. The barrel went around and the hammer came down and at the last possible moment she remembered the safe, and there was an instant of stupid hope that ended just as quickly—revolvers don't have safeties.

Chapter 9

The next day Stu limped out to the cliff face where the *Captain Jack* had met her end. He was supposed to be collecting fresh water and had the empty jugs to prove it, however he went to the cliff first.

Although the rain was, for the moment, pent up within the heavy brooding clouds overhead, the Pacific had wetted the edge of the freezing wind. He had recovered enough in the last day of sleeping for the cold to sting once more. It was a hurt that went ignored as he gazed down at the last of the wreckage, looking for a blue box.

It was embarrassing. He was twenty-one, but he was acting like a fourteen-year-old with a crush. Did she leave me a note? Does she want to go to the sweetheart's dance? Does she want to be my girlfriend? He groaned as much from his immaturity as from the pain racing across his body. He might have been acting like a fourteen-year-old, but his body felt like it was seventy-one.

Stu stood there letting the wind cut into him until the clouds finally let go, pelting him. He had on ill-fitting clothes; two sets in fact, as well as a coat, though this had been purposely torn into tatters as anti-zombie camouflage. The wind and the rain made their way through all of this to his battered flesh. Pulling up his hood, he hunkered into himself and headed south, not because the little town was closer, but because the wind would be at his back, at least on the way there.

The wind howled all around him, sweeping off the ocean unhindered. There was not a stitch of cover, not a tree or a bush from the cliff all the way to the edge of the town where trees had been planted as a wind-break. He wasn't worried about zombies. With his limp and his bedraggled, torn clothes, he looked like the dead. He didn't bother trying to "sneak up" on the town, either. It would have been impossible over such open ground, and he just didn't have the energy for it.

He didn't know exactly where they were and didn't really care. To him, this was just another fading and forgotten town that had likely been picked over a hundred times by then.

With every step, the wind and the rain became more unbearable and by the time he got to the line of trees, the air was so full of whipping water that he squinted through a grey haze. Caution went completely out the window as he stumbled through the thin belt of trees guarding the town and found himself confronted by a nearly unbroken line of fences.

Beyond the fences were the backyards of what had once been multi-million dollar homes. They were set well apart from each other with plenty of brown, weed-riven space between. Although the weeds were thick and frequently waist high, Stu didn't have any fear of stepping on a rusting bike or a hidden rake or even the crumbling remains of a lawnmower.

Rich people's homes always had such a strict orderliness to them that it bothered him. It was almost as if a person had to give up his sense of self to own one. They had to regiment their life and exist in a state displaying outward perfection to belong to the tribe.

"And now it's all crap," Stu murmured as he crossed through the rampant winter weeds and went up a short flight of steps to a great expanse of warped decking. Before going in, he had to duck under a leaf-filled gutter that had partially fallen from the edge of the roof. "My, what would the neighbors think?"

Past the gutter was a smashed-to-pieces sliding door that led to an immense kitchen; there were granite countertops as far as the eye could see and hardwood floors that were once someone's pride and joy. Both were littered with glass and shards of porcelain. The place hadn't just been searched, it had been destroyed.

"I think the maid missed a spot and these carpets..." There was a short, seven-foot long hall between the kitchen and the dining room. The deep carpet had once been beige, now it was grey-green with mold. To the left was an open and barren pantry; not even crumbs remained. To the right, was a wall with a half-dozen pictures of the Ling family.

In every picture, pretty Mrs. Ling eyed the camera with a nervous look—she didn't trust the cameraman. Mr. Ling had crow's feet at the corners of his dark eyes and he always had a hand on one of his two children in the pictures, as if he thought they might run off to play before the flash went off. The children, a boy and a girl had identical smiles, but different attitudes: the boy was stiff, doing his duty by getting his picture taken, but not relishing it. The girl loved the camera and the camera loved her.

All four of them were dead.

More than likely they had been eaten or turned from a scratch or a bite. Then again, they might have starved to death or killed by raiders. If Mrs. Ling had been really lucky she might be still alive and a slave somewhere. With 99% of the world dead, those were just the betting odds.

Stu didn't have any more snide comments. He gave the house a very quick once over and hurried from it as if ghosts were chasing him. Fleeing next door, he kept his eyes from the dusty, professional portraits that the Melendez family had paid a gob of money for thirteen years before. All Stu cared about was finding clothes that were warm, clean and dry.

Mrs. Melendez, a stout and homely woman, had birthed three sons, all tall and handsome—Stu didn't let his mind stray at the very great possibility that they were long dead—and was soon dressed and warm. He flayed a dry coat and tugged it over a second one. Together they were tight through the shoulders and as he stood there in the oldest son's second floor bedroom, easing his arms around and grimacing from the pain from the many wounds he had suffered, he gazed out the window.

The Melendez family had once had wonderful views from almost every window and this one was no exception. It looked southwest over a little town and beyond it to a snug little harbor.

"Huh," Stu grunted, suddenly knowing exactly where he was: Bodega Bay. Not only had he been to the town twice before, he had stood in this very room three years before when he and four others had been out on a week-long scavenging trip. The drab of winter and the grey day had turned the picturesque town dull and ugly; nearly unrecognizable had it not been for the harbor, the low hills surrounding it, and the Pacific beyond them.

Bodega Bay was thirty-five miles north of the Golden Gate; they had drifted much further than Stu had expected. It was a good start, but they weren't far enough away for his liking. If even a rumor that they were still alive made it back to San Francisco that would be the ruin of Jillybean. Her ex-Corsairs would rebel; they would destroy her. Likely, they would throw her off the same tower they had threatened to throw Stu, Jenn and Mike off of.

The very thought was enough to churn his stomach. It really didn't matter how he felt about Jillybean since he would probably never see her again, but he knew he didn't want her to die, or to suffer in any way. And he wanted her to be happy and…

He had been staring absently at the town while his mind filled with Jillybean, and it was only after a minute or so that he realized there was a curl of black smoke rising from a house down near the harbor. As if his legs had been kicked out from beneath him, he dropped to the soft carpet and only slowly edged back up to spy with a far keener eye all around the town.

With the wind, it seemed as if every bush was moving toward him and every shadow held some slinking criminal. His initial panic gradually abated until a new thought struck him: what if whoever this was had seen the smoke from their fire? Like lightning, he ran down the hall to the youngest son's bedroom, which looked north. Far in the distance, out on the barren highlands overlooking the ocean was the house Stu had carried Mike to the day before. If there was smoke coming from its chimney, it was either lost in the grey backdrop or the wind was swirling it away.

Stu felt weak with relief, however that relief gave way to a quietly grinding anger. Pretty much the only people who would be here would be runaway Corsairs—and he hated Corsairs. As much as he blamed Jillybean for starting the war, Stu knew that it had been inevitable. They would have come sooner or later, and the death toll would have been far worse.

He did not know it until just at that moment, but he burned with a desire for revenge, and before he knew it, he was slipping down the stairs, the Sig Sauer in hand. With the cold and the slashing rain, he guessed the Corsairs were sitting tight and enjoying their little fire. They wouldn't expect him or anyone, not even zombies, since it was common knowledge that they did not care for the rain.

Still, he was very careful. He used the cover of the intervening houses to slip in close. It seemed strange to him that they had chosen a smaller house, instead of one of the big mansions that were scattered like salt all around the town. It was strange until he got close. The house sat on a little nub of a hill and from its back porch was a set of stairs that led right to a pier on which was docked a black sailboat.

The boat, a thirty-three footer, sat prim and proper, looking ready to go at a moment's notice. These weren't runaways. One did not take a Corsair boat and then park it a quarter mile from the ocean. You took it and ran as far away as you could. And these weren't stragglers left over from the battle. The boat was in perfect shape; there was nothing stopping it from heading north.

"Then why are these guys here?" Stu wondered aloud. He didn't want to hang around to find out. The spark of anger in him had been extinguished as much by the sight of the boat, the rain, his own exhaustion and the fact that they had only one pistol between the three of them.

He left the town from the same direction he had come, stopping at the house with the broken gutter to fill his jugs with cold rainwater.

Mike had been in a groggy state all morning, but when he heard about the boat he sat up straight and dug a finger into his ear. "There's a boat and it's not being guarded? Did you say that right?"

Before Stu could answer, Jenn put her hand on Mike's arm and said, "I don't know about you guys, but I'm sick of boats and the water. Oh, and the cold. I don't know if I'll ever get warm again."

"We need a boat if we're going to get anywhere," Mike insisted. He paused, a shadow of doubt overcoming his handsome features. "Where are we going anyway?"

For the last day, they hadn't mentioned the future once. It was almost taboo. The future meant decisions and doubts and maybe death. Staying by the fire and nibbling away at the food Jillybean had thought to pack was a far better way to spend a day than thinking about the terrible and extremely limited choices open to them.

Traveling on foot with winter already on them was exceedingly dangerous. Because they were almost completely without provisions and supplies, they'd have to scrounge as they went which meant their pace would be snail-like—seven or eight miles a day in good weather and half that in bad. Worse, the probability of attracting zombies would be practically a hundred percent.

Then they would have to choose a direction. East into the mountains would only pack on more danger. The mountain bandits were deadly in their rock kingdoms. They had fortified all the passes which meant attempting to hike along deer trails that could reach 10,000 feet along the Sierra crest. Food and shelter would be scarce and with night time temperatures dropping well below freezing, death would be a constant companion.

North meant more bandits until they reached the Redding Five, which was run by five mafia-style families that were in a near constant state of war with one another. The only people they hated more than their rivals were outsiders. After that was wilderness until they reached the radiation belt around Portland. The three had seen firsthand the horror of that and not one ever wanted to see it again.

That left heading south and to the Guardians in their walled city. They were stoic, stout-hearted fighters. From the rumors brought by the traders, there were at least a thousand of them and were so well-provisioned that they could withstand a siege of a year or more. They were also fanatically religious. It was said the sinners were encouraged to scourge themselves using an eight-headed flail. Attending church services on a daily basis was compulsory.

They were so stern that both Mike and Jenn would admit to being frightened of even the women Guardians.

Unfortunately, they were doomed as a people. Jillybean had set her sights on them and no power on Earth seemed capable of stopping her.

The three of them discussed these terrible options in a dull monotone, not one of them able to muster any energy to care about the fate awaiting the Guardians, which wasn't going to be pleasant. To retain her hold on her people, the Queen would demand kneeling and oaths of loyalty, something the Guardians were unlikely to agree with. Some would choose martyrdom and Eve and some of the other personalities inside Jillybean would gladly give it to them in some horribly disgusting form.

"What's south of the Guardians?" Jenn asked. "Maybe something better?"

Stu shrugged, leaving it to Mike to say. "No one knows. The traders never go south to Los Angeles. Probably for a good reason." There were rumors that suggested there was another fallout belt south of Los Angeles. And there were others that said the desert had encroached from the west and had eaten up everything, and that sand covered the city three-feet deep.

It sounded bad, then again, it almost seemed as if there were rumors about every place they had ever heard of. Most of the rumors were completely wild and unprovable: Utah was said to be filled with cannibals; Las Vegas had zombie snakes and scorpions that could inject the zombie disease with just a bite; in Kansas, the zombies were corn-fed and stood fifteen feet tall. Even Jillybean herself had been a rumor. In her case, the "Girl Doctor" had been proven to be an actual person.

One true story out of hundreds of crazy tales were Mike's kind of odds and with a boat involved he was willing to take the risk.

"You know what?" he said with a touch of his old boyish enthusiasm. "I say we snatch the boat and zip south past the Guardians and see what's true and what isn't. If we find a fallout area like we did up in Cathlamet, we can always scoot around it, you know? And if there are bandits or giant deserts, we can go around them, too. We'll be able to fish for meals and maybe sneak ashore here and there for fresh water. It'll be perfect."

Jenn tried to smile. She tried to pretend the idea of a journey by boat was a great idea. She nodded as pleasantly as she could and tried with all her might to come up with a better, safer idea. The shipwreck was still fresh in her mind and would be for some time, perhaps even forever. Every time she closed her eyes she saw the boat tear apart beneath them as if it was made of tissue paper. She thanked God that the anchor had held just long enough so that the greater part of the wave had already struck when she and Mike went under. Even with that blessing, she had been within minutes of freezing to death, within seconds of drowning, within inches of having her head caved in by the rocks. Her body was raw and aching, nowhere near ready to move. She didn't have the energy to steal another ship. It was simply beyond her.

The same sort of thoughts were crossing Stu's mind as well. The idea of getting on another boat had a strange visceral effect on him. He could *feel* his cowardice swell in his gut like a black cancerous flower blooming. It was an embarrassing sensation and that alone might have prodded him toward siding with Mike, but there was another, far more logical reason to take the boat. He had already made the very short, two-mile trip to Bodega Bay and back, and it had left him drained and lethargic. He needed a nap, a long one.

"We're not ready for any sort of journey," he told them, his voice a rasping whisper. "I don't think I could walk more than a few miles today."

"That's why we need the boat!" Mike said, butting in.

Stu nodded. "And that's why we need the boat. We can't stay here. We can't risk being seen by those people."

Wearing matching looks, they both waited for Jenn to agree. They wouldn't do anything without her and she couldn't do anything because her fear of the ocean overrode their version of logic—her version of logic said: *Keep away from the sea at all costs, it's trying to kill you.*

That was the truest thing she had ever thought, but Stu was also right. They couldn't stay and she was too weak to go.

Would it be different on a boat? Their energy levels would be even lower. The cold would sap them and leave them vulnerable, and with the storm still going strong, being out on the water was too dangerous.

It seemed as though they couldn't go and they couldn't stay—could they fight? Was trudging to town and killing these Corsairs the answer?

The burning logs in the fireplace took that moment to collapse on themselves—a sure sign in Jenn's eyes. They weren't going to fight, which left fleeing by foot or by boat. She stood, went to the window and pulled back the curtain. Everything about this simple act was painful.

As she stared out, the wind howled under the eaves of the houses. The wind was a sign in itself. "We can't leave with the weather like this, not by boat at least."

"But the storm is the perfect cover," Mike insisted. "We could get in close and be gone before anyone has a clue." With growing strength, he turned to Stu. "Did they have a guard?"

Stu shook his head. "I didn't see one, though there could have been someone in the boat itself. Remember how it was back at Grays Harbor?" There was someone asleep in every boat, which had come as quite a surprise.

Mike looked ready to discount a lone guard, who was likely armed with a much better gun than their pistol, as hardly even a speed bump on their road to escape. When it came to boats, he was eternally optimistic.

Jenn held up a single finger to keep him from white-washing away the very obvious problems with stealing the boat. Jillybean had called her a queen. The truth was, however, that she was only a fifteen-year-old girl who looked and felt like a sewer rat that had been pelted with stones to within an inch of her life. The only queenly thing about Jenn was the knowledge that for a few brief days she had been a true queen. She had worn the mantle, she had made decisions when others wouldn't and although she felt as though she had failed, she had not backed down.

All of which had changed something about her. That one finger silenced Mike. "We'll wait until dark," she said, speaking as if her words carried so much more weight than Mike's and Stu's. "If the wind is calmer, we'll take the boat. If not, we'll go on foot. We'll let the signs guide us. They haven't let me down yet."

Chapter 10

Stu opened his mouth to object. He had heard the commanding, royal tone in her voice and he didn't like it. He hadn't liked it when Jillybean had pronounced herself queen. It hadn't been right, and it seemed that so much of what had gone wrong in the past week could be laid at the feet of that choice.

She could have made herself president or prime minister and could have given herself the same dictatorial powers. The difference in his eyes was that a president or a prime minister could not have arbitrarily ordered the three of them to their deaths.

But would the ex-Corsairs have followed a president or prime minister? Maybe? Perhaps, under the right circumstances. He didn't know and he didn't want to think about it. He just didn't want to go down the same road with Jenn, yet he didn't say anything.

Tired and beat up as he was, Mike had that over-eager look in his eyes when he thought there was a boat to command. If Stu stepped in, even if he was on Mike's side, it would end with them leaving at that very moment, throwing caution to the wind.

"If that's the decision, then I think we should get as much rest as we can," Stu said. "And maybe some more pain meds." No one disagreed with that and Jenn was quick to hand out a full dose of Dilaudid even though it was too early. "Slow down there. Maybe half a dose. You don't want to turn us into addicts."

Mike gave this warning a shrug, while he only said, "I'm willing to risk it. Jillybean said she was getting addicted to whatever she was taking, and she had no problem, you know, not being addicted."

"That was her. We're different. We're…" Weaker. It was true even though he didn't want to admit it. Jillybean was crazy and somehow she was able to harness her craziness for her own purposes. "You don't want to be an addict. I remember what they were from *before* and it wasn't pretty."

Cutting back the dose and feeling a miserable hunger within her, made Jenn think she was already halfway to becoming an addict. It was the pain in her joints that had her craving a new high. The pain made sleep, even drug-induced sleep far from easy. The three of them tossed and turned on the mattresses Stu had hauled down, unable to find any position that would suffice for more than a few minutes at a time.

The blustery, wet day wore away and towards sunset, Mike began coming up with more reasons why they needed to steal the boat as fast as possible. He even packed their very meager belongings, finding two pieces of carry-on luggage and a black backpack. Even the medical books were taken, although why Jillybean had stuck them in the box in the first place was a mystery to Mike. Someone as smart as her should have known that books could be found anywhere. Still, he didn't want any excuse to tarry even if it meant hauling what felt like useless bricks.

When the room began to grow dim, he went to the door and cracked it, listening to the wind carry on without let up. "It'll calm once the sun goes down," he said just as Jenn opened her mouth. "It always does."

Jenn waited twenty minutes and then proclaimed: "It's dark. We have to go. We have to put some miles between us and them. Stu?" He nodded. As much as he wanted to take the boat, the wind was blowing fiercely out of the west. There was a good chance that the second they slipped out of the little harbor they would be pushed right onto shore. Yes, they could wait, but with every passing hour, the odds that one of the Corsairs would discover them increased. Maybe they'd catch a glimpse of the firelight or smell the embers, or maybe they would see a muddy print.

Mike sighed wearily, feeling his pains even greater than before. "Fine," he grumbled and picked up the heaviest of the bags. Stu poured water onto the fire and followed Jenn out into the rain where Mike was grinning and Jenn was staring up as the rain fell straight down into her eyes. It was a moment before Stu realized that the wind had died.

"It's a sign," Mike said, nudging Stu.

Stu scratched his jaw where the stubble was coming in thick now. He didn't believe in signs or omens. What he believed was that without the storm masking their presence, stealing the boat would be that much harder. "We're going to need a plan," he said in his rasping growl. Each looked from one to another. Planning was not their strong suit, especially since they only had one gun between them.

"Maybe we can start a fire like Jillybean did," Mike volunteered.

Jenn tried not to look confused at the suggestion but she wasn't sure how that would help them get the boat. She waited for him to fill in the rest of his plan; after a few moments, she snuck a peek at Stu. In the dark his expression was hard to read.

"That'll just get them, I don't know, nervous," he said. "Or, you know extra vigilant." He dropped to a knee and drew out a quick map of the boat, the dock, the harbor and the house. He then looked up, hoping that someone had a better idea than just lighting a fire. No one did. He rubbed his chin again, not seeing the plan. He even thought: *What would Jillybean do?* and came up completely empty.

"Wellll," Stu said, with a shrug. "I think we might just have to wing it. We'll try to, you know, tiptoe down the dock and uh, you two undo the mooring lines and shove off. I'll go down into the cabin. They probably won't shoot right off the bat. I bet." He was going to bet his life on it, but he really didn't see any other choice.

Neither did Jenn or Mike. They both nodded, not seeing any better option. With their "plan" in place, the three began trudging through the dark, cold rain towards the town. From above, the rain soaked them to the bone and from below, the mud sucked at their weary feet. In no time they were exhausted and when the wind shifted into their faces, they could barely make headway against it. By the time they had made it to the edge of town, they were forced to take an hour-long break to recover. They took that break in the Melendez house, where Stu willed himself up the stairs so he could keep an eye on the one house by the harbor and the Corsair boat.

There was nothing much to see. The house remained dark and the boat was only a shadow. The Corsairs were there, however. As they had approached the town, the smell of smoke mixing with the earthy scent of rain-scrubbed air had grown until there was no doubt of its source. He should have been scared. So much could go wrong with their barebones plan that they should have been trembling. He was too tired to be scared.

Eventually, he came down, which was Mike's cue to help Jenn to her feet; they held each other to keep from falling over. Her role in the plan was to keep quiet, untie one of the two mooring lines, shove off when Mike told her too, and not get left behind. It seemed like a lot to ask. When she didn't immediately reach down and grab the backpack, Mike slung it over one of his shoulders.

"If something goes wrong, we'll meet back at the other house," he said.

Stu thought there wasn't even a remote chance of that happening, especially for him. He had the gun and he would use it and he would likely die, which was strangely sad. It was strange because for the first time in days, he actually didn't want to die. He grunted at the realization that he was no longer suicidal. It was all the excess energy he had left.

After checking the Sig, he stepped out into the rain, the gun in one hand and the handle of a little powder-blue piece of luggage in the other. He dragged the carry-on along behind him like an unwilling dog until the mud clogging its wheels finally fell away. Then it rolled smoothly, making a light *thump* every time it ran over a crack in the sidewalk. There were many such cracks.

Jenn hissed, warning him that he was making too much noise. Stu didn't slow and he didn't even think about picking up the piece of luggage. His left arm was still weak and somewhat mangled from the bullet he had taken.

He led them, going in a loop so they would approach the house and the harbor from the side. Once at the harbor's edge, the cement sidewalk gave way to a rickety boardwalk and the *thumps* from the carry-on became regular: *thump, thump, thump*. And they grew louder, but so did the sound of the falling rain, and the endless crash of the ocean. It was a rumbling roar that had started off as background static but had grown steadily as they got closer.

Fifty yards from the boat, Stu slowed and cast a quick peek behind him. Jenn was fifteen feet back, walking with her head hanging and swinging from side-to-side. Mike was dragging under the weight of the backpack and the carryon, his breath panting in and out. Together the two pieces probably weighed forty pounds, but he was so beat up and exhausted that it looked to Stu like he was hauling the weight of a baby elephant along.

It was apparent that they already needed another break, only they couldn't stop right there out in the open. The house of the Corsairs sat on a little hill frowning down upon them. It was so close that Stu could hear a quiet murmuring coming from within; every once in a while, there was a cackle of laughter. If someone came out to smoke a cigarette or to get more wood, or even just to take a leak, the three of them would be caught and killed.

A break would have to wait a few minutes longer. The next few minutes were do or die for them. Stu started forward again and the luggage went *thump, thump*. He stopped and tried to pick the piece up. It was too heavy and after a few steps he had to put it down again. He wanted to ask Jenn for help, but when he had stopped earlier, she had looked back and saw Mike struggling, and now she was acting as a human crutch and was doing what she could to keep him upright.

Stu wished he could just leave the carry-on, but he had picked up the one with the medicine and the food. He started dragging it again when a piercing white light blazed full on him. The light stopped him in his tracks. Like a deer in the headlights or an escaping felon trapped in the circle of a searchlight, he froze, unable to move as the light poured over him, forming a shadow on the dark water to his right.

He didn't even try to bring up the gun to shoot it out. It sat forgotten in his hand as he saw the silhouette of a huge man hurl something at him. At first, he thought it was an odd-shaped hand-grenade. It struck the side of the hill ten paces up from him and rolled down to stop at his feet.

"What the hell, Stukey?" the giant growled. "I know a rat when I see one." He hawked up a big ball of snot and spat it at Stu.

Being spat at got Stu moving. He might have been only a shadow of his old self just then, but he wasn't going to take being spat on by anyone. Up came the gun in a sweeping move and he aimed just as the man pulled the window shut and yanked the curtain back. Stu was in the dark again and very confused. Fearing a trick, he kept the gun pointed at the window, uselessly as it turned out.

It did not open again.

A few seconds of Stu standing like a statue passed before Mike whispered, "What was that about?"

Stu held a finger to his lips. He didn't know what had just happened and his only clue lay at his feet. Grunting down to one knee, he saw that the feared bomb was in fact the charred remains of a cooked rat. Some guy named Stukey was serving rat for dinner—there was meaning behind this, which, for the life of him, Stu couldn't figure out. Jillybean probably would have been able to discern volumes of information from the nasty-smelling rodent and the man's distaste for it.

"I'm not her," he said under his breath. Slightly louder, he said to Mike, "They didn't see us. Come on." He kicked aside the rat and in a second the carry-on luggage was again muttering softly: *thump, thump, thump, thump.* Softly or not, it was the only sound that wasn't the patter of rain, and it seemed to Stu that the closer he got to the boat, the louder the *thumps* became. He slowed and now the piece of luggage spoke with a deliberate cadence: *thump-thump-thump-thump.* Stu was afraid that anyone in the boat would be able to hear it, and someone did, only that person had his own fear.

At twenty-four, Rob LaBar was the youngest of the Corsair recon team who had come south the month before on the thirty-three foot, *Wind Ripper.* As such, he had pulled the worst guard times and was the butt of every prank. The pranks were a daily occurrence. Unlike the others, he didn't dare sleep on guard duty and, after accidentally putting a bullet-sized hole in the *Ripper's* hull in a fit of terror, he kept his AR-15 on safe and on the cushion beside him, instead of in his sweating hands.

LaBar was developing an ulcer. He had heard the *thump-thump-thump-thump,* coming closer and closer; nothing had ever sounded so dreadfully ominous to him. This wasn't his friends playing tricks, he was so sure of it that his sweating hand had crawled along the cushion like a spider going for the AR-15...only to stop an inch away.

What if I'm wrong? he thought, remembering the panicked shot that had put the hole in the boat. It had been ten days ago and he still hadn't lived that down and probably wouldn't for...

The boat suddenly rocked as someone took a step on board— LaBar's hand grabbed the AR-15, his thumb sliding to the fire mode selector. He hesitated, wanting to laugh aloud and say: *Alright, who's being the wise guy,* only he knew in his trembling gut that this wasn't one of his friends. This was exactly who he was guarding the boat from in the first place: a stranger.

Above him, the stranger took three unhurried steps to the stairs that lead down to the cabins, down to where LaBar was sitting. With each step, LaBar's heart beat faster and faster, but when he saw the first muddy boot and the rain-soaked edge of the stranger's blue jeans, his heart felt like it stopped. No one in the recon team wore blue jeans. They all wore camouflage.

Stu heard the scrape of the gun as LaBar slid it across the table. He knew exactly what the sound was and knew that with every step down, he became more and more of a target. "You don't want to do that, son," he growled. Although Stu was only twenty-one, he had the gravelly voice and the steel in his eye of a much older man.

There was movement on deck and for a moment LaBar took his eye from the boots. There were others! He could tell they were at the mooring lines...and now *The Wind Ripper* was being shoved off.

"S-Stop or I'll sh-shoot," LaBar said in a whisper.

Stu had no choice but to go on. He was halfway down and if he turned around and went back on deck, he didn't know what would happen. When he reached the bottom step he had to pause to allow his vision to catch up to the intense dark below deck. It was a few seconds before he saw LaBar and his AR-15 which was pointed right at him.

"Stop," LaBar said again. "You can't have the boat. You got it? It's my job to stop you. Got it? Do you understand?" The stranger, tall and lean, was shadowed in such darkness that he seemed to be without any features.

"You think this is your job?" Stu said, low and gruff. "Let me tell you, dying isn't much of a living, boy." They both had their guns trained on the other, their fingers slowly squeezing back on the triggers; if one fired, the other would as well just as a matter of flinching. They were two scorpions in a bottle, with subtle differences. Stu was too tired and already in too much pain to really be frightened. And he had nowhere to go. He couldn't turn around and leave; he could only press on and he did so, literally.

Stu walked deliberately forward until he stood over LaBar, the black bore of the AR touching his jacket. He didn't say a word because he didn't need to. Every second that he remained alive was another second Mike had to get the mainsail raised and the rudder adjusted and the jib prepared.

Jenn wasn't much help, so it was a blessing that Mike could do all this in the dark. But he was moving slowly, tripping over the lines and lurching into the shrouds in a way that wasn't like him.

When LaBar realized that *The Wind Ripper* was being stolen his ulcer began to ache. "You can't take her, they'll kill me if you do."

"And I'll kill you if you try to stop me, so that leaves you in a bit of a pickle. If living is what you want to get out of this, I'd hand over that gun. We're not Corsairs, we're...we're with the Queen." This was only a little lie since Jenn had been queen once. "She's compassionate. She won't kill you for doing your job."

Time was slipping away from both of them. Stu could hear Mike struggling to get the boat out into the narrow channel so she wouldn't run aground in the middle of the harbor. LaBar was running out of time to do anything. If he didn't stop these people he would die a horrible death, a far worse death than getting shot in the heart.

He knew what he had to do, but he couldn't pull the trigger and when Stu reached out a gentle hand and pushed the tip of the barrel away, he didn't fight it.

Stu quickly took the AR from him. "Up the stairs, now," he snapped, gesturing with the black pistol in his hands. When they got on deck and LaBar saw an unarmed teenage girl slouched by the wheel and what looked like a schoolboy, still wearing his backpack, trying to coax a meager wind into the boat's sails, LaBar realized he had been tricked.

"Cover him," Stu said to Jenn, handing over both the pistol and the rifle. He then moved off to help Mike. "What can I do?"

"We're not moving. I think we're grounded," Mike hissed, feeling frazzled and embarrassed. He had not expected such a small boat to have such a deep keel. "I'm going to need you to help push us off."

Going into the icy water was the last thing Stu wanted to do—second to last. It beat getting shot. Stu yanked off his coat and pulled off his boots, took a deep breath and dropped over the side. He let himself sink to the bottom, where everything was murky. Thankfully the boat had only been painted black to the waterline and he was able to see the long slope of the boat and the deep keel. He swam to it, braced his feet in the silt at the bottom of the harbor and heaved with all the strength in his back and legs. Pain raced through his body and bubbles erupted from his nose and still, he struggled against a boat that weighed nearly three-thousand pounds

By all reason, Stu shouldn't have been able to budge it much, if at all. It was a sprightly, quick-tempered boat, however and it yearned to be free and racing with the wind. It ground forward an inch and then two and then it suddenly lurched in a brown cloud and for just a panicked second, Stu feared it would shoot away and leave him behind.

Kicking off the bottom, he swam to the boat, which Mike was scarcely able to hold in check. "Hurry, Stu," he whispered, turning *The Wind Ripper* up into the light wind to keep her from bolting back into the shallows. At the stern, Jenn was also urging him to catch up. She should have been keeping a closer eye on LaBar.

He saw his chance and flung himself at Jenn, grabbing for the gun and screeching, "They're stealing the boat!" One hand found the gun and the other, balled into a fist, found the side of her head and sent her flailing backwards.

All around Stu time seemed to speed up. In what felt like a blink of an eye, Corsairs were pouring out of the house, guns in hand. Mike looked as though he had instantly forgotten his weariness and pain; he launched himself at LaBar, who had pulled the Sig Sauer from Jenn's limp fingers.

Stu swam as hard as he could for the boat as the two fought for the gun. LaBar had the upper hand. With the heavy backpack, Mike did look like a schoolboy compared to the much bigger Corsair. *I'm not going to make it*, Stu realized. The boat was drifting into the deep channel, away from Stu. He saw that he would catch it just in time to be confronted by LaBar and the gun.

He wasn't wrong. Just as he reached the stern ladder, LaBar twisted the gun from Mike's hands, fumbled with it for a moment before he was able to turn it on Mike. LaBar grinned just as his friends forty yards away on shore opened fire. The grin disappeared as it felt as though someone took a baseball bat to his left leg. He was spun halfway around before collapsing and falling down the stairs into the cabin.

To Stu's surprise, Mike wasn't hit in that first barrage. Bullets flew all around him and left him miraculously untouched. Mike's mind was only on protecting Jenn. He turned to rush to her side when a bullet got him, hitting him in the back with a meaty thump that sent him sprawling on deck, unmoving.

Chapter 11

The blow to the head had scrambled Jenn's brain. She couldn't seem to connect the very obvious dots: gunshots plus LaBar writhing and hissing in pain, plus Mike struggling to breathe and making a wheezing *huah, huah, huah* sound, meant what? And why was the boom swinging around? That meant something too, something important, she just didn't know what.

A soft voice called to her: "Turn the wheel, Jenn."

Wheel? What wheel? A car wheel? The wheels on the bus that goes round and round all through the town? "Huh?"

"Above you, damn it!" The soft voice had been Stu's; it was no longer soft. His normal growl managed to cut through the fog in her head. She reached up and there was a wheel above her; a boat's wheel. She started turning it, not really knowing or caring if it was the right direction because just then she realized someone was shooting at them.

Under the echoing booms of the guns were hissing crackles that seemed very close.

"Jenn!" It was Stu, sloshing toward the back of the boat. The rain was coming down in fine sprinkles, which didn't account for the water dancing in zipping lines in front of him, behind him, all around him. It took a second for her to understand: they were shooting at him. And the hissing crackles that seemed very close meant they were shooting at her, too.

What about Mike? Ignoring the danger, she sat up and saw Mike on his back, his spine arched, desperately trying to find a way to breathe.

"Jenn! Turn the wheel the other way."

She wanted to scream: *I don't care about the damned wheel!* This wasn't Stu's fault, however. It was hers. She had taken her eyes off the Corsair for two seconds and now Mike was shot, and the boat was heading back into the shallows and Stu was within inches of having the top of his head blown off.

Hoping she could fix everything with a flick of the wheel, she gave it a spin and tried to rush over to Mike's side. Her head spun as quickly as the wheel and with the boat suddenly shifting in a new direction under her feet, she tripped and fell down the cabin stairs, landing on top of LaBar, who threatened her with the Sig.

"Help me or else I'll…"

She pushed off of him and climbed back up the stairs. There was no threat he could make that would keep her from Mike. She came on deck just as Stu climbed on board, bringing with him ten gallons of seawater. Before she could rush to Mike, Stu grabbed her by the ankle. As she dropped, bullets whizzed just overhead. The shooters on shore were deadly and precise. They were trying to keep from hitting the hull and sail and even with the dark, fifty yards was not too far.

Jenn kicked away Stu's hand and was again about to go to Mike's side when LaBar suddenly yelled, "Stop shooting! Cannan, it's me, LaBar. I got them covered." Just edging up over the top of the deck was LaBar. He swiveled the pistol back and forth from Stu to Jenn.

"How many are there?" Captain Thomas Cannan called over the water.

"Two and one dead," LaBar yelled back.

Mike wasn't dead yet. He was still making that terrible, harsh noise as he tried to breathe, but it was fading. Jenn stared at his strangely arched body as the night grew amazingly calm. The rain became a soft drizzle, and the wind only sighed, gently pushing the boat along through the deep channel.

The calm crept into Jenn, infecting her. She should have been freaking out, screaming and throwing herself at LaBar to tear his eyes out. Instead, she stood and, ignoring the gun LaBar jabbed in her direction, she went to Mike. He was wild-eyed and red in the face, but his grip was still strong. He squeezed her hand hard enough for the pain to cut through to her.

"Get away from him," LaBar whispered, afraid that Cannan would think he was letting things get out of control. Cannan wouldn't hesitate killing him along with the prisoners. "Come on, move! And you, swing us around…" His mouth kept moving but no air was coming out.

Stu had used the distraction that Jenn had caused to grab LaBar's AR-15, which had been propped up next to the wheel, forgotten. "Here we are again," he growled. "You gonna pull that trigger this time, boy?" When LaBar hesitated, Stu laughed, quietly. "That's what I thought. You were awful tough punching a defenseless girl. Let's see if you got the balls to trade bullets. Or are you too chicken, boy?"

Normally Stu wasn't this chatty. He needed to buy time. *The Wind Ripper* was very slowly edging down the harbor. In another thirty seconds or so, they would be more shadow than substance to the men on shore.

"You're not going to shoot," Stu went on in a murmur. "We both know it. And if he dies," he jerked his head toward Mike, "She is going to kill you. She is going to take out her knife and stab you in the throat and there won't be anything you can do about it because if that gun moves even an inch, I'll put a bullet in your eye. Your only chance is to drop your weapon and beg for mercy. It'll help if you tell them that you're going to bring the boat about."

LaBar shook his head. "I won't."

They were running out of time. The Corsairs on shore were waiting. "Then I'll do it," Stu told him. Raising his voice, he called out, "I'm coming about." He wasn't, of course, he just needed a reason to let the sail fill and float further away.

"I-I'll tell," LaBar said, channeling his inner seven-year-old.

"And I'll shoot you. What you're missing in all this boy, is that I'm not afraid of dying. Are you?" Stu knew he was. It was all the leverage he needed because LaBar knew it, too. Realizing this, the Corsair backed down into the cabin, with his gun pointed steadily at Stu until he could dart to the side, where he leaned against a bulkhead, breathing heavily. His leg ached and there was hot blood leaking down into his left shoe. He had no idea what to do. His options were terrible. If he said nothing he'd be taken hostage and probably killed when they were out to sea and if he called out now his friends...

Stu seemed to be reading his mind. As he turned the wheel to get the most out of the meager wind, he whispered down to LaBar, "If you call out, your friends will open fire on us and chances are the boat would be shot to pieces. You might get hit. You might even die. I might die but I guarantee you I will set this boat on fire before I do. In fact, it'll be the first thing I do."

Jenn had been trying to get the pack off of Mike's back when she heard this. She turned to see if this was a bluff and caught Stu's hard gaze. He wasn't joking. The three of them had run out of options. They couldn't allow themselves to be captured and if the sail was reduced to rags, they would lose the ability to steer and would run up in the shallows where their only choice would be to swim across to the bare sandy spit of land on the other side of the harbor where they'd be trapped.

"Oh crap," she said under her breath and gave up on the struggle with the straps of the pack. She had found a tiny folding knife with a pearl handle at the house they'd spent the day in; it was not even two inches long and dull as a spoon when she had dug it from a junk drawer. During the long hours of recuperation, when she hadn't been sleeping, she had honed the blade and oiled the elbow joint.

It came open with a flick of her wrist and in seconds she had cut away the pack and slid it out from beneath Mike.

"Oh, lord...that's better," Mike said as he rolled to his side. "How bad...is it?"

So far it was great. It was something of a miracle that he was breathing again; it was a harsh wheeze for sure, yet he was still breathing well enough to form words. Using the knife, she sliced up the back of his shirt and then froze. Other than a deep, ugly purple welt that she could fit her thumb into, he was unharmed.

"It's. It's, hold on," she said, feeling as though she had been slapped on top of being punched. Grabbing the bag, she saw the hole where the bullet had hit the pack; what she didn't see was the exit wound. Quickly, she tore the pack open and looked in at the jumble of items. What jumped out at her was one of the medical books; there was a pinky-sized hole in the front just above the title. Turning it over, she saw that the back cover was pushed out.

"Holy-moly," she said and pried back the cover to expose a blunted, distorted hunk of metal.

"What is it?" Mike asked, nervously. When she showed him the bullet and the book, he breathed out, "No way." He tried to sit up, only to feel a dreadfully, sharp pain in his back. "I think something might be broken in me."

Just then there was no time for a diagnosis. *The Wind Ripper* was slipping between the green, algae-coated buoys that marked the deep channel. Stu was running in a zigzag pattern because for every ten feet forward they went, the boat would slip ten to the left, closer to the shallows. Mike could see he didn't have the boom angled correctly. He tried to get up but the pain felled him. Then he tried to point at the boom, only just then someone from the shore yelled to tack back.

"What the hell are you doing, LaBar, you moron?" Cannan demanded.

They were seventy yards away now. "Tell him the rudder isn't answering totally," Mike whispered. "Tell him the wheel is only going a quarter turn."

Stu relayed this message to which Cannan bellowed, "Then drop the damned sail! It's not going to fix itself. Son of a bitch, you're dumb."

"Right. Sorry," Stu yelled. More quietly, he said, "Everyone lay flat." Ten seconds went by before the first shot rolled down the bay like an explosion. The bullet streaked by between the sail and the deck; a terrific shot especially as they were a hundred yards away now, and they were essentially a black boat against a black background.

The next shot streaked over Stu's prone body, causing the air to stir across the nape of his neck. He shuddered and screamed out, "Stop shooting! We give up! There are women with us!"

"Drop the sail this instant or else!"

Unbelievably, Stu started to get to his feet. "Okay! Just don't shoot. You got one of us, okay?"

"This is your last warning! Drop the sail!"

"What are you doing, Stu?" Jenn demanded. "Don't do it. Are you crazy?"

He limped slowly over to the mast with his hands in the air. "The only way these guys are this accurate is if they have a thermal scope." The shots had been scary-close, too close for any marksman they had ever heard of.

Jenn's blue eyes were almost bugged out of her head. "If we give up…"

"We're not giving up and I'm not really going to drop the sail. I'm only trying to give us a little more time." The question was: how much time? If he dawdled for one second too long the sniper would put a bullet between his shoulder blades. "J-Just stay down."

She hunched lower, pressing herself against Mike's chest until he groaned. "I should be the one protecting you," he said. "Or better yet, where's that book?" It was laying just within reach on the deck; it was heavy and hurt to grab it. That was okay: feeling a little pain was better than being dead, any day. He leaned it against Jenn's back. "You know what? I think this book is like an omen. It saved my life. Maybe it means you were meant to be, like a surgeon or something."

"I don't know. There's so much pressure and…" A gunshot stopped her; a fraction of a second later Stu fell near the mast. He was grinning.

"That was a close one," he said. Jenn sucked in a breath, looking as though she was about to say something. He cut her off. "Hold on. One-one-thousand. Two-one thousand." Suddenly, he rolled to his left just as another gunshot rang down the harbor. Fiberglass splinters exploded where he'd been.

The grin was gone as he whispered: "One-one-thousand," and rolled again. This time the miss was by three feet. Again, he rolled, this time without counting. There was a pause and then the gun started firing faster. Stu hopped up, pushed the boom over to the side, sending them zigging at a new angle for the harbor entrance.

Just as the boat heeled slightly in the light wind, he threw out his arms and dropped again. There was a pause in the shooting in which he whispered, "One-one-thousand. Two-one thousand." Once more he began rolling from one side of the deck to another. The sniper fired twice more before he stopped. By then they were over two-hundred yards away and the thermal image had to be extremely fuzzy.

"Everyone okay?" he asked, still hugging the deck.

"I can't say as I'm exactly okay," Mike answered, "I'm not dying if that's what you mean."

Jenn sat up and looked around wearing a pensive, pinched expression. They had been flailing from one disaster to another and a part of her was resigned to the idea that nothing would work out for them. Nervously, she touched her arms and hugged herself. She was unhurt and *The Wind Ripper* had fewer holes in it than she expected which was a good thing since they were heading for the ocean.

"I'm fine," she said. *For the moment*, she didn't add. Stu still had a bit of a grin about him which was so rare she didn't want to spoil it. Yet there was a big question hanging over the boat, or rather, within it. "So, what are we going to do with the guy down there?" She pointed at the deck.

Stu's mood wasn't going to be dimmed by a coward. "We can just wait until he dies," he said loud enough to be heard by LaBar. "I saw his wound and unless *you* do something for him, *Doctor*, he doesn't stand a chance." Jenn was confused and the way Stu was staring at her with his eyebrows raised up on his forehead and his chin going up and down in an exaggerated nod was only making her more confused.

Mike caught on. "Do you think he even has a chance? It looked pretty bad to me." In truth, he had no idea what sort of wound LaBar might have. "The internal bleeding is probably what's going to do him in. It just sneaks up on you." Mike began to groan himself into a sitting position when LaBar spoke.

"It's just a scratch. I'm fine, so stop trying to scare me." He was more than scared and the wound was more than a scratch. There were two holes in his thigh and both were leaking blood at an alarming rate. The wound was going to kill him one way or another. In his mind that was pure fact. He was out of options. Even if the people on deck let him go, it wasn't like he could go back to Cannan. "He'd kill me."

And he couldn't go to San Francisco and try to join up with the Corsairs down there because they had all gone over to this new queen. The intel on her was all over the board. Some of their spies said that she hated the Corsairs with a burning passion and that she was driven by revenge. Others said she would take anyone as long as they swore allegiance to her.

One way or another, everyone knew he was in Recon and when the Queen found that out she would torture him for information of which he had quite a bit. He knew the names of the spies in San Francisco. He knew how they communicated with the Recon team and he knew the radio frequencies and codes.

And he knew that he would be hunted forever by the Black Captain if he said anything at all.

"I'm screwed," he whispered, biting at an already ragged fingernail and studiously avoiding his wounded leg.

His whisper carried up to the deck. "You're not that screwed," Stu told him. "We have a real doctor up here. You know, like from before." LaBar scoffed at this. There were no more doctors. The closest thing to a doctor LaBar had ever heard about was a sullen, alcoholic crone of a nurse that the Black Captain kept around to keep the men from faking sickness. The nurse killed more men than she ever saved.

"It's true," Stu said. He picked up the medical book with the hole in it and tossed it down into the hold. LaBar picked it up and squinted at it in the dark. He could read the word medical which was in a bold white font, but everything else was something of a blur.

"Is she going to fix me? Just like that? No questions or nothing?" Skepticism so dripped from his voice that he crossed the boundary into rudeness.

Stu casually checked the AR-15 and said, "You can trust her or you can bleed to death. Take your pick."

Jenn wished she had a say in all of this. She wasn't a doctor and barely knew a thing about medicine. Still, she knew they couldn't have an armed enemy below deck. "I can take a look at him if he behaves," she said, trying her best to imitate Jillybean's highbrow, imperious mannerisms and speech pattern. "And that means no gun. Do you hear me?" She thumped the deck twice.

He had heard. LaBar sat in the dark for a good five minutes before his head began to spin. Only then did he agree to give up his gun. As soon as he did, Stu frisked him, tied his hands and got three lanterns burning, one of which sputtered and wavered as if angry at being awakened so late in the evening. It soon went out. The two remaining lights pushed back against the gloom just enough to show Jenn that she was in way over her head.

Judging from the blood gushing out, a good-sized vein had been nicked. It would mean a repair job without anesthesia beyond a few pills, that is, and without IV replacement fluids.

"Until morning, I can't do anything but cinch the wound down and dress it." She used an old shirt as a bandage and a belt as a tourniquet. Begrudgingly, she let him have two of their pain pills. He was then locked in a small cabin near the bow of the boat. By then it was after midnight and they were out on the ocean, a mile from land.

The wind died, the rain became a fine mist and the waves had become only gentle rippling swells; a fortunate turn since none of them had the strength to battle the elements. It was hard enough battling to stay awake. Stu took the first watch and, bundled as he was, almost to the point of being swaddled, he lost his battle and promptly fell asleep and did not wake again until a soft dawn light managed to creep past the thick morning mists.

"That's embarrassing," he grumbled, mad at himself. So many terrible things could have gone wrong, but only one had. Stu was just standing and stretching his worn body when he heard soft laughter. He froze in midstretch, realizing that they were either fifty feet from shore or there was another boat very close by.

The laughter was followed by a low murmur and when Stu squinted through the mists in the direction of the sound, he saw the fuzzy outline of a black sailboat.

Chapter 12

Just before Deanna pulled the trigger, she saw something of the boy in Neil again. Up until the moment he had allowed himself to be ravaged by zombies in order to save her, Neil had always been amazingly boyish. It was as if time had come and gone, flowing all around him and leaving him untouched. At thirty-four, when the apocalypse had started, he had still been getting carded at bars.

The bullet wounds and the claw marks and the half-bitten off ear had turned him instantly old. But just as the cylinder of Joslyn's .38 snub-nosed pistol went around, she saw the boy in the man once again, and her sadness became close to overwhelming. She almost couldn't watch as she blew out his fried brains...almost.

Survival had toughened Deanna and she knew that if she closed her eyes she would likely only blow off a chunk of his head—and it would take a second shot to finish him. With her teeth gritted, she pulled the trigger and the hammer crashed forward.

Click!

Her hands remained steady, but her heart convulsed in her chest. The gun had dry fired. Confused, she looked down at the gun, and reflexively pulled the trigger again: *BAM!*

This time it fired, sounding like an explosion which echoed throughout the school, causing the undead to let out howls of rage. The bullet just missed Neil's nose as it went on to embed itself in the far wall next to the cafeteria door. Deanna was even more confused and this time it felt like her heart had stopped. Once more she looked down at the gun and whispered, "What the hey?" With her ears were ringing, her voice sounded muffled.

Deanna opened the cylinder and saw that Joslyn was one of those strange people who kept the first chamber empty. Deanna closed the chamber and found herself staring into Neil's open eyes; they were very dark with a tinge of red to them.

"I was having a dream," he said. "It was a good one of Sarah. We were back in Georgia. In the CDC. With Sadie and Eve. It was nice. Shoot me or let me go back to bed." He closed his eyes again and in seconds, he was snoring.

"Sorry, Neil. I won't mess up this time. I hope all your dreams are...are..." She pulled the gun back as something struck her: people didn't dream once they were bitten. She had never heard of such a thing. There was always a pattern: during the first few hours, they were too frightened to sleep. Then came fierce denial and sullen anger and growing pain. There was always so much pain that sleep was impossible. Normally, they would be in a rage-filled delirium by now.

Which meant what? "Maybe that means he won't die."

Filled with frantic hope, Deanna leapt up and turned in a circle, not knowing what to do first. "He's sick and sick people need medicine."

This was such a no-brainer that she raced for the front door. "He would also need an IV and more pain meds, and a gurney so we can…" She stopped, suddenly remembering the assassin. If she went running around without thinking, the assassin would find out in a snap that he or she had failed to kill Neil. If so, they might make another try.

As if the assassin was somewhere in the dark building, Deanna pressed her back to a wall between two bulletin boards which were covered with faded twelve-year-old notices for math tutors and science clubs and the coming "Winter Snow-Ball!"

"I'll have to find all the medical items here," she whispered, remembering all the crazy stuff Jillybean did to the undead. "She had to use some sort of medicine on them." But was it "normal" medicine? Would it kill a man? Would she accidentally poison Neil? "I'll just start slow."

She was halfway down the hall to where Jillybean carried out her gruesome practice when the front door came open. Deanna spun with the gun leveled, but it was only Joslyn. She was framed perfectly in the doorway, her hands curled protectively in front of her chest.

"Hey, it's just me, okay? I heard the gunshot. Is it done?"

Deanna shook her head and was about to tell her what happened when she remembered what a gossip Joslyn was. If she told Joslyn what was happening, it would be the same as whispering it directly into the assassin's ear.

"Yes," she lied, giving Joslyn a perfected politician's smile. "He's dead."

The smile, the lie, and the gun dropping to hang at Deanna's side calmed Joslyn's fears and she started forward with her arms out. "I'm so sorry. Here, let me take the gun and let me take care of the body. I'll get Norris to help. I had been thinking about burying him up in the cemetery, but since he was infected maybe we should…"

"No. I'll take care of this. He was my friend. If you could send Emily in, please. I want her to be a part of this. I think it's important, you know? I can't coddle her."

"Right, I'll get her," Joslyn said, and with a last look over Deanna's shoulder at Neil splayed out on the tile, she left.

Deanna had no time to waste. She needed a body to truck out of there in full view of everyone, one that was preferably Neil's size and preferably already dead. On both counts she struck out. The closest she was able to find was a female zombie that was a little over six-feet tall. It dwarfed Neil. Still, it was ragged and skinny, and with a little *modifying*, it might pass. First, it would have to be put out of its misery.

She had found it in the Computer Sciences room, chained to eyebolts set into the floor. It roared at Deanna and tried its best to tear off its chained arms to get at her.

She was just looking around for something to smash its head in when she heard: "Mom?"

It was Emily. She was already inside and judging by where her voice was coming from, she was with Neil. Deanna raced out of the classroom and around the corner to where the offices were, to find her daughter standing over Neil, both crying and looking perplexed.

"Mom, I think he's still alive. He just snorted. Where did you shoot him?" Her eyes roved all over him. "You didn't do it? That's okay, mom. Someone else will do it. It doesn't have to be you."

By then Deanna was right up on her daughter. She whispered, "I don't think he's going to change over. Look, he's sleeping. Infected people don't sleep, Emily. They never have. Ever. He's still immune."

For two seconds, Emily grew excited, then a thought hit her like a bat to the face. "What if Uncle Neil is experiencing a different kind of change? You know, like a slow one. Maybe it might take him a week or something before he goes all the way to becoming one of them."

"Then we wait a week and see," Deanna stated, flatly. "In the meantime, I need you to find a place to hide him. The assassin has to think he's succeeded. And while you're doing that, I'm going to get a replacement that we can bury." Emily's eyes went wide as the haunting screams of the dead echoed around them.

She didn't ask to help with that job and Deanna wouldn't have allowed her anyway. Killing any zombie, even one chained hand and foot, was dangerous work. It was also mentally and spiritually trying. Not everyone passed those tests. During the height of the apocalypse there were some who took their own life rather than face the challenge of living, and there were some who only became weaker with every trial.

Deanna had passed her trials eleven years before, when she had been all that stood between the army of the Azael and her crippled, leaderless people. Every problem since then paled in comparison to that, including killing the chained zombie.

Always cautious, Jillybean kept weapons inside, as well as outside, every room that held the dead.

Because she was tall and still strong, Deanna chose an axe and, after knotting up her long blonde hair, she made a mess of the thing's head with two swings. Next, instead of searching for a key to free the corpse, she used the axe to tailor the zombie to a size more equal to Neil. Kicking aside the hands and feet, she pulled the corpse into the center of the room and ran for sheets.

Once it was wrapped, the corpse took on a sad appearance. It was no longer a hideous monster; it seemed human once again.

Emily stared at it with her mouth gaping. She had never seen a real corpse before, at least not like this. Two years before, a young woman named Lilly had fallen asleep one night with a headache and had never woken up again. Emily had caught just a glimpse of her in her gleaming casket before it was weighed down and sunk in the sound. She had looked as though she were still sleeping, and Emily had to fight the ugly desire to go shake her and yell in her face.

She had no such desire concerning the body wrapped in the sheet. If she were to shake it, there was a chance it might come alive again. It had once before, after all, and so did every corpse in her nightmares.

"You take its…" Deanna began, nearly saying feet, except it had no feet. "Down there."

It was the lightest part of the body and she only had to carry it outside. Still, she was winded by the time they set it down on the sidewalk in front—she had been holding her breath, secretly afraid it would spring out of the sheet.

From there, her mother took over and soon the body was hustled out of sight. "Chains and weights," Emily could hear her mother. "Neil was never a stickler and since he was infected, we may have to hold off on a service until tomorrow."

For the moment, the assassin seemed to be forgotten by everyone, except eleven-year-old Emily, who lingered in the dark school, alone except for vicious giant zombies and perhaps one smallish one. She had not chained Neil but was beginning to think it would be a good idea. There was still a good chance he would turn.

The only room she could find with chains and locks ready to go was the Computer Sciences room, where her mom had left a huge pool of blood, two hands and two feet. It looked like a murder room. A shiver of fear ran up her back and if there had been someone she could turn to for help, she would have left to get them in a blink. There were only three people she trusted for this sort of thing: Neil, Jillybean and her mom.

"It's on me," she whispered. Moving into the room, she made a face, her nose squinching and her full lips almost disappearing as they pursed. The look remained in place during the cleanup, and for some time after as the bleach fumes were strong enough to induce a headache.

Neil remained asleep as she dragged him from the closet where she had hidden him in and hauled him by one foot to the Computer Sciences room. It was only when she had cuffed him that he cracked bleary eyes.

"W-What are you doing?" he mumbled, sounding like his mouth was full of marbles. His eyes were fiercely red, and his tongue looked almost crimson. *Like a demon*, she thought as she jumped back.

"I was just trying to, you know, help you."

He tried to stand and that was when he noticed the handcuffs. He gave them a rattle and then pulled at them with all his might. He had never been a strong man and just then was no different, yet his veins stood out and his teeth were clenched tightly and barred. "What the hell!"

"It's for your own good," Emily replied, backing further away. "You-you might turn into one of them." She pointed back toward the door, where the howls of the zombies echoed throughout the building.

"Then kill me and be done!" he yelled, "Or not. I don't care. Just don't stand there staring at me with those hurt blue eyes. Oh, poor me. Mister Neil is being mean. How can I ever live being perfect just like my stinking mother? What? Are you going to cry? Then do something about it and shoot me!"

He was definitely turning now, but shooting him was out of the question. "I would, 'cept I don't have a gun."

Neil jutted his chin toward the bloody axe. "You can use that. You can be like...what was her name from when we were kids? Mary? Miss Mary had an axe and gave her father forty whacks...no it was something like Miss Mary took an axe and gave her *mother* forty whacks. When she saw what she had done, she gave her father forty-one. Ha! That was it." His grin was maniacal.

"You know what you have to do," he said. "Take the axe and give me forty whacks."

She didn't know whether she could give him even one. The thought was both horrible and consuming, so much so that she didn't realize how much danger she was in. Neil's hands were chained, not his feet. While she was staring at the axe, he kicked her in the back of one knee. Her leg immediately buckled and before she knew it, she was falling backwards into him.

In a flash, his legs were wrapped oddly around her; one across her shoulder, the other around her waist. The heat of his fever radiated off him like she had backed into a small fire. She tried to escape, but he squeezed with his legs, crushing the air out of her lungs.

"Now, whatchu gonna do?" he whispered. His breath coursing along the nape of her neck was shockingly hot. "I'll tell you what, you're gonna give me those keys or I'm going to take a big chunk out of your pretty little neck."

Chapter 13

This will never work in a million years, Ipes declared with his usual negativity whenever explosives were involved.

"You're in luck, it's not even 'splosives, not really. Just because it can 'splode doesn't make it an 'splosive."

The zebra threw up his floppy hooves in exasperation. *I'm pretty sure that's the very definition of explosives. And look! Right there on the tanker are warning signs, and sure my eyesight might not be as good as a hawk's, but it's good enough to see the big fire warning sticker.*

"Yeah, I see the fire warning sign, too, you big dunce." She wiped the sweat from her forehead—accidentally leaving a smear of oil in place of the sweat—and pointed her screwdriver at the sticker. "It's a warning about fire, not 'splosions, sheesh. You ever see a plane 'splode before?" It had been a year since the beginning of the apocalypse and already their memory of planes jetting across the sky on a near constant basis was fading. Now the sky generally sat blue and empty, save for the occasional cloud or bird.

"No, you haven't, and they used to fly around chugged full of this stuff." The seven-year-old waited with her hands on her hips for Ipes to reply, which he did in a sullen manner.

Fine! Play mini-scientist, just count me out. If you could be so kind as to drop me back off at the hotel and fetch some cookies along the way, that would be great.

Jillybean gave him a fully-disappointed *Humph!* which blew the hair from her face. "Cookies!" That called for a second *Humph!* They hadn't seen cookies since Missouri. "It's almost like you're trying to rub Saltines into my wounds." She didn't have wounds exactly, just scrapes on her knees and palms from crawling through a drainpipe to escape a big jerk of a monster that had tried to eat her that morning—and why anyone would waste perfectly good Saltines putting them on wounds was beyond her.

"You can stay right where you are, mister. Watch and learn." She had gone dizzy in the head getting the jet fuel from the truck and into the large drum, where the fumes were now shimmering the air. Carefully she carried a gallon-sized gas tank of it to her first test vehicle: a 2010 Honda Accord.

The moment she began to pour the foul-smelling stuff into the car's tank she regretted her choice of apparel yet again. The sundress was a stunning vibrant yellow and offset the hand-stitched daisies perfectly. Had she been going to a church picnic or a family reunion or even second grade picture day she couldn't have chosen a better outfit. What it was not good for was hot-wiring cars and siphoning gas.

Already there was a nasty old smudge on it just above her tummy. And she had gotten rust stains on her bottom from sitting on the fender of the gas truck, and now some of the jet fuel jumped right out of the nozzle and put some stinky stains right where her boobs would be, if she had boobs that is.

"Oh man," she grumbled, her face scrunched from the smell and the general unhappiness surrounding what had really been a fine dress. Once the jet fuel was in the tank, she put all her measly weight against the small car and began pushing it back and forth to mix the normal gas and the jet fuel. She understood that the act of pouring it in had done most of the job and Brownian Movement, the erratic random movement of microscopic particles in a fluid, as a result of continuous bombardment from molecules of the surrounding medium, would do the rest, however she had a seven-year-old's mentality and if something wasn't stirred with a stick or shaken until it frothed, it just wasn't stirred proper.

"That should do the trick," she said, a minute later, unconsciously wiping her stinky hands on the pretty sundress. "Now is T-minus go time. I just need..." Just then she saw that Ipes was gone. He had been sitting on the hood of the Accord and now he had disappeared. "Ipes? What are you up to?" She walked around the car, more annoyed than frightened. "You aren't mad, are you? We'll get cookies on the way home, I promise."

He didn't make a peep. She bent down to look under the car. He wasn't there. He had run off! "Which is just like him," she grumbled. "At least he didn't take the keys." They were sitting on the ground in the middle of her very long, thin shadow. It was a strange shadow and it was only then that she realized it was still morning...or had just become morning. She couldn't remember, she only saw that the sun was just coming up out of a haze that enclosed her, the Accord, and the back half of the aviation fuel truck. It almost seemed as though there was nothing beyond the haze, as if it went on forever in all directions.

"Curiouser and curiouser." She stood back from the Accord for a few minutes, knowing that something was off, that something about the moment wasn't right.

Murmuring a low, "Hmmm," she picked up the keys to the car and sat down in the driver's seat. A glance showed her the wooden blocks she had glued to the gas pedal. Everything was ready to test the effect of a 50-50 mixture of regular unleaded gas and jet fuel on an average car.

She was ready, yet she hesitated. Somehow, she seemed to know what was going to happen even as she turned the key. The engine purred into life and yet, disappointment cloaked her as she sat there waiting. "Waiting for what?" she wondered. The answer came almost as soon as the words left her mouth. The engine coughed, chugged, coughed some more, wheezed, and then stopped with a jerk that shook it on its wheels.

"At least it didn't get blowd up," she said. "Somehow I just know this is Ipes' fault. He probably jinxed me with his..." She had just been climbing out of the Accord, but froze, wide-eyed as she spied something moving in the mist out beyond the fuel truck. At first, she thought it was a dragon, its wings stretched thin and membranous, like a monstrous bat's wing.

The sight of it struck a nausea-inducing fear into her. She nearly crawled back into the car and only just managed to keep her wits about her; she'd be trapping herself if she went into the car. A better idea was to hide beneath a car, it would allow her to run in any direction.

Quick as a squirrel, the little girl dropped and scooted beneath the car, getting more dirt on her dress in the process. She didn't care since she was very close to puking all over the dress anyway. A moment later, her fear reached its peak as she saw the dragon wing slip silently to the right and then around the back of the car. It was circling her! Turning on her stomach like the hands of a clock, she followed the wings and discovered something almost as horrible as the wing: not only had Ipes disappeared, the fuel truck had as well.

It was just her, the deep haze and the dragon.

Jillybean wanted to rely on logic, only it felt like she was in some sort of dream state, where anything could and, apparently was, happening. She was terrified almost beyond reason. Reason had always been her strongest defense and it suggested that she was either in the middle of a dream or trapped in a dissociative state. It was also reasonable to assume that actual physical danger was highly unlikely since in either the dream or the dissociative state, the terrifying illusions were the product of undue stress and could not cause actual injury by themselves. Though in case studies of patients with classic signs of pathological...

"Wait. Hold on. I'm seven." She looked at her small hand and saw the day-old dirt and the amateurishly painted fingernails. It was the hand of a seven-year-old. "If I am seven, how do I know anything about a dissociative state? I didn't begin studying psychology until I was nine." Oddly, this knowledge was immediately helpful because it meant she was either dreaming or in a dissociative state just as she had predicted. Her stomach-churning fear became only a nervous thrill that kept her breathing high in her chest.

Hoping she was in a dream, she crawled out from the Accord to confront the dragon. "Are you a talking dragon? Do you like to be petted?" Warily, she began to edge into the mists, hoping to catch sight of the creature. It was an elusive thing and acted even more frightened of her than she was of it. It kept just out of sight, always showing little more than a bit of a black wing.

With her frustration mounting, she charged at the creature as fast as her little legs could carry her until she brought it to bay, and in the dim mists, she saw it wasn't a dragon at all. It was...

"It's *The Wind Ripper*, alright."

Sadie felt a moment of confusion as her mind blurred. Jillybean had been right there, so close to the surface that Sadie felt her peering out of her eyes. Then she was gone again, and Sadie was alone with a bunch of vile, barely controlled, barely civilized, and barely potty-trained pirates; they kept peeing over the side of the boat. She wasn't the most squeamish of girls, still she ordered them to hold it while she was on deck.

Next to her, Mark Leney had a pair of binoculars up to his eyes. Beneath the black plastic, his face was a mass of unruly beard, twisting white scars, blue-green tattoos, and yellowed teeth—he didn't look completely human. "She's sitting strange. I don't like it, your Highness."

When he handed Sadie the binoculars, she wiped the lenses furiously as if Leney had some sort of eye kooties, which he just might have as far as she knew. She took a long look as the sailors on board *The Wind Ripper* seemed to be taking their time raising the mainsail. "What don't you like? Isn't this pretty much where we were told the boat would be? I think I wouldn't like it if it wasn't here."

They hadn't been told in the traditional way. Horrible, horrible torture had been used to pry the information out of the spies. It had been so bad that Jillybean had fled rather than face it, leaving Sadie in charge. It was a sickening, thankless job and she would have passed it on to Ipes if she could have, only he was with Jillybean playing house or skipping stones.

Eve had jumped at the chance at being in charge of their body. That wasn't going to happen if Sadie had anything to do with it. And that left Ernest Smith. The phantom was in among the Corsairs, dressed like them, laughing when they laughed, peeing over the side of the boat, trying to blend in. At forty-two feet, the *Hell Quake* was a good-sized boat, though with so many people on board it seemed small and crowded. Ernest moved through the men, taking their bodies and using them to grin up at her with that sly, knowing grin.

"What I don't like is why aren't they in the harbor?" Leney replied. "That's where we were told they'd be. Why sit out here?"

"Zombies," Sadie said. "Maybe there were too many in the harbor. They said it was more like a lagoon than a real harbor."

Leney made a face as if he wasn't buying it. "Maybe, I guess. But what explains all that, your Highness?"

Sadie really didn't know what "all that" entailed. As far as she could tell, the boat was getting ready to flee. Yes, they seemed to be moving a touch slowly, which Sadie chalked up to a nearly complete lack of wind. There was so little wind that the mists barely stirred, and the *Hell Quake's* mainsail sagged in a sad, jowly way. She only lifted a shoulder in a half-shrug. This lack of a response was not what he'd been expecting, so he gave her a long, deep look.

He knows you're not her. The words came from the crowd in a soft whisper. *He knows you're faking it. And soon they'll all know and then what will they do? What will they do to you?*

That was best not thought about. She was, after all, one rather small woman. "I'm not a sailor, Leney," Sadie said, arching one of Jillybean's soft eyebrows; she was only eighteen and these were still somewhat downy. "Why don't you tell me what you *think* I'm missing?"

"Sorry, your Highness," he said, quickly dropping his gaze. "They are moving slowly. I know Cannan, he would've had every stitch of canvas going by now."

"You don't think he's on board?"

Leney took the binoculars back and studied the distant figures. There were only four of them on deck, moving slowly about. Where were the other three? Dead? Eaten by zombies? He shook his head. "He's on board, all right. Cannan liked a weak crew. Not physically weak, but weak-minded; you know, like cowardly a little. They're more afraid of him than they are of any zombie."

"Soooo, what?" she asked, once more taking hold of the field glasses. "What's got you spooked?"

A low growl escaped him. "I don't know. It seems impossible, but maybe it's a trap. Maybe they smoked us out somehow or were tipped off. I'd like to suggest we try to get seaward of him, that way we won't be trapped close to shore if they are trying to pull us in."

It seemed like a sound enough idea and Sadie agreed. She stepped away from the wheel and the commotion, leaning against the gunwale with one leather-clad foot on the lowest rail. Her ex-Corsairs either ducked back into the hold to get out of the way, or sped about sending up a pair of triangular jibs at the front of the boat to get all they could out of the slack wind.

Half a mile ahead of them, *The Wind Ripper* was one step ahead and had their own jibs flying.

The chase was a slow one with each boat gaining a few yards here and losing them there. At times Sadie could have walked faster than the boats and for a girl who could run faster than the wind, the chase was an achingly dull one. It didn't help that Ernest Smith kept whispering his terrible thoughts into her head.

He wanted in. He wanted to slither his way into Jillybean's mind and once there, he'd never leave. Sadie hated him even more than she hated Eve. At least Eve had reasons for the way she was. Eve claimed she was the first. In fact, she claimed to remember being born, which was really weird to Sadie. It was a story she never wanted to hear.

At some point years before, Jillybean stopped denying her connection with Eve. Sadly, the two would never be separated. Eve was Jillybean's ID, that part of a person's psyche that is the source of their bodily needs, wants, desires, and impulses, particularly their sexual and aggressive drives.

It was true, Sadie thought that Eve had the mindset of an infant. She could be annoying and overly demanding and nasty—but she was a million times better than Ernest Smith. Ernest was inexplicably evil. He wanted ultimate control. What he would do with it once he got it was anyone's guess. The last time he'd been in control, Sadie hadn't just drowned in the darkness of Ernest's subconscious, she had died. It was even more than just ceasing to live, it was almost as if she had been eradicated.

Nothing was worse than Ernest, so it was an embarrassment that he was getting into Sadie's head and wearing her down. He had a comment for everything and his voice kept getting louder and stronger, while hers felt weaker and even less decisive than usual. She wished Ipes was there.

You're just going to go along with everything Leney says. He says jump and you have the Queen asking: How high? He says go to seaward and do you even ask what's out there? Is there an island we can crash into? And now it looks like you lost them.

"Huh?" Sadie had been staring into the grey sea. Looking up, she saw that the mists had solidified into heavy clouds and that these were moving southwest in a tearing hurry. Her wild hair began to swirl around her head and at the same time the *Hell Quake's* sails began to fill and snap. Someone was elbowed and cursed at to: "Stop the damned luffing, Greenie!"

The boom was edged back until the sail was tight and there was a fair-sized collar of white water on the bow.

The boat then grew eerily quiet as thirty sailors strained to hear anything from the now invisible *Wind Ripper*. "They're listening for anything that might suggest a course change, your Highness," Leney explained. "That damn Cannan is a slick one. He might double back on us, or he might head north."

"Or he might just keep going," another sailor added.

"Not likely," another hissed. "Everyone knows the *Wind Ripper's* best point of sailing is beam on. He's not going to let us eat into his lead by sticking…"

Leney whistled low and sharp, quieting the crew. "Zip it! Keep your eyes open and your ears sharp."

You too, Ernest said into Sadie's ear, causing her to jump. After the jerk, which everyone saw, she stared straight ahead, afraid to look back. *You should be afraid. You should be very, very afraid. If you're not careful, missy, and you look too crazy, they'll turn on you. They'll string you up from the mast. Say, have you seen the mast? Do you know what those stains are? Those reddish-brown stains? Kinda looks like old blood to me. What do you think?*

Sadie couldn't help it and she began staring up at the mast. There were stains up there just like Ernest said there would be.

He will parade you all over the bay, so everyone will see, so everyone will know. She wanted to ask who would parade her. *But you already know who. Leney. He already speaks for Jillybean. It's almost like he's the real leader here. There's only one thing stopping him from taking over.*

Suddenly, she felt a noose around her throat, choking the life out of her. Her fingers dug and tore at the rope as her feet kicked wildly and her body writhed. She swung like a pendulum as the deck shifted back and forth far below her toes...

"There she is," Leney said, pointing.

In a blink, Sadie was back on deck, her hands at her neck where the straps of the binoculars had been twined around her throat. She gagged for air and then had her breath stolen a second time as she saw a dragon's wing in the mist. "What?" she whispered, as her world greyed out. Ernest was in her head now, banging on the door to her mind. "No," she whispered, blinking rapidly, finally seeing the dragon's wing for what it really was: *The Wind Ripper's* mainsail.

A cheer went up all around her. It was drowned out by the laughter inside. *They're after blood and they're going to get it. And you're going to have to watch and smile and call for more. Just like last time.*

"I don't know if I can do that again." She knew she was weak. She had courage enough for ten men and was faster than anyone alive, but she wasn't mentally tough. It had always been a failing that she had tried to hide.

You can't hide it from me. I know all your secrets. I know what you've done. I know what you really are. You're not a ghost. You're nothing but a wisp of an illusion that Jillybean uses to hide...

"I need to use the bathroom," she said to Leney. Her voice had been as thick and as croaky as a frog's; Leney hadn't heard; he was busy barking out orders and swinging the *Hell Quake* straight north, racing after *The Wind Ripper*, which was only three hundred yards away and making a poor showing of it. The smaller boat had turned to tack straight east only to unexpectedly spin right around and shoot west.

It almost looked as though it was charging right down at them. All around her, men were either laughing or pulling their guns from their backs. The words, "Suicide run" and "We got ourselves a turkey shoot," vied with Ernest's nonstop blathering. It was enough to drive a girl insane.

She tried to flee down into the hold, but the stairs were clogged with greasy grinning sailors, their bloodlust showing along with every yellowed tooth.

Just let me in, Ernest said. *Let me take care of this for you. You'll be able to relax. All your worries will be gone. Doesn't that sound great?*

It did. It sounded wonderful, except for the sick excitement in his voice. And what would Jillybean say? "I just need time to think, okay?" It wasn't okay. There was no place and no time to think. *The Wind Ripper* had made another turn so that the two ships were running parallel courses two hundred yards apart. All around her men had their weapons up and ready to fire.

"Just say the word." She thought it was Ernest saying this and she ignored it, but it was Leney. After a moment, he took his eye from his scope. "Your Highness. Give the order now, before it's too late. Their boat is faster than ours. If we don't get 'em now, they could get away."

She was being pushed from one side and pulled from the other until she felt stretched and thin, and about to tear. It seemed her only choice was to order the murder of these Corsairs or have Ernest do it. She couldn't let him in, no matter what.

Taking a deep, shuddering breath, she called out. "Ready! Aim!" She paused to put the heavy binoculars to her eyes. The first thing she saw was Jenn Lockhart. The young girl was bedraggled and pale, and hardly looked like herself. And next to her were Mike and Stu, ragged and exhausted.

The sight of them sent an electric jolt through her. She jerked, nearly dropping the binoculars in the process.

"Wait," she whispered. Someone mistook the command and a single rifle fired. The bullet missed wildly, but that didn't stop the rash of goosebumps that flared over every inch of her flesh. "Don't shoot, damn it!" She pressed her eyes deeply into the binoculars, unable or perhaps unwilling to believe what she was seeing.

Was it really Jillybean's best friend? Was that the man she loved? *Or am I crazy?* she wondered. *Am I seeing things?* It definitely looked like them. But they weren't acting like themselves. Mike was a great captain, why wasn't he fleeing into the remains of the mists to get away? Why was Stu seemingly giving up? Why was Jenn standing as tall as she could, making a perfect target of herself?

"They want to die," Sadie realized.

And they're going to one way or another, Ernest whispered. *And they're going to take us with them. Don't you see what's going to happen when your men see that Jillybean didn't really kill them? They are going to come after us, and you saw what they did to those spies. It'll be ten times worse for you.*

A shiver went up Sadie's spine. "So, what do we do?"

We have to sink that boat! Give the word to fire, quick. Then just tell them to keep shooting until it goes down. It's our only chance, Sadie. And this is their only chance at a quick death. Jenn might be your best friend, but you know deep inside what will happen if they're taken alive.

Chapter 14

"What the hell are you waiting for?" Leney demanded. He had a bead on the short pale man and needed only the word to blast his beardless face in.

Sadie was looking at the same person through her much more powerful binoculars, and even though she had her great mass of auburn hair pinned up under a hood, there was no mistaking Jenn Lockhart for a man. She was just about the last person Sadie expected to see on a Corsair boat out in the middle of the ocean. The fifteen-year-old had changed. The poison she had taken had worn her down and aged her. She seemed sad, as if she was ready for the death that was coming.

Next to her, Stu's fierce glare could be felt across the water. He hadn't changed much at all. For such a young man, he had always been grim. Grim and tough.

And handsome.

The thought had not come from Ernest. It had come from somewhere deeper—from Jillybean? "Please come back," Sadie whispered.

"Hey!" Leney hissed in his own whisper. "It's time. Give the order or I will."

You can't let him get away with that, a strange multi-toned voice said inside her head. It was as if eight people were saying the same line all at once. She heard Eve's strident voice and Ernest's softly evil one, and Ipes slightly nasal tone, and even her own quarrelsome, incredulous teenage one. The one voice she hadn't heard was Jillybean's.

With the words ringing in her head, Sadie turned to Leney. "You're going to do what?" Sadie hadn't known she was going to say this; she hadn't planned to say anything and nor had she planned to go for the closest weapon within reach: Leney's hunting knife. She was no longer in charge. The body was up for grabs and had they been alone, it would have been a tussle to see who came out on top.

But she wasn't alone. She was surrounded by enemies. The ex-Corsairs weren't her friends or her allies, they were lions—mangy, dirty, vicious lions for sure, but they were still lions. They would turn on her and eat her if she ever showed weakness. Luckily for her, insanity was not a weakness in their world.

Leney knew he had overstepped his bounds. He saw his death in the twitchy look in the Queen's eyes. There was a shrieking, dangerous madness in them. The sort of madness that would completely ignore the boatload of ex-Corsairs who had known, feared and respected Leney for all these years. These were hand-picked men; they would kill her if he ordered it. That madness in her simply didn't care.

For the briefest of moments, he considered killing her. He had always planned on it, when she had set things up properly, that is. Once the bay was fully under control and they had their running water and their electricity just like those softies up in Bainbridge, he planned on taking over. He would rape the crap out of her and then turn her over to his men, because that was the right way to do things.

That would be hard to do if she kept embarrassing him left and right. He would lose the respect of his men; just like the Queen, he knew his men were little more than animals. They had to both fear and respect him if he was going to lead.

It would be easy to kill her. She was a tiny thing, surrounded and weaponless, while he had the M4 in his hands and a Ruger SR40 at his hip. All this went through his head in half a second. The problem Leney faced was all of that went through her head as well and it went through it in a tenth of a second. Even tipping the edge of crazy as she was, she knew what he was thinking even before he thought it and in a shocking blur of motion she was on him, almost hugging him and then sliding around him as he tried to spin. The rifle at his shoulder slowed him just enough that she had his knife at his throat before he could do more than flail and squawk.

"What are you going to do now?" she asked in the softest, silkiest, coldest voice he had ever heard. "Give the order or I will; is that what I heard come from that woman's mouth of yours? Say it again so everyone can hear you. Come on! Say it again and we'll kill you."

Just then, Leney regretted the razor edge he had put on the knife. He was already bleeding. Leney knew she could plunge the blade seven inches deep in a flash, just as he knew that a great part of her wanted to. He had no choice except to grovel. Swallowing his pride, he said, "I'm sorry, your Highness. I didn't mean it. You give the orders around here, not me. I know that and I really am sorry." Someone snorted laughter and Leney felt his ears burn in shame.

"Is this funny to someone?" she demanded. "Who is it? Who finds insubordination funny?" No one was willing to admit that they did. They dropped their gaze and shrugged. She glared at the shrunken men around her, the knife's edge quivered as the hand holding it shook and the arm tensed. Blood trickled down Leney's collar, collecting in a pool in the hollow of his throat.

"Okay then. What about this? Does anyone find this funny?" Before Leney could do a thing, she drew the knife across his throat. Her hand had been shaking before, now she was in complete control and the blade never went more than an eighth of an inch deep. For a second, it looked like little more than a red line, then the blood came in a wave, hot and wet, drenching his shirt.

Nothing vital was touched, yet Leney's knees gave way and he fell, gasping. She stood above him, her black coat flapping and her hair undulating with the wind. The boat had been quiet before, now nothing could be heard except for Leney's ragged breathing. He was having trouble understanding that he was still alive.

"That was your one warning, Leney," she said. She wasn't Jillybean just then or even "The Queen." She was a strange amalgam of churning personalities, each one desperate to be heard and felt and noticed. They had one thing in common, they were angry. Even Sadie was angry. Her life had been taken from her. Snuffed out by men very much like these pirates. Deep in her heart, she hated them as much as Eve did.

Together they pulled the rifle from Leney's hands and ordered another sailor to take his Ruger. "Man the wheel and do as I command, *without* question. Do you understand?"

Leney bowed his head and was thankful she accepted that. He didn't trust his voice just then, afraid that it would crack and that she would hear the seething anger within it. With one hand at his bleeding throat, he went to the wheel and shoved aside one of the sailors. He didn't know which because he wouldn't look up.

Staring out of what felt like a dozen eyes, the Queen watched him for a few seconds and then casually tossed the bloody knife into the ocean. The ripples it made were quickly left behind as the *Hell Quake* sped along, keeping pace with *The Wind Ripper,* which hadn't deviated her course an inch in the last few minutes. The predicament the Queen was in had not changed either.

We need to sink her, Ernest said. *You all see why.*

There was a murmur of agreement, but not from Sadie. She was mentally weak but also loyal to a fault. She wouldn't kill Jillybean's best friend or the man she loved or even Mike, who she knew butted heads with Jillybean more often than not. They had been friends. It wasn't something you threw away.

Ipes lined up with her way of thinking, while Eve went with Ernest. The other voices inside her were too small to make a difference.

"We need Jillybean," Sadie murmured, bringing the heavy binoculars up to her eyes. She thought she knew one way to bring her back: Stu Currans. She centered the field glasses on the rangy Hillman and felt nothing but a twinge. Next, she scanned Jenn and felt the same result.

You're wasting time, Ernest snapped. *The Corsairs are getting angry.*

There was something of a hissing buzz going on behind her and it only got worse when a low cloud momentarily blocked sight of *The Wind Ripper.* The sailors feared that they would lose their prize and weren't exactly pleased that their queen was being unnecessarily crazy. So far, her insanity had either been entertaining or had worked to their advantage somehow. This felt different to them and different almost always meant worse.

For Jillybean, the vagueness of its mainsail in the mist was actually very familiar and it brought her back more than anything had. Sadie could sense her deep inside her mind.

"It's not a dragon..."

It's a sailboat. The whispered words were now in her ear and they were in Jillybean's voice, or rather her voices. There was the child Jillybean, whom Sadie had loved and protected when she was alive. And there was Jillybean's normal voice, which Sadie would describe as know-it-all but impish at the same time. Finally, there was her imperious voice. This last had been the loudest.

"Yes, it's a sailboat and look who's on it," Sadie said and once more panned the binoculars across the deck, pausing on Jenn and Stu the longest. She only gave Mike a quick look and yet the sight of him dragged Jillybean almost all the way back.

That look...

Sadie swung the glasses to the handsome mariner again. "What look? What look are you talking about?"

"It's his look of intense concentration. He wears it when he's feeling the ocean and the rudder and the wheel. They're not giving up, Sadie. It's something else." Jillybean was concentrating so intently on Mike that she didn't even realize she was on a boat or that Sadie and the others had sunk back down into her subconscious.

When she did realize it, she felt terribly lonely. She didn't even have Leney to keep her company.

And right there, almost close enough to call out to, were her friends. It would have been disastrous to call out to them and worse to attempt to capture them. Ernest's idea of sinking the ship was so farfetched as to be ludicrous. Sailors love boats. They'd be the last people to sink a boat without proper reason and if Jillybean gave the order, she would lose even more standing in their eyes.

No, Jillybean's only real option was to discern what Mike was going to do and react to their benefit before he could make his move. They had no hope of escape, otherwise. She studied Mike, his expressions, his moves, even his lips when he spoke, and unfortunately could not tell what he was up to beyond waiting.

He was holding steady, biding his time, obviously waiting for something to happen. Jillybean swung her gaze straight west, however the low clouds kept her from seeing anything.

"Leney! What is *The Wind Ripper's* best point of sailing? What direction?" He swung his arm to the right, to the north. "And ours?"

"With this wind? I'd say almost dead south, your Highness. Now compared to her, it's a whole 'nother story. Compared to her, this is it. That's why I was trying to warn you, your Highness, she's sprightly. She really might get away."

Jillybean drummed the rail with her fingers. Had she not been in the process of hounding her only friends to their deaths, she would have enjoyed the cold breeze and the chill spray in her face. She had been so deep inside of herself that normal tactile sensations had been impossible. Everything she had touched in that strange dream world had the quality of a stale memory.

"So, it would seem she *could* get away if she were trying," Jillybean said, mostly to herself. "Which begs the question, why isn't she trying? Why expose themselves to possible death or capture? Are there any rocks or islands ahead of us?" All the sailors on deck shook their heads. "Then there's only one possible reason for their actions: we are being led into a trap. Leney, please turn us due north."

The possibility of a trap killed the swagger and bravado among the sailors. Their eager smiles vanished in an instant. "Uh, your Highness?" one of the closer sailors asked in a meek voice. "We live south now. San Francisco is south. And begging your pardon, if there's a trap shouldn't we be, you know, getting out of it?"

She smiled benignly at him. "If we were craven, afraid of our own shadows, then maybe we would. You fellows aren't shy, are you?" Once more the crew shook their heads in unison and some even looked offended at the suggestion, and yet when she turned to gaze through her binoculars at *The Wind Ripper,* they all craned their heads to look westward to see what might be coming for them.

Nothing could be seen through the low-hanging clouds. If there was a trap, its jaws were not yet ready to close.

Who is out there? Jillybean wondered as the *Hell Quake* swung north. Corsairs more than likely since Mike was still flying the black flag. Were the Guardians out in force, it would have made sense for Jenn to fly her white and gold flag or perhaps no flag at all.

"Leney, strike our colors and prepare..." He froze, wearing a puzzled look. "It means that I want you to take down our flag. I would've thought you knew that term, though I suppose it is more naval than strictly nautical. Get one of the *old* Corsair flags ready. You know, just to amuse our unseen guests."

The word amuse was muttered in a circle around the boat by the sailors until it came back to Jillybean. Leney was more confused by the word than he had been by the term colors. "Why would we want to amuse anyone? If the Black Captain is out there, he's not going to be amused."

"It's just an expression. In this case the word is synonymous with confuse. If the Black Captain is indeed out there, he might see our old Corsair flag and hesitate. Sometimes even the slightest hesitation is the difference between life and death."

"Ahh," Leney exclaimed, as did many of the other sailors when they understood. Jillybean thought it comical how just the idea of such a simple ruse was enough to fill her men with new courage. She held her smile in place though she wanted to roll her eyes. To keep the urge from becoming a reality, she glassed *The Wind Ripper.*

Mike had changed course along with them, heading northwest, opening up more distance between the two boats, and giving himself more options. Soon, he'd have enough room to tack back toward land at great speed, or turn north with a bigger lead, or suddenly dip southwest and try to hide among the low clouds.

"If there's someone else out there, which would he do? If they were still feeling the effects of the poison, then fleeing toward land would be the last thing they..." A distant shadow behind one of the clouds stopped her. Its darkness swelled to take over the cloud completely. *It's the dragon!* was her first thought, and in a way, it was.

The Black Captain had arrived in person and not only had he brought a fleet of a hundred and twenty ships, he had also brought a storm with him. The clouds began to fuse into one immense grey bank as the wind began to blow and the rain whipped.

"Run up the black flag!" Jillybean ordered as she caught sight of the first sail. The Corsair flag went up so quickly that someone might have thought it had been there all along. She had the binoculars pressed so tightly to her eyes, she couldn't blink even if she wanted to—more sails could be seen gliding through the clouds until the grey bank was nearly dark as night.

"Should we come about?" Leney asked. The clotted cut at his throat was all but forgotten as he held the wheel with both hands ready to spin it, and there were twice as many sailors needed to heave the boom around.

"Not yet." Had they been alone on the ocean facing the Corsair fleet, she would have gotten out of there as fast as possible, but she had to worry about Jenn, Mike, and Stu. They were clearly playing the frightened mouse fleeing the cat. They needed to be chased just a little longer to give them a chance.

Mike now had a three-hundred yard lead and he edged *The Wind Ripper* to a north-by-northwest heading. As if she couldn't see the dozens of Corsair boats crowding in on a converging tack to intercept her, Jillybean changed her course to match his. Slowly, she counted to twenty as around her the tension and the fear began to build. Someone hissed a curse.

Jillybean turned to look at the offender with a cocked eyebrow. He had been one of the more eager torturers of the spies; now he couldn't look up at her and all she saw of him was a lesion-covered bald patch. She snapped her fingers at the man standing next to him. "Hit him."

She turned to stare back at the Corsair ships. There was a thud and a grunt. Neither had been very satisfactory. "Again. Harder." There was a hardy thump and a much heavier groan. "Good enough," she said, before turning to one of the sailors at the stern, "Get a smoker ready. Sticky Jim, get my flag ready; I want it hoisted on my command."

Everyone expected her to turn around then and get the hell out of there, however she waited until the lead Corsair boat was only a half mile away. Only then did she begin barking out orders: "Come about,

Leney. Get us out of here! Sticky Jim, strike those colors and hoist mine. I want this deck cleared this instant. All nonessentials get below."

"Y'all wants me ta light the smoker?" the sailor at the back end of the boat asked. It was Sticky Jim's near toothless friend. He was so ugly that Jillybean had trouble looking at him in his tattooed face.

"Yes. Light it and let her go, but don't cut the tether. I want it to drag for a bit." The tether was ten feet long. Because it was so close, from a distance it would look as though the boat itself was on fire. The Black Captain would not be fooled by it. By now she figured he had accurate intelligence concerning her methods.

The billowing smoke and the clouds obscured their vision of the chasing boats but not before she saw Mike bringing *The Wind Ripper* around as if he too were giving chase. It was a smart move and she grinned, appreciating it, knowing that he would use the first bank of clouds they came to make a course change and run west. With that in mind, she had Leney head for the thickest and lowest hanging clouds in their general direction.

They went into it with only a quarter mile lead on the lead Corsair boats. Already some of the pirates were taking a few ranging shots.

"Cut the smoker!" she ordered after a minute in the cloud. The moment it was away, she barked, "Hard to port!" The boat swung east with the wind on their stern; it fairly hurled them along, though in the clouds as they were it was hard to tell exactly how fast they were going. The few men on deck were stone silent, listening for anything that might suggest the Corsairs were catching up. In a stage whisper, Leney suggested adding a third jib. It boosted their speed by a knot and when they finally burst out of the clouds, they seemed to have left their pursuers far behind.

"Point us south," she told Leney, gesturing at another set of low-hanging patchy clouds. She turned to Sticky Jim's friend. "Get another smoker ready, if you please." It pleased him so much that he showed her all of his remaining six teeth in a big lunch-delaying smile.

Everyone except Leney and Jillybean was looking back and when the Corsairs groped out of the clouds, they groaned even though the *Hell Quake* had a half mile lead on them.

"You boys worry too much," she said, cheerfully, laughing at them. Unlike everyone else on board, the sight of the Black Captain's fleet was an unlooked for godsend. Nothing else could have saved her friends, who were well on their way to escaping, or so she figured from the lack of gun shots—they would not have allowed themselves to be taken alive.

Just as good was the possibility of not just destroying the last of the Black Captain's fleet, but also killing the Black Captain himself. *He* was here. She felt it on a gut level as well as a logical one. After so many debacles, there was no way he would let another subordinate command the last of his ships.

No, he was here and he would stake everything on a victory. He would take chances he wouldn't normally take, and she would crush him.

First, she had to escape.

"Leney, take us in," she said, pointing at another dark squall that hovered just over the tips of the waves to their southeast.

Before going in, Jillybean had the next smoker lit. "Cut it," she ordered as the cold, penetrating rain pelted her. This time she didn't alter course, even though Leney and Sticky Jim waited on pins and needles for her to. As she had guessed they would, the Corsairs slowed before going into the cloud; some turned west, others east and some eased into the darkness.

It wasn't half as big as the last cloud, yet the *Hell Quake's* lead had grown even greater and it wasn't long before the Black Captain began recalling his ships, perhaps in fear of a trap. He was right to fear it. If she had been in the position to spring one, Jillybean would have been able to rip a third of his fleet to shreds.

"Get us home, Leney. We need to prepare for our guests."

Chapter 15

Emily's mind wasn't so much as racing as it was spinning in circles. Somehow, her sweet and somewhat dainty Uncle Neil had become unbelievably strong. And where before he would limp when it rained and complained about his back when she wanted to play soccer with him, he was now twisted around her like a vine or the tentacle of a giant squid from some '50s B-movie.

"Do you want me to bite you?" He hissed his hot, diseased breath directly into her ear. "I told you to be good and did you listen? Nooooo. And do you know what happens to kids who do not listen? They get punished."

"I-I-I'll be good," she whimpered. "Just don't, please."

He squeezed her harder, getting a better grip with his legs. "Don't what? Bite you? Hmmm, I don't know. I've never seen a neck so tasty. Not since Sarah. She had a beautiful neck. Did I ever tell you that? I used to love to kiss it."

Neil bent and kissed Emily's neck and then breathed her in deeply, running his scarred nose along the nape. She stiffened, and Neil's anger came back more viciously than ever. He squeezed so hard her back popped and her ribs were crushed into her lungs. "What? Do you think you're better than me? Or better than Sarah? That's it, isn't it? You think you're better than her. You think you're all that because of who your mom is. She's only a politician and who do you think started all of this? Politicians, that's who!"

Emily began to shake. She felt it first deep in her chest; soon it radiated outward into her limbs and jaw. Neil was going to bite her and then she would be infected too, if he didn't kill her that is. He was going crazy from the zombie virus and she had the feeling if he saw or tasted blood there'd be no coming back. In this situation, she didn't ask what Jillybean would do. The Jillybean she knew had always been quirky to the point of being eccentric, and despite the rumors had never been violent, at least around Emily.

And Emily didn't ask herself what her mother would do in the situation. Her mother's adventuring days were long past. Neil was right about one thing, Deanna had become a politician, skilled in the art of making it seem as if she were intently interested in each person she met.

No, instinctively she wondered what her father would do. To Emily, he had become the *fabled* Captain James Grey. Everyone had sung his praises for so long she assumed that there wasn't anything he couldn't do. He had been the strongest, the fastest, the most noble, etc. etc. She sometimes wondered how such a man could be killed even when facing two-hundred to one odds.

A running theme throughout the many stories she had heard concerning her father, was that he always seemed to keep his cool no matter what terrible things were happening around him, and Emily had always hoped she had inherited that trait as well. This was her first test and the courage gene seemed to have deserted her. She felt a terrified scream building inside of her that was only held back by the fact she couldn't breathe. If he released his hold, it would come exploding out of her.

He did the opposite.

His legs were clamped so tightly that her face went from pink to red. "C-Can't...breathe," she said in a high, strangled whisper. "C-Can't..."

"What?" he demanded. "What are you jabbering on about? Are you going to pretend your mom isn't a politician?"

She could only shake her head. Her thick, blonde ponytail swatted him in the face, causing him to lean back and turn his head. This gave her enough room to take a partial breath. As fast as she could she sucked in enough air to spit out: "Y-you t-told me it was Yuri Petrovich..." another thin breath, "who started this...and that he was a Russian scientist, not a politician at all."

"Yuri!" Neil raged, this time accidentally squeezing the air out of her worse than before in his anger. "I hate that bastard! If he was here, I'd tear his head off and drink his blood straight..."

In his fury, he had forgotten Emily. His legs relaxed their grip for just a second; it was enough for a strong girl like Emily to rip herself from his grip. She backed away from him, panting and holding her ribs. Neil looked confused.

"What are you doing?" he asked, his face livid with outrage. "We have to go get Yuri and we have to kill him. You and me, Emily. We can do it together. It'll be just like when Jillybean was little. We'll set the world on fire!"

"I don't want to set the world on fire, Uncle Neil. Neither do you. It's just the fever talking. Do you want some more medicine or some water?"

He stared at her as if trying to figure out what she was talking about. "Water? I said fire? Like the ferry boats, remember? I thought I was a goner just like Ram. Did I tell you how he...oh, wait. I am just like Ram. I'm going to turn into one of them just like he did." With a tired sigh, he sat back, his chains clinking. "Maybe I can use some water. My head is killing me."

Emily backed out of the room. Once in the hallway, she ran for the front door and thought she was going to dash out to freedom; however, the door was chained shut from the outside—she was locked in! With not just one monster but five or six of them. Panic had her by the throat and she found that once more she could barely breathe.

She wanted to hammer on the door and scream for her mother, only she knew that would attract the dead. It was common knowledge among the younger kids that the dead could smell fear and it made them stronger than ever.

Rather than screaming, Emily hid in a mostly empty classroom. The only item in it was an unwieldy machine set in a metal rectangular box. Partially filling the box was a soft slime of algae. Perhaps possessed by some lingering spirit of Jillybean's curiosity, Emily touched the slime.

"Gah," she cried, pulling her hand back. It had been beyond greasy and it moved like a jellyfish over a few feet of stagnant water. The slime was so nasty that it effectively killed her panic as well as any curiosity she had over the machine and why it had so many huge, toothy gears and gleaming pipes. It was a mystery she didn't care trying to solve.

Wiping her hand on the wall, she inched back out into the corridor to try to reevaluate her fears. Yes, she was afraid of the zombies, "Only they're all locked up with big chains. If they were going to escape, they would have by now." She decided that it was silly to be afraid of zombies when there was a killer on the loose.

"First things first," she said, picturing her Uncle Neil. She knew what she had to do: she had to put him out of his misery as gently as possible. "I don't have a gun and even if I did…" She pictured herself trying to shoot Neil and she felt the blood drain from her head. Guns were not for her. They were messy, imprecise tools, something Jillybean had warned her against using when better options were available.

"I'll have to OD him," Emily decided. Jillybean had taught her to be careful concerning certain medicines, that taking too much could kill a person. Sometimes it was a slow debilitating process and sometimes it was quick and painless.

"Like a good kind of poison," Jillybean had said.

Emily had only given her a strained smile at the time, but now she understood that there was a time and a place. This was one of those times. She went to a locked closet next to the principal's office which Jillybean had turned into her personal pharmacy. It came complete with a massive book, detailing the uses and side effects of every medicine known to the people of before.

It took so long to match the pills available to the job needed that Neil was sleeping again by the time she got back to him. He was snoring like a chainsaw and looked so peaceful that Emily decided she could wait to kill him. "When he wakes up," she told herself. She settled down to wait. It was a long wait and the lateness of the evening was too much for her. Emily fell asleep across from a zombie and, strangely enough, the two were probably only ones on Bainbridge to get a good night's sleep.

Everyone else was on edge, wondering where the assassin would strike next.

Deanna oversaw the burning of the zombie body before she redoubled her efforts to catch the assassin. The wall guards were all questioned, the harbormaster was brought in and even the fishermen who went out over the last two days were interrogated—Eddie Sanders was one of these.

Joslyn Reynolds handled his interrogation. It was the middle of the night and yet she was perfectly made up, her deep brown hair washed and brushed, her grey pantsuit showing sharp lines from her iron. In front of her was a folder, half an inch thick. His name was written in red ink along the tab. He felt like throwing up.

A folder could only mean they knew about him. For how long? Had they known from the beginning? Had he been played like a fool for all this time and now they were going to charge him with treason? It couldn't have been simply happenstance that they had asked to talk to him in the one police station on the island.

Joslyn smiled at him. It was a wide, easy smile and Eddie didn't trust it one bit. His breathing began to pick up in speed and there was a seismic flutter going on in his chest. "C-Can I smoke?" he asked, trying, and failing, to smile back at her. "I-I don't n-need one, it's just I'm w-worked up over this whole thing. I mean a spy? Here? In, uh Bainbridge? It's crazy, right?"

Her brown eyes narrowed. "Spy? The worry is of an assassin, but you may be right."

"No. I, uh, meant like a uh, like a uh, like a uuhhhh…" His mind had gone completely blank. He had no idea what he was about to say and now he was sure his guilt was stamped squarely on his forehead.

She looked pained as she asked, "Are you saying like James Bond? Is that the sort of spy you envisioned?"

"Yes!" Eddie practically cried. "The-the name was almost right there, you know? Yes, James Bond. That's the sort of guy we should be looking for. Someone slick like that could come and go in a cinch. He might even have disguises or something." Now Eddie was on firmer ground. What he needed to do was point the eye of justice away from little Eddie Sanders who was a redheaded nobody, and onto the "spy."

"You know what? He probably got on the island right at sunset. You know there's a shadowed area right by tower nine. I told, uh…" He was about to say *my wife*, but he didn't want to bring her name into any of this. "Uh, McGuinness. Yeah, I told Danny, I thought it was a perfect place for someone to get on the island. But you know what? That was months ago. He might not remember. He probably doesn't."

Joslyn looked troubled and that made the fluttering in Eddie's chest come roaring back. "You seem pretty nervous there, Eddie. Try to relax. No one thinks you've done anything wrong. You have a new baby. A man with a baby would never do something like this. That's what I told the Governor and she agrees."

She had just inadvertently called him the worst excuse for a dad in the history of the world and he let that blow right past him. There was hope in front of his eyes. "So, what am I doing here? I don't know anything, I swear."

"I told her we had to cover our bases. After all, you took the Scamp out alone. McGuinness said you practically demanded to go out alone. He even said you offered him a bribe and asked for the Scamp in particular."

"Because it was the only boat and he said that...well, he said someone might be using it to go behind someone else's back because it has that cabin. And he was the one who suggested a bribe. Two nines to fudge the reservation. That's what you should be investigating. Everyone knows he's dirty."

Joslyn bent over and began to scribble a note. "And what did you say to the offer? Did you turn him down?"

Eddie swallowed convulsively. "Yes I-I did. But you know what I did do. I suggested that we try to keep those two people apart, you know, to keep them honest. For that, I suggested I could give him half a nine to use the boat. For me that wasn't so much. You know how lucky I can get scrounging."

"Yes, Gina's always talking about her 'Lucky' Eddie." Joslyn began tapping her pencil up and down. "I think that's all the questions I...Oh, wait. What did you cross the Sound for? More scavenging?" He bobbed his head like a balloon on a string. "Were you lucky?"

His mouth came open to spill out another lie; however the truth was better. "No. I wish I had never gone."

Chapter 16

Jillybean began dictating orders to her fleet in San Francisco when they were still twenty miles away—which was the very limited range of the handheld radios. The words flowed nonstop from that restless mind and there wasn't a person who called themselves a royal subject who didn't think this was going to be the final, crushing battle with the Corsairs.

Oh, and they couldn't wait.

At one point or another, every one of the ex-Corsairs had found themselves stuck in the middle of one of Jillybean's terrifying traps while its steel-edged jaws clamped mercilessly shut on them. They knew the dread and the hopelessness as the billowing smoke grew so thick that it shut out the daylight, and they felt the terror as explosions went off here and there all around them, like someone was playing hopscotch in a minefield. And the screams that followed became so deafening a person didn't know if they were screaming or it was the man next to them.

But the worst were the endless rotting corpses which began to pile up like pyramids, a foul mixture of clotting blood and runny mud seeping from beneath the piles. Sometimes the blood ran like little rivers and sometimes it pooled. A man could never tell how deep one of those steaming pools were.

Having managed to survive the living hell that Jillybean had created, the ex-Corsairs were particularly eager to be on the dishing out side for once.

And yet, those on deck of the *Hell Quake* weren't thrilled with the orders being given out. It seemed, in their limited understanding of the situation, that Jillybean was throwing away a huge opportunity by not fortifying the Golden Gate Bridge as she had the first time they had attacked. Every one of them remembered the slow-motion nightmare as their ships ran up against the heavy ropes that had been strung from buoy to buoy across the mouth of the bay.

Sticky Jim had been on board *The Devil's Eye* when it had tried to break through. Of the twenty-one men on board, he had been the only one to make it out alive as rocks rained down like God's revenge, killing everyone on deck in minutes. He and half a dozen others had been below, cringing as blood poured in through the many holes. At least, at first it had been blood.

Sea water had rushed in next, drowning those who hadn't been put out of their misery from the thrown rocks. He still walked with a limp from eight crushed toes and even days later, he woke in the night bathed in sweat.

"She's letting them in so she can trap 'em in the bay," Leney assured those who could hear his whispering. "Don't worry about that. Once in, bam! She'll slam the door on them. Then it'll be the world's biggest turkey shoot, boys. They won't have anywhere to go. We'll drive them into one of them little bays and then we'll send in the torps."

The idea of blowing up a fleet sounded even better than dropping rocks on them, and they all listened with excitement for Jillybean to move their hundred ships into position for just such a stroke, but again they were disappointed. Unbelievably, she had the fleet sail out of the bay altogether. She had them skirt along the southern edge of the coast before sending them out to sea...out into the sloppy sea, where the waves were growing, the wind was running hard and the visibility was sometimes less than a hundred yards.

Even the dullest sailor knew that their homemade torpedoes were not the most reliable to begin with and that trying to steer them through an ugly chop made them even less effective.

To make matters worse, she pulled all the remaining men who had been left defending Alcatraz, the *Floating Fortress*, and even Treasure Island, and had them hurry to the barren, fire-swept hills north of the Golden Gate. The only people guarding the southern approach to the bridge was a platoon of near useless Islanders, most of whom were women armed with bells of all things.

This had the sailors shaking their heads in complete disbelief. None of them could understand taking men from perfectly good stone, metal, and earthen fortifications, and sticking them on a ridge where there wasn't any cover and the only way to camouflage themselves was to roll around in an ash-mud-stew.

As the *Hell Quake* passed the hills, Sticky Jim looked to Leney and in a hissing, garlic-stinking whisper said, "I don't get it. That is the one place the Black Captain would never attack. Look at them hills, Leney! Only a fool would try to slog across open ground like that."

Leney took a long look at what had once been the picturesque Marin Headlands. The fire Eve had lit a month before had turned it all to ash, and now the rain of the last two days had turned the ash and bare dirt into a foul slime that made the hills treacherous and had turned the low points between them into bogs that could suck a man down and hold him there, perhaps forever.

"What does she thinks ack-sually gonna happen, huh?" Sticky Jim's friend demanded in a slightly louder, slightly more aggrieved whisper, one that bordered on treasonous. They called him Deaf Mick because he tended to only "hear" orders that he liked. "Is it her i-dear the Black Captain is just gonna attack like a complete idiot? Huh? She thinks he just gonna walk, derp, derp, derp, right up a hill that ain't nobody got no bidness being on in the first place?"

"Quiet down!" Leney snapped. "Maybe you forgot that Gaida attacked right up that very hill. And you wanna know why? Because he wanted to flank the damned bridge. Maybe she thinks the Black Captain is going to do the same thing."

Sticky Jim spread his hands in confusion. "Gaida did it *because* the bridge had all them ropes on it. Now she went and took them all down, there ain't no reason to flank the bridge. You see what I'm saying? The Captain ain't no idiot. He ain't gonna come close to them hills. He's gonna see the bridge ain't defended and he's gonna rush in and take the prison and all the islands and then it'll be us whose gotta attack him."

"Yeah," his friend agreed. "And what good will our torps be against an island, huh? Ain't no good at all is what I say."

Leney nodded and smiled as though he had a mouthful of week-old eel. "I'll talk to her." With his throat still stinging from where she had slit it, and his pride in tatters, he made his way to the bow where the Queen stood, eyeing the terrain as they passed.

Before he could say a word, she said, "Trust me." Although the thrum of the rain and the growing wind drowned out the whispers, she knew the mood of the men by the way they made eye contact with one another and the way they made sure to paste bland expressions across their faces when looking at her.

"I do trust you," Leney lied.

She saw the lie and understood; how do you trust someone who'd been muttering or laughing to herself half the morning, and who was now suggesting that they throw away every apparent advantage they had?

"You don't trust me, but you should. Do you know why I didn't cut your throat wide open earlier?"

Leney swallowed, feeling the pain of the shallow laceration once more. "I don't know. Because you need me?"

Jillybean laughed at that. The laugh bubbled out of her high, sweet and painfully honest. "No, don't be silly. I need you as much as I need any of these clowns. I didn't kill you because you are a tool, Leney. The sharpest tool in a very dull shed. You are my voice when I'm not around to speak. Do you understand?"

"I think so."

"For your sake, I hope you do. Right now, you should be my number one cheerleader among the men. These moves you see are only the preliminary moves in a chess match between me and the Black Captain. They may not make much sense at first, however they will soon enough. You understand 3-D chess, correct? Well, this is 4-D." Leney's lips drew into a tight smile and she asked him, "You do understand the dimensions?"

"Like in space?"

Jillybean held back the laughter this time. "Not exactly. And I shouldn't have stated it as I did. Everyone understands the dimensions whether they know it or not. Height, width, depth and the fourth that's frequently forgotten, is time. The Black Captain is unlikely to have forgotten time and I have to assume that he hasn't, which in this case means he's not fighting the last fight."

"Then why put your men on that hill? It's the last place he'll attack."

"It's also the last place we would defend," she said, cryptically. "In chess, you can't stick to the obvious choices or you'll fall into trap after trap and before you know it you're hemmed in and forced to abdicate."

Leney, who had never played chess in his life, gave her a knowing, "Ahh, yes," though he didn't understand at all.

She wasn't fooled, but let it go. She didn't have time to walk him through her convoluted thinking process, which entailed considering every ramification from her point of view, the Black Captain's view, and her men's. Until only a couple of days before, they had been bloodthirsty Corsairs themselves; she couldn't pretend their loyalty was absolute.

She was deep in thought when a buoy's bell made a tinny *clank!* Leney had taken the wheel and was piloting the *Hell Quake* under the massive bridge. She saw he was doing his best to pretend that it was just fine that the span was completely deserted save for the twenty black and silver flags hanging from it.

"It's all part of the plan," he told the others. "Trust me, the Queen knows what she's doing."

"And what is the plan?" Sticky Jim asked, under his breath as Leney turned the wheel.

"Don't worry about it. Just do your part and everything will work out fine." He even managed to tip him a confident wink, though he still didn't have any idea what the battle plan was. About the only thing he knew was that Jillybean was going to run the battle from the north tower of the bridge. Leney, and a retinue of twenty men, were going to act as her personal guard, while Sticky Jim would take the *Hell Quake* and the rest of the men and dock her at Alcatraz.

"Like a damned prize for the Black Captain," Sticky Jim muttered so low that only his gap-toothed friend Deaf Mick could hear. Deaf Mick shushed him anyway since there were others near.

The two were soon separated as Deaf Mick joined the small crowd on the port side of the boat trying to simultaneously keep the *Hell Quake* close to the great cement base of the bridge tower as well as fend it off as the waves heaved them at it with enough force to smash the boat into a thousand pieces.

Leney left the boat first, leaping from the gunwale of the *Hell Quake* and landing on the moss-slicked cement island. A rope was thrown and he tied her loosely to a stanchion. Two of the more sure-footed sailors came after and then came the Queen. She stepped with light confidence onto the tower base and then immediately headed for the rust-colored door set squarely in the side of the tower. It was a squat little, creaking door that led to a narrow, suffocating staircase.

As she entered, black water rained down on her from what appeared to be an endless, living darkness. From out of that darkness came a long, deep-timbered moan, which was followed by a second moan that was almost identical. There was a pause and then the first moan repeated. It sounded like a pair of shadow giants speaking in some alien language.

"What the ever lovin' crap is that?" Deaf Mick asked as he jostled his way inside.

Jillybean knew precisely what the sound was and could have gone on at length expounding on the external environmental stressors being applied to the immense structure from which an infinitesimal portion was being released in the form of kinetic sound energy. She could have written a dissertation on the complexity of it all, if she wasn't suddenly stricken with terror. It wasn't the tower that frightened her, it was the dark and the creatures whispering to each other within it that made her tremble.

"That's the tower itself," Leney said, putting his hand on one of the walls and gazing upward, his face going pale beneath the tattoos, making them look a vibrant green. "This sucker's gonna fall one of these days."

"Probably not today," Jillybean stated with a great deal more confidence than she felt. She couldn't appear afraid in front of her men no matter how badly the darkness scared her. It reminded her of the darkness inside herself. That was an infinite night and within it were the souls of the people she had killed. There were thousands of them.

Thousands, the darkness agreed. *There are thousands of us down here and if you slip and come tumbling down, we will eat you. We will eat you alive. We will devour every...*

"Come on," she growled and began stomping up the iron stairs. *Now is not the time!* she warned, inwardly. She couldn't have an "episode" with a battle looming. For all she knew, it was only minutes away; she could emerge from the tower and find the Corsair fleet massed on the horizon.

She grit her teeth together, ignored the voices and went up quickly, while behind her came Leney and her guard of ex-Corsairs, every one of whom had once been among the most feared men on the planet. Just then, they were far more fearful than fearsome. The groaning tower and the deep darkness were bad enough, but it was the metal stairs that were falling into ruin which frightened them the most, especially as they mounted higher and higher. Some of the stairs groaned beneath their weight, others sagged as the welds began to give way, and others broke altogether.

One man let out a yelp of pain as ragged, rusted spears tore open his knee. Jillybean plowed ever upward without looking back. The sounds coming from the depths below her were magnified and given texture by the men, making them far more real than anything ahead of her.

After a time, it sounded as if demons were creeping among the men, hurting them, making them whimper and curse.

She hurried even faster. By the time she came to the door which opened onto the bridge, she was dripping sweat and wild-eyed—but she had made it. Gulping down air and throwing aside her fears, it was the Queen who stepped into a grey, wet day. She smiled despite the drenching rain and the fact that she was two hundred and twenty feet in the air and being buffeted by stray winds—the Corsair fleet was indeed before her.

A hundred and twenty ships throwing signals up and down their mainstays in a confusing array of colors and shapes—confusing to most people that is. Jillybean quickly picked out the cipher as a derivation of the one the Corsairs had used in their previous attacks. They were trying to form into three squadrons, however the weather kept pushing some far to leeward, which made them scramble their teams, resulting in the southern team being the weakest of the three.

"Nice flags, jackasses," she said wearing a grin. Feeling vastly superior, she flicked on her radio. "Come in, Captain McCartt."

"McCartt here. All ships on station. Over." His voice was clipped and precise. She could almost imagine him standing at attention on his heaving deck.

"Move to your second position. Let me know when you're there."

A burst of static from the radio startled Jillybean. "Hey, this is Melissa Chatman, over. We're in place, over. Everyone but Will Trafny, over. He says it feels like his lung is filling up with water, over."

Jillybean sighed and waited for the Islander to go on. When she didn't, which was surprising, Jillybean explained to her, "Only use the word 'over' at the end of your communique, when you'd like me to respond. It's not like sending a telegram. And tell Will to take the expectorant I gave him and stay indoors. Now, are the bells ready and is your team spread out enough?"

"Yes, I think so and sorry, over. Oh, wait. I wanted to let you know I can see the bad guy fleet really good from here. If you want, I can keep you up to date on what they're doing, over. You know, like if they're about to attack or something like that."

We should've killed her ages ago, Eve whispered into Jillybean's ear, making her twitch.

"No!" Jillybean snapped. It was a moment before she realized everyone thought she was talking to Melissa. "Sorry, I meant no thank you. Keep dry and wait for my signal. Out."

Ernie says we should kill the weak, Eve said, as if Melissa had broken in on their conversation and was just picking up the pieces of it. *And there's some guy in here who thinks we should eat the weak. He says we can become stronger that way. Like we can take their spirit force or…*

"Shut up for once," Jillybean growled, mentally slamming the door on the darkness within her and forcing her mind onto the details of the imminent battle. She turned her binoculars north to the Marin Highlands, where her infantry force of nearly a thousand men and women were hiding. The Corsair's slow trip south from Bodega Bay had given them four hours to get into place and to prepare firing positions. These were situated along the land side of the hills overlooking Rodeo Lagoon, which was the only logical landing spot for any attacking force.

The next closest one was north of them at a tricky, rocky inlet called Muir Beach. Landing there would mean that an attacking force would have to endure a four-mile slog through more of the ash/mud mixture. The Captain's soldiers would begin the fight exhausted from the march, drenched to the bone, and freezing; reinforcements and resupply would come at a trickle along that same muddy route, and a retreat would be an ordeal few would live through.

No, if the Captain landed anywhere it would be at Rodeo Lagoon, and it would be a massacre. Jillybean's officer in charge, Alec Steinmeyer, the one-time leader of the Coos Bay Clan, had the lagoon surrounded on three sides. All they needed now was for the Captain to comply and attack.

Only he didn't.

Chapter 17

The largest ship left to the Black Captain was the fifty-five-foot catamaran, *The Courageous*. As well as being the largest, it was also the quietest ship in the fleet. There were no jokes, no laughter, no singing and almost no farting. If a sailor had to rip one off, he made sure he was far away from the Black Captain before he let it sneak out.

To say the least, it was an utterly unhappy ship.

From the youngest sailor to Captain Chuck Boschee, a constantly smiling North Dakotan with flat, dead eyes and a red/gold beard that he kept meticulously braided, everyone went about on pins and needles, afraid to say or do anything to bring the Black Captain's wrath down on them. His mercurial mood, once legendary, had been established as fact after he had shot one of Boschee's sailors for belching too loudly. Before the burp had barely begun, the Captain moved with speed that was in the realm of mythical, snatching one of his twin .44 caliber Colt Anaconda revolvers from its holster, firing and returning it before the belch ended.

And that had been on the first day before the weather had turned cruel. Now, after *The Wind Ripper* had seemingly disappeared in the puff of a cloud and the *Hell Quake*, never the fastest ship in the fleet, had managed to elude them, the Black Captain was in a tearing rage.

Boschee had once butchered a man alive, carving off bite-sized hunks of his flesh and shoving them down his throat. On another occasion, he had killed three armed men in an old west style gunfight, blazing away in a room smaller than the average kitchen. He had done these things and more, *before* the zombies had come, because sometimes life was unpredictable.

He was a deadly man and yet, even he feared the Black Captain.

"Take her in closer," he ordered Boschee. "I want a better look at the bridge." It was only a courtesy that he let Boschee give the orders to the crew. The Black Captain had commandeered *The Courageous* for himself, booting off half of Boschee's men and making life so miserable that the others wished they'd been booted off, too.

From the outside, the catamaran looked very large, both wide as well as long. Instead of having one huge hull, it had two much smaller ones, more or less like oversized canoes, though in this case they were enclosed with cramped areas for bedrooms and storage. Between the two hulls was a platform with more rooms. Under normal circumstances, *The Courageous* had a crew of eighteen with men "hot bunking" it, that is, sleeping in shifts. Now there were thirty men on board. It made for cramped conditions, especially as the Black Captain had the largest cabin for himself and did not share an inch of it.

With so many men on board, most of whom did little besides carry their weapons with the full intent of killing anyone who even blinked at the Black Captain in the wrong way, steering the boat was not an easy exercise. *God forbid the boom should make an aggressive move toward his royal pain in the ass*, Boschee thought to himself.

Thankfully, what crew he did have left knew their stuff, and with barely a word, *The Courageous* pulled away from the rest of the fleet. The beauty of a catamaran was on full display. Not only was it a lovely, graceful boat, its twin hulls gave it a smooth even ride as they glided forward. At a quarter of a mile, the Black Captain raised a single finger; the sail was hauled in with naval precision.

The Captain didn't seem to notice. He had a huge pair of binoculars trained on the bridge. Other than forty or fifty junked out cars and some dangling ropes, it seemed completely empty.

"What's her game?" he asked, speaking to himself. Slowly, taking his time, he inspected every part of the bay that he could: Alcatraz, a bit of Angel Island, the western face of San Francisco, the grey waste of the Marin Headlands. Other than the distant *Hell Quake*, moored snugly up against Alcatraz, there was no sign of this queen or anyone else for that matter.

Boschee was startled as the Black Captain handed him the binoculars and said, "Find the trap. It's there somewhere, I know it."

"Yes, sir," Boschee answered, with just a touch of unease. He had heard all the rumors and had read the Intel briefings concerning the Queen, and although he was certain her supposed genius was greatly exaggerated, he too was sure there was a trap just waiting to be sprung. But he couldn't find it. He scanned every inch of the bay and it looked deserted, ready for the taking.

"Maybe she's left," he suggested.

The Captain turned his dark eyes on Boschee. "Just left? She heard we were coming and ran away but left the *Hell Quake* just sitting there as a gift? Is that what you're saying? And all these flags." He gestured toward the bridge and then towards the city. There were black flags emblazoned with a shining silver crown flying, not just from the bridge but also from practically every building in sight. "No, she's here, Bosch. Trust me on that. But what's her game?"

Boschee gave the most obvious answer, "I bet she's lying in wait, hoping we come storming into the bay." He glanced once more at the six-lane bridge. Because of their low angle, he could only see the near edge of it. There could be a thousand men hidden up there, each with a pile of bowling ball-sized rocks. It would only take two or three good hits to sink a boat. He could picture his beloved *Courageous* taking a beating as they tried to get past the bridge: her sails ripped up, her elegant mast broken like a twig, rigging in a mess everywhere, and seawater gushing in from half a dozen holes.

It made him sick to think about and yet *The Courageous* was a bigger, tougher boat than most. How many others would make it through such an attack? Half? Two-thirds? And what shape would they be in to fight? It would be a given that once in the bay, the survivors would be set upon by the Queen's fleet. Its size was unknown though the Intel ran the gamut from thirty ships to ninety. Even if it was a mere fifty ships, they'd have the advantage in speed and maneuverability. They'd be able to swarm in and cause further damage and if the rumor of torpedoes were true…Boschee shivered. It would be the end of the fleet and the end of the Corsairs.

This was going through the Black Captain's mind as well. "But what if that's what she wants us to think," he murmured, half under his breath. "What if she's weaker than we think? What if she's betting everything that we *don't* go blasting straight through?"

"We could send in a recon squad of thirty ships," Boschee suggested.

"And if they are allowed past the bridge and are immediately attacked?" he asked this as if asking himself. "So many what ifs. Bluff and double bluff. She can't be strong everywhere, so what does she do? She attempts to appear weak everywhere. And succeeds. She's practically begging me to attack now, as soon as possible. What was it like when Gaida attacked? She held the bridge, but not in force. She was too weak to hold anything in force. Is now any different? No, it's not. She's weaker than she thinks…or does she know her weaknesses with her cobbled-together crew of the unwilling. Am I looking at a lie within a lie or the truth disguised by a lie?"

Boschee didn't know what to say and was glad he didn't have to make this particular decision. He couldn't fault Gaida for how he had attacked. Based on all the Intel they'd had, it made sense to drive home the attack without waiting. Had they done so a month before, when there was no queen, the little disparate groups would have fallen one after another with ease.

But now there was a queen. Supposedly it was the girl doctor from Bainbridge, the same one that the Black Captain had been considering kidnapping. Had it not been for the rumors of her insanity, he would have done it years ago. *A doctor and now a queen*, Boschee thought. She was more than that if she was causing the Captain to hesitate. He had never seen the Captain hesitate or second guess himself in all the years he had known him.

Or third or fourth guess himself for that matter, as he was doing now, pacing the deck of *The Courageous*, with his hands behind his back and talking through every possibility. He reminded Boschee of a gambler facing an all-in bet, and in a way, he was. A loss here would doom the Black Captain, and them all as well.

For a long, frustrating, freezing hour he paced back and forth, uncaring that Boschee's men were shivering in their positions. They were not the only ones suffering from this long wait. The entire Corsair fleet hung back a mile or so from the bridge, sailing in endless loops, struggling to keep in their formations.

Finally, he stopped and scanned the bay area one more time with his binoculars. "There is only one conclusion we can draw: she is weaker than we could have guessed. Still, we can't move blindly and throw away our advantage."

"Soooo..." Boschee asked, not at all sure what the Captain had decided.

"So, we wait. We let them stew in their fear as it builds up. We let them freeze in the rain until they won't be able to move when we bring the fight. We let them think about the storm of pain that will be coming their way and then, when the time is ripe, we strike."

He had Boschee run that very message up the mast as they tacked laboriously into the wind back to the fleet. It was a long message to send using only colored pendants. It was also the wrong message to send to men who had been living in cold, cramped conditions for the last three days. Waiting was the last thing they wanted to do. They were men of action. They were men who had never dawdled when attacking was an option.

It didn't sit well with them and, instead of throwing fear into their enemies, it stoked the doubt in their hearts. The aura of invincibility that had always surrounded the Black Captain had not dimmed when someone had dared to steal one of their boats, and nor had it faded when Tony Tibbs failed to take the Hill People in the first battle weeks before. But when Philip Gaida was killed, and half his armada was destroyed, and the other half became traitors, people couldn't help but look at the Black Captain and wonder if his time was coming to a close.

This doubt festered for three hours. The men grew stiff from the cold and snappish from the tedium of keeping station in one of the worst places possible to do so. They had to deal with the tidal current heading west, the ocean current heading south and the wind and waves that shot due east. The constant undulation made even some of the hardier Corsairs seasick.

The Black Captain was made of sterner stuff. Hard weather didn't bother him and nor was he hampered by doubt. He knew his men would rebound once they were moving again, while his enemies would quail at the sight of his black sails opening to their fullest. He came up on deck after a refreshing nap and immediately hurled his entire fleet straight at Rodeo Lagoon.

The men let out a great shout as the fell ships swooped down on the empty beach. It looked to everyone as though they were going to make a landing there, but at the last moment the flags were sent up, ordering the fleet to veer away.

As they did, smoke started billowing up in dozens of places behind the first line of hills. The Black Captain nodded at the smoke with a knowing look in his eye, as if he had expected it. Next, he had the fleet curl out to sea. With the heavy, low-hanging clouds they were quickly beyond sight of land and so it should have been a shock when they came shooting back, born on an eight-knot wind.

This time the fleet made straight for the west side of San Francisco. They were not greeted with fires, but rather with the sound of bells ringing in a wild frenzy. They echoed up and down the empty streets. Despite the alarms, no one came running to try to stop a landing. The Black Captain stood on deck with that same knowing smile of his, gleaming white in his dark face.

"I don't get it," Boschee said, scanning the approaches to the waterfront. As far as he could tell they could land unopposed if they wanted to. "Where is everyone?" The only "people" he saw were zombies pouring out into the streets, looking for the source of the bells.

The Captain's smile grew. "Hiding. They are hiding like weasels. The bells suggest weakness. They ring the bells to attract the dead to fight for them. They've done it before and this is their reminder to us. On the other hand, the fires to the north suggest strength. But do you really need strength to hold those hills?"

Boschee shrugged. "Maybe not, but you need strength to take them. If you think she's only got a handful of people up there, I gotta remind you what happened to Gaida. He put nearly three hundred men ashore and they got ripped apart."

"Trust me, Boschee, I know this, just as I know exactly what their little queen is thinking. So far, we're just tapping here and there, looking for her weaknesses, of which she has plenty. I doubt she even knows her main weakness. She actually thinks her men…MY men will fight for her when the going gets tough. They'll cave under pressure and it's going to be our job to supply that pressure."

"You have a plan?"

"Of course," he said, smiling that confident grin of his. When he smiled like that, all doubts were forgotten.

His plan was as simple as it was unexpected. Instead of immediately attacking somewhere along the shoreline of San Francisco or at Rodeo Lagoon, the Black Captain pulled his fleet back a second time and, under the cover of the clouds, they went north to Muir Beach. Once there, he ordered half his forces to disembark.

Anyone with any sense knew that seizing the Golden Gate Bridge was the key to winning any battle for San Francisco. Whoever possessed the bridge could put a stopper in the bay. He or she could dictate the flow of battle. They could decide when to attack and could maneuver freely up and down the coasts. The Captain needed the bridge and his plan was to attack the approaches to it from two directions at once: from the north coming through the muck from Muir Beach, and from the west from Rodeo Lagoon.

"Caught between two forces the defenders will be surrounded, hammered mercilessly and destroyed," the Captain explained to Boschee, smashing a fist into an open palm.

It was a fine plan and might have been a great one if the elements hadn't been against them. The wind picked up, making the landing at Muir Beach even more dangerous than expected. Because of the crashing waves and the heavy seas, the boats could only come in one at a time and discharge their men in thrashing water, ten feet deep.

After one boat was nearly swamped and six men were drowned, the Captain changed tactics and anchored three boats in a row, stem to stern. A thick rope was strung from the last boat in line through the surf and tied to a tree just above the waterline. Like an endless run of spiders, men went from boat to boat and then along the rope to shore. Although they were weighed down with supplies, no one else died.

It took two hours to get the entire attacking force on the beach. At first the men huddled together against the rain and the cold, but when the Black Captain came ashore to lead in person, no man would cower, especially not a ship's captain like Chuck Boschee.

He stood tall, hoping to be noticed, hoping to command the second force attacking Rodeo Lagoon. Instead, he and his entire crew found themselves slogging through foul-smelling mud that sucked at their legs in a way that made it feel as though they were stepping down into some sort of toothless mouth with every step.

The mud was annoying when it was only seven or eight inches deep it, but when it came up to their knees, it was a struggle to remain upright, it was a struggle to keep hold of one's shoes, and more than anything, it was a struggle to keep going. The energy the mud stole from them made the march a torture. To make matters worse, most of the Corsairs were smokers and all of them drank to excess whenever they could.

They reeled and gasped, but no one dared to complain, and no one dared question the judgment of the Black Captain, at least not aloud. Boschee had to wonder why they didn't find a nice dry port to hole up in for a few days. The Queen wasn't going anywhere, after all.

As he frequently did, the Captain seemed to read his mind. "She is in a worse state than we are, Bosch. Her men are probably on the verge of mutiny. They've been out in this for hours, waiting and waiting, freezing their butts off. And what happens?"

Boschee shrugged, knowing that the Captain would continue once he caught his breath. Currently, he was using the excuse of taking off his working boots to rest.

When they were tied and slung over one broad shoulder, he went on, "We up and disappear. They have no idea where we are. They don't know what to do. After a few hours, they probably think we are looking for someplace to hole up in. After another hour, they're grumbling about the rain, and very soon they're making a stink about leaving. And what can their little queen do, but give in? The fact is, we might come up on those hills and find them empty."

He made it seem so likely that by the time the rumor of his little speech made its way from mouth to ear to the last man in the long column of dead-tired men, his words had been changed to say that the Queen's men had fled altogether.

This buoyed them more than any rah-rah speech could have and with the last of their remaining strength, the men pushed on through the miles of muck until they scaled the last of the many hills and saw Rodeo Lagoon below them. In the grey light of the sunset, the little inlet was filled with Corsair boats, off-loading the other half of the Black Captain's men by the hundreds.

The only opposition to be seen from the Queen was a few dozen black pits that sent up little wisps of smoke. The way to the bridge was open, as promised.

Chapter 18

"Boschee!" the Black Captain called out, loud enough for all seven hundred and fifty men to hear. "You have one order: take the bridge."

Suddenly, the weariness of the long march fell away from Chuck Boschee. This was a true command, one that could catapult him into a real leadership role. Commanding a ship was great, but the perks of being one of the Captain's chief lieutenants like Tibbs and Gaida had been, were incalculable.

"Consider it done!" he answered, and quickly snapped off a salute. He gazed over the crowd of men and didn't see any recognizable faces. All he saw was a sea of blue-green tattoos, grizzled, wet beards and eyes that burned with revenge—the Corsairs had never had such a string of losses and each of them wanted it to end this day.

The problem was that the day itself was ending quickly. So much time had been wasted that Boschee didn't know whether he'd be able to get to the bridge before the sunset. It was only a mile, but the hills here were just as slick and muddy as the previous ones. He needed to get moving that instant.

He started walking backwards and, as he went, he yelled out: "I want all the crews of the boats that are forty-footers and larger on my right. Everyone else, on my left! Let's go! We'll form into teams as we go. Captains, find your men and lead them. I want you out front. *Courageous* on me."

At first, it was a mess as men went here and there yelling the names of their ships. Some had to be kicked into place and that was fine with Boschee. All he cared about was that he had sixty captains and sixty crews. When they were in place and marching in an uneven line toward the bridge, he turned to survey the land in front of him. In the fading light, it looked somewhat like a hilly version of the moon: grey and cratered.

Nothing lived and nothing stirred except the smoke rising from the fire pits. Boschee scoffed at them, wondering how this genius queen could be stupid enough to think they would fool the Black Captain. The pits lay in a diagonal line to his right, facing the lagoon where the ships were being off-loaded; the men looking small as they milled about on the beach.

"Lucky bastards," Captain Shae Larson of the *Orca*, grumbled. "They got a half mile walk, while we've been hoofing it forever." He was red-faced, his chest heaving.

Boschee wanted to tell the man to shut the hell up, however they were mounting another hill and already he was winded. Climbing its slick surface sapped the strength in seconds. Everyone bent double, using their hands and feet to propel them upwards. It wasn't a large hill, maybe only seventy feet or so. Still, they were all gasping and wheezing by the time they got to the top.

As much as he wanted to stop to take a breather, there was no time for rest at the summit and Boschee immediately went sliding down the other side. He had been in the lead and was halfway down when he heard a cry from the ridge where the last of his attacking force had paused.

"Damn it!" he seethed, embarrassed that his formation looked more like a bunch of strolling losers bopping about a mall on a Sunday than anything resembling a battalion of men about to go on the attack. They were yelling something about the boats, but the wind had picked up and was snatching their words from the air and drowning them in rushing static. What did come through had an alien tinge of fear to it, something he wasn't used to hearing.

Everyone turned towards the lagoon, where the ships were moving with stately calm, their black sails shortened because of the wind. A dozen or so were right up on the beach, getting as close as they dared, while another dozen were heading back out to sea after off-loading their men. More were in position, waiting their turn to come in, and behind them was the rest of the fleet.

"What the freak are you morons yelling about?" Boschee demanded, furiously. There wasn't anything wrong. The ships were exactly where they were supposed to be. The men should have been cheering instead of yelling and pointing.

"They're saying something about ships," Captain Larson said. He had an M16A2 with a scope which looked like it was wedged into his eye. "Yeah, they're ships, so what? Those are our ships, morons. You don't need to get excited seeing our...wait. What the..."

His last words were filled with such dread that Boschee yanked up his binoculars and finally saw what had his men so frightened. The ships further out to sea were black-hulled, black-sailed and streamed black flags, only on them were shining silver crowns. It was the Queen's fleet and it was larger than they had expected. Much larger.

And in seconds, the rumors of torpedoes were proven true. They were too small and the waters too rough for them to be seen, however the explosions were hammering blows that sent fire and smoke high into the air. The Corsair fleet was outnumbered and hemmed in from three sides.

They had no room to maneuver and even if they could, the wind was against them. Some tried to tack towards the larger fleet, only to be targeted by three or four torpedoes at a time; none survived. It was a scene of utter mayhem, chaos, and death. Broken bodies and wrecked hulls floated in and out on the tide. Ships burned with such fierceness that the rain could not stem the flames and smoke poured into the skies, turning the evening into a premature twilight.

The smarter captains tried to use the burning ships as cover, hoping the dying ships would protect them from the torpedoes, but the Queen would not be denied her victory. The torpedoes were steered around the wreckage and began to score hit after hit. Her plan had always been for a battle of annihilation and it was just what she was getting, much to the Black Captain's fury.

"Fight, damn it!" he bellowed.

All the fight had gone out of them. The remaining captains turned their ships to shore and made straight for the beach. From a military standpoint, just about any other action would have been preferable—they could have attacked all at once and at least caused the Queen to use up more of her valuable torpedoes—they could have anchored as close to the beach as possible and tried to find shelter under the guns of the three or four hundred men on shore.

Instead, every one of them ran their boats ashore, although none made it. Their deep keels hit the sandy bottom while they were still thirty yards out. As anyone with even a passing knowledge of physics could have guessed would happen, the boats spun broadside to the shore when the first wave hit them. Each boat was thrown onto its side when the next wave struck.

Their weaponless crews straggled to shore and stood uselessly, staring at the Queen's ships as they formed up in a double line facing north. No one could understand this strange formation until a black smudge appeared among the clouds. With a sinking feeling in his gut, Boschee turned his glasses north and saw his beloved *Courageous.* It was within the pack of sixty ships sailing back from Muir Beach and directly into the next part of the Queen's trap.

Everyone but Boschee began screaming and waving their arms for the ships to go back or to run away. Boschee was too sick to his stomach to do anything but watch as the inevitable came to pass. Even the wind was the Queen's ally it seemed. It swung around from the northwest, shooting the sixty ships down to their doom.

"I can't watch," Boschee said, turning away. He was the only one turned away and thus was the only one to see the crest of the hill opposite from them swarming with men. A wave of adrenaline washed over him with a zinging sensation as every inch of his flesh tented in goosebumps. Before he knew it, panic had set in. Not fear, or overblown anxiety, it was raging, mindless panic.

He found himself tearing up the hill behind him, running for his life without a thought for anyone else. Just a few feet shy of the top of the hill, someone saw the Queen's soldiers and let out a cry. Then all hell broke loose. Hundreds of guns went off at once. Men on either side of Boschee were killed in that first volley. More were killed ahead of him and rolled down the hill.

Like some sort of sick version of *Donkey Kong*, Boschee found himself leaping over bodies as they spun down at him and dodging bloody heads that seemed to be bounding everywhere as though his fellow Corsairs were bowling them.

By some miracle, he made it to the crest and had every intention of going down the other side just as fast as he could, only Captain Larson grabbed him. "What do we do? What do we do?" he screamed into Boschee's face.

"I-I-I don't know." He had no idea. In the old days, before the zombies, he'd had no affinity with the military and knew next to nothing about tactics and strategy. All he saw was a line of people looking to kill him.

It was up to the Black Captain to take charge. While Boschee was still gasping and running his hands over his body, trying to find the gun he had dropped while racing up the hill, the Captain appeared. "Get up, Boschee. Take command of the left flank. We need to make a fighting withdrawal."

"To where?" Captain Larson demanded, shrilly. "Our boats are gone, damn it. She destroyed them…"

Before he could finish the curse, the Black Captain drew one of his .44 Anaconda in a silver blur and shot him in the guts. The bullet was placed perfectly, missing all of Larson's major arteries. He would die, that was a given, it was just a matter of how quickly. Larson was still staring down at the blood leaking through his coat when the Captain turned him around to face the enemy.

"Die with some damned usefulness," the Captain snarled, using him as a shield as he watched the sea battle. The northern fleet of sixty ships, led by *The Revenge,* had mistaken the smoke coming from the burning ships for clouds. Almost at the last moment, the captain of *The Revenge* realized his mistake and, in a fine display of seamanship, spun his ship on a dime, dodged two torpedoes, and then zipped out of there, chased by three more, none of which could catch her.

By a stroke of luck, the Queen failed in her battle of annihilation. After dropping off their troops, one of the Corsair ships had run aground on Muir Beach and it had taken an hour to get her free. Thus the sixty ships had not been in the initial trap as they should have been, and now they were fleeing, racing either into the wind or out to sea as if the furies themselves were after them.

In reality, no one was after them. The Queen's luck had soured again as a good percentage of her fleet was almost frozen in place, fighting desperately against both a change in the tide and the wind. The captains were doing everything they could to simply not be thrown on shore like their victims had been minutes before.

The Queen was also in danger of letting a good portion of the Captain's soldiers slip through her fingers. Yes, the hundreds of Corsairs at Rodeo Lagoon were completely trapped, however Boschee had upset her plans by coming in a long, somewhat uneven wave instead of a compact one of three or four smaller columns. The very nature of the straggling meant his Corsairs were spread out so far that sweeping around them to ensnare the entire group in one great net was proving too much for the inadequate number of men assigned to Captain Ryley McCartt.

McCartt had half the number of men as the Black Captain and a concerted effort on his part might have turned the tables. Neither he nor Boschee could see this, however. The growing darkness as well as the shock of the sudden attacks had blinded them to the weakness of their enemy. All they saw were their own exhausted men being ripped apart by what looked like an invincible enemy bearing down on them.

"Up there!" the Black Captain yelled, pointing at a hilltop a half mile in their rear. "Get your men up there."

Boschee was shoved to the left where the men were either cowering behind the slope of the hill or fleeing down the backside of it. He knew he had to take control and make decisions, but the only thing he could think about were the bullets hissing just over head, and the screams all around him, and the drumroll of gunshots.

He ducked down next to a man whose face was unrecognizable because of the blood covering it. "Hey," Boschee said, grabbing his arm. "We have to get up to that…" The man fell over to stare up at the clouds as rainwater filled his open eyes. There was a hole in the side of his head from which half his brain had come shooting out. "Son of a bitch," Boschee whispered, leaning back from the body. He looked up at the next man, who opened his mouth to say something only instead of words, a great blast of blood and teeth came out, splattering into the mud.

"Hey, what? What the…what the…" Boschee said, blinking as mud and sand kicked up into his face. It was like someone was throwing rocks at him, skipping them across the side of the hill. After the fourth or fifth rock zinged past, it dawned on him that he was being shot at.

But by whom? And from where? He gaped about trying to make sense of the explosions and the tremendous din of a hundred guns going off at once. One of those hundred was being aimed at him. Which one? Which one! For a few seconds, he turned in place looking for the shooter. Then panic took over his mind again and he went running off down the hill, followed by the entire left side of the line.

He fairly flew down the hill, but when he hit the face of the next hill, his pace turned into that of a crawl. An agonizing crawl made worse because men above him kept sliding down into him and because he couldn't stop looking over his shoulder. *They* were coming and they were coming to kill him. Ten feet from the crest, his prophecy came partially true.

The Queen's soldiers had crested the hill he had just fled from and were shooting up and down the line, killing almost at will. Boschee looked back in shock and fright…and then in anger. He was sure he saw a man he knew among them.

"Rat-faced Ronnie!" he thundered once he was safely behind a boulder. "I see you, damn it! What do you think you're doing, attacking your own people?"

This caused something of a truce among the two sides as they waited for Rat-faced Ronnie to answer the charge. Rat-faced Ronnie did indeed have a narrow face and could only grow an ugly, thin little bit of fur on his upper lip and a wispy, childish beard on the tip of his jutting chin. His cheeks went suddenly red at being singled out.

"You don't know!" Rat-faced Ronnie shouted back. "She can't be beaten. She knows everything, Boschee. She knew you guys were going to attack right here and she knew where the fleet was going and everything."

Boschee knew this could only mean one thing: she had a spy close to the Captain. It also meant another opportunity. If he could find out who it was, the Captain would probably make him a lieutenant for sure. And if he could turn the tide of the fight right here, there was no telling how far he could go.

"Listen Ronnie, if you come back to us we can win. Think about it. The Captain will reward you beyond your wildest dreams. Anything you want, you'll get."

Rat-faced Ronnie laughed. "That's what she said you'd say! She warned us that you guys would make all sorts of promises you couldn't keep. She said it was a sign of desperation and that we shouldn't believe you. She said that we only got crumbs before and now that's all you got left. Crumbs and lies."

"Does a ship sound like a crumb to you, Ronnie? I can get you a ship. Think about that. It's what you always wanted."

Boschee chanced a look from behind the boulder. Rat-faced Ronnie was too far away to read his expression, but Boschee took his hesitation as a good thing. If one man doubted, it would infect the rest. The battle would pause long enough for everyone to remember they were on the same side. Once that...

"Whose boat would I get, Boschee?" Rat-face asked. "Yours? Would you hand over *The Courageous*? Because I don't think you will. I don't think any of you captains will." The other ex-Corsairs around him agreed with him; Boschee was losing them.

"I might be able to get you the *Orca*, Ronnie. It's no lie. Larson's dead and the *Orca* needs a new captain. It could be you, Ronnie. All you have to do is put down your guns. Just for a little bit. Once we get all this straightened out; once we put this bitch queen in her place, I guarantee that you will get the *Orca*."

Again Rat-face Ronnie hesitated as the rain came down in torrents and the wind began to howl. Just as Boschee thought he was going to reel Ronnie in, another man on the far hill shouted, "What about me? I want a boat, too."

This was followed by another man demanding a ship, and a third, then a fourth. Rat-face Ronnie had never displayed more than average intelligence before that day, but just then he took the reins of the battle in his hands.

"He's lying! He can't give us all boats. Hell, he probably can't even give any of us the *Orca*. None of us are even on the officer list. And what would her first mate say about getting passed over? Wes is a mean son of a bitch. We all know he'd hold a grudge."

"We can switch him out, Ronnie. You'd be able to pick your own men. Your friends can crew her. I can guarantee that."

"Your guarantee and your promises are meaningless. They're just empty words compared to what the Queen offers. She's offered us something like the old days. Like how it was, before. She doesn't call me Rat-face. She let me kiss her hand and when I did, she called me Ronald."

"And you'd trade that over having your own ship?"

Ronnie let out a harsh laugh and pointed to the west, where dozens of wrecks filled Rodeo Lagoon. "You see all that? She is the Queen of War. She can't be beaten, Boschee. The *Orca, The Courageous, The Red Death?* They are all doomed. If I took the *Orca*, I'd be better off slitting my own throat."

Chapter 19

Mark Leney watched all this through the scope of his M4. He had the crosshairs lined up on the back of Rat-face's head, just in case the conversation didn't go exactly as the Queen had envisioned. She hadn't known who would be speaking to whom, but she had known with uncanny precision that it would happen.

Watching it unfold had caused the little hairs on the back of Leney's neck to lift, making him wonder whether she had something going for her besides her intelligence. Something otherworldly or perhaps inner-worldly, like a second-sight or ESP.

Although not nearly as superstitious as the Hill People or the Islanders, he was still a sailor and few sailors were wholly without their superstitions; for instance, he would never consider challenging a light wind by whistling, since it was the surest way to kill it altogether. Ever since he had first laid eyes on her, his gut told him there was something about the Queen that spoke of destiny. It was a vague feeling that suggested it was not necessarily a good destiny, or even *her* destiny, that he felt.

Not everything had gone her way, after all.

Leney was close enough to her to know that it had been a trial condemning her three closest friends to death. He also knew that she found it repulsive to have to rely so heavily on ex-Corsairs to fight for her. She had to force her face from becoming queered-up whenever the likes of Sticky Jim and Deaf Mick were around.

Even this battle, as masterful as it had been so far, showed that destiny was not completely on her side.

Just when she could have ended the war at a stroke, the wind and tide had thrown their allegiance into the Black Captain's camp. Instead of destroying the Corsair fleet completely, half of it had escaped. From his place on the crest of the hill, he could see the Corsair ships fleeing north. They were beating against a strange wind that was quarter-on for them, but hammering directly into the face of the Queen's ships.

Unless something drastic happened to the Corsair ships, they would getaway. The only question was whether they would head back to Muir Beach and await the Black Captain or would they just run all the way to Grays Harbor with their tail between their legs.

Leney guessed that few of his old friends among the Corsairs would dare to cross the Captain while he was still breathing and still had an army at his command. Leney turned his scoped rifle back around to the action at hand, which was beginning to pick up again. The two sides were nearly equal now, with about six hundred men a piece.

Unfortunately, for McCartt, Leney didn't see him winning this battle, at least not in the manner that the Queen expected. Although there were hundreds of dead Corsairs strewn over the muddy hills, the remainder weren't ready to give up just yet and it would take an actual attack over open ground to defeat them.

McCartt was leading a hodge-podge force made up of ex-Corsairs, who weren't thrilled with the idea of killing their one-time friends, a few hundred Santas, who were still getting used to the idea of serving a queen and weren't sure how they liked it, and a handful of Hill People, Islanders and Sacramento men and women who had demonstrated surprising stoutheartedness, but were still civilians at their cores.

Still, McCartt had the Queen in his corner and she had both a keen sense of human nature and an eye for terrain.

From her commanding position on the bridge, she could see the entire battlefield and with her radios she was able to direct the action. "Captain McCartt, pull half your force back and send them along the base of the hill you're on. It runs for about half a mile before it reaches a trail that cuts northwest. If your men hurry, they can flank the enemy and cut them off. Over."

McCartt had always been a yes-man and instead of arguing about the extreme difficulties involved in maneuvering raw troops under fire, he simply said: "Roger. Out."

Leney turned his scope to the east and spotted the trail that the Queen was talking about. It looked firm, but Leney had his doubts. So far, everything had been absolute muck and he guessed that a "dirt" trail would be twice as bad—but if it wasn't…an interesting set of opposing ideas occurred to him and before anyone else could volunteer, Leney keyed his radio and said, "I'll lead the flank attack."

If the trail turned out to be an impassable bog, the attack would fail miserably without a shot being fired—something he could blame on the Queen or the weather. Either way, he would be relatively safe and still be able to make a claim of bravery and dedication to duty.

On the other hand, if the trail wasn't a complete mess, he saw how a flank attack could be a spectacular success and if it was, he would make sure he got all the credit. Both options were preferable to staying with McCartt's force. A flank attack would only work if the enemy was "fixed" in position and the only way to guarantee that was to engage it, which meant attacking up the barren face of the hill across from them.

That would take actual, no questions asked, bravery. Leney's bravery took only two forms: the "what's in it for me" variety, or the "I don't have any other choice, so let's do this," option. This particular mission fell within the first category.

Moving along the safe side of the hill, he took every other person —unless that person happened to be a woman, then he ignored her and went on to the next. In his mind, one of the perks of being a Corsair, current or otherwise, was that he could be a complete sexist and never even contemplate apologizing for it.

Despite his clear preference for male soldiers, two women joined his battalion: Colleen White and Ashtyn Bishop. He kept them because they were both young and pretty, and because he suspected that the Queen had ordered them to go, probably to keep an eye on him.

"Don't fall behind or you'll get left," he warned them, raising his voice as the rain picked up.

The two young women looked cold and wretched, and at first they lagged badly at the back of the formation, lacking the brute strength needed to heave their legs from the deeper mud pits. Leney really would have left them, however a few Sacramento men, led by Steven Yingling, went back for them and basically dragged the pair over the deeper sections of mud.

Soon they were all slogging along at a snail's pace. The ex-Corsairs, like their cousins on the other side of the hill, were drinkers and smokers, which saw them staggering like drunks after a few hundred yards. Had it not been for the trail, which turned out to be a clay-gravel mixture, the flank attack might have ended before it began.

It was nearly full dark before Leney got his men, and two women, into position. The fighting around the Lagoon during this hour and a half had been almost nonexistent as the two sides dug in. In the middle of the battlefield, McCartt had tried two frontal attacks with heavy losses. Now it was Leney's turn. Even with surprise on his side, he wasn't looking forward to ordering an attack.

"Well, we might as well get to it," he muttered under the sound of the rain. Louder, he ordered, "Everyone forward!" No one moved. His soldiers were spread out along another of the endless mucky hills, and instead of charging in a screaming attack, the men glanced to their left and right to see whether someone else was getting up to attack.

"Son of a bitch!" Leney barked. "Come on. Let's go." He stood taller and snapped his fingers at them. It wasn't much of a Patton-esque move and it didn't instill an ounce of fighting spirit in the men. "Alright, fine. Anyone who doesn't follow me is going to get shot." He pointed his rifle at the nearest person. The mud-caked man sighed and pushed himself up.

"And the rest of you! Come on. Let's go." There was a good deal of muttered curses as the entire group got to their feet. Leney scowled until everyone was up.

He started down the slope, more like an inept skier than a warrior. He slid and slipped and tripped his way to the bottom which was thick with deep mud. Slogging his way across, he started up the next hill, fully expecting to be shot at any moment. There was no shooting and really no sounds except for the rain and the whispered curses coming from the stunted battalion behind him.

At the top, he paused to catch his breath and survey what he could of the scene. There wasn't much to see. Higher ridges blocked his view of the ocean and the deepening dark made even the next set of hills little more than a shadow. Where the Corsairs were, he had no idea.

After gulping down a few deep breaths, he went on to the next hill. It took fifteen minutes to climb and at the top, he paused to let the rest of his force catch up. That took another twenty minutes as they straggled slowly to the crest. While he waited, he radioed the Queen and told her of the lack of enemy contact. She told him to press on with all speed. Looking around at his ragged force, he knew they wouldn't be pressing on anywhere with any kind of speed. The darkness made any movement especially tricky since it was impossible to tell if the next step would be into an inch of mud or five feet of it.

Still, he replied with a firm, "Yes, your Highness."

The attack, which had begun along a quarter of a mile hill, had turned into three dangerously narrow attacks in which a single leader went first, picking their way through the mud, trying to find a path that had some substance to it. At first there was little danger since the enemy seemed to have disappeared— then a shot rang out and Leney almost pissed himself as the bullet passed high up between his legs.

Everyone threw themselves flat and lay in the mud, panting, waiting for the next shot or the next thousand. It seemed as if the real battle was about to begin. Minutes went by and when nothing more happened, a few of Leney's men fired back, wasting their bullets as they hit nothing but dark sky or the darker hill.

Slowly, Leney stood in something of a Cro-Magnon crouch. He then scurried here and there, getting his force prepared to attack. It took another twenty-five minutes and, by the time they did attack with a shout and a blast of bullets, the Corsair who had taken the shot was a hundred yards farther away. He was set up in a good spot: a squat boulder to hide behind and a good path that would take him to his next shooting position.

There were ten others just like him covering the retreat of the Captain's main force, which was rushing north as fast as they could, back to Muir Beach. They already had something close to an hour and a half head start and, with every bullet fired by the covering team, they gained an extra twenty minutes.

It soon became apparent to Leney that they would never catch up in time, yet the Queen had them go on. "The wind could turn," she told him. The wind did not turn for many hours and during that long grueling night march, half of which was spent crawling through the mud, it was whispered that the Queen had met her match in the Black Captain.

Leney couldn't believe his ears when the whispers finally got back to him via Deaf Mick. "You gotta be kidding," Leney shot back. "That's got to be the dumbest thing anyone ever said. Who is spreading this crap?"

Deaf Mick wasn't sure how to answer this as he had just spread the rumor to Leney. "Somes are talking, is all. And that's all it is, just talk, no one's ack-sually gonna do nothing."

"Well, if you hear any of that again, you tell them that the Captain just lost again. He lost half of what was left of his fleet and more than half his men. I'd be surprised if the rest don't mutiny before they get back to Grays Harbor. If you ask me, the Captain is done."

Leney chalked this sort of talk up to exhaustion. It took hours to get to Muir Beach and by the time they got there, the last Corsair boat was being towed out of the inlet. There was nothing left to do but turn around and go back. The return trip was only slightly easier since no one was taking potshots at them. They didn't have to crawl, though some did. Some didn't even make it back that night.

Just over a hundred men crowded into the few beach homes that were still standing and slept snuggled in on each other for warmth. Some took the wide way around, cutting across the peninsula on an actual paved road, before going south through Marin City, Sausalito and even the hill compound where Stu and Jenn had grown up. It added miles to their return trip, which was offset by the lack of mud.

Leney led a straggling group back to the bridge, arriving just as the sun was rising over the battlefield. It was a sad, wet view. Between them and Rodeo Lagoon were a few hundred mostly naked bodies. They had been stripped of anything valuable and their remains left to the thousands of seagulls which were busy pecking the dead to pieces. They were not the only ones to feast. Unseen from his vantage were a few more thousand crabs and an equal number of rats gorging themselves.

The battle was not exactly over. Five hundred Corsairs were trapped on a jutting angle of land just south of the lagoon. A ring of massive hills protected them from direct attack. Nothing would protect them from starvation. They were surrounded: on three sides by the ocean and on the fourth by the Queen's men.

Leney barely glanced in that direction. The only things he cared about were getting warm and dry, eating anything he could get his hands on, and finding a bed. It should have been nearly impossible to get any of this on that barren wasteland, however the Queen had a genius for logistics that was completely unrivaled. While Leney had been tramping back and forth along the Headlands, she had harnessed the strength of the remaining noncombatants.

Food, fire, and a change of clothes were readily available, while shelter and clean beds were only a short boat ride away.

As much as he wanted to sleep, he thought he should check in with the Queen, who had a huge white tent set up in a sheltered spot called Battery Spencer. It was one of the many reinforced concrete "hard points" built to protect the Bay area at the turn of the previous century.

The Queen's tent was so large that it should've been called a pavilion, and it was so perfectly white on the outside that Leney expected to find a throne inside, or maybe a series of banquet tables overflowing with food and wine. What he found instead were thirty-two occupied hospital gurneys, blood everywhere, bodies wrapped in sheets and cast in the corner, two sleeping assistants, and a haggard Queen, who looked more tired than Leney.

She was also a bloody mess. She had her arms elbow deep in a man's chest. Leney swallowed heavily at the sight, causing the cut across his throat to sing out in sharp pain.

"It's Leney," she sneered upon seeing him.

"I can see that," she replied, with a quick smile his way. Leney hesitated and she shook her head. "Don't worry about Eve, she's being cranky."

"Any wonder why?" Eve snapped. "We could be sleeping or getting something to eat. Hell, I'd rather be getting it on with Leney than wallowing in all this blood and this wasted time. You know he's not going to live." The Queen shushed herself, which only made Eve angrier. "He's one of *them*. He's a Corsair, Jillybean. We should be saving your talents for someone who counts."

"Should I come back at a better time?" Leney asked.

The Queen's blue eyes were darker than usual and the sneer more pronounced. "A better time? Look, Leney, I didn't realize just how ugly you are. About that roll in the hay? It's a no-go unless you bring your own paper bag."

Jillybean suddenly made a bloody fist. "Shut up, Eve!" She glared until her eyes cleared. She then apologized to Leney and said, "If you'll give me a situation report, I would appreciate it. Any casualties from your attack?" Leney hesitated at the question. He honestly didn't know. His entire focus had been on finding the enemy, enveloping them, and destroying them.

"Not any to speak of," he answered, glad that the Queen was so focused on the operation that she didn't seem to have noticed his long pause. "We really didn't get into any action. They retreated, and we chased. We would have got them, I think, but they kept setting these little traps." He did his best to explain the difficulties he faced, but she didn't seem too impressed.

When he was done, he happened to glance down at the man she was operating on and realized that he recognize him. "That's Trevor Waldron of *The Hammer*. He's a Corsair, but not a bad guy compared to some. Do you really think he'll make it?"

"Fifty-fifty. He's a bleeder. It's what happens when you drink alcohol to excess. You can smell the gin wafting up." Her nose wrinkled and then twitched. "Could you do me a favor and scratch my nose, please."

He gave the tip of her small nose a light rubbing, saying, "I heard alcohol thins out the blood. So…any word on Waldron's boat? *The Hammer* was a good ship. Some say it was a little too flashy, you know. Still, it was a good, sound ship." It was more than just good and its reputation as flashy was well founded. It was a gorgeous forty-seven footer with a wide, accommodating deck and deep, spacious cabins that Waldron kept in a state of perfection.

"I have no idea about the boat. He was found on land, whatever that might suggest. Also, alcohol doesn't actually thin the blood. As the liver deteriorates over time from over-exposure to alcohol, it slows the production of blood components called platelets, which are responsible for clotting. Ah, here's our problem. The right gastroepiploic vein has been severed."

Leney turned away as blood fountained up. "I should be going. If you don't mind, I want to check on my men and then get some shuteye." He was really going to ask around about *The Hammer* and then get some sleep.

"Of course. You've had a hard night. Six hours is all I can afford to let you have. Sorry, but I want that pocket reduced by nightfall and in two days I want us ready to move out."

"We're going after the Black Captain so soon?"

"No. Even wounded as he is, the Black Captain is too great a foe for us in his home waters. He will have a hundred tricks up his sleeve, and if anything, the night's fighting has proven once again the ascendancy of the defense over the offense. As we must attack and attack sooner rather than later, we're going to need more men. In two days, we sail against the Guardians."

Leney made a sour face. "The Guardians? Really? I don't see it. Have you heard about their wall? It's not as big as the one up in Bainbridge, but it's still a beast. It's one of the reasons the Black Captain wasn't in a tearing hurry to come south. And the people…" He made another face. "You know they're Christians, right?"

"I do."

"I mean like super Christian. Even worse than before." When she cocked an eyebrow, the way that only she could, he began to stammer, "I-I mean like weirdly Christian. They go to church every day and they don't drink. I really don't think they'll mix with our kind."

The eyebrow sailed higher. She paused, a clamp in one hand and a bowtie of intestines in the other. "There is no 'our' kind, Leney, there is only *my* people. A person might have once been a blood-thirsty Corsair, or a diseased Sacramento girl, or Santa Clara gambler, but now he or she is one of my subjects. The same will be true of the Guardians. They will render unto Caesar, or else."

"Of course, your Highness. We just have to get past their wall."

The wall was the least of her problems concerning the Guardians. She needed a wall of her own to keep her evil contained inside…an image of a burning house flashed in her mind. It had only been three days since she had burned Kimberley Weatherly to death, and had stabbed Matthew Gloom in the throat, and hung some Corsair from the mast of her ship.

One "slip up" like that in front of the Guardians and she would lose them, likely for good. Did she dare turn to drugs to keep her other selves in check? Would her liver hold up? One pill too many would cause her to develop hepatorenal syndrome or spontaneous bacterial peritonitis, or simply send her into a coma.

"It'll be just for a few days," she told herself.

Chapter 20

"I'm sick of boats," Jenn groaned from within the pile of blankets which she kept herself wrapped in when not on deck or dealing with Rob LaBar's wound, which, sadly was not healing well at all. It seeped grey fluid on a constant basis and was clearly infected.

It was the third day since they had fled from the *Hell Quake*. It had been an eventful three days, especially that first day when they had been with faced black boats and guns at every turn. It had started with them waking up with the Queen's ship so close she had recognized Jillybean standing at the bow with the light wind in her hair and her black coat flapping around her.

Although he was still feeling the effects of the poison they had swallowed, Mike performed a miracle of seamanship and was in the middle of pulling off an unbelievable escape only to run smack dab into the entire Corsair fleet.

In an insane move, Mike turned *The Wind Ripper* into the heart of the black fleet. Jenn thought she was seconds from fainting dead away. Everywhere she looked were Corsairs. They were defenseless, and Jenn's disguise of a ski cap and a scowl wouldn't hold up under any scrutiny. Then Mike had given the fleet a cheer and began jerking the black Corsair flag up and down so it couldn't be missed. He then turned around again to make it look as though he were joining the chase as the *Hell Quake* fled.

In minutes, there had been Corsair ships ranging up on either side of *The Wind Ripper*, asking about Cannan. "He's dead," Stu yelled back, just as Mike ducked the boat into a low cloud, hauled her around and cut under the Corsair ship on their right. When the ships broke out into the open, the missing *Wind Ripper* was quickly noticed. This began a chase within a chase.

They fled south, ducking from squall to squall, doubling back, slashing through the Corsair formations, making the most impossible and unlikely moves until, after many stressful hours, they had finally managed to elude their pursuers. Mike and Stu were exhausted from the chase, and Jenn wasn't much better off. Unlike them, she couldn't rest; she still had to look at Rob LaBar's leg.

She was afraid that looking was about all she could do for him. Their medical supplies were terribly limited, and the bullet had done extensive damage. Still, she lowered the sails and restrung the main so that it hung over the middle of the deck like a tarp to keep the rain off of them. They had no anesthesia except for a few quarts of horrible bathtub gin that she found in a locked box in the captain's cabin.

Its smell was so pungent and sharp that it made her dizzy just opening the first bottle.

After watching Jenn lay out her surgical instruments, a white-faced Rob LaBar drank the gin until his ulcers ached and his head swam. With his blood loss, it didn't take much to get him drunk and once drunk, he backed himself into a corner and raved about torture and a girl named Rita. He had to be tied down just so Jenn could inspect the wound. When she cut open his leg to get a better look, he practically screamed and was so loud that Stu wanted to punch him into unconsciousness. LaBar then puked up blood and gin onto the deck of *The Wind Ripper*, which made the normally more reticent Mike want to punch him, also.

"No one's punching anyone," Jenn hissed as she squinted in at the gory wound. The muscle in his thigh was so torn up that she didn't know where to begin. In the dim grey light of the wet morning, it looked like a bowl of bloody hamburger, which she would have to turn back into steak. "Get him another drink of the gin. Just tell him it's from Rita."

Stu was able to coax another couple of tumblers into him, and much to everyone's relief, he passed out. Jenn went right to work, tackling the bleeders first so she could see what was going on. She had only gotten three clamped and was struggling after a fourth when there came the sound of a sail flapping from out of a low cloud.

Everyone froze, their ears straining to hear through the patter of rain and the growing wind. No real straining was needed, in truth. The sound of the flapping sail was punctuated by a cough, a low, grunting laugh, and a splash of piss as someone urinated over the side of a boat.

Very quickly, more and more of these sounds came to them until it became painfully obvious that they had become surrounded by a large number of boats. Each of them thought they had somehow managed to float back into the Corsair fleet, but, as they were about to find out, it was the Queen's fleet. It had taken up its secondary position, twelve miles due west of the Golden Gate Bridge, where it was hidden from the Corsairs by distance, the curve of the earth, and the desolate Farallon Islands.

Everyone on the deck of *The Wind Ripper* was frozen in place. Jenn and Stu, kneeling on either side of LaBar, didn't know what to do, while Mike at the wheel was afraid to do anything for fear of making noise and calling attention to them.

This state of inaction couldn't last.

"Wha? What are my handsh doin' like dis?" Rob suddenly slurred, trying to sit up.

Stu clamped a desperate hand over LaBar's mouth, while Mike rushed about on tip-toe to get his ship ready to flee as quietly as possible. He had barely tied off the mainsail before the wind blew away the mists and showed them that this fleet was even larger than the one they had just escaped from. A hundred and thirty ships surrounded them, bobbing gently up and down on the swell.

At first, no one seemed to notice that they were not ex-Corsairs, though in Jenn's mind it was painfully obvious. For one, they were a mismatched crew. The Queen's men wore either black clothes or camouflage, while the tiny crew of *The Wind Ripper* had on the odd scraps that they had found in the lone house after their shipwreck. Mike wore a striped sweater under a downy blue ski coat. Jenn had on a purple skirt over jeans and two coats, one green and one white. Stu looked rather puffed-up due to the three sweaters he wore, while the brown corduroy pants he had on made a *zwip, zwi*p sound every time he moved.

Of course, the most obvious thing that made them stand out like a sore thumb was the bloody man tied to the deck. He looked like he was in the process of being tortured.

"What's going on down there?" someone on a nearby boat muttered when he saw Rob LaBar and the growing pool of blood around him.

"Just an accident," Mike said, his voice so high that he sounded half his age. "He fell down the, uh, the uh…" He began to choke on the end of the lie; he was having trouble trying to think of anything on board a person could fall down that would cause a wound of that size. As he groped around for words, *The Wind Ripper* continued sliding along the grey waters.

"The stairs," Stu finished for him, speaking quickly. "He fell down the stairs."

"And landed on a knife," Mike added. A few of the ex-Corsairs were staring at him without comprehension. *He fell on a knife? That didn't seem likely. And why had they set their mainsail? They* wondered if they had missed an order. *Were we supposed to set our sails, too? Is it time to attack?*

Only one man among them noticed that *The Wind Ripper* was still flying the pure black Corsair flag. "Hey! I think that might be one of the Captain's boats," he called out, pointing an accusing finger. This had less of an impact than he thought it would—all the boats in the Queen's fleet had been the Black Captain's until very recently.

Once more Mike began to trip over a lie, stammering out, "We-we-we had the uh. I mean we lost our old flag…no this is our old flag. I meant we…"

"Just get us out of here," Jenn whispered to him. She had a hand thrown across her brow, trying to shield her face. "Hurry, hurry."

Mike turned the wheel so that the wind was directly on their stern. The sail went as taut as a drum and they sped for the receding mists. Behind them, even the dimmest of the ex-Corsairs realized that something was wrong. There was a smattering of low cries as Jenn cut LaBar loose and dragged him to the stairs leading into the galley, and Stu ran up a pair of jibs.

They all expected gunfire, however the confusion among the Queen's fleet was too great. No one knew if it was okay to shoot, since they were trying to surprise the Corsairs. Only when it was too late were a few smattering shots unleashed. Mike already had *The Wind*

Ripper in the clouds when the bullets zipped past, making little swirls in the vapors.

Once more the chase was on, only this time they were hounded northwest by the five fastest boats in the Queen's fleet. They weren't faster than *The Wind Ripper;* though it was dreadfully close. On two occasions, their pursuers were able to swing by on opposite tacks and let loose torpedoes at them; one on the first pass, and three on the second.

The first one came so close that Jenn heard the whine of its motors as Mike turned hard away from it. She didn't really understand what she was hearing. "What is that?" she had asked.

Stu leaned down from the deck and hissed in a strangled voice, "Torpedo," as if simply being loud would set it off. When they fired the salvo at them, she had held her breath, her face scrunched in anticipation of the explosion that would break the back of the ship and send what was left of her body to the bottom of the ocean.

Mike resisted the urge to turn about and race with the wind as it would put them even closer to the Queen's ships. Instead, he willed his boat to go faster. When that didn't work, he swung *The Wind Ripper* hard to port. The torpedoes had an edge in speed this way, however they weren't able to deal with the growing waves which kept pushing them off course.

It became an endurance test—Jenn's heart, which felt as though it were about to explode, against the longevity of Jillybean's batteries and the compressed air within the cylinders. Two of the torpedoes died after a few minutes, but the third slowly ate up the distance.

Mike leapt up onto the stern rail and watched the little killing machine with growing resignation. There would be no escaping the torpedo and even if he managed to, he saw that his pursuers were readying more. Every dodge, every jig, every unexpected turn he had made, had only slowed the ship down, allowing his enemy to keep up. And if he tried anything drastic now, it would only put *The Wind Ripper* in the path for more. A fatalistic and deeply tired sigh escaped him.

He probably would have watched the torpedo until it went off below him if it hadn't been for Stu who limped up next to him with their one rifle in his hands.

"You might want to look out," he growled as he raised the rifle. He fired once, twice, three times, cursed, and fired again, missing for the fourth time. The heaving boat was causing havoc with his stance, and the slashing wind was driving rain into his eyes. Even his hands betrayed him; they were still crimped from the poison.

Mike began to back from the rail. "Stu! Stop missing, dang it."

"It's not my fault!" Just as he took his next shot, *The Wind Ripper* almost bucked him into the sea and the bullet went into the clouds. Mike grabbed him from behind to steady him and had a perfect view down the length of the AR-15. On a calm sea, Stu couldn't have missed.

On this rough sea, he had to shoot at a target that was moving in at least two different directions at once: forward-ish and up, or sideways and down, while his own platform was sometimes moving in sync and sometimes churning and yawing simultaneously.

When the torpedo was twenty yards away, Stu began pulling the trigger as fast as he could.

The eleventh bullet did the trick. It punctured the air tank, causing the torpedo to immediately turn in short angry circles. Stu sagged in relief and Mike let out a cheer which was drowned out by a shocking *Throoom!* The man controlling the torpedo had decided to detonate it, causing an explosion of brilliant fire followed by white water leaping high into the sky.

Mike and Stu fell back in a tangle of arms and legs. "That was uncalled for," Mike said as he helped Stu to his feet.

"Jillybean might think she's got them under her heel, but they are still Corsairs at heart," Stu told him. "They aren't going to change any time soon."

"I guess," Mike agreed without much enthusiasm. His ears were still ringing, and his hands were shaking as he began tacking back and forth into the teeth of the same storm that would soon play havoc with Jillybean's battle.

It was not just the storm that would change the nature of the battle. Little did they know, but the appearance of *The Wind Ripper*, which was flying the black flag and had been mistaken for a Corsair ship, was the catalyst that sent the Queen's fleet into battle before the entire Corsair fleet was in place.

The trio was oblivious to this and even if they had known, they were just too tired to care. All they really wanted was to get south as fast as possible and start a new life.

It turned out to be an impossibility. Two of the Queen's boats dogged them endlessly, forcing them northwest until the sun set. In the dark, Mike tried to skirt around them by heading west, directly into the growing storm. Unfortunately, it kept heaving them back to where they had started. He would tack back and forth across the ocean to gain a few yards at a time, only to lose them to the irresistible tide.

By midnight, Mike was too tired to go on. He had no idea if the ships were still out there. When he and Stu finally gave up and staggered down into the galley, stiff and numb from the cold, Jenn was sitting at a table, her red eyes staring at a single, spluttering candle.

"I think the world, or the universe, or whatever wants us to go north," Mike said once he had eased himself down onto the floor. There were leather couches, but he felt more like a sponge than a person and didn't want to get everything all wet.

"Don't ya think signs are my thing?" Jenn asked, listlessly scratching at some dried blood that was peeling on the side of her face. She had spent almost the entire day trying to save Rob LaBar and had finally sown him up a few hours before. Considering the hatchet job she had done, it was a wonder he was still breathing. She would be the first to admit that surgery wasn't her thing, no matter how much Jillybean wanted to make her into a younger version of herself.

Telling the future was so much easier. The signs either came to her or they didn't, she really didn't have to work for them.

Stu smirked and made a sarcastic grunting noise. Mike shushed him with the hardest look he could muster up sufficient energy for: a brief, one-second glare. He turned back to Jenn. "Of course. What do the signs say? Which direction should we go?"

Across from her was a calendar opened to December of 2012. Above the little boxes was a picture of a drunk Santa Claus having just crashed into the North Pole with his sleigh. Even though she had never really had the full Christmas experience, the image evoked a sense of nostalgia. "North," she told them. Sometimes it was as simple as that. She needed a direction and there was the calendar picture, unnoticed until that very moment.

This time when Stu let out a grunt of laughter, Mike didn't bother with a look. He was confused. "But I just said north."

"Yeah," Jenn answered, "but I gotta be able to do something around here. Think of it like I was just giving you…validation. That's what Jillybean would have called it."

"Besides, even without the signs, north makes sense. West is turning out to be impossible. To the south are lurking ships. To the east are more of them and that leaves, north. If the Corsairs are all in San Francisco looking to fight Jillybean, we might be able to waltz right up to Bainbridge completely unseen and unharmed."

"Waltz? Validation?" Mike said with a smile. "Once a queen, always a queen. Just remember, I knew you back when the only thing you were queen of was hide-and-go-seek." He heaved himself up and stood against the wall as if he couldn't will his legs to go back out into the raw elements.

Stu gazed up at him. "You need some help?" He hoped to God that the answer would be a truthful no.

It was. "North is easy. Just as long as the storm doesn't get out of hand, it's just a matter of watching our leeward drift and we're so far out it should be nothing. Someone spell me in a few hours."

Jenn took over for a three-hour shift after him and Stu came after her. By then it was morning, though it didn't improve the visibility all that much. The clouds were fat and full, hovering a hundred feet over the grey swell, while rain and mist took turns hiding everything between sky and sea.

It reminded Stu of the nasty weather they had endured while the *Captain Jack* was sinking under them only a few days before. Because that was still so fresh in his mind, he was always uneasy when he came up on deck to take his turn piloting the boat. In truth, he had little to fear. *The Wind Ripper* was as dry and as snug a boat as there was and Mike's seamanship was second to none.

Even the storm wasn't one of those beastly creatures that seemed to have been created from the depths of hell to make widows out of sailor's wives. It wasn't good sailing weather by any means, but without the threat of being torpedoed, they made slow but steady progress northward.

Shift followed shift, becoming a dull routine in which they froze for a few hours on deck and then rushed down as soon as they were relieved to huddle close to the little fire which burned nonstop in a stout unbelievably heavy black cauldron that hadn't shifted an inch by the movement of the waves.

Gradually, almost without notice, the pain from their poisoning and the many minor wounds they had received from the wreck of the *Captain Jack,* slowly receded. Only Stu had cause to limp about. His leg was stiff from the damp and his left arm weaker than Jenn's. He might have limped, but he didn't complain. In fact, he rarely spoke beyond the occasional grunt.

Their weariness left them as well, mostly that is. It had diminished considerably from the terrible stupor they'd been in after the wreck; however the endless cold settled into their bones and wouldn't leave. It made sleeping difficult and going out on deck a trial. By degrees, their exhaustion became a part of their daily lives; they could function, but just in a different way. They grew clumsy, tripping over stairs and lines. Their knots were limp, and their sails sagged. Answers to questions came slowly, if at all.

It was this endless weariness that had Jenn proclaiming on the evening of the third day, "I'm sick of boats. Sorry Mike. If I never see another boat as long as I live, I'll be happy."

He would never speak such blasphemy and yet, he too needed time ashore, if only to sleep for one full and uninterrupted night.

"We should consider going to shore," he said after a moment's consideration. "We're getting low on wood, and we should find out where we are."

"And Rob needs real antibiotics," Jenn added in a hushed voice. She cast a glance the Corsair's way in case he was listening. "His leg is definitely infected. If we don't do something, he's going to lose it."

The Corsair was the least of their problems, in Mike's view, and Stu didn't hide the curl to his lip as he glanced at the man. "We'll see what we can do," Mike said. "I'm going to head east, so that means we're going to need to douse all our fires."

The Wind Ripper came about so quickly it was almost as if she was looking forward to the break as well. Her sails filled, and the rigging sang as she raced for the unseen beach. They had no idea how close they were…or how far. Everyone went on deck, including Rob LaBar.

They sat wrapped in blankets that smelled like old socks and campfires.

No one said much of anything, and if they did speak, it was in whispers. They were listening intently for any "beach-like" sounds: the cry of gulls, the crashing of waves, even the gentle lapping of water on sand.

The four of them were also listening for the telltale sounds of other ships. There wasn't a ship abroad this far north that they wouldn't run from.

They were further from land than any of them expected, and even with the slowly diminishing wind pushing them along, it was hours before they heard the first sounds coming through the dark: it was the distant crash of waves rolling into rocks. "Watch the boom," Mike hissed, as he swung *The Wind Ripper* from an easterly course to a north-north-east heading. "Stu, check our depth, please." The boat had a state-of-the-art depth finder that was useless without batteries or an engine. Instead they had to rely on a two-hundred foot length of twine attached to a hunk of metal.

Stu dropped it overboard and let the line run through his fingers for what seemed like a long time before it thumped into the sandy bottom.

"A hundred feet, at least," Stu said, softly.

Mike had him drop the line every few minutes; little by little, the bottom seemed to swell up at them. When the depth was fifty feet, Mike ran them straight north, running parallel with the shore. The sound of the waves had become unnervingly close, though it was hard to tell just how close they were with the dark.

Now, they listened for the waves as if their lives depended on it; a sudden shift in the unseen shoreline would doom them, and yet, they needed to get as close to the shore as possible to find a suitable place to make a landing. Because of the darkness and the storm, they had to get very close, foolishly close, or so it seemed. With Stu tossing the depth finder overboard continuously and calling out the measurements in an ever increasingly hard voice, Mike eased the ship gently back toward the sound of the breakers.

He was so cautious that it was an hour before Stu called out, "Twenty-five feet," just as they broke out of the clouds and into the clear. They had a perfect view of the foaming breakers rolling over with thunderous crashes, not seventy yards off their starboard side. From seventy yards, they could feel the unnerving pulse of the ocean through the hull.

Far worse, from Mike's perspective was the shudder coming up from the rudder. Although the ship was heading north, the winds and tide were also pushing it east, right at the rocky shore.

"Easy now," Mike whispered, mostly to himself as he edged the wheel over a quarter turn, away from the breakers and back into the clouds. When the shudder coming up from the rudder faded, he let out a laugh that was all relief. "Now, all we have to do is find a place where the sound of the waves drops away. It'll mean an inlet or a…"

In the middle of his sentence a bell rang somewhere ahead of them, causing Mike to go stiff at the wheel. Instinctively, he turned *The Wind Ripper* further away from the hidden shore. A bell at sea meant a buoy was nearby. These were set to warn boaters of peril. Fearing hidden rocks or a reef, Mike waited for the next ring, so he could pinpoint the location; however, the next bell that rang came from behind them.

It was a perfectly clear chime, not the clunky sound of the old, rusting buoy bells he was used to hearing. Confusion and a growing fear vied for supremacy within him as he turned to squint back behind them. All he saw were the dark mists and the foam trailing from the…

A third bell sounded, this time from far back behind them. In shock, he realized these weren't buoy bells, these were ships and whether they were Corsair ships or the Queen's ships made no difference. Either side would kill them without hesitation.

Chapter 21

"This can't be happening," Jenn whispered, after more bells began to ring ahead of them. Each let out a slightly different note so that it was almost like a song.

Now that they were not so dangerously close to the breakers crashing onto the shore, the sounds of ships around them could not be missed.

Although most of the ships were being sailed by sullen, half-beaten skeleton crews who knew better than to call attention to themselves when the Black Captain was in a towering rage, the ships themselves made all sorts of subtle noise that was becoming more and more apparent as the storm died and the winds slackened.

Their ropes creaked, and their masts groaned. The tops of waves splashed into the keels, and the hulls themselves let out little sighs as they came up out of the water.

Mike had missed all of this as they had passed through the formation of Corsair boats mainly because the formation itself had slipped dangerously to leeward, which was the reason for the bells in the first place. The first bell signaled a move to port and the second meant a return to their original northward direction.

"It'll be okay," Mike told Jenn. He had said this so many times that it was now a reflex on his part. "We'll just slip a little to the west and they'll never know we were here." Stu grunted his doubt while Jenn wore hers openly on her face. To her, it felt as though they were living on some sort of see-saw; their luck had gone back and forth between good and atrocious, with each dip toward the bad side getting worse and worse.

Did I misread the signs? she wondered, as Stu and Mike made the minor adjustments needed to ease them towards the wind. "Or did I just get lazy?" She hadn't given any thought to their direction at all when Mike had asked for a sign. The calendar had just been there. "Maybe it was just more bad luck?"

She was about to go back down into the cabin to look at the picture of Santa and the North Pole once more, when she heard the whisper of a boat coming towards them. She stopped and squinted into the darkness and the misting clouds; they all did. The Corsair ships were not in exact alignment and as Mike tried to slide *The Wind Ripper* out of the formation, he cut across the path of another ship. It appeared out of the darkness like a patch of perfect midnight.

"Look out, moron!" someone hissed from the boat. "What are you, deaf? The second bell was plain as day."

Jenn's only reaction was to hold her breath as the two boats passed within spitting distance of each other: a loogie was hawked at them and hit *The Wind Ripper's* gunwale.

"Get your ass in line!" another voice from the Corsair ship snapped. "And why the hell don't you have a second jib strung? Do you think you're driving some sorta yacht?"

"Sorry," Mike said, trying to pitch his voice low.

"Sorry, he says. Who is that, Rainbow Dave? You tell Cannan I'm gonna have words with him and you when we get back."

He went on muttering quiet threats and put-downs as Stu laid on another jib and Mike apologized and agreed that he was an "Ass" and a "Green Bitch." Slowly, he eased the ship away and back towards the shore. Soon the patch of perfect midnight became only a black shadow and then it disappeared altogether. "We'll let them pass by," Mike whispered, "and then scoot out west again. I think getting wood is going to have to wait."

It had been such a close call that no one argued about the wood. Jenn was just about to go below when Rob LaBar grabbed her arm. "I thought you said you were gonna get me some antibiotics. I don't wanta lose my leg, Jenn."

The near collision had driven his wound out of her mind. Her shoulders sagged as she asked Mike, "What about Rob? I don't know if he can wait."

Mike couldn't believe the request. Didn't she realize how much trouble they were in? He glanced toward Stu, who only gave a shrug, saying, "You're the captain. I just work here."

A sigh, one that was a perfect replication of how his dad used to sigh, came from Mike. He also shrugged as if he was in a position beyond his control. "I don't know what to say, Jenn. He's just going to have to try to wait."

Rob's face was set in a rigid mask of pain and despite the cold, there were sweat stains at his collar. "You want me to try to not be infected? Is that what I'm supposed to do?"

"I meant try to hold on. I-It might not be that long. I counted the second set of bells; there were seven in front of us and only four behind. I think we're at the very end of the formation and once they're gone, it'll just be us and a bunch of empty water. We can go where we want."

He based this on a false premise. Mike didn't realize that the Corsair fleet had been broken up into squadrons and that another one was coming up fast, following pretty much the exact same course the first had, which put *The Wind Ripper* directly in its path.

Thinking he had the situation under control, Mike shortened sail and had them tooling along just fast enough to keep from being pushed onto shore. He figured he would give the Corsairs a head-start and then slip in behind them. He didn't count on hearing another bell. It was clear and crisp, somewhere very close and hidden by the low clouds.

"Mike?" Stu whispered. "Which way?"

That was an impossible question. In a sense, they were stuck. They couldn't heave to the right because the shore was too close, and they couldn't go left because they would be broadside to the coming ships, and the possibility of being rammed was too great. Their only chance was to yank the sail tight and race forward as fast as they could. *The Wind Ripper* was a fast ship, though it took time for her to get to speed from what was practically a stand still. Stu gave her all the sail he could, as quickly as he could, and she fairly leapt forward, she just didn't leap as fast as any of them wanted.

Emerging from the clouds was the forty-five foot *Silk Diamond*. The Corsair ship was so intensely black and so eerily silent, sliding through the water, that she looked more like a ghost ship than a real, tangible one, at least to Jenn.

Mike had a different perspective. Jutting from the very front of the ship was what looked like a huge spear and it was aimed right at his face.

He ducked just as the spear cut the air over his head. There was an explosion of curses from *The Silk Diamond,* while almost right above them was a huge voice roaring, "Hard to starboard! Hard to starboard!"

Mike cut his wheel hard to port, hoping to evade the huge ship by taking diverging courses. They were too close, and *The Silk Diamond* had too much momentum. In reality, the spear was the ship's bowsprit, which was something akin to an extra boom designed to hold a larger forward sail. In this instance, it worked like a modern lance and, as the two ships came together with a terrific jolt that sent Stu sprawling, the bowsprit ripped into *The Wind Ripper's* sail.

Ropes snapped, and the boom swung like an immense baseball bat just a few feet over the deck. It passed so close to Jenn that it ripped out a few stray hairs from the top of her head.

The impact sent *The Wind Ripper* spinning to the west with a high shrieking noise as her sail tore as easily as tissue paper. The *Silk Diamond* went to the right, her captain still roaring. "Who is that? What boat is that, damn it?" A bell began ringing and soon it was joined by others.

For a few moments, Mike didn't know what direction they were facing, and then their bad luck became atrocious as they drifted right out of the low clouds. Above them was a solid bank of grey and all around them was empty black sea.

"What do we do?" Stu asked. Mike didn't have an answer. As captain, he was responsible for everything. It was his fault that their main was shredded and their lines were flung about like spiderwebs after a storm. Guilt had him by the throat. He couldn't pretend to be the big man when everything was going perfectly and not be the goat when disaster struck. His first response was to look to Jenn.

She was gently touching her face with shaking hands, as if she couldn't believe she was still alive. "What are you looking at me for?" His eyes shifted to the terrible state of the ship and she understood: he was no longer master and commander of the high seas. He looked like a boy who had broken his mother's favorite mirror. And Stu had changed, as well. The tough as nails Hillman had drunk poison from more than just the little vial. His love for Jillybean had been toxic. It had corroded him. It had weakened him as a man.

And now they were both looking at her, a fifteen-year-old girl with no experience beyond a few days as queen in which she let valuable minutes slip away, one after another until they were all gone and she was drinking poison.

What did they expect of her?

Nothing, she thought. *They are just afraid to make their own decisions.* She understood. No matter what they decided to do in the next few seconds, it would probably lead to their capture, their torture and their deaths. It was hard to be the person responsible for that, even if there was no other choice.

The only thing being queen had taught her was that a queen didn't get to choose not to choose. For good or bad, she had to make a decision.

"Can we go with just the jib?" she asked Mike.

"Not very well and not very fast. And they'll see…"

She cut him off. "We'll use the jib. Hurry." The bells were still ringing in the clouds behind them and the angry curses were growing in volume.

As Mike and Stu ran up two jibs, Jenn went to the back of the boat to see if there was damage. The railing was twisted into something that resembled a warped spider web and was hanging by a single screw. Below that, the stern was bashed inward in the shape of a V. Luckily, the point of the V stopped a few feet from the water.

They weren't going to sink and that was some good news, at least. The bad news, as Mike explained a few minutes later, was that steering using just the jibs was problematic at best, and worse, their speed would be half what it was. "And," he added, ominously.

"There's an and?" She couldn't imagine an "and" worse than what she had just heard.

"There might be a lot of them. In this case, there's a real danger that we might lose the boom if we push things too hard. *And,* I think we're going to have to push as hard as we can. Whoever's captaining the boat that hit us is pissed off."

This was a bit of an understatement. They could still hear the captain bawling orders, one of which was: "Find that damned boat!"

"Man the wheel," Mike ordered her. He was already coming back into his own. "And keep watch back there. If you see a ship, let me know asap." The squadron had come to a stop and was still in the bank of low clouds. *The Wind Ripper* was a half mile away and slowly building up speed under the twin jibs.

"Let's hope she holds," Mike said to Stu as he ran a hand up the mast. It was already bending forward, letting out a light groan. If it caught a gust wrong, it would snap. He gave the mast a tug with both hands and heard Rob LaBar chuckle. Mike eyed him before asking, "What do you think? You've been on this boat longer than we have. What do you suggest?"

He chuckled again, a cold little laugh. "I think you should jump overboard and make a swim for it. You'll be caught if you don't, plain and simple."

"That's it?" Stu growled.

"That's it, squinty-eyes. You think you're so tough, but you walk around here like an old man, all creaky and crap. So yeah, jump in and start swimming before half a dozen boats zip up here and cut you off. It's not like there's anywhere to hide and how many boats look like they just got run over by an ocean liner?"

Stu cracked the knuckles of both hands, saying, "If I swim, you swim, so maybe you should think of something else."

Mike raised a hand to Stu. "Hold on, he might have a point. We need to make *The Wind Ripper* look less ripped up. In the meantime, Jenn, give me a half-turn to port. Maybe something as simple as a course change might throw them off."

While Jenn tried to hold a north-west course, Mike and Stu ran down into the lower deck for tools and more sailcloth. Once back on deck, they got rid of the broken railing and then cut a length of sailcloth to fit over the splintered V-shaped hole in the stern. Up close it looked like cloth stretched tight over a hole, but from further away, the black painted hull matched well enough with the black sail to make it look as though the boat was in one piece.

"I see a boat!" Jenn hissed. Three more followed the first out of the mists. From this distance it seemed that they were only the shadows of clouds, yet these shadows moved sideways to the wind.

Mike went to the wheel and tried to turn the boat further into the wind. The mast creaked and the lines running from it looked as taut as bowlines. They were very close to the breaking point. "Hold it here," he ordered Jenn. She had to strain to keep the wheel in place.

While she fought against the strength of both the wind and tide, Mike and Stu rushed to get their sail back in place. It would never draw wind like it used to, and would never be drum-tight, but that wasn't the point. They only had a few minutes to make it *seem* as though the sail was up and operational.

Staples and duct-tape made it appear whole, while a series of half-assed knots gave them enough rope to keep it from flapping around. They could only hope that no one noticed that the boom was loose and that the sail was little more than a giant weathervane.

"Now we need backstays," Mike said, "and a whole lot of luck." The backstays were lines that would pull back on the mast to help stabilize it against the forward pressure of the jibs. It could help them to eke out a few more knots of speed and perhaps they could get away completely. The ships behind them were already sniffing up the wrong path. They were still heading directly north, while *The Wind Ripper* was slipping away to the northwest.

The backstays were tangible things Mike could handle; it was the luck he couldn't do anything about.

The moment he and Stu went below, Rob LaBar screamed, "Over here! We're over here! Hey…"

By the time the two rushed up on deck, they found Jenn crouched over the Corsair with a glittering knife at his throat. There was blood, but not much. She hadn't killed him.

"What are you waiting for?" Stu asked, coldly. "He's a Corsair. A knife should be stuck into every one of them." Jenn's hand shook, and the tip of the knife slid deeper into his flesh.

"Don't," Mike begged. "Yeah, he's a Corsair, but this is something Jillybean would do. I think it would be wrong. I just…I just don't want you turning out like her. She had to start somewhere to get as bad as she…"

"Hey!" a voice hissed over the water. The word hadn't come from behind them, it came from their left, from the west. They all looked up to see a line of ten ships. The first was just crossing in front of them. It was another squadron of Corsairs that had been slightly off course but was now coming back in line.

They had *The Wind Ripper* dead to rights and this time the crippled ship would not be able to get away.

Chapter 22

The outer wall built by the Guardians was truly an impressive engineering feat. It stood twenty-feet high, four-feet wide and ran in a two-mile long arc encompassing a small peninsula that bulged out into the Pacific. It was made up of concrete blocks and rebar. Inside its hollow structure were ladders and platforms and murder holes, allowing men move and fight within it.

No zombie was strong enough to do much more than scratch this wall and no human army had ever considered mounting an attack on it, for obvious reasons.

"What did I tell you, your Highness?" Mark Leney asked, his hands planted squarely on his hips. "The Black Captain's intel is almost always spot on. Don't ask me how he has so many spies, I just know they are good."

"I don't see it in this case."

Leney jerked his head around in surprise, causing the partially healed cut across his throat to zing with pain. "They got it all perfectly right. Every last detail. This place can't be taken, at least not by a frontal attack. It would be a complete nightmare. No offense, but those pills you're taking might be messing with your head, your Highness."

Despite still being exhausted from the battle, she had sent him into San Francisco with a shopping list the previous morning. Among the different odds and ends were a number of pills. She had downed two the moment he had gotten back, making him wonder if they had been the entire reason for the trip and all the other things he had picked up had only been window dressing.

"I'm fine," she answered, curtly. In truth, the Zyprexa made her sleepy and the night before she'd had eight hours of continuous sleep, something that hadn't happened in years. Although she felt refreshed, she wasn't happy about it. There was still so much to do to be wasting time uselessly sleeping. She had patients to attend to, the Corsairs trapped around Rodeo Lagoon were going to surrender at any minute, she had to replenish her supply of torpedoes, bombs and batteries, and she had to compel the Guardians to accept her as Queen.

It was going to be a full day.

"Shaina? Binoculars, please."

Leney thought it was strange that the Queen had brought three "helpers" along with the seven hundred fighters who were arranged in tight companies behind them. They were the oddest set of assistants he had ever seen: lumpy-headed Shaina Hale, who was as skinny and angular as a stick bug and probably not quite as smart as one; a one-armed kid named Aaron Altman, who carried a pistol that looked like it weighed more than he did; and a seven-year-old girl named Lindy Smith. She skipped around like a butterfly, talking almost nonstop about absolutely nothing.

"Here you are, your Queen-ness," Shaina said, with a lopsided grin. "I mean, your Highness. I don't know why I said that. It just came out and…"

"Thank you, Shaina," Jillybean interrupted. After sending the battered woman back with the other two, the Queen put the binoculars up to her face and said, "Hmmm."

"Hmmm?" Leney asked. "Is that all you can say? Look how wide open the land is between here and the wall. There's not a lick of cover for two-hundred yards. Any attack will get smashed before it even begins. We'll be dead like that." He snapped his fingers for emphasis. "And we can't use smoke to cover our movement. The wind is against us; it'll blow right into our faces."

He purposely didn't mention a seaward attack.

As the Queen's hundred-ship fleet swept towards the peninsula, he had eyed the sea approach to the lair of the Guardians. With the rocks, and the surf, and the wall, an attack from that direction was insane. Their ships would be pounded to pieces by the surf and anyone who managed to live long enough to reach land would have to climb a slick, fifteen-foot cliff just to reach the base of the wall. Although the wall was shorter on that side, it was still an utterly flat eleven-foot wall. Without a ladder, no one could get up it.

"And," he went on, quickly, "those walls will hold up against your explosives, unless you got a whole lot more of them and some way to deploy them."

This, he left hanging in the air, waiting to see if she would confide in him.

She said, "Hmmm," again, which made him roll his eyes. She didn't trust him, but she needed him and his ex-Corsairs. For now, he needed her and so he said nothing, knowing that she would eventually cough up her plan—if she had one that is. He was worried that she would expect him to lead some sort of suicidal charge. The men would never go for it—hell, he would never go for it.

He didn't see any other way, however. The wall was too formidable. He was almost certain it would defy her crude bombs, unless she could figure out a way to deliver them without damaging them. They were fragile things that probably wouldn't survive being chucked by a catapult, and no one in their right mind would try to run a hundred-pound bomb at the wall.

Of course, Shaina wasn't exactly in her right mind. Leney turned slightly to take in the woman. *Dumb as a box of rocks,* Leney thought. Maybe the Queen is going to trick her into hauling a bomb up to the big, metal door set in the wall. That's what he would do, if he were in the Queen's shoes.

"So?" he asked when she had given the binoculars back to Shaina. "You can admit it, the wall is too much. The Captain's spies were right."

"I see that the only wall stopping the Captain is the one he erected around his mind. Take Lindy and arrange a meeting. And yes, I will be demanding their surrender."

"Lindy? That girl who won't shut up?" He took a deep breath, holding in the expletives that wanted to come shooting out. When he felt he was in control he asked, "Why?"

"Because your queen told you to."

This did not help to control his volcanic anger which was threatening to explode out of him. He smiled, pressing his lips so tightly together that it made his eyes bulge. Then, with a bow that was very close to mocking, he whistled for the girl as he would a dog and started stomping towards the wall.

The girl caught up quickly enough and of course her mouth started going the second she fell in step with him. "What are we doing? Miss Jillybean said I was supposed to come with you, but she didn't say why. I think it's cuz she's a witch in disguise. Not like totally a bad witch. No, she fixed up Aaron and Mister Trafny like magic and only good magic fixes people. And she can make fire and smoke, and 'splosions, and water pumpers, and…"

"And shut up for goodness sakes! I don't know why you're here but it's not to blather on nonstop. So, zip the lip, got it?"

Lindy nodded, wearing a hurt look. Leney rolled his eyes at the look, but refused to apologize. He began to march faster, making the little girl almost run to keep up.

"I need a white flag, not a stupid kid," he grunted as he saw men in grey lining the top of the wall. Leney counted a hundred and twenty before he gave up; quite a few of them were aiming rifles at him. With careful movements he unbuckled his hip holster and then let his black pea coat fall. The cold wind immediately attacked him, stealing down the neck of his shirt and taking his heat for its own.

"Put your hands up, Lindy. Just to be on the safe side."

The pair came within fifty feet of the reinforced steel door that had been set into the wall before they were hailed. "What do you want, Corsair?"

"And what's with the kid?" another man demanded.

Leney didn't know how to answer that, exactly, since he didn't know what she was doing there. "Her name is Lindy and I am not a Corsair. I'm…"

A burst of laughter came from the wall. "You're not a Corsair? Next, you're going to tell us those aren't Corsair ships lurking around our back door."

"They were Corsair ships," Leney admitted. "Now they are the Queen's ships. You might have noticed the crown emblazoned on them."

"What queen are you talking about?" an older man asked. Unbowed by age, he was tall with wide shoulders. He stared out over

Leney and Lindy at the distant figure of the Queen. She stood alone under her rippling black and silver banner. "There are no queens anymore."

Before Leney could say anything, Lindy piped up. "Yeah there is. That's her over there with the flag. She's the Queen of the Hill People. I'm a Hill Girl, case you were wonnerin' about that. And this is Mister Leney. He was a Corsair until the Queen blew them all up."

"It's Captain Leney, and she's right."

The older man blinked like an owl. "So, the Hill People have given up on that ridiculous coven and they replace it with a queen? Well, that sounds slightly less blasphemous, at least. But what's this about no more Corsairs? Is that true?"

Again, Lindy was quick on the draw. "Oh yeah. There's been all sorts of big fights going on and the Queen whips them every time. Now she ain't always what you'd call all good. She can be bad sometimes and crazy, too. There was this girl named…"

Leney clamped a dirt-tasting hand over Lindy's mouth. "Sorry, she's a talker. So, about the Corsairs, they did lose three or four fights. The Queen is something of a genius when it comes to, well a lot of stuff but she's especially good when it comes to warfare."

"And healing spells," Lindy added. She had squirmed out of Leney's grip. He grabbed her again.

"No, not healing spells. She is a surgeon, not a witch or anything. Ha-ha!" The laughter was forced, and while he smiled up at the men on the wall, he gave Lindy a quick pinch on the neck. "Look, she would like to talk on neutral ground."

The old man's eyes had narrowed at the talk of spells. Now, they were at slits. "What is there to talk about? The fact that your queen has brought an army into our lands? There's not much to say; come fight or go home. It seems to me that those are your only choices, and I would advise that you go home. Even the Black Captain knows better than to test our walls."

Leney agreed. "It would seem that way to me, too, but…" He let the word hang in the air for a few seconds, a sordid grin playing on his lips. "But you heard the girl, the Queen blew up the Corsairs. She can make explosives and she has used them. Two days ago, I saw her destroy a fleet of sixty-five ships in minutes. How many ships do you have?"

He had counted thirty-one tucked up inside a tiny harbor at one corner of the peninsula. It was guarded by some of the nastiest, boat-killing rocks he had ever seen, and the gap between them was so narrow, it was a mystery to him how they got in or out.

Finally, the old man looked uncomfortable. "Does she have artillery?"

"Maybe you and a couple of others should come talk to the Queen. You'll be perfectly safe, I assure you. She would consider it bad manners to kill you without first chatting and giving you an opportunity to surrender."

"Do you want to know what else is bad manners? Attacking people without provocation," the man replied. His name was Christian Walker and he was the commander of the Knights of the Cross, a title that had never felt nearly so weighted with responsibility. In the four years he'd been commander he had drilled his men for exactly this situation—well, almost this situation.

They had trained to fight the Corsairs, not some crazy queen. Anyone claiming to be a queen was crazy in his book, and it had been his experience that being crazy made a person dangerous, especially if they had a fleet and a small army. "Give us an hour. I will send an advance man to make sure there will be no guns. You may do the same."

The man with the horrid face tattoos and the little girl left; he walked in something of an uncouth shamble while she skipped or sometimes hopped on one foot. As a pair they didn't make sense.

"Did that guy really say he was giving us an opportunity to surrender?" Keith Treadwell, his second in command, scoffed. "Like that would ever happen. Did you see his throat? Someone nearly laid that joker's throat open from ear to ear. And that's who they send? And a little girl? They might all be bonkers, if you ask me." Everyone within earshot agreed with a great deal of nodding, some knowing grins, and a few "Amens," which were spoken with conviction.

Walker stared at the retreating figures and then at the distant woman standing under her flag. A sudden chill crept up his back; it wasn't caused by the cool morning. "A queen," he muttered. "That's so odd." Deep down, he knew it was more than odd and the situation was more than crazy, though exactly how and why eluded him at the moment.

"I have to inform the Bishop," he said to Treadwell, tugging him close and speaking into his ear. "While I'm gone, recheck everything. Ammo, food stores, water, wood, everything. That queen might test us directly in battle or she might try a siege. We have to be prepared for either."

As Treadwell snapped off a salute and began barking out orders, Walker went to the nearest port and ran down the ladder with the agility of a young man. With his snow-white hair and his sharp angular face, he looked much older than his forty-six years.

There was a crowd of people, two-hundred strong standing in a loose formation behind the single door in the wall. This was his reserve force; a nearly fifty-fifty split between those men and women who were slightly too old to fight and those not quite old enough. Most were armed with crossbows, compound bows or lances.

Walker waved over the reserve commander, a forty-two-year old named Jennifer Edgerton. He didn't slow, forcing her to run to catch up.

"How many are there?" she asked, huffing along under the weight of her armor and her stiff leather uniform. Unlike the rest of the reserves who wore a mixed array of modified football shoulder pads and kevlar vests, Edgerton wore the same armor as the Knights of the Cross: military style ballistic plate that covered the shoulders, chest, neck and arms. It could stop a bullet and withstand the claws of the biggest zombie.

Like many others, she wore a heavy gold cross on a thick chain. She kissed the cross, saying, "Mack said there were two thousand of them. Is that true? Are there that many of them?"

"I don't know yet. My count was seven hundred. Of course, she might have more, though I doubt it. She wants to talk surrender which suggests she's showing her full force to scare us."

"Seven hundred?" Edgerton was visibly relieved. "We can handle seven hundred even without the reserve."

Unless they have explosives, Walker thought. He stopped abruptly, gazing with blank eyes around at the little community which consisted of little more than a few hundred homes, dozens of greenhouses and a warehouse-sized church. In and around all of this was tilled land waiting for the spring planting. If the wall came down, his Knights would have to defend it.

"Maybe," he told her. "Perhaps even probably, however we can't take any chances. I need your soldiers to start digging foxholes. I want fallback positions ready as soon as humanly possible. I'll talk to Julia Jewett and have her release the civie teams to you. They can dig as well as anyone. Oh, and I think we can lose the lances for now. If zombies become an issue, it'll be their issue, not ours."

Edgerton went back to being visibly anxious again. Their community had been threatened a number of times: twice they had weathered the ravages of immense zombie hordes and once they had been threatened by the Azteca, who had come boiling up from south of Los Angeles, raping and pillaging as they came. These had been terrifying moments, yet she had never been asked to dig foxholes within the confines of the walls.

"It's just a precaution," Walker said, trying to reassure her. He even gave her a smile, though it was grim and looked like it had taken a great deal of effort.

Walker didn't have time for more than the smile. He had to explain the situation to the Bishop and there was no telling how long that would take. When the Bishop was in prayer, nothing short of a meteor strike would budge him and maybe not even then.

Faith Checkamian met him as he entered the doors to the church. Like the wall surrounding the community, the church was made of concrete blocks and rebar. It was not pretty, inside or out. The building was purely functional. In shape, it was a square with hundred-foot sides and a ceiling thirty feet high. There were no chairs or pews, or tapestries or statues or even paintings. Covering its floors was plush carpeting and in the center of the building was an altar resting on a raised dais.

As he feared, the Bishop stood in front of the altar with his arms raised, softly whispering prayers. Kneeling with heads bowed at the foot of the dais were four priests, two nuns and an ancient, creaking deacon with huge white caterpillar eyebrows, who had managed to live through the apocalypse "by the grace of God."

Walker was as devout as any of them, yet he groaned at the sight; an hour was not a long time, unless it was spent waiting for the Bishop to finish his prayers, then it felt like an age. Faith, dressed in the drabbest of grey dresses and the most sensible of her unadorned shoes, gave him something of a warped smile and whispered, "I will let his Excellency know that you would like to meet with him as soon as he has finished his prayers."

This was her way of telling the Commander to wait outside. Weapons and armor were not strictly forbidden within the church; they were, however, frowned upon and Faith could frown with the best of them. She had taken a long, hard road from Pennsylvania to California and when she was displeased, she could display that hardness in a way that made children behave and many men quail.

Commander Walker went outside to wait. As he did, he checked his M4, adjusted his grey armor so that he could move fluidly and thought about the idea of explosives. "She destroyed a fleet of sixty-five vessels in minutes. How?" If it was a sneak attack that was one thing… only the girl had said their Queen had whipped the Corsairs three or four times. From what Walker knew of the Black Captain, he would never allow a sneak attack to occur when…

"Hello Christian."

Walker hadn't heard the Bishop approach. Although Bishop Gary Wojdan was soft and round in every aspect from his dimpled face to his dimpled knees, he was as naturally stealthy as a ninja. He called everyone else by their designated title, but he claimed Christian's name was title enough for him.

"Your Excellency," he said, inclining his head. "We have an issue with the Corsairs. For one, they're not Corsairs. Supposedly, they used to be. Now, they are, well, I'm not sure what they are. They're being led by a queen, if you can believe it. What's more unbelievable is that she's demanding our surrender."

"A very cheeky thing she must be," Wojdan said. He turned slightly to stare at the looming wall. "No, not cheeky. She must be a great deal more than just cheeky if *she* commands Corsairs. That alone suggests she is a very formidable person. I would like to meet her."

Walker was relieved to hear this. He didn't like playing the part of go-between. He was a soldier not a message boy.

The Queen was still standing beneath her banner and with her were two children, the tattooed Corsair and a woman who looked sickly skinny even through Walker's scope.

"I believe we should match their number," Bishop Wojdan said, after taking a look through the scope. "And I like the idea of children being present. Their innocence might have a mitigating effect on any aggression."

"Perhaps this queen is using these kids," Walker suggested. "Perhaps she's trying to suggest she's not all bad since she likes children."

The Bishop lifted his round shoulders in a soft shrug. "Perhaps. Christian, why don't you fetch your daughter Ryanne, and Faith, will you please find one of the orphans. I think Ida might do. Ida Battenburg. Such an interesting girl with such an interesting name."

Walker wasn't exactly happy bringing his daughter into this situation. If the Queen was using the two children as props, would she hesitate to take his Ryanne and use her as a bargaining chip? Or worse, as a human shield? There would be no changing the Bishop's mind, however. It was no use even asking.

He returned with his chirpy, golden-haired daughter; his thick, scarred hand holding her tiny, soft one. Ida, a friendly thing who was completely unaware of any danger, took Ryanne's other hand and then asked for Faith's. Not to be left out, the Bishop took Faith's free hand and so the five of them walked through the doorway forming, what Walker felt was the most ridiculous formation he'd ever been a part of.

As they walked up the cracked and broken remains of an asphalt road that cut directly across the open field, Leney came out to meet them. His holster was empty, and he was once again without his warm black coat. He looked somewhat askance at the Bishop in his black, ankle length cassock and red sash that wrapped around his ample waist.

"I gotta frisk you, Father, sorry." Wojdan lifted his arms so that his gold cross winked in the sun. He said nothing as Leney expertly frisked them one after another. When Leney was done, he lifted his arms to be frisked in turn. "We're unarmed but you can send someone to check."

"That won't be necessary," Bishop Wojdan said. "To earn trust, one must give trust. Don't you agree, Captain Leney."

"Huh? Yeah, I guess that sounds about right." Except it sounded crazy to him. If he had been in charge, they would've had pistols stashed under nearby rocks and in seconds would have had what looked like two top tier guys and three hostages. But the queen was different.

She stood with her hands behind her back as her hair blew like flames around her head. After Bishop Wojdan introduced his small group, Jillybean gave Leney a quick nod. He gave his name and those of the others finishing with Jillybean, saying, "Her Royal Highness, Jillian, Queen of the Hill People and the Islanders. Queen from Sacramento to Santa Rosa to Santa Clara. Queen of the Pacific as far as her fleets may reach, and soon, Queen of the Guardians and all the land and people within their borders."

The introduction was bloated with self-importance, so it was something of a shock when she stuck out her hand to Bishop Wojdan so he could shake it. "As a man of God, I will not ask you to kneel, now or ever. The rest will, eventually."

He shook her hand; it was small, strong and warm. His was soft, pudgy and cold from walking about without gloves or a coat. As they shook hands, he looked into her eyes, which were startlingly large and brightly blue. They were intelligent, quick eyes that ran over him, picking out tiny details that informed her of his character.

"Yes, they will kneel," she said, once she was satisfied with her inspection. "But do not worry, your Excellency, your flock will continue to render unto God that which is God's."

"As long as they also render unto Caesar that which is Caesar's, I suppose," the Bishop replied, an eyebrow arched. "You are an impressive young lady, that I do not doubt, but your hubris seems boundless. First, you claim to be queen of this and that, and now you have the gall to compare yourself to Caesar? Beyond hubris lies destruction."

Something like fire brewed in her eyes for just a second and yet the smile that flashed was wickedly cold. "I have already proven greater than Caesar. In truth, what, beyond the forgotten battle of Ilerda, is there to prove myself against? For the most part, he fought against untrained barbarians and the rabble of a strife-torn empire. Had I compared myself to Hannibal, that would have been hubris."

He had only the vaguest notion of who Hannibal had been. "I accept that your knowledge of ancient warfare is greater than my own," Wojdan said, with a slight nod. "That being said, I have a wonderful wall, as well as five hundred trained soldiers that say we will only kneel before God."

Unexpectedly, the Queen threw back her head and laughed. "Please! I hate that wall. I detest it. I will preserve as much of your flock as I can, but that wall will come down. I swear it."

Chapter 23

For a few moments, the Queen wore a particularly savage look, one that was part feral animal, part pure evil. Inside, she felt both. She swallowed and tried to smile again, but it wasn't easy. The pills she was popping three or four times a day had her alternating between sleepy and sick. They were working, though sometimes she felt like she was drowning in chemicals.

She passed a hand across her forehead and when she looked up, she saw Bishop Wojdan studying her, much as she had studied him.

"Explosives were mentioned by your little helper." Wojdan gestured toward Lindy, who was busy eyeing her counterpart Ida Battenburg and wondering what sort of a girl she was. The Bishop went on, "We weren't told what sort of explosives. If you wish to compel our surrender, perhaps a demonstration is in order. I think I would like to see your big guns, or your tanks, or whatever it is that you will use to tear down our wall, brick by brick."

It almost seemed as if he were mocking her. *Brick by brick…he is…he is mocking you. Kill him…kill him. Build the biggest bomb ever and obliterate him, and all of them. Blow them up, up up, up…* This came sifting softly up from deep within Jillybean's mind. She clenched her hands into fists and gazed up at the grey sky, pretending to consider his words until the scattered voices went away.

"Tanks? Big guns?" she asked, meeting his eyes again. "I would think even a simple priest knows that these could not be carried in the type of boats we possess. Wouldn't you say that feigned ignorance is on par with actual lying? Or do you feel that adding: 'or whatever' allows you to dodge the sin?"

He chortled at this. "Worry not for my sins, young lady. It was an honest question though perhaps spoken glibly. I have no idea what the weight of these weapons are and nor do I know the carrying capacity of your ships."

Young lady…young, young, young…lady…lady…

There was laughter in her head. The voices knew better than to call her a lady. A lady didn't feed poison to her friends or set a house on fire when there were people inside screaming…

Jillybean plastered a fake smile in place. "Bishop Wojdan, you will refer to me as your Highness, and though you were never officially consecrated, I will refer to you as your Excellency. Yes, I am young and a lady but calling me such within this setting is your way of asserting dominance, and I won't stand for it."

He inclined his head again, never once taking his keen eyes off of her. "Your spies are remarkably well informed if they have dug that far into my past to know my position within the church. I suppose I should be flattered to have received so much attention. I must be quite the threat."

Jillybean made no answer and did not move so much as a muscle and yet she radiated such coldness that Wojdan inclined his head a third time, adding a late, "Your Highness."

"Thank you, your Excellency," she replied, nodding just as he had. "I'm sure you agree that titles have their importance even among enemies, though I believe that situation will be short-lived. And I don't have any spies. The ring you wear is not a normal bishop's ring. I'm no expert in these matters, however, you'd be surprised how one thing just leads to another. Somehow researching lead poisoning got me onto Gutenberg and his printing press which in turn led me to Pope Pius, this got me on the amazing story of the *Cadaver Synod* in which the dead body of Pope Formosus was dug up out of its grave and put on trial. I just had to know if he was wearing *The Ring of the Fisherman* during the trial, and this led to other inquiries of that nature."

"Someone dug up the body of a pope and put it on trial?" Leney asked, laughter in his voice. "Was he the first zombie or something? Did they find him guilty? What happened?"

"They did find him guilty, actually," the Bishop answered when Jillybean glanced his way, a sparkle in her eyes. She was testing him, which he found very interesting. "They cut off three fingers of his right hand. He was buried again, but soon after, his body was dug up a second time and tossed in a river." Jillybean nodded exactly like one of Wojdan's elementary school teachers had fifty years before. The Bishop had no idea what to make of the girl. All he could wonder was how many people left alive knew about the Synod or that the Pope wore the *Ring of the Fisherman*? Or he used to. Wojdan didn't hold out much hope for the Pope.

As these thoughts crossed his mind, Commander Walker stumped forward and cleared his throat. "Can we get back on track, your Excellency? We have an army threatening us. I for one would like to know about these explosives. Are we talking mortars? AT4s? We will not be frightened into surrender as easily as you might think…your Highness."

He looked as though saying "your Highness" had left him sickened. After clearing his throat a second time, he went on, "To destroy the wall would take a good deal of ordinance, which I doubt you have."

Jillybean's smile became knowing and tinged with evil. "I won't be using explosives to destroy the wall. I have bombs and torpedoes and all of that, of course. I don't think I want to use them this time. They've become too easy. There's no challenge. I don't want to get lazy, right?"

Walker glanced at Leney, who was trying not to react to the crap that Jillybean had just spewed. Leney wanted it easy. When it came to warfare, he thought the easier the better.

Walker saw the flick of Leney's eyes and the slight raising of his eyebrows and practically read his mind. Walker grinned. "You will find that we are a far superior foe compared to these *Corsairs*." He fairly spat the word out. "We have five-hundred soldiers who have trained to defend this wall. We know every inch of these fields and we have them dialed in. We will destroy anything that moves on them, day or night."

"Perhaps it won't need to come to this," Jillybean replied. "My goal is the eradication of the Corsair threat and the joining of the disparate people along the western coast under a single leader. I can't imagine that you'd balk at that or find the goal anything but noble. Though I do understand there may be trust issues. What may I offer as an inducement for you to become my subjects willingly?"

Walker stood straight and tall, his lips pursed and his eyes flinty. He answered, speaking shortly, "For starters, you should remove your army from our land. Then *perhaps*, we can begin negotiations."

"And there's the fact that we are a religious society," Wojdan added. "For now, you may look upon us as a theocracy. I do not rule per se, I simply follow the word of God and my flock follows me. It seems to work well enough for us that a queen is not needed." He added a belated, "Your Highness. The Knights of the Cross are soldiers of God and will not kneel."

"And if I were a manifestation of God's will?" Jillybean asked. She was staring past the Bishop and Faith, who stood just behind him, and past the wall and the town. Her eyes were unfocused seeing only the grey of the Pacific, mixing with the dull, iron sky.

The Bishop's dimples showed deeper as he smiled and asked, "Are you? I don't discount the idea, mind you, I would just like to know your mind."

"No, you don't, your Excellency." She shook her head, sadly, her eyes coming back into focus and settling with unnerving sharpness on his. "You don't want to know what's going on up there, it's generally… never mind. My thoughts are between me and God. And, as for kneeling. I will tear down your walls and leave your people vulnerable without having fired a shot or having used an ounce of explosives. Your people will kneel before me and accept me as their rightful ruler."

The two groups separated a minute later. There really wasn't much more that needed to be said between them.

"Can she do it?" Wojdan asked, as soon as they were out of earshot. Walker immediately started shaking his head. Wojdan put a soft hand on his arm. "Don't dismiss her. She commands Corsairs, which means she had beaten them in battle. How? With what force? Certainly not with those Bay People. The Hill People and the Islanders are too few in numbers. The Sacramentans have always been weak-willed and too tribe-minded to unite. And the Santas would have joined with the Corsairs rather than fight them."

"Maybe she scared them into surrender with her torpedoes," Walker suggested. "But sixty-five ships all at once? How does someone get a hold of that many torpedoes?"

Faith hurried ahead of the men so she could face them as she said, "She said she wouldn't use bombs or bullets on us. What does that leave? Wouldn't a rocket be the same thing as a bomb or an explosive? And if she doesn't use one of those, what will she use?"

Walker stopped and truly looked at the wall as it stretched in a gentle arc back from the reinforced steel door. A few stupid ideas came to him: parachutes, hang-gliders and hot air balloons; he discarded them. Sheer logistics would make any attack with them impossible. He turned, his ballistic armor creaking. The open area sloped gently upwards. "She has the high ground, she could set up a catapult or some sort of modern equivalent. It would be dangerous and probably wouldn't work. She would need a huge store of stones or ammo. And even if it did work, she would be vulnerable to counter attacks. I can't imagine her being able to build one with a range of more than a few hundred yards."

"What about a tunnel?" Ryanne asked. "She might could build one and then pop up right in the middle of church." She liked going to church so the idea of bad guys like the Corsairs breaking out in the middle of it was dismaying. Though she did like the queen-lady. She had cool hair and cool clothes and she seemed very fearless about the Corsairs.

"A tunnel wouldn't work, bugs," her father told her, using his gentle dad-voice and not the gruff one he used for everyone else. "A tunnel would need to be started beyond one of those hills. It would take weeks to build. Besides, the soil around here is a touch too soft. There'd be cave-ins anytime anyone even sneezed."

Having dismissed the possibility of the Queen getting over, under or through the wall, Walker considered the possibility of going around. They were vulnerable from the sea, but only barely. There was only a single landing spot along the entire shoreline and only a fool would attempt to attack from that direction. Twenty men could wipe out a thousand as they struggled ashore.

"The one thing we can't do is accept what she says at face value," Walker said. "If she has explosives, she will use them. I have no doubt about that. Why wouldn't she? I imagine her Corsairs would dig their heels in if she tried to get them to make some sort of suicidal attack when they could use bombs instead. No, she'll use them, alright. Never in the history of warfare has an aggressor failed to use a decisive weapon."

As logical as that was, Bishop Wojdan didn't know if he believed it. Why would she lie so blatantly? And why lie to a religious community like this if her end goal was to incorporate them into her domain? It didn't make sense.

Just like Walker, the Bishop planted his soft hands on his rounded hips and looked around, trying to fathom what the Queen was up to. He gave up after only a minute. Sighing, he said, "Warfare is just not my thing. Luckily, the Lord had provided the community with you, Commander. Take all precautions necessary."

Walker frowned at the word "luck" but Wojdan was already heading back to the church. He needed time to think and pray. He needed time to absorb all he had heard and seen. The Queen had been perfectly engaging, amazingly informed, and strangely confident. Whether she could destroy the wall remained to be seen. She certainly believed she could. There was no lie in that.

He was so taken up picturing the Queen that he was oblivious to the dozens of foxholes being dug behind the wall. In something of a fog, he passed through the immense construction zone followed by Faith Checkamian, who had the same questions hissed at her over and over.

What happened? Were they really Corsairs? Who was the woman?

"I'll tell you later," she repeated, though what she was going to tell them was something of a mystery.

The mystery only deepened as the Queen's entire army marched away, heading up into the hills. Their fleet disappeared as well, heading back north. It was seen briefly in the late evening skirting around to the south again. By then the foxholes were dug, the ammo was distributed, water from the town well was collected in buckets and jugs, and every sort of wild rumor had been spread.

Watches were set and, other than the Knights guarding the walls, the entire community attended the evening mass, hoping that the Bishop would explain what was going on. He spoke in his usual gentle voice as if he were utterly unconcerned with the day's events. This wasn't a brave face he was putting on. The Bishop was completely unafraid.

The same was true of his congregation. They were anxious, that was true. They weren't afraid, however.

When Mass ended, Wojdan explained the situation as he saw it and when he was done, what sounded like a sighing wind went around the church as the entire twelve-hundred person congregation began to whisper to their neighbors. These went on even as Faith took her place at the piano and hammered out the notes to *Onward Christian Soldiers*.

More hymns followed this one in a steady stream. Most people expected the attack would happen at any moment.

It did not occur that night or the next day, though there was a scare as the Queen's fleet hove into view just after the noon meal. The hundred ships found safe anchorage half a mile away and, as the Guardians watched through rifle scopes, binoculars and even three telescopes, six hundred men were off-loaded and made their way to shore on a variety of smaller boats and rafts.

The men were grouped into two companies: one armed, the other unarmed. The unarmed group carried Corsair flags, which they burned before forming a single line. This line proceeded, man by man to the

164

Queen, who sat on a high-backed chair. Each man came and knelt before her, kissed her hand and was then sent up into the hills.

After this, the ships disgorged crates and boxes by the ton and then left again, disappearing over the horizon.

"That's not going to be me," Keith Treadwell announced for all to hear. "I'd rather die first." Everyone cheered this pronouncement.

Commander Walker put a damper on the enthusiasm by saying, "She's trying to get it into your head that surrender is an option. Remember, she is just putting on a show. Nothing more."

The show was done for the day and on the third day it did not recommence. The open land around the walls remained empty and the silence that hung around the hills became cloying. Some of the men urged Walker to send out a recon force. He refused, worried that the Queen was delaying an attack, simply to draw him out. It's what he would have done. Once outside the walls, his men would lose a great deal of their advantage.

He decided to wait.

His wait was not long. An hour after sunset, when a grey twilight turned into a dour, cold night, a horn sounded up in the hills. It was followed a moment later by a second horn, this one much further away.

"To the walls!" Walker bellowed. "To the walls!" The church bell rang, two deep, solemn notes. The three hundred Knights ran to their stations while the two hundred men and women of the reserve force formed up behind the wall.

Minutes passed and at first, there was nothing and Walker was just wondering if the Queen was playing mind games when there came a rumbling sound from up in the hills that grew louder with every passing second, until, with a roar, Walker saw what the Queen had unleashed.

A grey wall of water, ten feet in height rushed down the old road that led straight to the single door in the wall. She had destroyed the Robinson Dam and had somehow redirected its rain-swollen waters for three miles until now it came blasting into the wall.

Men who would never hesitate in attacking an eight-foot-tall zombie backed away from the edge of the wall. "Steady!" Treadwell barked. "It's just water!" He turned to Walker. "We're safe, right? I mean it is just water."

Walker shook his head. "Back before when you were little, did you ever take a garden hose, turn it on high and point it at the ground. Do you remember how quickly you could dig a hole with a hose?" Walker could remember using water to make "gopher holes." It took half a minute to make a hole a foot deep. This was the same concept except the water was a million times greater in volume and strength.

"We have to get off the wall."

Chapter 24

After only a week, a miraculous change had occurred on Bainbridge. The island that had been gripped with an all-consuming fear of an assassin was now gearing up for their version of Thanksgiving as if nothing had ever happened.

The talk of murder died down quickly, being replaced as the topic of choice after the third day, by the announcement that Mr. Durnel had produced a bumper crop of blackberries and that he would be donating a hundred pounds of it to the Fall Festival—on Bainbridge, the main concern was who was going to win the annual pie-eating contest. The betting was running hot and heavy.

Very quickly, the assassination became old news and was rarely discussed. It was an unpleasant topic all around. Few people believed there had been an assassin in the first place. There certainly wasn't any evidence there had ever been one. There were no clues or eyewitnesses, and no shadowy figures had been seen lurking near Neil's house or anywhere else for that matter.

The prevailing wisdom was that Neil hadn't been murdered at all, but had been killed because of his own foolishness.

"He's the one who let her keep those ridiculous beasts chained up in that school of hers."

"What did he expect? You play with fire, you're gonna get burned, and if you play with zombies…well, it's just sad is all."

"Who would bother attacking Neil Martin in the first place? I mean, without Jillybean, who is he except some creepy little guy?"

Everyone figured Neil had accidentally allowed himself to get scratched by one of the zombies and either made up the story about an assassin because he was embarrassed or, that in his growing delirium, he had become paranoid. It was so much easier and much more pleasant to focus on the positive. And everyone loved the Fall Festival. Along with Mr. Durnel's blackberry pies, there would be vats of spiced pumpkin beer, sourdough pretzels by the twenty-score, apple fritters, and turkey done up in a dozen ways.

Along with the food and the pie eating contest, there was the Fall Float Parade to look forward to; it had been getting wilder and crazier every year. There were also dozens of games, the archery and crossbow contests, and the annual talent show.

The mood on the island during the previous week was one of growing anticipation, not one of fear.

Deanna Grey knew better. She had seen the razor blade, she had smelled the sickening stench of the zombie blood on it, and she had touched the underside of Neil's doorknob where the glue had dried in little ridges. There was no doubt in her mind that someone had tried to kill him; tried and failed.

Neil Martin was still alive. Sort of. He wasn't quite human and he wasn't exactly a zombie either. He was something in between and whatever that something was, it wasn't pleasant.

For the first three days, Neil had slipped in and out of a fever-induced delirium so intense, that more than once, Deanna had reached for her gun, telling herself that "this time" she would end his misery. Each time she had hesitated just long enough for some sanity to creep back into his bleary red eyes.

On the fourth day, she returned to the dark school with its terrifying grunts and howls, to find him in the process of escaping his chains. His hands were bloody and torn to ribbons from trying to twist an eye-bolt from the wall. It was halfway out when she walked in.

"Thank God it's you," he whispered, squinting up at her. "Were you kidnapped, too? What's going on? Where's Emily? Hey, what are you waiting for? Help me out of these chains, damn it!"

Deanna was frozen in the doorway, her mouth hanging open, a look of pure disgust on her face. It had been many years since she'd seen someone turn from human to zombie, but it wasn't something she would ever forget, and yet she had never seen or heard anything that looked like Neil before.

He had always been small; now he was hunched and contorted, looking more like a rabid animal than a man. The hospital johnny that he wore was soaked with sweat and plastered to his body. His straw-colored hair was limp and greasy. His disfigured face was ashen except for his lips which were bloody as well. He had bitten his tongue and there was blood in his teeth. What was worse, however, was the blood dripping from the corners of his ferocious red eyes.

Neil had become a monster.

"You weren't kidnapped," she told him from the doorway. "Someone tried to kill you. They infected you."

He immediately forgot his chains. Sitting back against the wall, he scratched his scarred nose, leaving a dripping red smear across it; he didn't notice. "That's right, I remember. There was a razor blade and they cut me on the…" He lifted his bleeding hands and stared in amazement as if noticing the flayed flesh for the first time. "Did they do this?"

"No, you did. Neil, I'm afraid they've made you into, I don't know what. Something like a zombie. Does it hurt?"

"I don't think so," he said, touching his face again, leaving more smeared blood. "I feel kind of weird. And pissed off. Yeah, I am pissed. That's what I'm really feeling. Who would do a thing like that? Huh? Do you know and you aren't telling me?" Before she knew it, he was up and straining at his chains, dark blood dripping onto the floor.

She took a step back, ready to run if the chains failed. "I really don't know, Neil," she said, holding her hands out, palms facing him. "I wish I knew. I really do." She had racked her brains over the question.

The answer wasn't as obvious as one would think. Neil had piled up a great number of enemies during the early years of the apocalypse. It could have been any of the hundreds of Believers still alive, or one of the thousand Azael who had been released at the end of the war in Colorado. Or perhaps it was the child of one of those killed? Or a spouse or sibling?

Deanna could only hope that it was the latter. With revenge out of their system, they would probably be done killing, especially if Neil were to quietly disappear, which was, sadly, his only real option. The people of Bainbridge would put up with a lot, however living next door to some sort of zombie-human hybrid was not one of them. They would drive him from the island if they found out—if they didn't kill him outright, that is.

As a friend, the idea was horrific; as governor, she understood. As much as people liked to think they were civilized and far removed from their primitive history, they were in fact ruled by their fears, justified or not. In this case, the fear was justified. Deanna certainly felt the cold edge of it up and down her spine whenever Neil's savage anger erupted, which was frequent when the subject was on their past enemies.

He was much calmer when she brought up the Fall Festival. Neil even became wistful, which was something to see. It was like watching a shark pausing over the remains of a surfer to consider its life.

Still, the talk of pumpkin beer and pies calmed him enough to allow Deanna the opportunity to retighten the eyebolt with a pair of vice-grips. "It's for the best," Neil agreed, giving her a sad, bloody smile. "Until I get better."

"Exactly," she replied, offering him one of her politician's smiles. He used to make fun of them because they were so obviously fake compared to her genuine smiles. This one; however, he soaked up. When she stepped away after tightening the bolts, she could feel a trickle of sweat down her back.

He wasn't going to get better. It was a sad fact, one that her daughter refused to believe. "I don't see why not," she told her mother, that evening when they were alone in the Governor's mansion. "He's not getting worse, right?"

Deanna really didn't know. She didn't understand what Jillybean would call "the mechanics" of being a zombie. "He's not dying anymore, if that's what you mean, but that doesn't mean he's getting better. Zombies don't get better."

"Yeah, because their brains are dead," Emily countered, stubbornly. "And Uncle Neil's brains aren't dead. He can talk and everything." Deanna didn't mention that "everything" also included spitting blood as he vowed to rip people's heads off. Emily wouldn't have listened, she was already concocting plans to house Neil indefinitely within the school. "Not as a prisoner, but sorta like a caretaker over the real zombies."

"That no one sees? Just like the Hunchback of Notre-Dame? It's not a life I think he'd like to live."

"We should ask him, don't you think? He should make that decision, not us."

It was kid logic. She couldn't see beyond the moment. What if Neil was dangerous? What if he decided to stray at night and was caught? What if he accidentally infected someone? What if one of Deanna's political opponents caught wind that she was keeping a "creature" in the school without informing anyone? They might all be hounded from the island.

All of this was counterbalanced by the simple questions of friendship: What if Neil didn't want to go? What if he was lonely or afraid out on his own? What if he got hurt out in the wilds and there was no one to help him? Deanna didn't know what to do and she hesitated—the fourth day turned into the fifth, which turned into the sixth and then the seventh.

She had delayed killing him and now she delayed telling him to leave, even though he wasn't getting better. His anger remained volcanic and volatile. Anything could set him off: a wrong look, a misplaced word, even the sound of the other zombies.

Deanna went back and forth on what to do about him, while Emily weathered it all with unfailing loyalty. Even though her class was putting together a "Mondo" float for the parade, she removed herself from school and spent her days with Neil, trying to find some concoction of Jillybean's that would calm his moods. "I know she's been working on something for her own use. She told me about it once, but I'm afraid I wasn't listening as closely as I should of. You know how she uses all them big words."

"It doesn't matter," Neil snapped. "Just start giving me some of whatever and we'll see what works." It was a profoundly poor method of finding a cure for anything and had Neil been his old self, it would've killed him. Emily crushed pills and added them to a honey and water mixture in what she jokingly called "potions." Poison was a more accurate term.

She wasn't entirely stupid about her methods. She started with small doses of everything. She started off by giving him 30 milligrams of Lithium. After an hour-long wait in which he was just as surly as ever, she gave 30 more. When that didn't do much of anything, she added 20 milligrams of Haldol.

"How do you feel?" she asked, gazing intently at him over the rim of her safety goggles. Along with the goggles, she wore gloves and a white lab coat, and in her hands she held a clipboard and pen. This was science, after all.

"Nothing. The same, I think. Let's try some more of that last stuff." The Haldol didn't work and neither did 50 milligrams of Thorazine or forty milligrams of Prozac. His only reaction to any of it was to puke up a golden mess of the nastiest vomit Emily had ever smelled. Neil licked his lips, saying, "Not bad. It tastes better coming up than down. Put that in your clipboard, will ya?"

He dipped a finger in the spew and she turned away as quickly as possible before he could taste it. "I'll, uh, go fetch some towels," she said over her shoulder.

Day six and seven were more of the same, except she added Pepto Bismol which helped…to a degree. After that point things became even worse; sweet pink vomit was the horrible result and Emily lost her lunch twice. After that, she kept stacks of towels handy. The most successful potion she made was a four-drug cocktail that didn't do much for his anger issues; however it did make him sleepy, which was better than nothing.

While Emily was busy with Neil, Deanna ran herself ragged. The Fall Festival took a lot of planning which entailed a lot of lengthy meetings, which took up a lot of time. In the few moments she could cobble together for herself, she combed through the records of the nearly sixteen hundred people living on the island, trying to narrow down suspects who had come from Georgia, where the Believers had been, Missouri, where the River King had once ruled, or Nebraska, the home of the Azael.

There were surprisingly few. It turned out that cross-country treks in the middle of an apocalypse were a rare event. No one claimed to have come from Georgia, eleven people listed Missouri as their state of origin and sixteen had admitted coming from Nebraska. Of those twenty-six people, twenty of them had made it to Bainbridge well before Neil and could be ruled out.

Deanna visited the remaining six in person, showing up without notice, hoping to surprise one of them into tipping their hand. All six were as sweet as could be and she spent the rest of the day with her stomach aching from all the pie she was forced to swallow. Her stomach also bothered her for a separate reason: if the assassin wasn't from Bainbridge, where had he come from?

"The Black Captain," she whispered, feeling dread creep into her belly. The Corsairs had been their boogeymen for years. The pirates had cost the last governor her job when they had descended on the Sound in a series of raids that had stripped Bainbridge of most of their boats.

In fear, the great wall had been erected with Deanna nominally in charge, though it was Jillybean who drew up the plans and oversaw every inch of its construction. It was a monumental work that had propelled Deanna into the Governor's office. It had also nearly broken Jillybean's carefully pieced-together mind. She had lived and breathed the wall into existence at the expense of her mental health.

Still, the wall had done its job. Since the Corsairs couldn't hope to defeat it, they had kept to the Pacific for years.

Although she had built the thing, Jillybean did not trust the wall as the be-all and end-all of the Island's defense. She had advocated for open war against the Corsairs and when that was repeatedly shot down by Deanna, she had pushed for covert operations against them. "They are a cancer on this world and the wall is little more than a band-aide," she had insisted. "Sooner or later, they will have to be dealt with."

"And now she's gone and done something," Deanna said, sweeping back her golden hair, and gazing at the wall through the trees. Her gut told her that was the case and yet, logically the attack didn't make sense. Why would they come after Neil Martin? Only a handful of people knew Jillybean well enough to know how much she depended on him, and they were all people Deanna trusted.

"So that leaves me where?" It left her feeling uselessly paranoid and distinctly powerless. There was almost nothing to investigate. She didn't have witnesses to question or even a suspect to beat a confession out of. And she couldn't throw her people into a state of fear by making unprovable accusations against the Corsairs. If she shouted that the "Sky is falling!" right before the Fall Festival and the Corsairs didn't suddenly show up with their fleet, she would be toast.

The best she could hope for was that someone would notice a strange man in black lurking in the ruins of Seattle, preferably someone wearing an "I Heart Corsairs" T-shirt. Until that happened, she could only continue doing what she had been: nothing at all.

That fact had not been lost on the actual assassin, Eddie Sanders. It didn't make sense. Couldn't a blind person see that he was guilty? He went about with what felt like a lie stamped on his face in the form of a smile. When he nodded at his neighbors, the simple act was a lie and a confusing lie at that. What did the nod mean? That they were compadres? Friends? That they had something in common beyond proximity? Couldn't they see they were nodding to a murderer?

And when he commented blandly about the weather to Danny McGuinness down at the harbor, wasn't that a lie, too? Eddie didn't care about the weather. Rain or shine, he was still a killer. And when his "friend" Todd Karraker had him try his freshly brewed pumpkin beer, the sip tasted like bile, pumpkin flavored bile, but bile nonetheless. The acid burned all the way down. Everyone else seemed to like it and so Eddie smiled his lie and went along with them, even though he was on the verge of vomiting.

Everything was a lie with Eddie. Really, his entire life was a lie. He even secretly questioned his wife, Gina. How could she love a murderer? Or had she been faking her love for him all these years? If not, what did that say about her? What sort of woman would stay with a sleaze-bag like him?

Gina knew he was struggling, and she did her best to console him and he pretended it helped, but it didn't, not for a second.

His week had been hell. He had not slept through the night once, and was generally up by three in the morning, staring at the night sky, his mind blank, his soul nothing but an empty shell. His hair had begun falling out and the bags under his eyes had progressed from purple to nearly black. Every morning as the sun crept up, he would go out on his stoop and puff nervously on his morning cigarettes.

He smoked more every day, until his mouth felt raw and his throat was in tatters. He even smoked when he was out scavenging and hunting. It was terribly stupid; then again, he was stupid. For most of his life he'd considered himself slightly smarter than the average guy, only that had been a lie as well. It had to be. A smart person would never have let himself be blackmailed so easily.

Exactly one week passed before he saw the smoke again. Just like last time it drifted up from behind the Alki Point Lighthouse, across the chilly, still waters of Puget Sound. It wasn't a wavering grey feather this time. Now it was an angry black column that couldn't be missed...by anyone. Surely someone would suspect what it really meant. Eddie began to shake. It wasn't a tremble that made his cigarette dance; nor was it a shaking fit that came on gradually and left again in the same manner.

No, he saw the smoke and the next thing he knew, he was shaking from head to toe, his entire frame rattling. The cigarette dropped, unheeded. The fag was no matter to him. He couldn't have taken a drag from it if his life depended on it; his lungs were undergoing the same sort of seizure attacking the rest of him. He began to choke on nothing.

The fit went on and, in a disinterested way, he realized he could die. That thought didn't bother him for a second. He had naively thought that once he had killed for the Corsairs they would leave him alone to live his life in peace. He was a fool and a fool didn't deserve to live.

Gradually, the earthquake-like shakes diminished. Shivering like a sick man, he left his stoop and went inside and came to stand across the room from his wife. Gina was blank-eyed and mute as a hunk of stove wood. "I have to go," he told her, in a strangled voice. "*They* want me again." Gina didn't try to stop him when he left five minutes later, and Eddie didn't know what to think about that.

His mind was in a fog when he passed the Governor. He didn't say hello or smile that lie of his. She didn't notice because Deanna Grey was in just as deep a fog as he was. In a blink he was at the docks, fumbling over his words, asking for a boat and not able to give a reason why; he had forgotten his pack and bow at home.

"Scouting," Eddie was eventually able to come up with. Danny McGuinness didn't care. He was almost at the end of his shift and he liked having as many boats out as possible when his replacement came on duty. It made the change-over quicker.

Eddie was gone so quickly that the gate barely had time to open before he slid through. There was no messing around this time. He didn't piddle about with any false moves, but instead went straight for the church, thinking that if he saw the strange hump-backed man he would give him a piece of his mind.

"It's over!" he growled as he strode into the church. It was empty as always, or at least it seemed that way. "I said, it's over!" His voice echoed around the empty building. Furious, he went to the usual hiding spot, pulled out the note and saw that it wasn't over. Along with the note was a picture of his baby boy. There was no threat; the picture, the very recent picture said enough.

Eddie began crying as he read what they had planned for him next.

Chapter 25

In the dark, each of the boats in the Corsair squadron appeared immense. The tips of their billowing sails looked like they were cutting the bottom out of the clouds and the huge black flags streaming behind them made them seem twice as long as the crippled *Wind Ripper*.

With her mainsail taped to hide the gaping holes, she was struggling along with only her two small jib sails. Her speed was no match for the squadron which came rushing up, white foam at their prows. Mike Gunter could only turn parallel to their course to keep the *Wind Ripper* from being run down and cut in two.

"Do something!" Stu rumbled to Mike.

"Like what?" Mike answered. With angry ships to the south searching for *"the bugger that tore up my boat!"* and the misting clouds dissipating in a growing breeze, they had nowhere to run. And no time, either.

The new squadron turned slightly towards them and the distance closed rapidly. "Keep that guy quiet," Stu ordered, meaning Rob LaBar, "And act natural."

Jenn had no idea how to act natural while straddling a man and holding a knife to his throat.

Rob had no intention of acting natural. He knew that going to Bainbridge would result in him dying one way or the other. Either his infected leg would kill him, or they would execute him for being a bloodthirsty Corsair. No, he had to get away now, while he had the chance. The girl was small and weak. Even with his leg numb and useless, and his strength nowhere close to what it used to be, she couldn't hold him down and she wouldn't be strong enough to clamp a hand over his mouth.

She knew this as well as he did. All she had was the knife. "I'll use it," she whispered.

"You won't," he told her, betting his life on the timidity he saw in her blue eyes. Even in the dark, the doubt was obvious; she didn't want to kill him.

"Who is that?" a voice came hissing from the third boat in line as it slipped by. Jenn leaned closer to Rob so that their shadows merged. As she did, Rob made a grab for the knife.

The two began to squirm and grunt in a desperate, near-silent struggle. Mike couldn't leave the wheel, or the boat would flounder, and Stu was on Mike's other side, too far away from them to do anything. He worried that if he even looked in their direction it would alert the Corsairs that their enemy was just within reach. The only thing Stu could do was growl out: *"Wind Ripper,"* in the same sort of angry voice that Cannan had used in the hope that the man's fearsome reputation would be enough to have people looking away.

"Tell them our main went by the board," Mike said, speaking in urgent whispers directly into Stu's ear. He waited until Stu had repeated this before adding, "Tell them we caught a rogue and it just tore us up. Say it like that."

The Corsair snorted laughter and told his shipmates, who also found this funny, though why, Stu couldn't understand. Seconds later, the ship was past. Their relief, if it could be called that, was over before it began as the next ship came gliding up. The man at the wheel leaned over to look down at them. In the dark it was hard to tell, but it looked to him like two of the men on board were wrestling.

"What ship?" he asked.

Stu had taken only a single step toward Jenn and Rob. He stopped, saying, "*Wind Ripper,*" and made the same excuses he had a few seconds earlier. Next to him, Mike turned the wheel ever so slightly to put more distance between the two ships.

Just like the last Corsair, this one laughed. "It won't matter what your excuse is, Cannan. The Captain will have your ass if he finds y'all out of line. You can snug in behind us for a price. That blonde you been keepin' for yourself sound 'bout right. Just for a few nights is all."

At that moment, LaBar gained the upper-hand on Jenn Lockhart. He outweighed her by eighty pounds and with a twist of his sinuous body, the two switched places; now he was on top, the weight of his upper body bearing down on her knife hand, pinning it in place. She tried to grab the knife with her other hand, but he shoved that beneath his leg.

"I don't think so," he growled into her face.

The barely seen Corsair high up on his big boat was confused, thinking it was "Cannan" who had spoken. "I won't hurt her none. You know me, Cannan. 'Sides, it don't look like you got any choice." They were ranged up almost parallel to the Corsair ship and if Mike was going to slip into line, it was now or never. They couldn't dangle at the end of the line and allow the next squadron to catch up.

"Fine," Stu said in that harsh growl. "Just don't dirty her up too bad." He glanced over at Mike and shrugged, not knowing what else to say. Mike shrugged back and then began the laborious process of trying to get *The Wind Ripper* in line; steering while only under the jib took a lot of embarrassing and unseamanly back and forth, first overcorrecting in one direction before overcorrecting in the other.

Only feet away, hidden by the useless mainsail, Jenn and LaBar continued their near silent duel—she had basically lost. Rob could yell out at any time, but he wanted more. If he yelled, he would have to be "rescued." It was going to be bad enough that he would have to admit being captured in the first place. There would be jeers and endless snide remarks, but if he could "take back" *The Wind Ripper* from a team of assassins who were planning on killing the Black Captain, why then he'd be a hero.

The three of them would have to die of course—dead men tell no tales, after all. Rob planned on shooting the three and then emptying the magazine around the boat to add to the image of a life and death struggle. He even considered winging himself.

First, he had to get the knife from the girl. Had he been at full strength, it wouldn't have been an issue at all. As it was, his head was swimming and his muscles shook; bad things to be sure, and yet he had one hand free and she did not. He grabbed her by the throat and leaned his weight forward.

She immediately started to gag. Stu edged closer and Mike abandoned the wheel.

"Not so fast," Rob whispered. "Unless you want her dead." Both stopped in their tracks. "I can kill her with just a squeeze of my hand. Got it? Get us in line, Mikey. And Stu, I'm going to need a gun. Don't even think about trying anything. If you shoot, they'll be all over you. You guys can't escape."

Rob was right. They all knew it. Even without a gun, Rob was in a position to scream and yell. And with a gun…Stu didn't want to think about that. He didn't know what to do, especially as Mike was no help. *The Wind Ripper* was in danger of crashing yet again as another Corsair boat was coming up strong, its sailors hissing curses and demanding they fall off.

Only Jenn really had a chance to do anything. Rob had leaned back to keep her from making too much noise as the Corsair ship passed so close she thought she could stretch out and touch the farthest reach of its boom. Rather than doing that, she slid her hand up around Rob's thigh and grabbed his wound as hard as she could.

"Son of a bitch!" Rob cried as he jerked away from the pain. In that brief second, Jenn squirmed beneath him and freed her knife hand. It flashed up to his neck.

In the shadow of the Corsair ship, the two locked eyes over the shining blade. Jenn pressed the knife into LaBar's flesh until he ground his teeth. "I dare you," he growled. He knew the girl was spineless; she wouldn't kill him, she'd only threaten. She'd had every opportunity to kill him before and hadn't been able to summon the courage or dispel her morals long enough to do the act; and nothing had changed.

"What are you waiting for?" Rob whispered. The knife dipped, dropping away from his throat. He smirked. "That's what I thought. One shout on my part and they'll be all over you. Your only chance is to trust me."

Trust a Corsair? Jenn had never heard of such a thing, and yet, what choice did she have?

You could kill him. A cold wave washed down Jenn's back. It hadn't been a crazy voice, it was a calmly sinister, murderous one, and it had not been a voice from nowhere. It had been her own voice and it had originated right there among all the rest of her thoughts.

Is this how Jillybean started? she wondered. Had there been one stray thought that just hadn't fit? Had it just seemed louder than the rest? More urgent? Had she listened to it, and had that egged it on? Or had she tried to ignore it only to hear it get louder and louder?

You could kill him. There it was again, even louder. *You should kill him. You can't trust a Corsair.*

Jenn jumped as something thumped into the side of *The Wind Ripper*. Someone from the other boat had stabbed out at the side of *The Wind Ripper* with a boat hook, marring the paint and thrusting her away.

"Say a word and you die," Rob warned.

This had Jenn's head spinning. Why would he want her to keep quiet? What game is he playing? She had no idea, she only knew that she couldn't trust a Corsair. Ever.

No one seemed to move as the Corsair boat slipped by with more curses being tossed across at them. The tension was so thick Stu held his breath until the boat was gone.

They all let out a breath, except for Rob. His diaphragm was paralyzed by the knife sticking out of it. Jenn had slid it up through his abdomen, beneath the notch in his chest and into the very tip of his heart.

There was an adage that she'd heard time and again for the last ten years: *The only good Corsair was a dead Corsair.*

Rob took three minutes to die. Stu held him down while he convulsed, and his feet kicked out spastically. Jenn could only watch for so long before she fled below and hid in the dark. A part of her expected to hear voices either congratulating her on yet one more murder to add to her list or laughing at the tears that wouldn't stop. Thankfully, she heard only reality: the splash of waves, the unsteady thumping of Stu's boots on the deck, and the occasional bell.

She cried for an hour, mourning not for Rob, who she considered little more than a beast, but for some lost part of her. That part was ineffable and unnamed. It would have been easy to label it simply as her "innocence" only that had been dying by degrees for months and her first mercy killing had started a fire that would cremate its remains, leaving her mouth tasting like ash and her soul stained by soot.

No, this loss within her was subtly different and far worse because it was so jarring. It was as if she had suddenly lost the ability to smile, as if she would never again wake up on Christmas morning filled with excitement, or feel the least bit of wonder at a sunset, or feel joy when a baby laughed, or know the pleasure of playing kick the can in the long twilight of a July night.

It was as if she had gone from fifteen to fifty when she had slid that knife into Rob. Her world had dimmed in that one move, or perhaps she had only just realized it had been growing dim for some time. She didn't know. She only knew that crying was the right thing because she had lost some part of her that most people held onto for years.

Jenn was still crying when she heard Mike come down into the cabin. He squinted around the dark shadows until he picked her out by the paleness of her face. It seemed to have an ethereal glow. Without saying a word, he held her and it was strangely perfect. They were like an old married couple who thrived with the simplest acts of intimacy. Even with his touch, she didn't regain what she had lost; he only made it bearable.

When the last tear fell, she murmured, "You're letting Stu pilot the boat. You must really love me."

It was a joke and he allowed a smile to show, though he didn't laugh. "We turned east just before I came down. The wind is on our stern."

"East? Already?" Though she might have lost some ineffable part of her, she could still feel fear. There was only one reason the squadron had turned east: they were getting close to the mouth of Grays Harbor, where the lair of the Corsairs was hidden.

"Yeah, we should hear the approach buoys any minute. From there it won't be long. At least, I hope it won't. The wind has been dying."

Jenn's fear edged up, as did her depression. It felt as though nothing was going right or ever would. It would be just their luck for the wind to die just as the sun came up. They would be caught ten times over. Even as stern and gruff as Stu was, he still looked his age, and Mike with his golden-hued "baby beard" and his friendly smile was the polar opposite of a Corsair. Then there was Jenn; she would have to hide uselessly below deck and hope no one wondered why the Black Captain's recon ship had magically appeared among the remains of the fleet.

She followed Mike on deck and did not immediately see the land in front of them. Her eyes were drawn to where she had left the body of Rob LaBar. It was gone. Only a dark stain remained.

Mike saw where she was looking. "We said a prayer and…you know." He jerked a shoulder toward the sea. "If someone saw."

"Yeah, it's okay. He was a Corsair. I wish I could care, but they started all of this." In truth, Jillybean had been the one who had started the war. Jenn wasn't going to blame her, however. She was past recriminations. All she wanted to do was start over.

A bell clanked in the distance. The three of them immediately recognized the sound as that of a slowly corroding buoy bell. They were getting close. Mike stood up on the gunwale and strained to peer into the dark ahead of them—Jenn looked back. Beyond the sail of a shadowy forty-foot the clouds had become patchy and a few bolder stars could be seen.

As far as signs went, they meant nothing and yet, a breeze blew back her auburn hair as she stared. It was a healthy, steady wind that filled sails. In front and behind *The Wind Ripper*, Corsair boats leaned over and took in the wind. Masts creaked, flags flapped, and once more, white showed at the waterline of each of the boats. The entire squadron surged forward.

The Wind Ripper lagged as they came to the harbor, and it seemed like a good time to duck away; however the second squadron was also flying along, gaining on them quickly.

"If we go into the harbor we might be stuck," Mike told them. "So should try to slip south along the beach, instead? We might be able to circle around them and head north."

Jenn looked back once more, and once more ignored the boats. The stars were being covered over again. "No," she said, quickly, feeling the sign more than understanding it. "This is our window. I-I think any ship seen heading south will be viewed, like bad or something. Once we're in the harbor we might hide, or we can take the same land route to Bainbridge that Jillybean showed us."

"Go in," Stu agreed. "A Corsair boat can probably go anywhere within the harbor without really being questioned. We just have to be out of sight before sunrise." This was their cue to stare at the sky to the east. It was still dark, but was it as dark as before? None of them knew.

Mike did his best to keep up with the squadron in front of them. In fact, he did too good of a job. The harbor was triangular in shape; it narrowed towards the Corsairs' lair and as it did, there was some congestion as the ships in front slowed to wait their turn to be pulled up the narrow river that sheltered the fleet.

Thankfully, they hugged the northern shore, giving Mike opportunity to slip away toward the south. One boat hailed them, not to offer help but to make jokes at their misfortune. Mike made sure to play up that misfortune by giving his torn sail some wind and letting it rip completely in two.

This brought on howls of laughter, to which Mike cursed like a Corsair. Jenn raised an eyebrow at the vulgarity, but said nothing. Even knowing that it was all for show did not make her feel any more at ease, realizing that the man she loved could sound as crude as one of *them*.

Soon they were safely hidden by Rennie Island and letting the gusting wind take them slowly up the Chehalis River. The wind was so perfectly placed that had the river not become too shallow, there was no telling how far they could have gotten. They made it only two miles before the sun came up over white-capped Mount Rainier, which stood tall directly to their east.

Two miles seemed far too close to the Corsair Lair for Jenn's liking and she wanted to leave the ship and go. Mike looked aghast at the idea. "It's a *ship*," he told her, as if he thought she was proposing to leave the Baby Jesus behind. "What we have to do is hide her."

"What about hiding us?" Jenn asked.

"First things first. We might need the boat later. You know, like for a getaway if things don't work out in this direction. What if we run into a horde?"

Jenn only nodded, saying nothing. Deep inside, she wanted nothing more to do with boats. The sight of the stars from a few hours earlier came to her. They had shone brightly for only so long before the clouds came. It meant they had to get under cover, and yet Stu agreed with Mike about the boat.

Stu took the AR-15 and Mike had the Sig Sauer. Jenn was only armed with her growing apprehension as they climbed down to searched along the banks of the river for a place to hide the boat. The Chehalis was not a boating sort of river. They hadn't passed any docks, boat ramps or abandoned trailers on the way so Jenn figured that it would be a miracle to find one now.

She was right. Luckily, they did find an almost perfect little arm of water that stuck out from the river. They crept forward to inspect it and found it was heavily shrouded by bushes, a hairy growth of jungle-like vines, and a few cherry trees that leaned over the water like pretty maidens hoping to catch a glimpse of their reflections. Jenn was just imagining them in the spring when their branches would be clothed in white blossoms, when she heard a growl.

Her ingrained survival instinct kicked in and she froze, holding her breath, while she tried to peer through the morning shadows and the thicket of wild bushes to their right. On either side of her, Mike and Stu did the same. In their scrounged and mismatched clothing, they were both terribly conspicuous—instead of blending in with their surroundings, the three stood out, obvious even to half-blind zombies.

The growl came again and this time the bushes and reeds began to move. Branches snapped like brittle bones. One of the dead was very close; no one said a word, and no one moved a muscle, but it did not matter. Suddenly, there came a tremendous crashing and roaring. The ground seemed to shake as a great, grey beast blasted through the thicket, charging at them.

Jenn felt the shock of its charge right down to her core and she was perfectly paralyzed at the sight of the zombie. It looked as tall as an elephant and seemed almost as strong as it laid one of the cherry trees on its side with a single smash of its fist. The creature's immense mouth hung open showing a black tongue the size of Jenn's forearm, which it ran along jagged teeth. Its eyes were nightmare red and filled with rage.

Calm and cool as the morning, Stu shouldered the AR-15 and fired round after round into its huge head. Mike did the same with the Sig Sauer.

The zombie's rage and power were such that it took fifteen shots to finally drop the beast right at their feet, where it twitched and jerked as if connected to electric cables.

Jenn found herself panting and swallowing convulsively and was just reconsidering her stance on boats when there came more growls and crashes through the underbrush. She should have run, she should have hidden, she should have done something more than stand there as two more zombies broke through the thicket, with a third hurrying behind.

Mike fired first, putting a neat but very tiny hole in the first zombie's cheek just below the eye. The eight-hundred pound beast didn't even seem to notice it. Mike went to fire a second time only to discover he was out of bullets. Stu's gun emptied after his third shot blasted away chunk of the beast's scalp.

Even before the greasy chunk of flesh and hair splatted against a tree trunk, Stu knew they were in trouble—they were out of ammo and the only weapon they had left between the three of them was Jenn's hunting knife.

"Run!" Stu ordered, giving Jenn a shove and pulling Mike behind him. There'd be no running for Stu. With his hurt leg, he knew he had no chance.

Chapter 26

Stu dodged around a tree and, to give his friends a few more seconds to get away, he cried, "Over here!" The beast, which had only one eye, heard Stu, but lost sight of him. It saw Jenn perfectly.

With horrid, dream-like slowness, she turned to run, only to stop in her tracks as something almost as frightening as the zombies came rushing right at her. It was a fiendish, hideous brute of a man...no, it was a hideous Corsair, wearing not just the usual head to toe black, but also a scrap of cloth across his face and a long cloak made of dyed animal furs and crow's feathers.

With one huge arm, he swatted Jenn aside, sending her sprawling in the mud. He was past her in a dark blur, bowling Mike over in the process. Mike had still been half-turned and didn't see what had hit him until the Corsair was charging at Stu.

"Look out!" Jenn screamed.

Stu ignored the scream. The closer zombie was the size of an ogre and was tearing apart the tree he was hiding behind. It was literally shredding it limb from limb. It was a young pine and it came apart like kindling. Stu went flailing backwards, falling to the damp ground as branches struck him on his bad arm and more raked across his face.

He wondered if he'd been hit on the head by something as a man with the wings of a crow flew over him. In his right hand was a four-foot long, double-headed, dead black axe that had been forged to hew flesh, not wood.

One-handed, the man swung it in a high arc so that it came down on the crown of the beast's head and buried itself half a foot deep. The strength behind the blow was fantastic. It stopped the monstrous zombie in its tracks and it collapsed where it stood.

The man had no time to retrieve the deeply embedded axe. The second of the three zombies was on him too quickly. This one was a female, not quite seven-feet-tall. Her form was that of an exaggerated egg. The girdle of her hips had to be five feet across while her shoulders were a little over three feet. One of her arms was long and strong, while the other was a feeble ragged stump that ended above the elbow.

Because of this weakness, the man dodged to her weak side, keeping low, causing her to spin awkwardly. At first glance, the Corsair had appeared tall and strong, but now he seemed just as awkward as the zombie. Although he moved quickly, he did so with a limping, sideways, crab-like gait. His body was deformed with one leg twisted and shorter than the other; his left arm was encased in black metal from his elbow to his wrist. The metal was capped, ending abruptly; there was no room inside it for a hand. His torso was hunched and humped.

When he dodged away from the grasping hand of the female zombie, the cloth covering his face blew back, revealing a visage that made Jenn gasp. What flesh he did have was pocked and scarred. He had no lips and only two slit-like holes where his nose should've been. Half his head was covered in mottled scar tissue from the same long-ago fire that had eaten his face.

It was no stretch to say that he was almost as gruesome as the zombie he was fighting.

On the plus side, he was lightning fast and as strong as he was deformed. The bicep of his good arm was huge, and his forearm was knotted with muscle.

From somewhere under his cape, he ripped out a foot-long dagger and plunged it through the back of the creature's right knee. When he dodged away a second time, the beast grabbed wildly at him only to fall flat on its face as its leg buckled.

Without a pause, he leapt on its back and stabbed at the base of the skull. The beast nearly bucked him off. He stabbed downward again and was about to stab a third time when the last of the zombies came stomping up towards him. It was even larger than the first one had been and when it swung its enormous arm at the man, there was a *CRACK!* The man went flying.

Stu didn't think a person could sustain such a blow and live, and yet the man was just getting to his feet as the beast rushed over and picked him up as if he were little more than a child. He had held onto his dagger, but Stu had no idea what good it would do against such a monster. It was one thing to use an over-sized knife against a smallish, crippled female, it was quite another against a giant like this thing.

It also didn't look like he was going to be able to use the dagger at all. The zombie opened its mouth and was all set to bite the man's neck wide open when he shoved his metal-encased left arm down its throat. When the beast bit down, shards of teeth went flying. The zombie looked confused and the look, an odd one on any zombie, froze in place as the man drove the dagger into the thin bone of its temple.

The two went down in a heap.

"Well, that sucked," the Corsair growled as he struggled up; the words sounded as if they might have come through a mouthful of rotting wet cabbage. Right away he adjusted the veil of cloth making sure that it covered his disfigured face. As he did, he gazed at the three of them, his eyes lingering on Jenn the longest.

Mike stepped in front of her. Aggressively, he puffed out a defiant chest to which the man only laughed. Like the rest of him, the laugh was harsh and ugly.

"Don't bother to thank me," the man said, sarcastically.

"Sorry, thanks," Mike muttered.

Jenn stepped around him. "We really do appreciate it. And Mike didn't mean to be rude. It was just such a shock. All of it." She almost pointed to his face and stopped herself just in time.

"I suppose it was a close one. You three look a bit out of place. You guys lost?" The question was not difficult unless one was deep in enemy territory talking to the strangest of strangers. Mike looked to Jenn, who looked to Stu, who only shook his head. "Okaaay," the man drawled. "Do you at least know your names. I know this one's name is Mike and you are?"

He had asked Jenn. "J-J…" She had been about to say her real name, which didn't seem prudent, then she had almost said Jillybean's name. It had just popped into her head. In the end, after a three-second hesitation, she answered. "Julie."

His eyes crinkled over the mask. He was smiling, though what a lipless smile looked like she didn't want to know. "Okay, J-J-Julie it is. And you?"

"Steve," Stu answered. The two men appraised each other and as they did, Jenn appraised them both. From the eyes up, they could have been father and son. They both had smoldering dark eyes and almost black hair, though the stranger's was streaked with grey, where he had hair, that is.

"My name's Gunner." He didn't hold out his good hand; it was wet with black blood. He seemed to notice it for the first time and went to the edge of the river to wash it off. Now that the fight was over, his crabbing, sideways walk was more pronounced, and he settled deeper into a hunch. "You guys will probably be needing some help hiding your boat."

"What was that? A boat?" Mike asked, in a voice of pure innocence.

Gunner snorted laughter. "Oh, so that's not your boat back there. Then I guess I'll claim it as my own."

"It'll be the last thing you do," Mike said, going over to the corpse with the axe sticking out of its head and yanking it out. It was surprisingly heavy, and he held it in both hands.

When Gunner turned around and saw this, he brayed laughter. He laughed so hard he had to sit down in the mud. Honest tears formed in his eyes and he used his little veil to dab at them—Jenn had to look away when she caught sight of bone showing through at his jaw.

"Stop! You're killing me," he said, his voice pitched high as he struggled for air. "You should see yourself, kid."

"I'm not a kid," Mike said, planting his feet, and giving the axe a trial swing. It was ungainly and wanted to twist in his grip. Still, he figured he could make mincemeat out of the Corsair if it came to blows.

Gunner sighed. "Well, you aren't a man, son. At least not a smart man. A smart man would know when he's overmatched." He stood and swept back the mottled fur and feather cloak. Underneath it he wore military style armor that had been reshaped to fit his misshapen physique. At his hip was a Glock as scarred and ratty as its owner.

He caressed the butt of the weapon, his eyes narrowing into menacing slits. A second later he shrugged his cloak back into place, hiding the weapon. "Then again, I don't need a gun to kill the lot of you. All of you look like warmed-over death; scarred and beat up. It must be quite a story you have to tell. Let's get that boat hidden and then you can tell it."

The three of them stood there in something of a daze as the man scrambled sideways back to the main section of the river.

"Do you guys think he's a Corsair?" Jenn whispered.

Stu shook his head before shrugging. He had no idea what the man was, other than dangerous, that is. Gunner had just killed three zombies as if it were nothing. He could have killed them as well—or taken them prisoner, just as easily.

"He's crazy is what he is," Mike answered. "Who fights zombies with an axe when he's carrying a gun? Maybe he's out of ammo. Either way, I don't want him touching the boat. He's not the gentlest of persons, that's for sure." Mike could picture him climbing aboard and scraping *The Wind Ripper's* paint with his odd armor. It gave him a chill. "Come on."

Holding the axe near the double-bladed head, Mike hurried after Gunner, catching up to the semi-crippled man just as they came abreast of the boat. "Oh, look at her," Gunner said, with a gleam to his eye. "Torn up sails, bullet holes, and what's going on back there? Did you get rammed? Ooh, and a splash of blood! An adventure on the high sea! That's gotta be some story."

"Uh, it's actually not," Mike lied. "It was really more of a, uh, an accident than an adventure. And that blood was, uh, mine. I cut myself on the uh…"

"Stop it, son," Gunner growled. "You owe me a story. If you want, you can change the names to protect the innocent. Oh, right, you already did!" He cackled at this as he untied the mooring rope. The sound coming from beneath the cloth across his face was strange and wheezing. It wasn't a good or merry sound by any means.

He gave the rope a tug with his one good hand and dragged the boat along as if he were taking an exceptionally large dog for a walk.

Mike said nothing, even as some low-hanging branches got caught up in the torn sail and ripped it even worse. He did cringe, which had Gunner cackling again. "Ah, I bet she was a beauty when you first got her. Where was that, exactly? Alcatraz? Caramel? Maybe Coos Bay?" Gunner's dark eyes were all over Mike's face, looking for clues.

"That's enough," Stu said as he caught up. "Our past and our stories are our own and we don't have to share any of it with you."

"Yeah," Jenn agreed. "Thank you and all for saving us, but there is a matter of trust. This is the wild after all, and we just met you. You could be a Corsair spy for all we know. Are you?"

Gunner grinned behind his veil. "If I were a Corsair would I have saved you?"

"Maybe if you…I mean just maybe." Jenn had been about to say: *Maybe if you knew who we were.* She recovered, saying, "Maybe this is how you get people to talk."

"By saving their ungrateful lives? Yeah, that's how we do it, missy. We Corsairs go around battling zombies and saving morons just so we can figure out they stole one of our boats from somewhere. Jeeze! I have half a mind to turn you over to them. You know how much I can get for you guys?"

More than you suspect, Stu thought. Aloud, he answered with his own question. "How would you know how much? Maybe you aren't a Corsair. Maybe you just work for them."

"And maybe I'm an independent contractor," Gunner replied. "I work for myself. I do for me, first and foremost. Yes, I could've taken you even before the stiffs showed up and I can still take you, and I just might seeing as you aren't being exactly sociable. They'd give me a thousand for the boat, alone. What you three should be doing is changing my mind. All I asked for was a story. Really, it's not like we have cable anymore."

"When we put a few miles between us and the Corsairs, then we'll talk," Stu said.

Gunner's eyes crinkled again. "Do I have your word that you aren't just going to run when I'm not looking?"

Stu glanced at Mike and Jenn, who both nodded. "Yes, we won't run or try to hurt you."

"Ha-ha!" the man cackled. "You're from Alcatraz. I knew it." He started hauling the boat again, shaking his head and laughing. "Those Guardians in Caramel wouldn't have sworn to anything unless it was on a stack of bibles five feet high, and anyone from Coos Bay would've said yes faster than a man could spit. Lying comes second nature to them, you know."

"I didn't know," Stu said, feeling suddenly stupid.

"Oh yeah, it's a fact. They are born to it. Never trust them, is my advice." They were at the opening to the inlet and Gunner casually waddled into the water to heave the boat away from the shallows. The icy cold water didn't seem to bother him for a moment.

Mike nodded in approval, his mind taken up with the boat. Next to him, Jenn wore a pinched, nervous look. She didn't like how any of this was going and she especially didn't like the look or even the name of the man. A person named "Gunner" could clearly not be trusted.

She arched an eyebrow, giving him a cool look reminiscent of Jillybean. "You seem to know quite a bit about the Corsairs."

"I know a lot about a lot of stuff. Now how 'bout you lend a hand. We're going to have to get her up this little tributary a ways and she's going to want to get stuck in the mud."

It took all four of them, standing shoulder deep in the cold water and straining at the lines, to get the boat into the arm of water. The

186

water was too shallow and the boat sat canted over. Mike wanted to add more rope to keep her from washing away in case of a flash flood, and weights to counterbalance her, and more fenders to keep her from sinking.

"It'll be fine," Jenn said, giving him a wan smile. It was now close to eight in the morning and, other than Gunner, they were all tired from the long sleepless night. They couldn't rest, however. They were far too close to the lair of the Corsairs.

"Which way?" Gunner asked, a knowing smile mostly hidden by his veil. When Stu only said northeast, the smile grew as if the direction had never really been in question. Gunner had his own pack which he put on under his cape, giving him an even greater hunch. It was hard not to stare as he led the way.

Although his gait was crab-like, he made even less sound than Stu as he went from shadow to shadow, from one tree to the next, his eyes always up and his head cocked on its gnarled neck as he listened for any sound that might mean danger. He marched them nonstop for an hour, winding up into the hills to a small home hidden by the overgrown forests. Nature had also devoured the long driveway.

"There's some clothes that will fit you guys upstairs," he told them as he laid his pack down in the living room and fished out a fresh set of black clothes.

Jenn had been wet and miserably cold all during the march; she was the first upstairs. There was little for her to choose from. One of the people who had lived in the house had been a junior in high school and her taste in clothing was nothing short of scandalous. Jenn found shorts that were so short they could have doubled for a pair of panties. Skirts that were only a light breeze away from baring everything. Even the jeans were skintight.

In the end, she went with a pair of yoga pants, shorts and one of the skirts. Over the top of this she put on a t-shirt and a man's sweatshirt that still had a hint of cologne clinging to it.

Mike and Stu wore extremely baggy jeans and dark sweaters that made them both appear gaunt.

Gunner had slipped away and did not return until nightfall where he found the three of them sleeping in a single upstairs bedroom. They had pulled mattresses in from the other rooms and lined them up. Jenn woke first and found the twisted man staring at her from the corner, where he sat with his legs stuck out in front of him. His veil was off and in the starlight, she could see his long teeth and scars.

"Sorry," she whispered when he caught her eyes lingering.

He covered up quickly. "I have meat when you're hungry," he intoned and walked out of the room.

The meat turned out to be a wild turkey. Even without the yams and gravy it was delicious eaten right off the spit. When they were all full, Gunner sat down on a rocking chair, stretched his legs out again and began to rhythmically sway. "I saved you, I protected you while you slept, and I've fed you. Now it's your turn. It's story time, just like you promised."

Chapter 27

Mike and Jenn glanced nervously in Stu's direction. They had all agreed he would tell any story if it came to it. Because of the slow way he spoke, they figured he was the least likely to reveal anything best kept under wraps. "What do you want to know?"

"Everything," Gunner answered. He wasn't smiling now. He was staring with fantastic intensity at Stu. His eyes were like two wet hunks of coal. "I would start at the beginning."

"That'll take some time," Stu drawled, thinking he would spin out such an overstretched yarn that Gunner would be soon asleep. He started by admitting they were from Alcatraz, originally. "I came with my brother not long after all this started. Back then the island was crowded. It was a real good place to keep safe from the zombies, but we were starving half the time. We fished every day from the rocks or the pier, but it wasn't long before there wasn't a fish left alive.

"When we couldn't catch anything, we begged or starved. I remember we stayed alive for a few weeks by eating seagulls we'd catch with nets. We ate every part of those birds, except the feathers and the beaks."

Gunner nodded, enjoying the story. "How'd they taste?"

Stu couldn't remember the exact taste, not in a way he could describe other than saying, "Greasy. Nasty. The situation didn't last. Not so many people lived through that first winter. Some sort of disease killed off a bunch of us. It got so bad that people began stealing the boats and disappearing until we were left with very few. It wasn't long after, that Julie's dad came and sorta set things right."

"Would you say that was ten years ago?" Gunner asked, eyeing Jenn now. She felt his gaze and she knew she would wilt before it, so she stared into the glowing fires.

"Right around then," Stu answered. "He was a good man and a strong leader. He basically adopted me when my brother disappeared." Jenn had never heard this story; of course, she barely ever heard any stories from Stu. This might have been the most she had ever heard him say in one sitting.

Gunner seemed uncomfortable by the sudden silence. He drummed his fingers on the wooden armrest. "And was he your real father, *Julie*?" The way he accented the name told them he didn't believe it was hers at all. She didn't trust herself to speak, so she nodded. He rumbled displeasure at her silence and asked, "How old are you?"

"F-Fifteen."

He didn't believe that either. "Really? Stand up and come a little closer. I want to take a better look at you, *Julie*." It was not a request, it was an order that she could not deny—his good hand was on the butt of his ancient Glock and Jenn was under no delusion. She was sure that he could pull it in a flash and kill the three of them with ease.

Except for the soft crackling of the fire, the room was dead silent as she stood with jerking, almost robotic motions and went to stand before him, where, she was inspected from head to toe like an award-winning hog. He even had her bend down so that he could look into her eyes. She felt naked, her mind an open book, her soul laid bare. On the other hand, his mind was impenetrable; his thoughts and feelings hidden in the inky darkness of his watchful eyes. Still, she trembled. He was loathsome and sinister.

"Alright," he said, at last. He allowed her to sit back down and laughed loudly when he saw Mike glaring. "I'd keep an eye on her, son. She's worth a pretty penny to the Corsairs, one way or the other."

"What's that supposed to mean?" Mike asked through gritted teeth. "One way or another? What ways are you talking about?"

Gunner took a long time to answer, "I think we all know." Eyes shot around the room and he laughed again. "Slaves, son. The Corsairs like their slave girls. They snatch them up whenever they can. That's why you need me and that's why you're going to have to put up with me. I can keep you safe or I can drag you all back to the harbor in chains."

"And all you want in return is stories?" Mike asked, dubiously.

"He wants information," Stu corrected. "No one is lonely enough to risk their lives to hear fishing stories. Are you something like a spy, Gunner?"

Gunner's eyes crinkled, though this time it didn't seem as though he were smiling. "Come back when you look like me and then you can tell me all about loneliness. Until then, I'd keep your mouth closed on the subject."

Stu nodded, his face impassive. "Fair enough. But you didn't answer the question. Are you a spy?"

"Like James Bond?" He cackled again and then when he saw the old reference meant nothing to the three he laughed again, this time shaking his head. "Who would listen to me?"

"The Corsairs for one," Stu answered.

"Because they like fishing stories so much? No, you're just paranoid, which makes me wonder why? What are you afraid of letting out? Something exciting? Something interesting? I think you should finish your story." His eyes flicked back to Jenn for just the briefest moment.

Stu knew he couldn't say anything interesting at all as it would just lead to more questions, which would only lead to more lies and he wasn't a good liar, especially under the proverbial gun. His best bet was to stall for time until he could think of some dull, relatively simple reason why they had been on a Corsair boat and why they looked as though they had fought a recent battle, and why there had been fresh blood on the deck. He nodded slowly, stared into the fire for what felt like ages, and listened to the far-off howl of a zombie.

190

He took his time coming to the realization that no lie would suffice. "You know I don't think tonight is a good time for more stories. We're all pretty tired. I know I am." He stood and stretched, letting loose with a fake yawn. "Tomorrow, I promise." Mike also stood and stretched. Jenn stood up, turned partially away from Gunner; she could feel his eyes crawling all over her.

Other than those searching eyes, Gunner made no move or sound at all. It became uncomfortable. Even Stu felt the odd need to say something and he blurted out: "We'll see you in the morning. Bright and early. Good night." Still nothing from Gunner. He watched them file past and head up to the room they shared.

Mike locked the door behind them and put his ear to it as Stu and Jenn held their breath a few feet away. He listened for over a minute before he straightened up and whispered, "I can't hear anything. He's probably down there whittling human leg bones into flutes. Is it me or is that guy the creepiest thing on two legs?"

"It's not just you," Jenn said. "He wigs me out, too. We all know he's after Jillybean. We should just tell him that I'm not her. Maybe he'll leave us alone."

Stu was at the window, pulling back the blanket they had hung over it. He stared out, saying, "And maybe he'll turn us over to the Corsairs since he won't have need of us anymore. I think we should try to string him along until we can overpower him or slip away. All it'll take is a second where he's not paying attention. Then we hit hard and fast."

"Do you want to kill him?" Jenn asked. "He did save us."

"We don't have to kill him, if you don't want," Stu said. "But we have to disarm him no matter what."

They all agreed to this. After pushing a dresser in front of the door, they fell asleep quickly, even though they had spent the better part of the day in bed.

Stu was up before dawn. Alone, he lifted one end of the dresser away from the door and crept downstairs. Gunner was gone, and Stu had the impression that he had been gone for some time. Perhaps all night. Even a few hours were long enough to get to Grays Harbor and back again with a posse of Corsairs.

He turned on his heel and rushed back upstairs. Throwing on his still damp boots, he hissed to Mike and Jenn, "This is our chance!" In under a minute the three were dressed and out the door, each pausing only long enough to grab a chunk of the leftover turkey. They had been traveling northeast; now Stu led them directly east where the sky was beginning to glow along the edge of the dark horizon.

After half a mile, he slowed their frantic pace and began to pick his way with more care. At night, zombies were almost blind; now that the sky was beginning to brighten the danger from them increased a hundredfold. They began to creep through the thin winter forests, always on the alert.

They came upon a paved road that was carpeted in wet leaves. As if they were dodging sniper fire, they took turns running across it, or in Stu's case, limping across it. Mike frowned as he watched him. "Shouldn't your leg be better by now? How long has it been?"

Stu had no idea. Without the constant reminder of calendars or work or school, days tended to run together in a blur. "A month maybe? I'm not sure. I think the muscles are healing wrong. It'll be okay once we get to Bainbridge. How far do you think it is?"

He had been loopy on pain meds for most of the trip south and time had taken on a deceptive nature. They might have been traveling for days or weeks. Neither Jenn or Mike were sure since a good part of their trip had been by motorized boat. They added "map" to their growing list of needed items.

Finding a house in that wilderness was difficult. There were endless hills to climb, icy and swollen streams to cross, and zombies to dodge. Without weapons, they had no choice but to hide from the dead. It was miles before they came to the first house, which was a little box of a place with a detached over-sized garage that had once doubled as a barn. Now it was the home of an owl which glided silently away as they approached.

The house had been picked over many times and was stripped of all the essentials: food, guns, and gas. It did have plenty of dusty, but dry clothing. Jenn found herself in boy's jeans and a hoodie with a matching vest, the latter two items in *Seahawk* blue and green and emblazoned with the *Seahawk* logo.

Stu was decked out like a lumberjack, complete with flannel coat. There were no other coats, so Mike wore layers of sweaters and shirts to stay warm. The three also took the time to fashion quick and easy ghillie suits/ponchos out of blankets and torn-up clothes. They had a vagabond sort of appearance to a human eye. To zombies, they were a confusing mishmash of stripes that did not look much like a person at all.

The ghillie suits had their first trial ten minutes after leaving the house. Stu kept them on an eastward course until the land began to open up into what had once been farmland. They began to skirt around to the north where the pine forest gave way to fruit trees that had once existed in perfectly manicured rows, and were now almost hopelessly intertwined. The cool air was ripe with the sickly-sweet stench of rotting apples.

Over time, the orchard had attracted a number of zombies that had grown immensely fat and huge. One mountain of a beast was so large that it could bend the thickest of branches down to its gaping mouth. It not only ate the apples but also leaves and twigs. The zombie appeared ponderous and slow and yet, when another came too close to its feeding grounds the larger zombie attacked with shocking speed, tearing off the newcomer's arm and beating it senseless with it.

Mike's stomach had long before digested the bit of turkey they'd taken and had been growling at the smell of the apples. That all changed as he watched the black blood squirting from the downed zombie.

"Let's go around," he whispered.

They quickly followed his lead and found themselves on a dirt trail, heading down yet another hill. The trail ended at a scum-covered green pond. When they turned to head back, they heard the unmistakable sounds of a zombie forcing its way down the trail—it was the beast zombie, its enormous belly leading the way. Although the creature probably wasn't the tallest zombie they had ever seen, it was easily the fattest. The trail was five feet across and it broke branches on both sides as it came down.

Stu reacted first. With only seconds to hide, he pushed the others off the trail where they squatted among the frost-withered ferns, pulling their blankets over their heads. Although it was foolish, they peeked out and watched the thing go by. When it entered the water, Jenn sighed and drew the sign of the cross. She was about to huddle back down beneath her blanket to wait out the zombie when she saw a curious sight: a pair of black eyes staring at her from the other side of the trail.

It was a man!

He was hiding fifteen feet from the edge of the little path; close enough for her to see the tattoos beneath his eyes and his long straggly beard. He wore a stained black leather coat and even dirtier blue jeans. It wasn't a man at all, it was a Corsair. She quickly jabbed Mike in the ribs and pointed. In turn, he poked Stu.

"Damn," Stu breathed. The only thing he could think to do was pull the empty Sig Sauer and aim it at the Corsair.

Unbelievably, the man smiled and mouthed: *Go ahead and shoot.* Even if he had bullets, Stu wouldn't have shot unless his life depended on it and the Corsair knew it. The beast of a zombie would be on him in seconds if he did. Since the Corsair seemed equally impotent, Stu decided that their best bet was to try to slip away while they could.

He gave Jenn a nudge and nodded for her to head back in the direction of the pine forest. She started inching away from the trail and the pond as quietly as possible. Mike followed, and Stu was about to go when the Corsair unexpectedly yelled: "Hey! Over here!"

Stu's first thought was that the Corsair had a dozen or so friends with him; anything less would be suicidal. He spun around in time to see the Corsair throw something high in the air and then drop back into the undergrowth.

The zombie turned as well, his dull eyes following what Stu saw now was a spinning branch as it flew straight at him and almost landed on his head. He jerked in response, throwing his hands up as the branch came down. The branch thumped into his shoulder; he'd probably have a nasty bruise, but that was only if he lived through the next few minutes. When he peered down at the pond a second later, he found himself looking right into the zombie's face with only thirty yards of open woods between them. For the second time in less than a day, he yelled: "Run!"

Chapter 28

At three minutes past midnight, the water that had been swirling beneath the wall's foundation finally began to erode its footing. A long section of the wall, running from the gate to the arc in the northern wall where it swung west, began to lean outward and as it did, it let out a titanic groan. It sounded like it was dying.

Cracks appeared next and then hunks of cement began blasting off it, causing some of the townspeople to back away.

"Keep digging!" Commander Walker bellowed, marching along the trench. He marched with his usual confident gait: his shoulders back, his thick chest thrust out and his strong arms swinging—not even a second later he was sprayed with dirt; he didn't flinch and he didn't chastise the soldier. His armor was already filthy and yet he looked pristine compared to his men. They had been digging for hours, trying to carve out an arcing ditch three-hundred yards long.

Although he wanted it deep enough to divert the waters away from the interior of the town, flooding was a secondary concern of Walker's. What he desperately needed was another defensive line, even one as archaic as a moat, which was what the trench was laughably being called.

Militarily speaking, a seven-foot wide moat wasn't much of an obstacle, but he didn't have any better option. The wall had been so large and so grand that no one had ever thought it could be destroyed by anything short of artillery and, as everyone knew, there was no more artillery. In short, the Guardians had put all their defensive eggs in one basket and now the Queen was grinding that basket beneath her heel.

More dirt flew, flicking off his armor as his men put in a last frenzy of digging. Although it had been inadvertent, Walker knew he deserved it. There was no denying that he had failed as a "Guardian." It had been his job to prepare his Knights for any challenge, be it from zombie or human, and now people were going to die because he had lacked foresight. He deserved more than just dirt being flung at him.

"It won't be long now," Bishop Wojdan murmured, appearing out of the dark like a small, soft apparition. He was still in his cassock and would likely remain in it throughout the fight; he liked to joke that it was his uniform. Walker shot him a look and saw he had his round head canted back. The Commander expected him to be staring at the wall; however he was gazing placidly up at the constellation Orion.

Walker let out a grunt as he glanced briefly up at the sky cowboy which was pitched well over, practically lying on its side. "Nope, not long," he said, shortly. He didn't have time for stargazing when there was still so much to get done. "If you don't mind, your Excellency, I have…"

"What do you think, Christian? Will they attack as soon as the wall comes down?"

"I have no idea," Walker answered, honestly. "It's what I would do, but with her, there's no telling."

The Bishop sighed and placed his soft hands behind his back. "She is devilishly tricky, that one. I think we can only plan for the unexpected." He smiled up at the tall commander, expectantly.

A scowl bent Walker's brows down—did Wojdan want him to start spitting out wild guesses as to what the Queen was going to do next? By their very nature, unexpected attacks were purposely vague and, although he knew next to nothing about this queen, she had already proven to be just as the Bishop had said: devilish.

Walker was glad the dark hid his scowl. He had as much respect for the Bishop as anyone; perhaps even more. Walker had been with him since the beginning, back when he had been Father Wojdan, back when the zombie hordes had roared across the earth in unstoppable masses. In the midst of all that terror, Wojdan had not only never lost faith, he had used it as a shield to protect his flock. He had singlehandedly held the community together. Whenever things had looked their darkest, the priest would intone: "God will provide," with complete assurance, and God had provided.

"Whatever her plans are, we are limited in our responses." He was curt, hoping that the Bishop would leave, to make his rounds among the people. The man had a calming influence which was needed among the civilians.

Walker's Knights were another story. They needed to be amped; they needed to have righteous electricity running through their veins. He needed them to be an extension of God's right arm, smiting without let up or mercy, until that time in which mercy was called for. With Corsairs, mercy was a flexible concept. The war that had been thrust upon the Guardians had been expected for some time and it was thought that to shorten it and saves lives in the long run, sadly vicious actions had to be more than just condoned, they had to be a part of their strategy.

But were such actions needed against this Queen? Devilishly tricky or not, when the wall came down, she would still have to mount a frontal assault against trained fighters, who would have their backs to a moral and metaphorical wall. His Knights would not run away and they would not surrender. They would sell their lives at a dear price.

How many casualties would the Queen or her army endure before they broke? Walker guessed that it would be far fewer than the Queen was anticipating. Twenty percent was a high guess. Historically speaking, ten to fifteen percent casualties would suffice to stop practically any attack. Those were numbers he could guarantee even if there were more surprises.

The wall groaned again, this time sounding like it was in pain. "Not long at all,"

Walker said, under his breath. He felt an odd sadness overcome him, almost as if an old friend was dying. "Excuse me, your Excellency. There are some last-minute things I have to attend to in person."

The Commander walked down the length of the new trench, nodding to his men as they hacked at the earth. A few saluted him, while others threw themselves even harder into their work. Only a handful let their fear show. Next, he inspected the new "fortification" that was being hastily prepared behind the trench.

Dirt from the moat was being piled up, patted, wetted, and smacked with shovels in a doomed effort to form a new wall. The best that could be managed under such short notice was little more than a squat, sloping mound which was wider at the base than it was tall. Regardless, Walker smiled and praised the workers as if it were the equivalent of the Great Wall of China.

It will provide some cover at least, he thought to himself. It was better than nothing and if the Queen was telling the truth about not using explosives then the mud wall could make all the difference. "Didn't she also mention not firing a shot?" he muttered.

"It's a trick, Commander," Keith Treadwell said. He had come hurrying up, his armor clacking and his chest heaving. "She probably meant that *she* wouldn't fire a shot. You know what I'm saying?"

Walker hadn't thought about that. "I wouldn't put it past her," he answered. "What's the word on the wall?"

"That's what I came over to tell you, there's water coming through on our side of it. It's not going to be long before it comes down."

"That's what everyone's saying. Have you cleared it completely?"

"Yes, Sir. Just like you asked me. I walked through it myself from end to end, not twenty minutes ago. It's empty." Treadwell sighed. "Empty and a little sad. I'm going to miss her, you know what I'm saying? She's been around for so long."

Walker thought it interesting that he had just been thinking the same thing. "We'll make the next wall even stronger. And we'll put the moat on the other side of it."

Treadwell started to grin at the little joke, only the wall groaned again, an immense, deep sonorous sound that filled the air and vibrated up through the ground. Everyone stopped what they were doing to stare as the front section of it slowly began to lean further and further away. The groan took on a high-pitched wail as the intertwining lattice of rebar which connected the entire structure like a skeleton, began to stretch like taffy.

The wall stood, improbably tipped for close on a minute before it suddenly collapsed. In the dark, it was impossible to see the destruction completely; it could only be felt and heard. It started with a vast, deep rumbling that grew to a frightful, thundering roar, which faded to echoes that carried on and on like the distant sound of thunder.

When the echoes finally ended, the entire community stared about in shock. Save for what looked like stunted wings on either end, the wall was gone—just as Jillybean had sworn, she had torn down the walls and the Guardians were indeed vulnerable—suddenly the little ditch and the thigh-high mound of dirt seemed terribly pathetic, even childish.

"What's that?" someone asked, in a high, strained voice. Everyone had been standing with their ears cocked, expecting the Queen's attack to commence right away. Instead of the sound of boots and gunfire, there was the innocent gurgle of water as the Queen's river trundled over the remains of the walls, washed gently down the fifty yards of open ground, and began filling the ditch.

To a man, the diggers began to leap out of the moat as if it was acid pouring over the side instead of cold, dark water.

Walker frowned at the display; it smacked of cowardice. Dropping to one knee, he made a show of drinking the water. Although it was gritty and unpleasantly earthy, he smacked his lips. "Not bad, not bad. The Queen has been kind enough to give us a new source of fresh water. Once we destroy her army, we'll have to thank her."

The Knights laughed at his show of bravado and a few tasted the water as well, to demonstrate they weren't afraid, either. Walker smiled on them with easy benevolence before turning to Treadwell and calmly ordering: "Get everyone to their battle stations and have Melinda check out the remaining parts of the walls. Unless a feather could knock those parts down, I want some of the reserves up there pronto."

Treadwell saluted smartly before hurrying to bellow and bark at the company commanders, who in turn bellowed and barked, and in some cases, shoved their people into their new positions. It was a mad, jumbled scene, with men throwing down their shovels and snatching up rifles as they ran here and there, looking for their helmets or their rucks, or the right section of the low mound they were to defend.

There was Jennifer Edgerton giving out last minute instructions to a group of reserves, and Denise Woodruff, who was rushing the nursing team back to the three-bed hospital. He saw his daughter, Ryanne holding Ida Battenburg's hand as they and the other small children walked in a two-by-two line to the church.

They marched past the four priests who had taken up positions at intervals behind the mound. Each had a nun and a deacon in attendance. Behind them were the older children who would act as ammo runners, and the middling teens who would become stretcher bearers. Even the very old and the lame took part in the defense. Some kept watch over the approaches to the harbor while others braved the remains of the wall. They carried only crossbows but were deadly with them.

During the chaos, the Bishop found Walker once more. Wojdan fell in beside him as he marched behind the low mound. "I wonder if she will actually attack," the Bishop remarked. He was so utterly devoid of fear that he might have been commenting on the weather. "She did say she would compel our surrender without explosives or firing a weapon."

This same sort of question was being asked up and down the line. It seemed it was all anyone could talk about. In Walker's opinion, anyone who believed it was being foolishly optimistic.

"She's going to need to shoot, alright," Walker said, speaking louder than necessary, knowing he would be overheard. "Unless she's got some new trick up her sleeve, her Corsairs are going to have to come at us right down Broadway." He stuck an arm out, pointing due east to where the gate had once stood. "For all her smarts, she wasn't able to destroy the entire wall and with our flanks secure, she's going to have to attack into the teeth of our defenses."

The long pile of earth didn't look as if it had much in the way of teeth, Walker would be the first to admit that. Still, there was a tremendous advantage in firing from cover in a stable position.

"And you believe the remains of the wall will stand?"

Walker fought the desire to shrug. "It almost doesn't matter. What matters is if she thinks they'll stand. If so, she won't risk a flank attack. And if she does, we'll meet the attack and tear it apart."

"I wonder," the Bishop said again, stepping forward to inspect the moat which was already half-filled. "I fear we have only caught a glimpse of what's in her bag of tricks." He did not have to wait long to be proven right. A few minutes of tense silence passed before an orange light shot into the air from behind the hills, causing the entire town to gasp in unison. It went up a good two-hundred feet and then seemed to hang in the sky, pulsing strangely.

"That's a flare!" Treadwell shouted from far down the line. "It's time! Get ready, Knights!"

The Knights were as ready as they could be, crouched down behind the mound or lying across it, their rifles at the ready. But it was not time. The one flare slowly settled onto the ground where it burned itself out. Within a second of its landing, another was shot into the sky and it too took a minute or so to drop to the earth. After that the flares came at steady intervals—when one went out or hit the ground, another was sent up.

"I don't get it, Commander," Treadwell said, walking over, his body partially turned toward the latest flare as if he were afraid to turn his back to it. "If those are signal flares, where's the attack? And what kind of signal is that, anyway? One or two flares is a signal. Different colors is a signal. Just shooting the same ones up, over and over again isn't a signal. Is she just messing with our heads?"

Walker didn't understand the flares either. He too didn't see the point in them as a signal and nor were they at all effective in lighting the battlefield. They were far too small and looked somewhat like floating chandeliers. Despite their apparent uselessness, they made him nervous, especially as they were fired on trajectories that steadily brought them closer to the edge of town. Essentially, they made him nervous because he couldn't figure them out.

The Bishop seemed to be able to read his mind. "It's almost as if she sees us as primitive men with a primitive man's fears. Do you see how she plays upon the fears of the uncivilized brute in all of us? We fear the dark and she works in the dark. We fear what we don't understand, and she gives us puzzles. We fear the unknown and her actions are hidden and unknowable."

This didn't sit well with Walker and it didn't help that those men and women who were close by had crossed themselves at the mention of the unknown and were nodding along with the Bishop. Walker trusted in God as much as the Bishop did and yet he also believed that God helped those who helped themselves. "What we don't fear are queens, Corsairs, and mind games," Walker stated, a little more gruffly than he meant to. He gave an abbreviated bow and added in a softer tone, "Your Excellency."

For some reason, Treadwell also bowed before saying, "Of course we aren't afraid, but maybe we should think about sending out one of the recon teams. You know, because of the unknown and all. Forewarned is forearmed, right?"

Walker hated giving in, even to the specter of fear, and yet the flares were drawing ever closer and the entire point of the recon team was to discover what the enemy was up to. "Fine," he grunted. "Send out Holt and his men."

Chapter 29

As always Troy Holt carried his spear and had his rifle strapped across his back. Before saluting the Knights Commander, he dropped to one knee and kissed the Bishop's ring. Wojdan drew the sign of the cross on the young man's forehead and told him, "The Lord God will be with you and protect you on your mission."

Troy grinned, his teeth white against his freshly blackened skin. He and his five-man team had daubed their faces with ash in preparation for the mission. "Amen. Thank you, your Excellency."

The Knights Sergeant then stood at attention and snapped off a salute. "Holt reporting, Sir." Beneath the ash and the camouflage, Troy was clear-eyed and apple-cheeked. At nineteen, he was the youngest of the Knights. He was also the bravest, which was no small feat, as the men around him were known for their bravery. He put his complete trust in God.

Walker pointed up at the latest flare. "I want you and your team to find out the purpose of the flares. We need to know what the Queen is up to. Chances are it's her way of prepping us for an attack. She might think she's getting under our skin, I don't know. Your job is to find out. Do not engage if you run into heavy opposition. Evade and assess, only. Do you understand?"

Troy answered with an exuberant: "Yes, Sir!"

"Be a good lad, and have your men blessed before they leave," the Bishop Wojdan said.

"They're with Father Amacker now, your Excellency."

The Bishop beamed. "That's fantastic. I'm sure you and your men will do us proud. Now, off you go." Walker watched him go with a heavy heart. Wojdan read the worry on his face. "You're afraid that you promoted him too quickly. You fear that he trusts *too much* in God, if such a thing is possible. And you are full of doubt that you missed some step in his training that will lead to his death."

"Yes," Walker, sighed.

"Heavy is the weight of leadership. Young Troy and I are fortunate. Our steps are chosen for us. Ours is simply to do and die. You, on the other hand, must assign the dangerous paths on which your men walk. It is a burden, though in this case, I feel you have not chosen wrong. He is the very essence of Christian chivalry."

Despite his deep faith, Walker looked for more than Christian chivalry in his Knights and doubly so in those who were in leadership positions. So far, Troy had passed every test set before him. He had faced cartel pirates out of Diablo Canyon, and Mendota hill bandits, as well as zombies by the score.

He was quick and agile, both mentally and physically. He was also patient and calm when the situation called for it, which, more than his vaunted bravery, was why older men put their trust in him. Not that he led men who were all that much older.

The oldest man on his Recon team was twenty-four-year-old Justin Regis. He was tall and rangy, and never seemed to tire, no matter how hard Troy pushed the pace. The next oldest was Shamus McGuigan, with his beak of a nose and his habit of painting flowers on his M4. Then came Eric Gothier with his trademark slouch that made even his armor seem relaxed. Stocky Bob Duckwall was one of the strongest men among the Knights—he liked nothing more than wrestling men twice his size and bending them into human knots. And finally, there was Chris Baker, who hummed instead of speaking, as his tongue had been cut out by a hill bandit eight years before.

The five waited quietly in the dark and were unsurprised by the orders Troy relayed.

"They are weird," Shamus remarked, giving the latest flare a glance as it floated lazily along. The ash on his nose was marred, showing his skin. He was overly sensitive about his long nose and had a tendency to touch it frequently.

"You know what I think?" Eric asked. "I think it's a sleep thing. You know, like deprivation. Her people are probably snoring away while we're here frightened of a few lights. I bet it'll be drums next and then a few gunshots. Then tomorrow they'll act like they're just about to attack and then pull back. A few days of that and we'll be going batty. That's how you win without firing a shot."

Baker hummed in agreement; however, Regis shook his head. "Not this queen-chick. She's got Corsairs working for her, so you know she's evil right down into the pit of her stomach. Here's what I think: I think she's going to poison that river. Easy-peasy. No shots fired." He wiped his hands together as if brushing away dirt.

"Then what's with the flares?" Eric demanded.

Before Regis could answer, Troy interrupted, "That's what we're going to find out, *if* you guys will stop arguing. Now, since this is so straightforward, we're going to travel light." Normally, they carried equipment and supplies for at least three days but with the flares puffing into existence almost over their heads, Troy figured they'd run into trouble fairly quickly.

"We're not taking spears, are we?" Regis asked. "If there's any dead around, they'd be going after the Corsairs."

Troy hesitated. The ten-foot long spears were bulky and would slow them down, yet if they ran into even one zombie, they would be forced to use their rifles and ruin the element of surprise. "Take them." Along with their spears, each man took only his M9 bayonet, ninety rounds of ammunition and an M4 carbine.

When they had ditched all their gear led, except for two coils of rope, he headed toward the tiny, rock-strewn inlet which doubled as their harbor. It was surrounded by sharp, slick cliffs and Troy knew that if they could escape the town without being seen by any of the Queen's spies, it would be there. Getting down to the harbor itself was easy. The Guardians had built retractable ladders especially for the purpose.

Once on the craggy beach, Troy began to sneak south, picking his way through the rocks and trying to keep as close to the looming cliff as he could. What little noise the six of them made was drowned out by the endless crashing waves, breaking not far from the low tide mark. Sometimes, with the last of their energy, the dregs of these waves would wash over the toes of their boots and at other times they waded through waist deep water.

After half a mile, Troy began to look for a place to climb the cliff that wasn't so steep. Had this been a training mission, he would have chosen the hardest spot he could find. Just then, they couldn't afford to take any chances.

When he found a favorable spot, he unslung one of the lengths of ropes and handed it to Duckwall. Although he was the shortest of them, he was easily the best climber. His hands were so incredibly strong that he could hang by the tips of his fingers for minutes at a time. Without breaking a sweat, Duckwall worked his way to the top, tied off rope and dropped the loose end down to Troy, who climbed up, going hand over hand. The six spears were hauled up next, then came the other members of the team, one after another, without incident.

"Here's where it may get hairy, so keep sharp," Troy warned. "God be with us."

The six had trained and fought together for the last year; they did not need any more instructions than this. Each man knew his place and position. Each knew what to do if they ran into enemy fire, and each knew what their fellow teammates' reactions would be. As always, Troy went first, moving slowly, his eyes and ears straining to catch the slightest indication that the enemy was nearby. It wasn't easy since the night was dead black, and when he could differentiate between shadows they were in constant motion as the wind swept unceasingly off the ocean. The wind also masked every sound except their own, or so it seemed.

Troy barely heard the rock kicked by Regis, and Eric's light cough, and when Duckwall accidentally let the butt of his metal spear scrape the ground, the *clank* it made seemed to radiate to the far corners of the earth.

"Sorry," Duckwall mumbled.

They went straight east at first, but after a few hundred yards, Troy turned directly north, directly towards where the flares were being fired. He expected to run into Corsairs at any second, so he slowed to a crawl. It wasn't a literal crawl, though it was very close. He moved in a crouch, his M4 now in his right hand and his long spear in his left.

Gradually, he moved closer and closer to where the flares zipped up into the sky with a rush of sparks and *zzzsswwwwiissh* sound. They reminded him of something, but he couldn't remember for the life of him what it was. It was something from before the zombies had come. He had been seven at the beginning of the apocalypse and felt that he should have remembered far more of that time than he did. Almost all of his memories were shrouded or strangely choppy; a face here, a scene of a boy running, a ball bouncing, a tree lit with thousands of lights.

This memory was annoyingly just out of reach. It wasn't until one of the flares malfunctioned and burst into flame on its way up that Troy remembered. "Independence Day," he whispered. It all came back to him in a flood: the parades, the picnics, the hamburgers cooked over charcoal—"Never gas," his dad had always said. There had been pies and three-legged races and baseball and fireworks. He should have remembered the fireworks. They had been spectacular.

When the flare exploded, Troy dropped to a knee in the waist-high brown grasses, and in the light, his smile could be seen. It was a child-like smile as the memories flooded in. It faded when the flare hit the ground a hundred yards away. For just a second, right before the fire went out he had caught a glimpse of a figure hurrying toward it.

It had been a big figure.

"Was that a zombie?" he whispered to Shamus.

"I think so, but it doesn't make any sense if it was. How'd it get past their guards?"

"How did *we* get past them?" Troy asked, looking around. "We're awful close to where they're shooting those flares off. Wouldn't you post a defensive perimeter further out than this?" The flares were being shot off from the next hill. In the dark, it was hard to tell how far it was, though Troy didn't think it could be more than eighty yards.

Shamus stood up slowly and turned in a slow circle. When he slunk back down, he said, "I think you're right. We gotta be within their perimeter."

Eric crabbed over, hunkered low. His sharp ears had picked up the conversation. "Or, what if they don't have a perimeter at all? Remember what I said about the sleep deprivation? Maybe they just have a few guys here while the rest are a few miles away sleeping like babies."

"Either way," Shamus said, "I think we should go after them rockets. If it's like Eric says, then maybe we can turn the tables on them."

Troy tapped the cold metal of his spear as he considered his options. "Our orders are to discover what the Queen is up to with the flares and I was told not to engage the enemy. I think in this case we can't do one without the other." Shamus' eyebrows shot up and he nudged Eric, who grinned. Troy gave them a look. "Hold on, you two. First, we have to find out if it is really just a few of them."

He meant to accomplish this by splitting his team in two; Regis would take his three-man team east around the back of the hill, while he took Eric and Chris Baker around the front. He figured his route would be more dangerous because of the zombie and because if there were guards, they'd be more alert and trigger happy the closer they were to the town.

It turned out that it wasn't *one* zombie he had to worry about. There was a whole slew of them. After the team divided, Troy hadn't gone fifty feet before he heard the first low, grumbling moan. His team dropped down into the dead grass and watched as an immense shadowy beast emerged from the darkness. It lumbered along without seeing them and passed between Eric and Baker.

"That was freakin' close," Eric whispered. "It almost stepped on my hand. How many zombies are we gonna run into?"

Troy put a finger to his lips as another zombie stumbled into view. Seeing three zombies one after another was rare this close to the town. It was part of a Knight's training to hunt them, and each twelve-man squad was required to make a spear kill every six months. Troy demanded much more from his team. He and his five men hunted every month.

"The Corsairs must be attracting them," Troy answered. "I think we should go white, just in case." Each of them pulled out white "scarves" and attached them to their spears just below the foot-long bladed tip. The scarves were used to distract zombies long enough to allow a teammate to attack from the flank or the rear.

As tough as his recon team was, Troy hoped they wouldn't have to put the spears to use. Fighting a zombie in the dark was one of the most dangerous things a person could do. All the training in the world couldn't overcome the slightest misstep on a steep hill.

Troy had just affixed his scarf when Baker hummed in a low register. Another zombie was coming. This one fell down the hill, rolled past them in a wild jumble of grey arms and legs, and stopped only when it thudded heavily against the stump of a tree. Before it even stopped rolling, another could be seen as a colossal shadow some ways off.

"If the Corsairs had a perimeter, it's being overrun by the dead," Eric said. "I think we should make straight for the rocket…"

An echoing roar interrupted him. It had come from the back end of the hill where Regis was. Without a word, Troy ran towards the sound with Baker and Eric right behind him. They crossed a shoulder of the hill and stopped. Off to their left was a twenty-foot long, windowless, dark box on wheels; the flares were being shot from the back of it.

There was no time to give it more than a glance. Right in front of Troy was a zombie, a smallish seven-footer with a strangely out of proportion huge, shaggy head, while farther down the hill were half a dozen more surrounding Regis, Shamus and Duckwall.

The shaggy-headed beast was half turned away and didn't see Troy or his ten-foot long spear as he swept it in an arc. The head of the spear resembled a great double-edged dagger and when he slashed the blade across the back of the beast's knee, it sheered through one of its hamstring tendons.

It added its roar to that of the others as it turned about to face Troy. Before it could; however, Chris Baker caught its attention, jabbing his spear into the thing's face. He aimed for an eye while the scarf attached near the end flared, further distracting it. This allowed Eric to slash at its knees. In seconds, it was down and clawing after them as they raced into the real battle, which had been desperate from the very start.

They could see Regis was down, with three of the beasts fighting to eat him alive. Shamus and Duckwall were dodging and weaving, flashing their spears around trying to save him and themselves, simultaneously. So far, their speed and training kept them just out of reach of the long arms. From an outsider's point of view, it would have made more sense for both of them to run away and leave Regis to his fate. Although he was lying face down, he had not screamed or cried out in any way, which meant there was only a tiny chance that he was alive.

None of the three charging down the hill had much hope and yet they would never leave a man behind if there was any chance of saving him. Troy was the fastest and he swept through the fight, slashing at the throat of one beast and drawing black blood. In a blur, he was past the first and jabbing at another's face; aiming for the eyes. A blind zombie was the next best thing to a dead zombie.

Then he was onto the beasts surrounding Regis. They were on their knees pulling his body in three directions at once. Troy used the spear as an axe and swung it for the back of one tree-trunk-sized neck. Had it been a real axe, it might have taken the thing's head clear off. As it was, it bit hard, went three inches deep and stuck.

The zombie jerked and nearly wrenched Troy off his feet. Since playing tug of war with a 600-pound monster would only end in his death, he had to give up his weapon. It was no matter. Regis's spear was lying on the ground not far away. Troy jumped for it, snatched it up and then backed away quickly, spinning it like a baton. The flashing metal in the dark confused the two zombies who had been charging him. One reached out a clawed hand and tried to touch the flashing spear. As Troy stopped the spin and raised the spear tip high, both of the creatures tried to grab it.

This practiced move allowed Chris Baker to attack them from behind, once more going for the vulnerable soft spot behind the knee. It had long been known that zombies were not magical creatures. Their bodies were essentially human and operated along the same set of natural laws that normal human bodies did. Without tendons attaching muscles to bone, the bones would not move.

Unfortunately, normal tendons are exceedingly tough which meant that zombie tendons were like steel cables. Baker's slash did nothing except draw the zombie's attention. But it was slow and he was fast. He was already attacking another zombie by the time it turned around and when it did, Troy hacked at the same knee finishing the job. Its leg buckled and down it went.

Reversing the spear, Troy drove it through the neck of the closest zombie, with all his strength. He then wrenched the haft of the weapon to the side as hard as he could, turning an inch and a half wide hole into a huge, gaping wound. Hot black blood gushed down the spear as he yanked it out. The creature lunged for him, not realizing that it would be dead in seconds.

Troy began twirling his spear again when Duckwall ran past. The stocky Knight was rushing to attack one zombie from the rear while being chased himself. Troy aimed the blade of his spear for the chasing zombie's knee. He connected; it was like taking a full swing at a brick wall with a baseball bat. A shiver of pain ran through his hands as his spear sprang out of his grip and bounced away. Troy ran for it. He scooped it and spun expecting an attack, but not knowing from what direction.

"My Lord!" he cried at what he saw.

His team wasn't fighting six zombies, as he had thought, they were fighting sixty zombies!

They were everywhere, charging from all points of the compass.

In that second, it dawned on Troy what the Queen's plan really was. The flares weren't a signal at all; they were being used to summon the zombies from as far as the eye could see. She really wasn't going to beat them by firing a shot; she was going to let the zombies do her killing for her.

Chapter 30

"Retreat!" Troy bellowed as he unslung his rifle. Despite the cry, he walked in the opposite direction of safety, firing the gun, half-blinding himself with every pull of the trigger. It didn't matter much if he could see or not. Although he would have loved to kill every one of the monsters, his main reason for shooting was to get them focused on him so his men could escape.

But they weren't escaping. They were unslinging their own guns. "No!" he yelled. His ears were ringing already and he couldn't tell if he was screaming loud enough to be heard on the moon, or not loud enough to be heard over the dozens of roaring zombies. "Run! Now, before it's too late!"

He could only hope they were following orders as he marched forward, firing as he went. He would run as well, just as soon as he checked on Regis. The man had been cast aside and lay unmoving; he was missing an arm and his neck was stretched as if he had just been pulled from the gallows.

There was nothing Troy could do. With his left hand, he drew the sign of the cross in the air and then ran up the hill, firing at the zombies that got in his way until his magazine ran dry. With practiced hands, he switched in a new one and fired just as an eight-footer with half a face blundered up. Two headshots dropped it at his feet and yet it was not wholly dead. A steel grip closed on his ankle just as he was getting to run again.

He was down in the dirt and before he knew it, he was being dragged toward the beast's great bloody maw. Troy's bullets had blown out the thing's teeth so that when it bit down on his boot, it was more disgusting than deadly. Still, he was in a dangerous situation, which he remedied by sticking the hot barrel of his M4 against the thing's head and pulling the trigger.

In its death-throes, the huge hand wrapped around his ankle spasmed, and for a moment, the grip on his leg was like someone was crushing his ankle with a vice. A groan escaped him as he kicked himself free and tried to stand, only to nearly fall again. He could barely stand, though it hardly mattered. Running was out of the question. When he looked around, he saw that he was completely surrounded by a wall of the undead. They had turned from chasing the shadows of his men and were completely focused on him.

"The Lord is my shepherd; I shall not want." He fired. "He maketh me lie down in green pastures; He leads me beside still waters." He fired again and began limping forward up the hill, toward the ocean, towards home. "He restores my soul and leads me in the paths of righteousness for His name's sake."

Troy didn't count his shots. When he ran out, he ran out. For him there was no saved last bullet; there would be no suicide.

"Yea, though I walk in the valley of the shadow of death. He reloaded and fired again. "I will fear no evil for You are with me; Your rod and Your staff, they comfort me."

Now the zombies were coming so thick he only had time to shoot, and shoot, and shoot, and reload, and shoot…

Sometimes the beasts got so close their diseased hands would knock him back or twist him around. Still, he fired, building a mound of bodies around him. There were so many zombies that only a miracle could have saved him. He knew that no hand of man had a chance. His people were too far away. Even if his team came rushing back, it would be in vain. And the only other men nearby were the Corsairs, whose evil could not be doubted.

No, only God could save him. The question in Troy's mind was he worth saving? Had he been righteous enough?

The M4's bolt shot back—he was out of ammo. Throwing aside the rifle, he pulled his bayonet. It was deadly sharp and yet, compared to the size of the zombies, it might as well have been a baby spoon.

"Just one," he whispered, hoping to take out one more before he died. He got lucky because the closest of the zombies tripped over the pile of bodies surrounding Troy. He raised the bayonet and just as he did, the box on wheels shot up a flare unlike any of the others it had sent up.

It was a true flare that blossomed into painful brilliance a hundred yards over head. Every zombie within half a mile turned to stare into the piercing light. They were brainless beasts. Troy didn't have that excuse. He also stared, but only for a second before he came to his senses.

This was his chance to escape. The zombies were blind but wouldn't be forever. He had minutes to find somewhere to hide before the flare died and they regained their ability to see. The problem Troy faced was that the hills were barren—other than the hundreds of zombies there was nothing but grass…and the box-like vehicle.

Despite the pain in his leg, he grinned, thinking that he could hide beneath it until most of the zombies had moved on. "And then I'll burn it," he growled around the grin. There was enough old dead grass within arm's reach to cook a full-grown elk and if he bundled enough of it into small bales he was fairly certain he could torch the Corsair vehicle.

If he were lucky, the heat would set off the remaining rockets and hopefully draw the zombies away from the town.

It was a good plan and he began limping towards the vehicle as fast as he could. It was the strangest sensation to pass among the dead like that. They were huge, grotesque statues cast in an amber light that made them even more disgusting than ever. Seeing them like that made it hard to believe they had ever been human. They were so terribly warped and bloated and savaged that they were more like demons from a nightmare.

"Or from hell," he whispered to himself. He could easily imagine that he had died, that the undead had killed him and dragged his soul back down to hell. The pulsing light lent a surreal quality to the world. It blotted out the stars so that it seemed as though he were surrounded by endless darkness above and a vast lifeless prairie below.

The thought was absurdly unsettling and, with his face twisted into a grimace of pain and fright, he concentrated on getting to the box. It reminded him of a small camper, but only in size and shape. It had no windows and only one door set in the exact middle of the side facing him. It was black and seemed to be made of crudely welded metal plates. Under the light, it too had an unsettling quality, as if the rockets were being worked inside it by dozens of imps with reptilian skin and mouthfuls of wickedly sharp teeth.

In his mind, they were being whipped into working by a larger demon with hoofed feet and red eyes...

Troy shook his head to clear it. He had been on the verge of freaking himself out. *I'm not in hell*, he told himself, *And there are no demons in there. It's only...*

Just as he was thinking this, the door opened and out spilled red light. It was a strange, dim sort of light that did little to push back the darkness. Standing in the center of the doorway, framed by the light, was a black figure that seemed so much more demon than human that Troy stepped back, fiercely gripping his bayonet.

"Do not be afraid," the person said in a low voice. It was a woman. Was it the Queen? Was it one of her helpers? The very fact that it was a woman had him hesitating. Had it been a man, Troy probably would have hurled the bayonet at him and rushed off into the dark.

"Hurry, the flare is not going to last," she whispered. "I won't hurt you." It was then that he noticed she held a gun. She made a show of holstering it. When it was out of sight, she added, "Drop your knife and come in." Amazingly, she stepped out and held the door open for him.

It was such an odd thing to do that he found himself hesitating until it was too late. The flare was barely thirty feet off the ground when she sighed and stepped back inside. It was the sigh that got Troy limping to the door. The sigh had been tinged with sadness.

She stopped him at the door. "The knife?" She held out her hand. If this was the Queen, he could stab her in a blink of an eye and perhaps end the war. She had to know this and yet she was perfectly calm, her hand completely still. She wasn't afraid and she had no reason to be. It would have gone against everything he believed in to kill her just then. He was no assassin to stab the unwary.

He gave her the knife and she allowed him inside, shutting the door behind him. "I will ask that you do not shout, make noise, or otherwise interfere." She gestured to a couch that was built into one of the walls. "Take off your boot so we can see that leg. Donna, if you would be so kind?"

Another woman, this one a good deal older, helped Troy to the couch. There were six people in the room, which was smaller on the inside than he had expected. The other four were men, three of which were undoubtedly Corsairs. They were scrubby, bearded and covered in tattoos. They eyed Troy with matching sneers.

"He looks like he got all dressed up to go trick-or-treating," one said. The other two sniggered, while the fourth man smiled, nervously.

"Am I a prisoner?" Troy asked as Donna started untying his boot. The older woman looked up but didn't say anything.

The others glanced to the Queen, who had her face propped in front of an odd view-finder that hung from the ceiling on a short tube, similar to what would be found on a submarine. She worked it around in a circle, whispering to herself. "That's a lot of them. Maybe too many. How do I know how many is too many? I just think it looks like too many."

One of the Corsairs cleared his throat. "Your Highness?" His sneers had evaporated. He was suddenly nervous. "The puppy you rescued had a question."

"Hmm? What's this about a puppy?" Her eyes went wide at the sight of Troy. It was as if she had never seen him before.

She was playing some sort of game and he didn't appreciate it. "Am I a prisoner?" he repeated, coldly. "If so, there should be…" His words dried up as she leaned in close, peering into his ash-covered face. Her eyes were uncommonly large and brightly blue. She smelled of shampoo and lilac perfume. The scent wasn't strong and yet her over-all effect, her beauty, her aroma, her wild, uncouth hair was so beguiling that Troy leaned back, awash in uncertainty. No woman among the Guardians had ever looked like this or smelled like this or acted like this.

Troy was struck by the most ungentlemanly desire. He couldn't look her in the eye.

"The Queen doesn't take prisoners," she said and then laughed quietly. "Not for long, at least."

"Then you plan on killing me?"

"For what? Did you do something wrong?" Her eyes shot even wider as if an obscene thought had struck her. She turned away, hissing, "You need to stop that, Eve." When she turned back, she wore an odd, fixed smile. She excused herself and went to the only other door in the room. When she opened it, a bitter chemical odor wafted out.

She left and there was a strained silence that was surprising. Troy expected the Corsairs to make some lewd or piggish comment concerning the Queen's behavior. The Corsairs were infamous for their crudeness, after all. They said nothing. One went to the periscope to look out, while the other two just lounged back on chairs.

The only person who said anything was the fourth man in the room. He didn't seem to like being near the other men. "Y'all ran into a hell of a fight back there. Say, y'all get scratched or bit or something?"

Troy ignored the use of the word "hell" and answered, "I don't believe so. One of them grabbed my ankle and squeezed it cruelly when I killed it."

"It's not scratched," Donna said, flicking a lighter and inspecting his ankle with raw flame. "It is bruised pretty good. A bone bruise can smart for a little while. I can wrap it for you if you want."

"Really? You would wrap it?" The very idea was completely at odds with what he knew about Corsairs. It was common knowledge that they were violent, thuggish and evil. They were proud to admit their tortures, all of which were sadistic in the extreme. He half expected them to set his hair on fire and kick him out of the trailer; placing bets to see how long he could run before the undead ate him.

"I take it she's not going to kill me…"

A sudden *whoosh* from the other room made him jump. One of the Corsairs laughed at him, while the man at the periscope muttered, "It's going deep, deep, deep and off to the left." He pulled his eye from the viewfinder and gazed baldly at Troy. "She must like you." The third Corsair opened his mouth to say something only at that moment, the Queen came back in and he locked away his comment behind tight lips.

She paused in the doorway, taking stock of the room. "Good, it's only been a minute."

"It was a short one, your Highness," Donna assured her. "We barely even noticed. But next time, maybe don't go out there like that. There's no sense putting yourself in danger."

The Queen did not reply to her. She walked over and gave Troy a once over. "That was some stiff odds you were up against. I'm surprised that you made it. Surprised as well as happy. We'll need men like you."

"I hate to disappoint you, but I will never become a Corsair. If that means tossing me out, so be it. I would just like my knife back before you do, if you don't mind."

"It's good that you hate them," she answered. "I hate Corsairs too, and my goal is to rid the earth of them. What's your name, trooper?"

"Knights Sergeant Troy Holt, ma'am. And if you hate Corsairs, why are you in league with them?" Troy cast a look at the Corsair at the periscope.

The Corsair was Mark Leney who smiled, showing crooked teeth. "We're reformed Corsairs," he said around the false smile. "We've seen the error of our ways. You're a Christian, right? You must believe in forgiveness. If so, then you can start by forgiving us, though I don't remember ever doing anything to wrong you, Knights Sergeant Troy Holt."

"You helped tear down our wall and now you're sending a horde of zombies to kill my people."

"Well, there is that," Leney agreed. "You got me on that one. Though in my defense this whole mess really is political. I'm just following orders, probably just like you."

The Queen shot him a look and Leney's mouth clamped shut. "This is actually beyond political," she explained. "We're in the realm of geo-political. The fate of humanity hangs in the balance." She held up thumb and finger so that barely any of the red light slipped between them. "We are this close to extinction as a species. Not only must we stop the depredations of the Corsairs, we have to unite the various groups under one banner and pray that humanity can recover."

"And you think you can do that by sending a zombie horde after us? It sounds to me like you're trying to speed our extinction along."

"That's because you lack foresight. Donna, if you'll wrap him up and Captain Leney, if you'll be kind enough to give him a weapon and escort him back to his town." Leney's eyes went wide and his mouth fell open, but only for a second. After that his eyes went to squints, the red light adding a touch of the demonic to them.

Troy was sure the man was plotting to kill him, and was probably even then thinking up the lies he'd tell when he got back alone.

Jillybean must have sensed the same thing and said, "You will have nothing to fear, Knights Sergeant Troy Holt. I *will* find you whole in the morning, right Captain Leney?" Her eyes pierced him and his scheming look failed.

"Of course, your Highness," Leney said with a short bow. "Of course."

Chapter 31

Leney glanced suspiciously over at Troy just as Troy was doing the same to him. "What are you looking at?" Leney challenged. He hadn't liked the Knight from the moment he had come stumbling into the trailer. Even covered in ash and zombie blood, Leney could tell he had that annoyingly perfect all-American, starting quarterback look that he despised and was jealous of in equal measure.

"I'm looking at someone who wants to get eaten by zombies, apparently."

"You think I'm scared of them or you? Hardly." Leney scoffed and then began to mutter angrily, just on the edge of being heard. "Damn Queen. What the hell is she thinking sending me out like this? Crazy is what she is, making me go with this pathetic, little mother fu…"

"Excuse me!" Troy hissed, grabbing his arm. "You need to quiet down, this instant. Look around you for goodness sakes. This is not the time for a tantrum. If you want to go back, then go. I would like nothing more."

Leney wished he could go back. It was insane to simply walk into an enemy camp, especially one that was about to be overrun by a horde of the dead. If he could go back it was something of a toss-up as to whether he'd go back as a sniveling servant begging for forgiveness or as an assassin.

He had no doubt the Queen would win this fight with the Guardians, and Leney would bet his life that she would also beat the Black Captain and any other enemy she set her sights on. There would be riches and power beyond anything Leney could have ever dreamed —but it would come at a price to his dignity. Yes, even a murdering Corsair had his dignity and the Queen was constantly tearing his down.

She kept pushing and pushing as if looking for his breaking point, as if a part of her hoped that he would rebel, or maybe come after her one night when she was alone. He had thought about it a lot, especially after she had cut his throat. The problem lay in the fact that killing her would be harder than it looked. Yes, she was tiny; even with her long black coat and high boots she probably only weighed a hundred and ten pounds. Tiny but fast. Tiny but always alert like a fox. Tiny but deadly.

She didn't just push him to the edge, she pushed everyone, herself included. Leney secretly wondered which would crack first: her or her army? More and more, she would talk to the wall or to a lamp. More and more, it was up to him or Donna or anyone with guts to try and straighten her out.

The men had found it quirky and funny right up until she seemed to have lost her marbles altogether three days earlier. Instead of fighting the Guardians, she had set them to digging! Corsairs were not diggers, especially when there didn't seem to be a sane reason for all the hard work.

They dug here, they dug there; they dug up streets and widened ditches. They went at it for three days and nights until Leney had to warn the Queen that anymore and she'd have a mutiny on her hands. She didn't listen. Instead, she had them throw the last of their strength into taking down a dam. Leney feared she had gone a step too far.

But she had not erred in her judgment that men were simply: "Big boys with better toys."

Almost all of them were eager to see what would happen when a dam burst. They went at it with more gusto than Leney would have guessed and when the water came bursting out, they capered and cheered.

Her pushing had worked out this time, but one day she would push it too far and when she went down, Leney knew he'd go down with her. The two were close to becoming irrevocably connected, and it grated on him to know that he would either be fated to be strung up beside her or be her chief whipping boy for all time.

Since neither option was acceptable, he knew he'd have to jump ship, eventually. He just had to pick the right time and just then wasn't it.

"I'm not going back," he growled at Troy, lying through his nearly clenched teeth. "I have a duty to see you safely to your town." Of course, duty had nothing to do with it; the Queen's anger could be volcanic, and he had the slowly healing scar across his throat as proof of it.

For his part, Troy didn't want the escort, nor did he need it. The Queen had aimed her latest rocket slightly to the south of the town and its ruined walls, and now the hundreds of zombies were stumbling in that direction with their grotesque heads thrust back, and their vacant, uncomprehending dark eyes staring upwards. With a direct route open, Troy could have made it back on his own. Even his leg had warmed up and was only slightly "twingy" if he stepped on something oddly.

As he hurried along next to the still-grumbling Corsair, Troy tried to make some sense of the Queen and found it next to impossible. For reasons that were beyond him, she had saved him from certain death, and was now delaying her attack so he could make it back home. Was it guilt that drove her? Was it simple insanity? Or was it some terribly intricate scheme that he had no hope of unraveling?

He feared it was the last of these.

"To what end?" he muttered.

Leney grunted out a laugh and whispered, "Stop trying. You'll never figure her out. Sometimes I think I got a handle on her and then…"

Troy dashed at him and hauled him down, clamping a hand over his mouth. Rage exploded in Leney and he was just reaching for his knife when a shadow moved. What he had mistaken for a boulder was a hugely rotund zombie. Its girth was so fantastic that its arms looked like the stubby wings of a penguin. It had fallen and was now trying to roll itself back to its feet.

The two men crept away, crossing over the side of one of the hills when they saw Highton a few hundred yards away. With its walls in ruins, it looked old and ugly, as if it had been deserted for years. It was far from deserted. Even then they could hear a faint growling and the occasional clank of metal on rock. Not all the zombies had followed the flares the Queen had been sending up. Some had been pulled along by the steady slope of the hill and found themselves in the town.

There were more of the beasts between the two men and the meager safety of the town. Some were stooped at the edge of the new river, drinking, while others were heading toward the muted sound of battle.

It galled Troy that he was both wounded and without an adequate weapon. The AK 47 he'd been given was a weapon of last resort, and his bayonet was far too feeble to do much damage. If he'd had his spear, he would have rushed among them, and crippled half a dozen before they even knew he was there.

For his part, Leney had no intention of doing any fighting unless absolutely necessary. He tapped the Knight on the shoulder and began to slink around the dead, moving in a wide circle to the north before approaching the town. They were challenged by forty-eight-year old reservist Kaitlyn Renee.

"I know you're human," she hissed. "And I got you dead to rights, so put those hands up or I'll shoot." Kaitlyn had always been more of a storyteller than a proper Knight and Troy recognized her voice. When he gave his name, she gushed: "Oh, praise the Lord! I heard a rumor that Duckwall said you were dead. Is that Justin you have with you?"

"No. Regis didn't make it. I checked him, personally. This is a Corsair. It's a long story that I don't have time for." Troy was already picking his way through the mud and the pools of muck and the broken hunks of concrete.

Kaitlyn watched him for a moment, a perplexed look on her face. "But he has a gun. Troy? Why does he have a gun?"

"Because I'm not a prisoner," Leney told her. "If anything, all of you are my prisoners."

Troy turned around to object to this only he slipped in the mud. Leney caught him and roughly set him back on his feet. "There you go, junior. Papa's got you." He took his muddy hand and tousled Troy's brown hair, much to his embarrassment.

Leney's swaggering manner grew even more pronounced once they were past the broken jumble that had once been the wall. He rooted for a zombie that was being stabbed to death by half a dozen Knights, and he laughed aloud at the moat, saying, "We created a river ten miles long, and this is all you guys could manage? A ditch?"

The Guardians close by were appalled at both what he'd said and how loud he'd said it. Troy took him by the arm and pulled him along, saying, "As of now you are my guest, but if you can't control your tongue I will have you jailed." The two glared hard into each other's faces and Leney was tempted to test the young Knights Sergeant, only he knew more zombies were on their way and he didn't relish the idea of being chained to the wall when they crossed the pathetic moat and tore apart the town.

"Sure, whatever you say, junior."

"I say follow me and keep quiet. Come on. I need to find the Commander. Does anyone know where he is?"

One of the men hissed: "He and Duckwall just went to the church a few minutes ago. Is there really a zombie army coming our way? That's what Bob said."

"A small one," Troy told the Knight. "We'll overcome it, don't worry."

Leney laughed again. "A small army? I thought you Jesus-freaks weren't supposed to lie? We have enough zombies to swallow this place whole."

A long silence hung over that section of the moat until Troy said, "It's no matter to us how many zombies you have fighting for you. We have the Lord God on our side and our cause is just and righteous."

"We have the Queen," Leney countered. "And here on Earth, I don't think there's anyone who can beat her. I've seen her tear apart the Black Captain's fleets. I've seen her grind his armies beneath the heel of her boot, and she crushed the Santas without even trying. They say she can think five steps ahead and has a plan for…"

"That's enough!" Troy barked. "I don't have time to listen to this garbage." He took a smirking Leney by the arm and hurried to the church. With fighting going on inside Highton, his adrenaline was pumping, and he barely felt the pain in his ankle. When the two reached the building, they saw nothing of Bob Duckwall except muddy prints that were mixed with black zombie blood.

The prints led up the steps and inside. The two followed them just past the foyer to where Bishop Gary Wojdan and Commander Walker stood together wearing matching looks of surprise at seeing the Knights Sergeant alive. Troy went to them, but before he knelt, he kicked Leney in the back of the legs and pulled him down to his knees.

Leney growled and was about to fill the silent church with curses, but then saw the stern look on the Commander's face and how his hands were clenched into fists. Some battles were not worth fighting and Leney figured this was one of them.

Wojdan held out his ringed hand to be kissed by Troy, saying, "This must be some story, Troy. Back from the dead, and look at this creature. Have you brought the prodigal son with you?"

"I heard about that one," Leney said. "One son takes off with all the money and then comes back when he spends it and is all broke, right? Only I never knew which one was the 'prodigal' son. Was he the good one or the bad?"

"Prodigal from the Greek," the Bishop explained, "meaning recklessly or extravagantly wasteful; utterly and shamelessly immoral."

Leney grinned and elbowed Troy. "Ha! That's me to a 'T.' They made a Bible story about me. So, where's my fatted calf or pork tenderloin, or whatever you guys got?"

Having kissed the Bishop's ring, Troy stood. Leney started to stand as well, but Troy put a heavy hand on his shoulder, holding him down. With the other hand he saluted his commander and gave a very brief report concerning what had happened to him. He finished by adding, "I also believe our current dispositions are incorrect. The area around where the wall stood is a barrier in itself. That should be our initial defensive line."

Walker frowned. Since becoming the Knights Commander, no one had ever second-guessed his tactical positioning. Still, he trusted Troy. "Have Treadwell move everyone up." Troy left at a run.

The Bishop watched him until the door snicked shut; he then turned a cold eye on the Corsair. "What are we to make of you? You're certainly not here in any diplomatic sense. Are you a hostage? An unwanted threat to the Queen's power? Or are you exactly what the Queen claims, an escort for a wounded man?"

"Holt seemed fine to me. Perhaps he's a spy?" Walker suggested.

"Hmm, I don't think the Queen would be so obvious."

Leney rolled his eyes and got to his feet. "Unlike you Catholics, my knees can't handle the kneeling. And no, I'm not a spy. What's there to spy on, anyway? With your wall down, it's just a matter of time. The zombies will get you, and they'll eat your kids and your women. It's not too late to stop all this. All you gotta do is kneel to the right person."

The Bishop felt a twinge deep inside. Whether it was guilt or doubt, he couldn't tell. "Maybe I was wrong about your diplomacy. You seem to speak with some authority, Captain Leney. Are you sanctioned by your Queen to treat with us?"

"Treat? Like in treaty? Well, I am her…" Leney was about to say that he was the Queen's second in command, however, he wondered if he really was. He spoke for most of the Corsairs, but not all of them. She still looked to McCartt when dealing with the Magnum Killers, and Steinmeyer with the Coos Bay Clan. She had Donna as her go-to when she spoke to the Bay people, and an oddly young girl named Lexi May for when she wanted to address the Santas.

Still, he was close enough to being her second in command. "I can accept your surrender and the sooner the better if you ask me."

Walker shook his head. "No. There will be no surrender. Every man among us has fought their share of zombies. This time will not be any different, so go back to your mistress and tell her exactly that."

Leney grimaced, his embarrassment coming out as anger. "I can't exactly. I was told I'd be picked up in the morning."

"That's just precious," Walker said, laughing. "You want all of us to think we're going to die but your queen forces you to stay? If you ask me, I think your queen wants you dead, which is one thing we have in common." The Bishop tut-tutted him, making the Knights Commander sigh. "Sorry about the joke; it was uncalled for. Still, I should warn you that I don't have the manpower to babysit you, so if you stay, it will be under lock and key."

This put Leney in a pickle. What if the Queen was trying to kill him in a way that no one would question? If he went back, she could demean his courage and ruin his reputation among the Corsairs even more. He'd be out of the inner circle and since he didn't have a ship anymore, he'd be just another flunky digging ditches or fighting her battles. If he stayed, he could end up someone's main course with no way to defend himself.

He had to find a middle ground. "Actually, my orders were to keep that Troy guy safe until morning. I can't very well do that chained to a wall."

Walker started laughing again, but sobered as he saw the Bishop considering the notion. "Excuse me, your Excellency, Knights Sergeant Troy Holt is our best fighter. He doesn't need a babysitter, especially one who might stab him in the back."

"I'm going to allow it," the Bishop answered. "I don't know much about warfare but the Queen seems to want to fight with some sort of honor. I don't think we can always assume the moral high ground, sometimes we have to earn it. Let Captain Leney fight."

Commander Walker bowed to the leader of their community. "He will fight, but he will fight as we fight." He held out his hand for Leney's weapons.

Leney felt like a child being asked to give up his favorite toys and squeezed the strap of his rifle to his chest with both hands. "No way. You want me to fight with a spear. Like, like some sort of savage?"

"No," Walker said, with a gleam in his eye. "We want you to fight like a man."

Chapter 32

"Run!" Stu cried in muted panic as the gargantuan zombie surged out of the water with a frightful roar. When it reached out to pull itself up the hill, it uprooted young pines with its bare hands. That didn't slow it down at all. It looked as though it would tear down the entire hill to get to them.

Mike ran. He just didn't know where he was running to exactly. Nowhere seemed safe. They couldn't go back up the hill; it would put them in the orchard, which was filled with more of the titanic battleship-sized zombies. They couldn't go to the right; that was where the Corsair had been hiding and when there was one Corsair, there were always more.

His only real choice was to the left, where the forest grew gradually thicker until it was as dark and overgrown as a jungle. He charged toward this, dodging trees and pushing through the vines. Quickly, he found himself blundering blindly through the dense woods; he had to practically swim through it all. Twigs and branches tore the homemade ghillie suit off his back, while twisted roots and hairy, brambly vines tripped him with every other step.

Behind him, he could hear Jenn making high frightened noises and begging him to hurry. Lagging behind her was Stu, grunting as he limped along as fast as he could.

Despite nature doing everything it could to stop him, Mike thrust on, moving along the slope of the hill, hoping to come across a path or a road or anything that would allow them to move faster.

The beast chasing them plowed through the growth, leaving a wide path of destruction behind it. Nothing seemed to slow it. And yet, after a few minutes, the sound of breaking branches and tree trunks snapping in half diminished. With a surge of hope, Mike chanced a look back and saw that the zombie had caught up with Stu.

The Hillman was desperately trying to keep one of the thicker trees between him and the monster. He was going round and round it, just managing to keep out of reach of the thing's long arms. Mike knew his friend would not last much longer and he did the only thing that he could think of. With a shout, he scooped up a broken branch, rushed at the zombie from behind and slammed the branch down on its head with all the strength in his arms.

The branch, which was as thick as his forearm, broke square in two as it split the beast's scalp. The inch of rock-hard bone beneath remained completely intact.

"Oh crap," Mike whispered as the zombie turned on him. Stu was behind the only tree big enough to slow the creature, so Mike couldn't play the same ring-around-the-rosy game. He had to find a new way to escape a creature that was faster than he was on the open ground, one that would never tire, and one that could bash its way through the forest with ease.

He couldn't fight it and he couldn't logically hope to get away by running, which left only illogically fleeing without any thought as to direction or outcome. The animal in him instinctively turned downhill where he would gain speed with the help of gravity.

The zombie gained that same bump in speed. What was more, it didn't care if it ran a stick into its eye or if it tripped and snapped an ankle. It came on, full steam and halfway down the hill, its claws fastened on the hood of Mike's coat and yanked him back. At that point, the two were barreling along, both basically out of control. The yank on Mike's hood bent back his upper body, while his frantic feet kept up their pace.

Something tore and he fell. The zombie was so close that it fell over the top of him. The two rolled in a strange mash of dead and nearly dead. Mike was crushed in foul-smelling darkness, then splashed with light and then crushed again. Pain shot through his chest as the air burst out of him in a whoosh. Light again, then his face was slapped by old wet leaves and then came the crushing sensation once more. Everything spun and spun until there was a long moment of free fall. It ended with a thunderous explosion of white, foaming water.

Jenn screamed his name, but the high, frightened sound was muffled and far away as he sank deep with a thousand pounds of thrashing zombie meat above him. Mike was so disoriented that at first, he didn't realize they were in the pond; he thought they had somehow made it back to the ocean. He tried to swim as he normally would have however a ripping pain in his left side kept him from extending his arms fully. His legs worked well enough and he began to kick toward the surface, with the zombie well within arm's reach.

Thankfully, it was partially turned away when they both broke the surface, which gave him a ten-second head start. That should have been enough. Zombies were terrible swimmers, while Mike was an excellent swimmer, normally that is. Just then he was limited to swimming with only half his body. It felt as though he had broken a rib or three. It was hard to tell; he just knew it hurt to move or to take a full breath, and he needed to do both.

When the beast finally saw him, it went crazy, thrashing at the water, clawing at it, doing anything it could to get to Mike and tear his head off. Slowly it ate into that head start. Mike's head began to spin, and he sank lower and lower in the water. He found it too difficult to propel himself both forward and upward.

Even without the zombie after him he might have drowned if the pond had been any bigger.

At the halfway point, he began to wonder why he was still going. Once he got out, he'd be in an even worse position. He'd be even slower compared to the zombie and any lead would evaporate in seconds. Supposedly drowning was an easy death—it sure would be easy enough to accomplish since he was halfway there.

He risked slowing even more to take the largest breath he could manage. He was about to yell over to Jenn and Stu to go on, when he saw Stu hurl a rock right at him! It missed, landing with a splash a few feet away. Now Jenn threw one and this came closer to hitting him. It was when Stu threw his next, again missing behind him that Mike realized they were throwing at the zombie.

It was a feeble attempt to save him that would never work. The rocks were so small that when they missed, it didn't notice and when one bounced off its huge dome of a head, it only made the thing more furious, which in turn made it faster. Jenn noticed the problem first and hissed for Stu to stop. She needed some way to slow the beast down. Uselessly, her mind turned to Jillybean and pictured the wild-haired girl making a zombie-proof net out of the vines around them. That would take more time than they had and the vines...

"Come on," Stu whispered, grabbing her hand and hurrying around the pond. The pond had started out as a deep fishing hole, which had been widened and turned into a retention pond designed to limit flooding in wet times and to act as a reservoir in dry ones. Mike was swimming in the general direction of an outflow pipe that looked big enough for a man to squeeze into, but not a monster like this one was.

When Jenn saw the pipe and realized where Stu was leading her, she hissed across the water. "There! Over there!"

Mike made a last-ditch attempt to get to the pipe before the zombie got to him. He did everything he could, but his head began to spin and his arms grew so heavy they felt like they were shackled with anchors attached to them—he wasn't going to make it. After the brief spurt, the zombie again gained on him in their torturously slow race and it looked like Mike was going to be caught just short of the pipe.

Stu wasn't going to let him die, even if he had to jump on top of the zombie and attack it with his knife in a poor imitation of Gunner. As much as he distrusted the gnarled and stunted man, Stu secretly hoped he would show up just then and save them all again. He stared around as he ran without seeing him. His eyes did fall on something that gave him an idea and some hope.

A long limb had broken from a tree and was hanging in the vines in a manner which made Stu feel as though it was being presented to him. He grabbed it and then scooped up the next longest one he could find as they ran. "Get in the water," he ordered Jenn when they got to the pipe.

"Huh?" She couldn't see what he was planning. The branches weren't very thick; they wouldn't do much to hurt the zombie. And getting in the water was crazy. It would only doom her along with Mike; she wasn't a good swimmer.

Stu didn't have time to explain things. He shoved her in and then waded in himself. Right away, the icy water had his injured leg cramping and his heart fluttering. "T-Take a b-branch in each hand. W-We'll form a chain," he stuttered. "You'll be in the middle."

Anger turned to excitement now that she saw what his plan was. He held onto the edge of the pipe with one hand and reached out as far as he could with the first branch. She swam out and took the end of his stick and then extended her own as far as she could toward Mike.

Mike was flagging badly. His body was squeezing in on itself, gradually forcing him into a fetal position. It wasn't a matter of pain or will power, he simply couldn't extend his torso, to allow him to do more than the doggy paddle or a mangled, abortive version of the side stroke. Neither was any better than the other and it wasn't long before he felt the zombie's fingers brushing against his feet. All it would take was one to hook him.

Jenn reached as far as she could, but it wasn't far enough. She let go of Stu's branch and swam out to meet Mike. She didn't know the first thing about being a lifeguard and her swimming skills were best described as adequate. But she had a branch and a fierce determination not to let Mike die.

She swam until he was close enough to grab it. When he did, she pulled with all her might and scissor kicked with her legs. She was too strong and yanked the branch out of his hands. There was no give up in her and she tried again. This time he held on but because of the weight difference between them she found herself going hand over hand closer to him *and* the zombie!

Somehow, she had made things worse. The branch was now in the way and they were too close to each other to really swim properly. "Go," he whispered, breathlessly. "Leave! Hurry. I'll get to…" The hood of his coat was suddenly yanked back. His head came along with it.

The zombie had finally got a hold of him.

Jenn did the only thing she could, she took the branch and jabbed it like a spear into the creature's face, running it up into its right eye socket and bursting the dark orb like a swollen grape. The zombie didn't seem to notice the grey pus-like substance dripping down its cheek. It was trying to pull Mike into its open mouth and bite his head off, but Mike grabbed the branch and pushed back. The zipper of his coat bit cruelly into his throat, cutting off his circulation, and in seconds the day began to dim, and he was suddenly disconnected as if he were falling asleep.

His hands began to slip and Jenn grabbed him, matching her paltry strength against the zombie's. She leaned back and heaved with all her might; the branch bit into her one hand while the coat was slowly pulled from her other hand. She screamed in frustration as her hands grew weaker and weaker. At the end, she crushed her eyelids down tight, not wanting to see what was going to happen.

In the midst of her scream, there was a tearing sound that she feared was Mike's head being torn from his shoulders, but when she opened her eyes she saw that his previously torn hood had ripped right off.

The zombie stuffed the hood into its mouth, while Mike laid across the branch, gagging and gulping in air. Jenn knew that swimming was now out of the question for him. She pulled him to her end of the branch and his weight nearly sent her under—as long as she held him, swimming would be out of the question for her as well.

They were barely managing to stay afloat when the monster began thrashing the water again, trying to finish them off. All Jenn could do was fend him off with the branch and kick madly to stay afloat.

"You're almost there," Stu said, from behind her. She glanced back and saw that the zombie was moving all three of them steadily closer to the pipe. A crazy laugh burst from her and she found the energy to kick harder.

They were very close when the zombie broke the branch in half with one of its flailing swings. "Mike! Reach for the stick!" she urged, pushing him towards Stu. "Come on, get it!" He seemed more dead than alive but still managed to find the end of the stick and hold on as Stu pulled him in. "Get him in the pipe," Jenn ordered, as she swam for shore. Without Mike's weight she suddenly felt free and light as a feather.

She got to shore so quickly that she was in time to help hoist Mike into the pipe. Like an earthworm looking for a place to hide from the sun, he moved sluggishly inside it. The zombie was almost to shore by then. Stu picked her up next and his adrenaline must have been pumping like mad because he practically threw her inside. She immediately started shoving Mike further on, hissing for him to hurry.

Stu waited until the last second to get inside with them. He didn't like the idea of all three of them climbing into a pipe that might not lead anywhere. With the zombie struggling along the muddy bottom of the pond, Stu crawled inside the pipe and wiggled on his stomach until he collided with Jenn's feet.

Behind him the zombie stuck its head inside the opening and breathed a plume of horror over them. The ghastly stench had Stu choking and pushing at Jenn's feet. "Go. Move. Please." She somehow got Mike slithering up the pipe and just in time. The zombie withdrew its head and stuck an outrageously long arm into the pipe and began to paw and scrape about, searching for Stu's wet boots.

Even with pulling in his legs as far as he could, it was close. When the zombie failed to catch hold of him, it tried to stick both its arm and head inside. Grey flesh peeled off its shoulder in one long skein like someone was peeling an apple. The top of its scalp was sheared right off

224

and black blood welled all around the edge of the opening. And still it kept coming, forcing its bulk into the small opening.

"Hurry, Mike. We have a Winnie the Pooh situation down here."

"Winnie the what?" Mike looked back and all he saw was the pale blur of Jenn's face surrounded by pure darkness. "What's that mean?"

Jenn had the same question but when she cranked her head back, she couldn't see anything. The dark was sinister and felt unnervingly heavy, as if the weight of the world was bearing down on the pipe, looking to crush it and bury them alive. She turned her head back so quickly that she thumped her temple on the concrete. It was worth the pain to see the trickle of light slipping past Mike.

"Get going," she begged.

Mike began to inch along the pipe again. Pain radiated out of his chest and every movement made it worse, but he could hear the fear in her voice. "It'll be okay, Jenn. We'll be fine when we get out. I can see the opening. It's only another fifty feet."

His reassurances helped, and he kept them up even as the bars over the far end of the tunnel began to firm up in his vision. *They're old and rusty*, he told himself. *They'll break. Or its part of a gate and its open.* He was wrong on all accounts. The bars were thick and strong, and set only inches apart. In vain, he gave them a shake.

"What's wrong?" Jenn asked, straining to look past Mike. He took up most of the pipe, but when he moved his head to the side she could see the tops of the bars. "Oh no," she breathed.

"Oh yes," a hissing voice, laughed. It was Gunner. He appeared on the other side of the bars. She could just make out his angry dark eyes and part of his burned scalp. "Looks like you've got yourself trapped. I could help, but..."

"But what?" Mike said. He meant for it to come out as a tough growl; however, he still couldn't take more than wheezing sips of air.

Gunner ran a dirty finger along the bars. "But I don't want to. Not for free at least. I saved you guys and what thanks do I get? You run off the first chance you get. Not very Christian of you. No, if you want me to save you, you'll have to tell me your story and you're going to start by telling me everything you know about Jillybean."

Chapter 33

"Jillybean?" Mike asked, feigning ignorance. "Th-that's an odd name."

His transparent lie earned him a snide laugh from Gunner. "It sure is. You know what's more odd? I have it on good authority that you three were traveling with her. You snuck out of Bainbridge weeks ago. It's odd you didn't remember that."

"Oh, her. Her name was Jillian. That's what she liked to be called."

"Uh-huh," Gunner replied, dryly. "Let's talk about her then. Where did you go? What did you do and where is she now?"

Before Mike could say a word, Stu's voice rolled up from the tunnel like the voice of an angry god. "Don't tell him a thing!"

Mike pointed behind him. "He is the leader, so maybe we'll tell you what you want to know, if you get us out of here. I think that's a good compromise. What do you say?"

Gunner reached up under the cloth and scratched his face with his good hand. "I'll have to think on it for a while. I'll come back in an hour and let you know." He stood and stretched his deformed body, gave Mike a wink and disappeared.

After a few seconds, Mike whispered Gunner's name without receiving an answer. "He'll be back," he assured Jenn. "Or maybe the zombie will give up and go away." To make that a possibility, they all quieted down. Jenn fought her new found claustrophobia, which had spiked when Gunner left. At first, she concentrated on the light sneaking past Mike. She made it her whole focus, which didn't do a damned thing. After ten minutes, it still felt like the world was crushing down on her.

It even felt like the pipe was shrinking, closing in around her. This grew worse as a shriek built up inside of her. She tried counting to take her mind off the fact she was buried alive. Then she tried tracing her father's face on the pipe above her. That stopped when a piece of the cement broke off. To keep from screaming, she bit down on her tongue.

It was Mike who saved her from going mad. She began to worry over him far more than herself as his breathing did not improve over the miserable course of the long hour. He wheezed constantly no matter which of the many positions he tried to get comfortable with. Nothing could make the bare cement comfortable. Worse than the hardness of the cement was the cold that emanated up from the pipe. All three were soaking wet and although it was a forty-eight degree day, inside the dark tube it was ten degrees cooler.

They were all shivering by the time Gunner came back and lounged by the opening of the pipe, wrapped in his ugly crow feather and fur cape. "I've come to a decision," he told them without bothering to moderate the volume of his voice. The beast let out a fearful roar, which he ignored. "Here's my deal: I'm going to let you tell me everything I want to hear and only then will I let you out. You can either tell me now or if you're feeling exceptionally tough I can come back in two hours. By then, it'll be downright chilly. Don't you worry about me I have a fire going in my place. I'll be fine."

More than anything, Mike wanted to give in. Instead, he lowered his head and closed his eyes. Jenn was even more desperate, but also said nothing, less out of loyalty to Jillybean and more because she cared about Stu and knew he still loved her. If anyone was going to say anything, it would be only if he allowed it.

"Go ahead, Mike," the Hillman said. Gunner wasn't bluffing. He would wait exactly two more hours and Stu was afraid what shape they would be in then. He'd heard Mike's wheezing and Jenn's teeth chattering. His own hands were painfully numb, and his feet were like blocks of wood. After two hours everything would be far worse. Mike would likely add a phlegmy cough to his wheeze and Jenn would be borderline hypothermic. Stu knew he would give in then, for their sakes, which, in the end, would make their suffering pointless.

Mike began his story with the *Calypso* and the rescue in the San Francisco Bay of Remy and Jeff Battaglia, which led to Aaron Altman losing an arm and William Trafny getting shot in Sacramento. He talked about Jenn's visions and how she slew the giant zombie, Frankenstein that everyone had been deathly afraid of for years.

Gunner kept saying, "Uh-huh, uh-huh, then what?" He seemed to want Mike to hurry, so Mike spoke quickly, hitting the highlights: The stormy trip north, the crazy people of Cathlamet who shot Stu, meeting Jillybean and how Neil Martin basically hijacked the *Calypso*.

Gunner interrupted. "Tell me about this Neil. Everything about him."

"He's small," Mike began and then went on to tell Gunner the little he knew about the man. This led to questions about Deanna and then to Emily. The answer elicited a rumbling sound from Gunner that was as close to an evil purr that Mike had ever heard.

"Did the girl mention any hobbies?" Gunner asked. "Fishing or boating, or anything like that?"

Jenn answered quickly, her voice rising enough to aggravate the zombie. "No! She's too young to leave the island, you sick…"

Stu squeezed her ankle hard enough to make her wince and to bring her to her senses. He didn't want to anger Gunner and risk being trapped in the pipe forever.

"She didn't mention anything," Mike said, hurriedly. "Sorry. Where was I? Oh, we had lost the *Calypso*…" He went on, describing how they stole the *Saber* and the chase that followed. After that came the first battle with the Corsairs, which he quickly blurred with Jillybean becoming queen of the Sacramentans. He was eagerly telling about the *Floating Fortress* when Gunner pulled him back.

"Did you call her the 'Mad' Queen? Forget the damned boats for a moment and tell me about that."

Mike explained about her being crazy. He was painfully truthful which made it all the worse. She came across sounding more evil than anything else and he finished up by saying, "But she's not all bad."

"No one ever is," Gunner replied, softly, with what Mike took to be regret in his voice. "Go on, but if you mention the different types sails any of these boats had or their damned rigging one more time, I'm going to leave you here until dark." Mike did his best, though he thought his story suffered especially when he wasn't able to describe the final battle aboard the *Saber* and how he had tacked counter to the other boats, holding the edges of his flaming mainsail in his bare hands.

When he finished, Gunner sat quietly for a long time, gazing westward towards Grays Harbor and the lair of the Black Captain. Finally, Mike asked in a weak voice, "Are you going to let us out? I told you everything."

"Hmm? Let you out? That's a tough question."

Mike didn't see what was so tough about it and wanted to remind Gunner of his promise. He didn't, however. He did his best to keep a friendly, neutral look on his face, knowing that promises meant different things to different people, especially to Corsairs. Although Gunner claimed not to be one, he was still clearly in league with them.

Five achingly long minutes passed before Gunner made his decision: "Yes, I think I will let you out on the condition that you three will do exactly what I say, when I say it. If you don't, I will leave you to fend for yourselves, which means you will die. Agreed?"

"Of course, of course," Mike said, hoping he didn't sound too relieved. "We can do that. Whatever you say."

Gunner smirked and then disappeared from view. Mike assumed that he had a hacksaw or something to cut the bars. Gunner had a simpler way out. He killed the zombie blocking the tunnel by driving his knife into its back and through its heart.

Having a ruptured heart only seemed to annoy the monster. With a scream of rage that partially deafened Stu, it yanked its huge body out of the pipe and promptly fell back into the pond, where it splashed about like an enormous toddler. Gunner looked to be in no hurry to kill the thing. He patiently waited for it to get itself turned around and then, rather casually, used the branch Jenn had tossed aside to puncture its one remaining eye. The zombie was harmless after that. It splashed and moaned, moving off to the left. Gunner didn't give it a second glance as he watched Stu worm his way out of the pipe.

They had to back out with undignified wiggles, and frozen as they were, they came out feeling prematurely aged. Stu was the oldest of the three at twenty-one, but his joints ached like that of a seventy-year-old who'd spent the night on a friend's couch. Because of his broken ribs,

Mike was even worse off and Gunner had to reach into the pipe and drag him out by the foot.

"You guys look like crap," Gunner blurted out. "Lucky for you, I don't judge people on their looks. Now, stay close and keep quiet."

Keeping quiet wasn't easy. They were exhausted, wet and shivering. Jenn walked hunched over like a crone and stumbled over everything in her path. Mike walked, holding his arms in close as if he were hugging himself; his ribs were so sore he couldn't scratch his nose without wincing.

After ten minutes of misery, Mike asked, "Where's this house you mentioned? Remember, you said you had a cozy fire going?"

"Oh, right. That was more of what I like to call an inducement."

"You mean a lie," Stu snarled.

Gunner turned on him and the two matched hard stares for a few seconds until Gunner shrugged and said, "No, it was an inducement. In case you forgot, it was you who put yourselves in that pipe. I was just trying to get you out. My fee for the service was information, which I knew you'd give me eventually. I was just trying to save you unnecessary pain and discomfort. You *should* be thanking me."

Stu dropped his eyes and mumbled, "You're right, thanks."

"Yeah, I am right. Even if there was a house or cabin within miles of us, a fire would be stupid. You have enemies nearby, or have you forgotten?"

They had all forgotten the Corsair who had sicced the zombie on them in the first place. "I remember," Stu said, leaving off the word "now" which would have been more accurate.

"Sure," was all Gunner said, before he turned and began marching them at a torrid pace. He led them through the hills, always keeping to the lower slopes when he could and when they had to cross any peaks, he found places where the slopes were tree-covered, and even then, he had them creep from shadow to shadow. Although they saw many zombies foraging for food, only once did one of them see the group.

It had been squatting behind the trunk of an old hoary elm, eating the remains of a crow. When it saw them it roared, spewing out a bizarre cloud of black feathers. The zombie was such an unusual sight that even Gunner was caught flatfooted as it charged.

Stu ducked around a tree with Mike following after. Jenn was about to go next, when Gunner grabbed her. "Cause a distraction," he ordered her and then basically flung her toward the zombie.

"A distraction?" she cried. He was already disappearing into the forest. The only distraction Jenn could think of was to run away as fast as she could. She sprinted away like a deer and, because of his love for her and his foolish notions of heroism, Mike ran, too.

In this case, heroism equaled being zombie bait. He tried to keep up, but couldn't with his broken ribs, and very quickly, he replaced Jenn as the distraction. At six and a half feet, it was one of the smaller zombies they had seen, and it was missing a hand. Still, it had all the ferocious rage of its bigger brothers and raced after Mike, its black eyes staring with greedy hunger at the young man. It didn't see Gunner leap out from behind a tree with his axe swinging like a scythe.

The razor-sharp blade took off the zombie's leg at the knee and the beast went rolling and sprawling, stopping at Mike's feet. Mike had stumbled when Gunner appeared and was so stunned by the suddenness of the attack that he didn't back up quickly enough. Heedless of its missing leg and the jets of black blood shooting from its stump, the beast grabbed Mike's ankle. Gunner calmly chopped the thing's arm off at the elbow.

"Let's go," Gunner growled, and began marching again.

The hand was still clinging to his ankle even without a body attached when Mike kicked it off and hurried after the others.

As before, Gunner pushed them to their limit and they were stumbling from exhaustion when they finally found a small community tucked away in the hills. Gunner left them hiding in the woods while he scouted to make sure the village was deserted.

He wasn't gone long. "Let's get that fire going that I promised you," he said, grinning behind his scarf. They didn't know if he was serious or not, but not only did he get the fire going, he also fed them and fetched water. As they ate he watched them, especially Jenn. "So, you are a queen?" he asked, after the silence became tense. "Should I bow?"

Stu glared and Mike began to get as huffy as his broken ribs would allow, which amounted to only strident breathing. "Relax," Gunner said, laughing at them. "I was just joking. It is interesting that you were a queen even for a little while. I wonder what the Black Captain would think about that? It's my guess that he probably doesn't know…yet." This wiped the glare off of Stu's face and Mike turned even paler than he had been. Gunner chuckled again and then stood to stretch his twisted body. "I've got work to do. Don't stay up too late."

Without any other explanation, he left. When she was sure he was gone, Jenn leaned toward the others and whispered, "What do we do? If the Black Captain finds out about me…" She swallowed loudly, unable to go on.

"We don't do anything," Stu said. "I don't know what his game is, but I get the feeling he's looking for a reason to turn us over to the Corsairs. We should just go with the flow, act nice and hope for the best."

"Maybe Jenn should look for a sign," Mike suggested. "I'd prefer to put my hope in her rather than in him."

Stu's initial gut-reaction was to wave away the idea, until he realized Mike was right: it was foolish to trust Gunner. "Okay," he said, giving his permission. He looked over at Jenn; she seemed so small and young—and taken back at the suggestion.

"You guys know I can't just make the future come to me," she said, defensively. She hated being put on the spot like this. The pressure to "see" something made her worry that she was just throwing out guesses or seeing false signs. Signs had to come to her. And in this case, they didn't. She stared into the fire and got nothing. She went outside into the cold night to gaze up at the stars and got nothing. She even studied the shadows of the nearby trees to see if they spoke to her. She got nothing.

"Maybe I'll see something in a dream," she told the two when she got back inside. Unfortunately, she slept uneasily and her dreams were so fragmented that she could only remember snatches of them: trees, the dark pipe closing on her, light rimming the end of the pipe in gold, and leaves falling. Five minutes after waking up, she could only remember the gold circle at the end of the pipe. It made her wonder how anyone could pour cement with such circular perfection.

She was still picturing the pipe when Gunner stomped inside bringing with him delicate fingers of chilled air which crept around them, making Jenn shiver. He also brought with him six small eggs and four partridges. Without asking, he shoved Mike away from the fire and began stripping the birds.

Even with only one hand, he made quick work of the carcasses. As he worked, he tossed a few of the small bones Jenn's way. "Bones for rolling," he said, with a wink. "You're a witch, aren't you? You see signs, right?"

He'd been eavesdropping on them the night before. None of them felt the least bit of surprise. "When they present themselves," she replied, shortly.

As always, he scoffed at her answer. "If you're going to put your trust in signs, you might as well go all in." He tossed another bone in front of her. She didn't touch it. She was not nearly so averse to touching his cooking. He made thin omelets that were deliciously gamey but small, and Mike's stomach growled after he had finished his.

"I'm with you there," Gunner told him. "I know where there are some apple trees. It's not meat but it's better than nothing."

They stepped out into a bright cold morning. Jenn felt the chill of it seep deep. Mike held out his hand, a gentle plume of winter breath coming out of his open mouth. It hung in front of him for just a second before dissipating. It hadn't blown away, which was strange since the branches overhead were swaying as if there were ghosts dancing in the trees. It had to be ghosts because there was no wind.

"What is it?" Mike asked.

Her only answer was to shush him. There was a sign in her presence and she was missing it. She spun in a circle and the high branches danced. They were barren of leaves and looked like spindly bones. Like thin finger bones. "Or chicken bones," she whispered to herself. "I'll be right back." She spun and ran back inside the little house to the fireplace where she found a neat little stack of bones. They had been stripped.

Feeling embarrassed, she grabbed them, stuffed them in her coat pocket and hurried out of the house, only to run smack into Gunner. She could see partially under his mask; the flesh of his throat looked like dripping melted cheese.

"Gonna roll them bones, aren't you?" he asked, wheezing and laughing. "Go ahead. I can wait."

"No. Not with you watching. Or anyone. I'll do it later."

This earned her another laugh and a shrug. Just like the day before, he began hiking at an exhausting pace. By ten, Mike was dizzy from the pain. Gunner sneered, calling him a "delicate boy."

Furious, Jenn called a halt and helped Mike remove his shirt, so she could inspect the injury. There was a wide purple and blue band across the left side of his chest. She gasped when she saw it, while Stu said, "Hmmm."

"Hold on," Gunner said. "Supposedly, the *Girl Doctor* was training you. What did she tell you to do in this situation?"

He was testing her. "We never talked about it," Jenn admitted.

A shrug told her she had passed. "If you had, she would've told you there's not much you can do except pop some pills." He reached under his cloak and produced a bottle of large white pills. He shook out three into the crook of his left arm, and when Mike hesitated, he swallowed them himself. "Come on, doctor's orders," he said, and shook out three more.

Mike swallowed them and then stood there waiting to see if he would start frothing at the mouth.

"They aren't poison, boy." With that he turned and marched on. They ate a bellyful of apples an hour later and while Stu and Gunner were filling a pack with more of them, Jenn went off by herself and rolled the bones. She had no idea what she was doing. She didn't know how many to use or if she was supposed to roll them like dice or put them in a teacup and plop it down.

And she definitely didn't know how to read them. Was there an art to it? A science? A code that could be looked up in a book?

Feeling a little silly, she picked out five bones at random and dropped them in the dirt. Next, she turned her head this way and that like an inquisitive dog, trying to see a pattern or a shape or a secret message. They were just bones: two tiny neck bones, what might have been a wing bone, and two very small "drumsticks."

They had fallen into what could only be described as a soft pentagon shape. "More of a circle, really."

"Do you see something?" Mike asked in a soft whisper.

Perhaps because she hadn't, she was suddenly embarrassed. She grabbed the bones and stuck them back in her pocket. Even though he was pale, with scratches on his forehead and a whopping big bruise on one cheek, he was still so handsome that Jenn felt inadequate and wished she could be something more for him. Something special. But the bones weren't showing her their secrets.

"No, nothing. I probably did it wrong."

"Then try again. I bet this sort of thing takes practice. I'll keep guard over you." The only thing he had to guard anyone with was a sturdy branch. "Go on. I trust you."

She thought those simple words were one of the nicest things anyone had ever said to her and she couldn't help the smile she wore when she spilled the bones back into the dirt. Again, she couldn't read them. They spilled into almost the same shape as before, except one of the bones was a few inches away from the rest, pointing at Mike.

"No," she whispered, "That's a stick." She plucked it out and looked again. "Does that look like a circle to you?" she asked Mike.

"I think so. What's it mean?"

By itself it meant nothing, but with the shards of her dream and the wind cavorting around her, high in the trees, she knew there was something trying to speak to her. "I think it means we're on the right track. We're going back to Bainbridge. We're going full circle."

Chapter 34

Mark Leney simply could not understand how he came to be fighting for his enemies against the very same zombie army he had helped to create, while straddling the broken remnants of a wall he had helped to destroy. It was something of a cosmic joke and he was the punchline.

What was more insane, was that he had maneuvered himself into the role of protector of a man who clearly did not need protecting.

Knights Sergeant Troy Holt was a scary man when wielding one of the Guardian's long spears. Sometimes he spun it as if he were leading a parade. Sometimes he waved it around as if it were as light as a conductor's baton. When he wished, it was as supple as a willow reed and at other times, it seemed as rigid and as hard as rock.

Leney, on the other hand, never quite got the hang of spear fighting. First off, he thought it was stupid to fight like a caveman when there were perfectly good guns available. And secondly, the damned things were heavy and ungainly. Yes, he could jab the spear with some efficiency, but unlike the others, he couldn't swing it with any hope the blade at the end would do anything beyond causing useless gashes in the zombies that lumbered out of the night.

When he tried to hack open a neck or cut through the vertebrae from behind, he always missed. There'd be an embarrassing *DONK!* sound, and then painful vibrations would run down the length of metal and into his hands. When that happened, Leney always felt as though he were part of a cartoon and if it had been quiet enough he was sure he would've heard a whimsical *bonnnng*.

But it was not quiet. The night had grown steadily louder. At first, the zombies came in dribs and drabs, and the killing was shockingly quick. As Knights distracted the charging beasts with their flashing spears and what looked like little flags, others would close in from the sides and back, striking savagely, cutting arteries and hacking tendons. A dozen Knights could bring down the average zombie in seconds.

That was all well and good; however, the Queen was not content to send her army forth in dribs and drabs. She sent them in waves that tested the mettle of the Knights as it had never been tested before. When the first wave broke along the line, the noise, the screams, and the inhuman roars were enough to cause even a hard man like Leney to waver. He had not heard anything like it since the early days of the apocalypse when the zombies swarmed in the millions and the army had thrown every ounce of ordinance they possessed into the hordes. The entire world had trembled from the fury of the fighting.

As more of the beasts staggered into the line of warriors, some men began to back away. Leney was among these. "Steady," Troy ordered, in a soft voice that carried through the violence of the battle. Somehow he could sense when his men were losing their nerve. "God will prevail." God was always his answer and because of that, he was utterly without fear.

Leney did not have any faith in a god he didn't even believe in— and he was scared out of his mind.

The very idea of fighting eight-foot tall, seven-hundred pound, enraged demons using only pointy sticks was ludicrous. They felt no pain, no matter how many spears were driven into them. Their strength was out of all proportion to their size; at one point, a single smallish female had driven back five fully grown men, whose combined mass doubled hers. Each of the men had driven their spears into her chest up to what they called the "Boar Guard." The guard was comprised of two jutting wings of metal at the end of the spear blade, designed to keep the zombie from working its way down the shaft of the spear and attacking the Knights.

The female beast ignored the spears and kept coming, bulling the men back until one had set the butt of his weapon into the ground. The steel spear bent into a silver arc and even though the boar guard tore a gaping hole straight through the brute, it kept coming.

And it had been a small one! The largest males weighed over nine-hundred pounds and could bend spears in half with a swat of their huge hands. These juggernauts were unstoppable, and it was best not to try. Leney was not far from one when it hit the line, throwing men aside like rag-dolls. To protect the injured, an entire squad closed in with weapons leveled. In seconds, only four of the eleven men remained standing.

"Idiots!" Leney hissed.

Troy heard and snatched the spear from his hand. "Shut up and fight, or go hide with the children, *Corsair!*" He spat the word, his chest heaving, his armor and spear splashed with blood. To the Guardians, being called a Corsair was the ultimate insult.

Leney was not above hiding and would have if he thought it would have done any good. No, he needed to fight and be seen fighting. If he had any faith, it was in the Queen. She knew what she was doing, even if no one else did. She had said she would see Troy in the morning which meant she didn't intend for the town to be overrun. If this was true, Leney couldn't hide or shirk his duty. He would fight, he just wasn't going to be stupidly heroic about it.

He picked his spots, always coming in from behind the beasts, or always making sure that there were Knights in front of him when there was a headlong rush. Sometimes he would "accidentally" stumble when everyone else was attacking, and at other times he would let out a bellowing way cry as he got in the last strike that would fell a beast already in the process of dying.

This worked for him for the first few hours and he was still relatively fresh when the night was just starting to fail and the lowest edge of the sky to the east was beginning to glow. It was then that the waves of zombies reached their peak. Hundreds came at once and no longer were the Knights able to use their swarming tactics. It became a bloody hand-to-hand battle where the dead piled up in mounds. Leney kept as close to Troy as he could. The Knights Sergeant attracted so much attention, exhorting his men, whirling his spear, and calling on God, that the dead barely saw the lurking Corsair until he would flash in and jab.

The Knights Commander threw everything he had into the fight, but his men and women were exhausted. They were hurled back to the moat. While they leapt across the seven-foot wide ditch, the zombies fell right in. This allowed the Knights to rally. They turned on their foes and butchered the beasts as they struggled in the muddy water.

There were so many of them that it wasn't long before the moat was filled with the hacked-apart remains of the dead. The water overflowed and the undead were able to tread over their unmoving brothers.

Now the fight became desperate. The Knights gave ground when they had to, falling back when the ferocity or the numbers of undead was too much. They would fight and slay, and then come roaring back to the line, but always with fewer men or with bent spears, or with weary lines etching their faces.

Leney knew they weren't going to last much longer. So far, their armor, their bravery and their unmatched fighting prowess had kept their casualties lighter than he would have believed. He had seen men trampled, men thrown twenty-feet or more, men raked and bitten—and he saw them get back up and keep on fighting.

But they weren't going to last. Exhaustion was setting in and slowing them down. Worse for the defenders, was that when the light of the new day swept over the battlefield, the nearly night-blind zombies would be able to see the Knights perfectly. Even worse, in Leney's view, he would no longer be able to lurk.

What the light would bring wasn't lost on Commander Walker. "Weapons free!" he bellowed. "Rifles at the ready! Every fourth man!" The depleted squads knew their business and the best shooters pulled their rifles from their backs. The firing began seconds later. Three spearmen would engage a zombie, while the fourth man would try to put a bullet into its brain. It was not an easy task and on average it took slightly more than two bullets to kill the beasts.

Leney, who was an excellent shot, snatched an M16A3 from a wounded Knight. "Sorry, kid. I'll give it back. Corsair's honor." It wasn't a kid, it was Knights Reserve Commander Jennifer Edgerton. She'd had her left arm yanked from its socket. "I mean, sorry, ma'am," Leney said, when he saw she wasn't a boy under all her armor. "You Knights can't shoot worth a lick."

He brought the rifle to his shoulder and didn't need to "scan" for a target, there were zombies everywhere. Some far too close for his liking. Had it still been dark, he would have slunk away to fire from further back. He couldn't do that now. Besides, Edgerton had fallen and, perhaps because he'd been fighting alongside actual Knights, Leney felt the tiniest spark of chivalry. He stood his ground and fired.

Seven kills in ten shots.

"Nice shooting," Edgerton said. She had managed to sit up, though it looked as if it had taken everything out of her.

Leney didn't notice; he was staring uncomprehendingly at the rifle. The bolt was back and the chamber was empty. At first, he had thought it had jammed, but now he saw it was out of bullets. "What the hell? You only had ten bullets in this thing. Gimme the rest of your ammo." He had his dirty paw out.

"That's all I have. Unlike you Corsairs, we don't have unlimited bullets." Grunting with pain, she turned on her side, struggled to a knee and pushed herself up. The world spun and she teetered. Leney didn't help her. He stood there, sneering, not really at her, but at the entire notion of not having enough ammo. It was repellent to him.

"So, that's why you guys use spears. I thought it was because you were stupid when really it's because you're weak."

Edgerton's eyes narrowed into angry slits. "We aren't weak. Now give me my gun, please."

He could have kept it if he wished; she was in no position to take it from him. "Then I guess that leaves only being stupid." He gave her the weapon and promptly turned his back on her, thinking to himself that the Queen hadn't completely wasted her time sending him with Troy.

Standing back, he began making a quick count. There were about four-hundred men with rifles. "So about four-thousand rounds between them all. And that number is going fast."

The dead were being brought down by the score. They came in herds, like stampeding buffalo, making the earth shake. The shooting picked up in tempo and the Guardians' reserve of bullets dwindled with every shot.

From the Knight's limited view, for every dead zombie, two seemed to rush up to replace it.

This was, in fact, not the case. The Queen had been waiting for the Knights to resort to using rifles and the moment they had she stopped shooting her flares; in essence calling off her attack. Of course, even she couldn't control zombies so easily and they kept filtering in for the next hour until the rifles were once more set aside and spears were taken up by weary Knights.

Finally, at about eight in the morning, the last of the zombies was slain and the survivors of the long night could look about in stunned horror. Thousands of the creatures had been destroyed. Their stinking, bloated bodies were everywhere and, sadly, among them were fallen Knights. As the men gazed about with tears in their red eyes, Bishop

Wojdan and his four priests marched onto the battlefield and began administering Last Rites to the fallen.

Troy knelt to pray and in seconds everyone but Leney was kneeling as well. So as not to look too out of place, he plopped down on the muddy ground and stuck his legs out. He didn't have any idea what they were praying for. "Mercy from the Queen, maybe. That's what I'd be asking for if I was them."

Leney began to trace the outline of a zombie footprint. The thing was over two feet long and right in the middle of it was a human shoe print that, in comparison, looked like it belonged to a toddler. The individual prayers were followed by a group prayer in which the Knights formed impromptu kneeling circles. Leney didn't join. He lay back in the mud, closed his eyes and fell asleep. Troy kicked him awake a few minutes later. "About time," he grumbled.

Troy glared. "It's morning, Corsair, you can leave now."

"Whoa! Where's all that Christian love I keep hearing about? And where's the thanks? I killed a freakin' gob of those things. If I hadn't, who knows how many more of you woulda been killed."

The glare on Troy's face faltered. "You are right. You fought by my side with what passes for bravery among the Corsairs. Breakfast is the least I can do. First we must check on the wounded."

Strangely, at least to Leney, there weren't many wounded Knights among them. During the battle, he had been oblivious to the young women of the stretcher teams who had been running here and there among the zombies and the soldiers, scooping up the more seriously wounded.

The pair found the hospital crowded, and were not let in. Commander Walker was sitting on the steps outside. One arm was in a sling and his face drooped with exhaustion.

"What's the final count?" Troy asked him.

A long sigh escaped the man before he answered: "Twenty-seven dead, thirty-one wounded *and* infected, twenty-two seriously wounded and not infected. It could have been worse."

"Almost a fifth of us," the Knights Sergeant said, in a whisper. No one looked at Leney, which was good since he didn't know exactly what he was supposed to be feeling. If the Queen thought that he was going to suddenly get all chummy-chummy with them just because they had fought together, she was going to be disappointed. In his view, they had been chumps before the fight and were still chumps now. Despite his general dislike for them, he wanted to give them advice: *Give up now, because it's only going to get worse.* He didn't bother. They still didn't understand what they were up against. If they had, they would've been begging him to intercede on their behalf.

"She'll be coming soon," he told them, gesturing in the direction of the low sun.

Troy peered east past the bodies and the ruined wall. Somehow he managed to look handsome even with the ash and blood covering his face. "Is she coming to fight?"

Walker knew better. "She'll be coming to demand our surrender." He sighed and stood. "We should get cleaned up. I don't want to look like scrubs when I tell her she can go pound sand."

Leney rolled his eyes. "I wouldn't if I were you. Listen to me. All this, the wall and this little fight, that was her being nice. She was just toying with you. She could have crushed you if she wanted to."

"Then why didn't she?" Troy asked. He was too tired for outrage or any back and forth. He wanted the truth.

Leney wasn't going to give him the real truth, which was that Jillybean was popping pills like they were candy to keep her other, more violent, personalities from taking over. So far, he had counted four other people in her head, and two of them were frightfully dangerous: Eve, the chaotic evil girl who couldn't go ten minutes without setting something on fire or lighting off a bomb, and Ernest who fell under the lawful evil alignment. He was a perfectly ordered, perfectly cool, perfectly logical murderer. They both frightened Leney.

But they couldn't know that about her, yet.

"Because she doesn't like to kill her people, but that doesn't mean she won't. I guarantee that if you piss her off you'll all be dead by this time tomorrow. Your only choice is to surrender."

His sincerity radiated past his hideously scarred and tattooed face and they believed him, though neither knew what to do about it. Ultimately, the decision to fight or surrender was the Bishop's.

Troy walked back to his little apartment in brooding silence. He was kind enough to find a fresh set of clothes for Leney, and even made him a somewhat grainy sandwich, made from hand-milled wheat and chicken salad. Leney was still wolfing it down when there came a cry from the lookouts.

The Queen was coming.

Chapter 35

No one knew whether she was coming to fight, or to bargain, or just to gloat over the effects of her diabolical handiwork. Walker wasn't going to take any chances and ordered the Knights back to their battle stations.

Leney accompanied Troy to his station where they discovered that his recon team was down to just him, Chris Baker and Bob Duckwall. Eric Gothier had one of his arms torn off and had died before a stretcher team could get to him, and Shamus McGuigan had been bitten by one of the beasts and had lost most of one shoulder. He was still alive, but it was now only a waiting game to see if the infection took him.

Sometimes it didn't. His chances were somewhere around one in ten-thousand.

The three of them, with Leney in tow, went to where the front gate once stood. Now there was only debris and corpses. Flies buzzed around in great black clouds and vultures wheeled silently above.

Duckwall, who had a pair of binoculars pressed to his face, informed everyone within earshot that, "She's putting up a tent!" He looked again and said, "Well not her, exactly. She has a small company of soldiers. Yep. That's a tent and…and…Lord bless me, she has zombies with her. They're just standing there, not attacking people or nothing."

Practically everyone turned to Leney. He could only shrug. They had been a surprise to him as well when she had turned up with them the day before. "She uses them sorta like draft horses. And yes, we think it's weird, too."

"That's not weird," Troy said, putting his hand out for the binoculars. "That's unnatural is what it is. And it's probably a sin." The Guardians agreed and, to a man, they crossed themselves and kissed their glittering crosses. There were mumbles about "witchcraft" and "sorcery."

Leney goaded them, saying, "Some call her the Queen of the Dead. They say she can summon them at will and that they will do her bidding. They also say that she sacrifices small children to them."

"Really?" Duckwall gasped, with such solemnity that Leney burst out laughing.

"No, of course not. Look at them. She's blinded them and popped their eardrums. They don't know up from down." Everyone looked to Troy for confirmation and he agreed that they did indeed seem to have been mutilated. This didn't have the impact he or Leney expected. The murmuring and the worried glances continued as the tent was being set up.

It was a great white canvas structure that leaned with gravity down the hill, but was pushed by the gentle wind into a more vertical position.

In every way it was more of a pavilion than a tent. Along with the tent, there were two of the boxy campers and what these were being used for spawned an entirely new set of rumors.

The rumors gained outlandish momentum when two figures were seen picking their way down the hill towards the town. Skinny, one-armed Aaron Altman carried a white flag, while next to him was Donna Polston in a charcoal grey pantsuit. The two paused just shy of where the carpet of dead bodies began.

Striding out to meet her were Bishop Wojdan, his four priests and Commander Walker. They picked their way through the bodies as though they were trying to avoid giant piles of dog crap. When they came through without falling, Donna went to one knee exactly as the Queen had instructed and kissed the Bishop's ring when he offered his hand.

She waited until Aaron did the same thing before repeating her rehearsed lines: "Queen Jillian wishes to invite his Excellency, Bishop Wojdan to speak with her. She also welcomes Knights Commander Walker, Knights Sergeant Holt and your chief surgeon to attend."

"I'm sorry," Wojdan replied, "Unless she is ill, we cannot afford to allow any of our medical staff to leave. As you might have guessed, they are hard-pressed because of the many injuries we have sustained due of the Queen's actions."

"This is why the Queen would speak to your surgeon. The hands of the Queen are the hands of a healer. She is an accomplished surgeon. I speak from experience, she operated on my arm after I was shot by a Corsair and I am practically good as new."

The Bishop steepled his fingers beneath his round chin for a moment in contemplation. "I will agree," he said, and then asked the youngest of the priests: "Would you be so kind as to fetch Denise." The young man was off like a shot and back again with a harried and somewhat angry Denise Woodruff. She'd been a nurse back before the apocalypse, but ten easy years in a pediatrician's office, giving out shots, band-aides, ear drops, and lollipops had dulled what skills she'd had. When the zombies had come she had adapted and relearned much of what had lain dormant inside her. Still, she was no one's surgeon.

"Do we trust her?" she whispered to Troy as they made their way through the mass of bodies.

Leney, who hadn't been mentioned at all and was irked enough about it to invite himself along, spoke loudly enough for Donna to hear, "I would trust the Queen. She doesn't think of you as enemies, exactly. You're more like wayward children. Or like that prodigal son guy. She knows you're going to come crawling to her, eventually."

Donna Polston shot him a glare. She had been briefed by Jillybean on what to say and what not to say. That anyone was going to "come crawling" was definitely something that would have fallen into the what not to say category.

"If you'll follow me," she said, hoping that no one would take Leney seriously. She led them to the pavilion where three operating tables were set up. Each had a tray filled with surgical tools next to it. She had them wait in the tent and was gone for a strangely long time.

After five minutes, Denise decided to inspect the tools, while Troy went to the far tent flap and gazed out at the zombies, of which there were four. They were on their hands and knees eating grass like cows. Leney came with him and grunted, "What'd I tell you? Nothing scary about them now."

It was another five minutes before Donna returned, walking behind the Queen, who was garbed in black as always.

Leney cleared his throat and made a show of kneeling. Walker came to attention, while next to Leney, Troy obstinately crossed his arms. Denise, who was shocked at how young the Queen was, didn't know what to do and looked to the Bishop for direction. He didn't notice. He was staring intently at the wild-haired girl. She was different that morning. Her eyes were shifty and her demeanor wavering between haughty and nervous.

"Your Highness," Wojdan said, with the slightest bow of his head. It was the action of respect between equals, which she copied.

"Your Excellency," she said, very quickly. "Thank you for coming. I know there is much for both of us to do this morning, so I will cut right to the chase. She...I mean *I* have kept my promise and have torn down your walls just as I said I would. I demonstrated last night that I have the power to destroy you with ease. Will you please capitulate and come under the protection of the Queen?"

She had spoken with little inflection, almost as if she had recited memorized lines. It was strange to Wojdan and he paused a full minute before answering. She began to fidget under his gaze. *Like a kid*, he thought to himself. *Or like a normal eighteen-year-old. And this wasn't any normal eighteen-year-old.*

"Protection?" Wojdan asked, eventually. "My dear, it's obvious that the only person we are in need of protection from is you."

It took a few seconds for the Queen to react, almost as if she was waiting for someone in another room to radio a response into her head. When she did react, it was as abrupt as it was unexpected. Her smile, which had looked fixed in place with invisible thumbtacks, turned into a nasty sneer.

"You have no idea how right you are." Her right hand dipped into her long coat while her left slipped behind her back.

For a second, Wojdan thought she was about to pull a gun or a knife or even both. His reaction was limited to a general stiffening of his muscles. Troy was just as taken by surprise, however his reflexes were better, and although he was a few steps behind the Bishop he jumped in front of him.

The Queen's body convulsed, her head snapped to the side and one shoulder went up. "Fine!" she hissed, but what she meant by it, no one knew. She turned back and stared at Troy, her blue eyes glittering with a strange malevolence that he had missed the night before. "The boy scout," she purred.

"Your highness!" Donna fairly shouted in the Queen's ear. "Jillybean! Can you come with me?" The Queen jerked again, looked nervously about and allowed herself to be led away.

Troy followed until he reached the edge of the tent, where he was greeted by two fearsome-looking Corsairs. He wanted nothing more than to bash their heads in, but they were on a diplomatic mission and so he smiled and stared past them as Donna pulled the Queen into one of the trailers. When the door opened, he saw that the inside seemed to be upholstered in foam.

"What is that?" he asked the Corsairs. Neither would answer and nor would Leney. He only plastered a bland look on his scarred face.

Donna returned and bowed to the Guardians. "The Queen is not feeling herself, but she will be out in a moment."

"What's wrong with her?" Troy asked. "And what was with that trailer? It was padded. They used to joke about padded cells being for crazy people. Is she one? Is she crazy? She was kind of weird like that last night."

Donna was not ready for these sorts of questions. They had not been part of her briefing. Still, she figured they would find out about the Queen sooner or later. "She is a little crazy," she said, holding her fingers an inch apart. "But that's not a padded cell. It's what she calls a sensory deprivation chamber. She gets, uh, excited when over-stressed."

"Perhaps she should consider a different profession than being queen, then," the Bishop advised.

"It's too late for that," Donna said. What they didn't know was that if Jillybean ever stepped down as queen, Eve would step in to fill her shoes and that would be a hundred times worse. The truth was, Jillybean or Eve: "She can't be stopped," Donna told them.

Troy doubted that. He could stop her right then if he wanted to. He could kill her without trying, if it wasn't a sin, that is—and she knew that about him. *Is she using our own morals against us?* The thought was disquieting. A nonbeliever didn't have to worry about rules or morals. They were unburdened by the thought of higher consequences, of anything greater than themselves. The only thing that truly mattered was their immediate lusts. They could do anything. Anything.

"Is she dangerous?" he asked. "I mean really dangerous at any time at all?" He was worried for the Bishop. The man was too trusting when it came to the Queen.

"She's only dangerous to her enemies," Leney answered, not knowing just how wrong he was.

Even then a part of Jillybean was hungry to wipe out every last Guardian. "We need to kill them," Eve said as soon as Sadie walked into the windowless trailer. "Starting with the Bishop, mister high and mighty, himself. I say we use poison and tell people it was a heart attack. We have stuff that'll do the trick, right?"

"We're not killing anyone," Sadie shot back. "Where's Jillybean? Is she here?"

"Of course not!" Eve yelled, as she picked up a candlestick and hurled it at the wall. Because of the triple layers of acoustic foam it bounced away harmlessly, which only made her angrier. "She's off in Neverland playing make believe with that stupid zebra, which is fine with me. She can stay away forever. I just don't see why you're in charge instead of me."

"Because you're crazy," Sadie answered

"How am I the crazy one? She's the one who talks to a stuffed animal. And she's the one who hangs around with dead people. Sorry Sadie, but you don't belong here. You need to cross-the-hell over to the other side. Run into the light, bitch."

Sadie bristled, her dark eyes flashing. "You want to have a go at me? Come on! I'm not the only one who's dead. I was there when Neil threw you into the fire. I watched you burn."

"Take that back! Or I swear…"

"Enough!" Ernest called out, his voice little more than a strident whisper. In the middle of the room was an immense leather recliner, looking like the throne every middle-aged American man had once dreamed of owning. Ernest was settled into it, though he didn't look comfortable. He reclined stiffly, as if he were in a dentist's office. "You know why you're not in charge, Eve."

Eve rounded on him, her wild mass of hair flowing around her head as if they were snakes and she the Medusa. "Who asked you, Stick-boy?" She laughed and advanced on him, seeming to swell in size, while he shrunk, looking so small that if she snapped the recliner back into an upright position, he might fly across the room to splat against the wall.

Ernest was not the man he'd once been. A week before he'd been the giant. He had crushed the others into tiny windowless boxes and had run Jillybean's body as if it were his own. But she had found a way to take his power and now his voice was small and his presence barely more than a shadow.

"I was just trying to get you back on track, Eve. You are right about the Bishop. He's got to go. He has too much power over them. They're almost like the Believers. You remember the Believers, don't you, Sadie?"

She would never forget the Believers and their insane leader, Abraham. "But they were crazy. These people are just, I don't know, religious. What's wrong with that?"

"Nothing," Ernest admitted, softly. "Nothing at all, right up until their leaders use their religion to further their own evil desires at the expense of their own people. That's what Abraham did and that's what the Bishop is about to do. Ask yourself, why hasn't he surrendered?"

"Maybe he's going to," Sadie said. "We haven't even talked to him yet."

"One thing is clear, *you* shouldn't talk to him," Ernest told her. "This isn't your bailiwick. And it's not yours, either Eve. This takes a cooler head and a clearer vision, because we all know what will happen if they don't surrender."

Eve grinned. "Yeah, we get to attack. We'll wipe them off the face of the earth and then nobody will ever tell us no again."

Sadie pushed her back. "Wrong. We aren't going to destroy an entire town. Jillybean won't allow it. And I won't allow it."

The two young women squared off, glaring at each other. They were almost evenly matched; Sadie was faster, but Eve was unpredictably deadly.

Ernest climbed off the recliner to come stand between them. "You're wrong, Sadie. If they don't surrender and we don't attack, our Corsairs will turn on us. They just spent three days of back-breaking labor creating a river and they expect a reward. If they don't get one, it'll be a 'stray' bullet during the heat of battle, or a knife in the back in the dark of night, or maybe Leney or one of the others will grow a pair and arrest you."

"And you think killing and enslaving a thousand people is the answer?" Sadie cried. "No! I won't stand for it and neither will Jillybean." She pushed past Eve, stormed through the tiny kitchenette and into the even tinier bathroom, yanking open the single drawer by the sink.

Eve saw what she was going for and sucked in her breath. "Don't! They'll pull you under, too." Sadie only lifted a single shoulder in response and dropped three pills into her palm. "What about our liver?" Eve begged. "The yellow is coming back. She's hiding it for now, but all the make up in the world isn't going to keep our liver alive."

Next to the bottle of Zyprexa was Jillybean's new makeup bag. She had taken to painting her face.

"It's only temporary," Sadie said and swallowed the pills. In a fury, Eve grabbed a heavy medical book and flung it at her. It flapped like a dead bird and thumped heavily against the wall. As Eve grabbed a second one, Sadie slammed the door. She put her weight against it and waited, expecting to hear another book hit or maybe the crash of Eve's boot.

Instead, she heard something completely unexpected: Christmas music!

Chapter 36

To put it mildly, Sadie was freaked out. Through the door, she could hear a woman singing *Silent Night* and it didn't make a lick of sense.

"Eve?" she whispered. "Is that you?"

The only answer she received was a sudden rush of feet drumming past the door. She leaned back and then leaned in again as the cadence of the feet changed and the sound dipped. "They're on stairs. What the heck is going on?" She stepped back from the door and was surprised when she didn't knock into the little sink.

Spinning, she saw that she was no longer in the trailer's cubby-sized bathroom. She was in an entirely different bathroom, one that was large and strangely, brilliantly white. It was clean! It wasn't the "mostly clean" one saw now that water was drawn by hand, it was aseptically clean. There wasn't a speck of dust anywhere, not even on the window panes.

It took her a moment to realize that there was something different about the windows: the curtains were pulled wide and the black-out curtains were nowhere to be seen. Instinctively, Sadie dropped to one knee, her senses tuned to catch the slightest movement of shadow beneath the door, the soft growl of a distant zombie, or the sour smell of a bandit's breath.

Her senses didn't need tuning; they were inundated.

Immediately, she smelled bleach, window cleaner and lavender soap. Beyond this was a woman's perfume and something that had her mind reeling. She couldn't believe the aroma was real, but: "Oh my God. Cinnamon rolls!" Closing her eyes, she breathed in deeply and all the scents were still there.

Ecstatic, she reached for the doorknob, but then her ears began to pick out their own details: a squeal of happiness, deep laughter, the crinkle of paper, a horn honking, and a rumble that caused her skin to flare in goosebumps.

"That's an airplane," she said and rushed to the window. Sure enough, there was an enormous metal bird disappearing into patchy white clouds, leaving behind a long stretch of fading thunder. When it was gone, she marveled at the scene below her: a winter wonderland, complete with a snowman in the yard, trees gilt with white, crystal spears hanging from the gutter, and a boy shoveling a driveway three doors down.

"Where am I?" she wondered. *Home*, a voice whispered in her head. It felt perfect and it sounded right, and yet it wasn't. Her home had been a cramped little apartment in New Jersey where she'd been raised by an overworked single mom. She rarely saw her father until, that is, when he wanted to use her to catch runaway slaves. No, this wasn't her home. This was the home of a happy, well-adjusted family—and she was trespassing. She didn't belong here.

Sadie was just testing the bathroom window to see if it would open without making too much noise when she heard, "Jillybean, hun, can you get your boots on?" It was a woman; a mom. Jillybean's mom. That meant they were in Jillybean's house.

It was only then that Sadie realized she had been in the house before. She had lived in it, in fact, after Ram had been killed and they had escaped from New York. "I peed in that toilet," she said, in something of foolish, reverential awe. She had to stop herself from touching the porcelain.

"What about the presents, Mommy?" Jillybean asked, in a voice very different than her usual one. It was high and sweet.

"They'll still be here when we get back. I want to drop off some of these rolls over at Mrs. Bennett's."

"But the presents! All I gotted to open was Ipes and he thinks there may be more zebras in some of them packages. Like a herd of 'em. A herd is what means a whole lot, like a hundred, and it wouldn't be fair…"

Her dad interrupted in a booming voice: "Boots on, Jillybean or some of those presents are going to stampede their way over to the Goodwill."

Sadie cocked her head and listened as someone small climbed dejectedly up the stairs. "He's only playing, Ipes. We'll save your family, I promise. They won't go over to the Goodwill. Say, you ever have a cim-im-nim rolls before?"

The urge to open the door and see Jillybean as she was before the apocalypse was too much. Sadie cracked the door as the little girl walked by. She was so tiny it broke Sadie's heart. She wanted to rush to Jillybean and crush her in her arms and tell her that everything was going to be alright.

It would be the biggest lie ever told. Her life would be hell. Her world was only months from being destroyed and everyone she had ever called family would be dead. And the death wouldn't stop with her parents and friends. Everyone she would meet after the apocalypse would be dead as well, everyone but Neil, that is. She could still count on him.

When Jillybean went into her bedroom, Sadie crept along the hall and watched through the open door as she pulled tiny pink boots over her adorable footy pajama pants, then hunted around for mittens. Sadie jumped when Jillybean's dad called from the bottom of the stairs: "Hurry up, Jillybean. They're getting cold."

Sadie darted to the side as the little girl, her hair flying in every direction, came bursting out of her bedroom. She had left Ipes behind in her rush. Sadie waited until the family was crunching through the snow before she went into the room. It was even more vibrantly pink than she remembered.

The zebra was splayed, face down on the bed. It looked dead. "Ipes?"

He came to life, jumping up so quickly that Sadie leapt back, thinking that the tiny stuffed zebra was about to attack her. She had never seen him move in real life and it was horrifying. "Sadie? What are you doing here?"

"Jeeze, that's crazy," she said, her face queered up as if watching a pigeon puking. "Where does the sound come out? You don't have a mouth."

Ipes touched the underside of his bulbous nose where his mouth should have been. "It's best not to think about that sort of thing. So, is something going on up there? Is that why you're here? Wait! Did Ernest trap you down here? Did he trap all of us? Oh boy, this is bad. Really, really bad."

He was waving his flappy hooves over his head in excitement and getting loud. Sadie wanted to pat him on the top of his spiky mane to calm him, however the idea of touching a living toy was too off-putting. She wrung her hands together to resist the urge. "No, he didn't trap us. He's been weak ever since Jillybean put him in his place."

Ipes' narrow shoulders drooped in relief. "That's good. I was worried that...hold on. If you're down here, who's running things up there?"

"I am...I think."

Ipes rolled his beady black eyes. "You think? That's not how this works. You can't run things from down here. You have to get back up there before Eve does something bad."

"That's the thing. Eve's getting strong again. We need Jillybean. Can you send her back up?" A happy, chirping voice from outside floated in. Sadie went to the window and saw Jillybean and her parents coming back home, trudging through the snow. The little girl was trailing by a few steps, trying to leap from one of her father's footprints to the next.

Suddenly Ipes was at Sadie's side. He sighed, saying, "I just love her so much at this age. She's so perfectly innocent that it's heartbreaking."

It was, and Sadie found herself staring until the happy family disappeared from sight and could be heard moving about below them. Then there came the sound of Jillybean running up the stairs.

"Hide!" wailed Ipes, as he ran for the bed.

The desire to hide was so great that it was practically an unquestionable demand. From Sadie's perspective, she was literally in Jillybean's bedroom. Everything was so amazingly real that it didn't feel as though she was striding around in a dusty, thirteen-year-old memory or in some sort of hazy, ever-changing mental delusion.

Everything about the room from the baseboards to the crown molding was so perfectly exact that it felt undeniably authentic.

Even the fear of getting caught in Jillybean's bedroom was substantive enough for her heart to start racing. There was no way that she, a teenaged goth chick with a spiked mohawk, was going to be able to talk her way out of a trip to the police station, something she didn't have time for.

She also didn't have time to find a proper hiding place. The room was sparsely furnished: a bed that was both narrow and extremely low to the ground, a squat dresser with unicorn decals decorating the drawers, and a nightstand that held a tiny lamp that used a bulb that was smaller than Sadie's thumb.

The only place to hide was the closet. Sadie ducked in and knelt among ballet slippers, cowgirl boots and a brand new pair of pink Keds. They were the same pair of shoes that Jillybean was wearing when Sadie first met her. By then they were scuffed and muddy and stained slightly grey from seawater. She was just reaching out to touch them when the door burst open.

At first, Jillybean didn't see Sadie. It wasn't just that her all black attire blended with the shadows, Jillybean was also dancing on one foot trying to get one of her snow-boots off. When she did see Sadie, the girl stumbled back, her big blue eyes looking cartoonishly large in her fright.

Before she could scream—clearly what she was planning to do— Sadie put out both hands and said, "It's me, Jillybean. It's me, Sadie. We're sisters, remember?"

Just as it would throughout her life, fear did not linger long with the little girl. It slid off her like rain from a duck's back. "I don't have a sister. Why is your hair like that? It looks pokey. And anyways, if I had a sister she wouldn't wear black. I like pink and sisters always like the same things. Becca's sister Janine is a red-head just like Becca and neither of them ever wear red or pink, because their mom says they'll look like pigs if they do, which I think is real mean."

She paused as if to hear Sadie's thoughts on the subject of Becca and her sister. "That is mean. And to go back to the whole 'sisters' thing, we're not really sisters, we just call each other that, because I swore I would always treat you like a sister. You made me pinky swear on it." Sadie held out her pinky, crooking it slightly.

"Are you sure you got the right house?" Jillybean said. "A lot of these houses look the same. My mom calls them cookie cutters and that's what means they look the same. Maybe you meant to be on Highview Drive. That's the next street over that way." She pointed south. "There's some kids that way, too. Some are big and ride bikes."

This was going nowhere and was eating up precious time. Eve could have massacred half of Highton by then.

"No. I'm in the right place and I have the right girl. I need you to come back with me."

"Back where?" Jillybean asked, taking a step away.

Sadie almost answered with: *Back home*. That would have been silly. Jillybean was home. She had built her own little slice of heaven. It was the perfect day: Christmas presents in the morning, a fire to warm the toes after an afternoon of sledding, a turkey dinner to stuff her belly and an evening of cuddling with her parents switching off between reading to her and tickling her. She would never leave on her own.

It would be up to Sadie to make it happen.

"Back here. There's a doorway to another world. Come see." Jillybean was properly skeptical and yet, she could be counted on to give in to her curiosity. She edged forward to peek past the strange girl. There was no one faster than Sadie. In a blur of black cloth, she darted out a hand, grabbed Jillybean's wrist and pulled.

For a second, Sadie was able to yank Jillybean's forty-four pounds forward with expected ease, but just as she crossed the boundary of the closet door, Jillybean's weight seemed to multiply a hundred-fold. She held herself back from the doorway, easily, an icy gleam in her eyes.

"You're a kidnapper," she accused. "I'll never go anywhere with you. And wait till my daddy catches you. He'll make minced turkey meat out of you."

Sadie was suddenly flung back by what felt like a huge, invisible hand. She jumped up as Jillybean slammed the door shut with a bang that echoed inside Sadie's head. The tiny closet was perfectly black. Not a mote of light escaped the edges of the door. It was as if the door and the closet itself had ceased to exist.

A hot clot of fear came to life in her belly. It wiggled and spun, growing larger. Ever since she had died, Sadie didn't like to be trapped in dark places. It hit too close to home. She didn't reach out for the doorknob, she attacked the closet door and exploded out of it, her breath coming in great gusts.

She took one step and nearly pitched face-first down a short flight of stairs. They were the stairs leading from the sensory deprivation trailer and consisted of only three risers. She managed to catch herself before face-planting.

"What the hell? How long was I gone?"

Go back, a voice whispered inside her head. Although the voice had been wavering and ghost-like, she knew it belonged to Eve. It was always easy taking advice from Eve; Sadie would just do the opposite. She began walking towards the pavilion, hoping she hadn't been gone too long.

Leney saw her coming first and went down on one knee as soon as she entered the tent. Donna cleared her throat and called out: "The Queen!" and did the same.

The Queen had been gone for seven minutes, which had been seven wasted minutes to Denise Woodruff. She didn't have time for kneeling or crazy queens, though she did need help desperately. She had four fractures to reduce and cast, two broken skulls—one with increasing inter-cranial pressure, suggesting a brain bleed. And finally, a Knight who had been crushed beneath a heap of the beasts for an hour and was urinating blood. Denise looked over at Troy and since he was standing at attention, she did as well.

Bishop Wojdan inclined his head and asked, "Are you Queen Jillybean?"

Sadie started at the question and looked down at herself, afraid that she was wearing her old goth skin. Her shadow was topped by an explosion of hair; she was in Jillybean's body, so why the question?

"I took the liberty to explain something of your condition, your Highness," Donna admitted, nervously, afraid of who was really in charge in Jillybean's head. "It seemed necessary because of the circumstances."

Sadie wasn't sure what circumstances Donna was talking about and she was doubly unsure how to proceed. Her job had always been as a place keeper, there to keep Jillybean's body alive and kicking until she got back. Everyone knew she wasn't smart; that she wasn't equipped to make real decisions. And she didn't like the entire business to begin with. Threatening good people wasn't right, even if was something of a necessity.

But what about what Ernest said? This voice was louder, stronger. *Your men will turn on you and when you're gone they'll swallow the Guardians in one bite.* A snapping sound, like a steel bear trap closing, erupted almost in Sadie's ear, making her flinch. Eve was getting too close to the surface for Sadie's liking. *And you'll do nothing about it. That's because you're weak. Everyone knows it. It's why your own men will frag your ass if you don't...*

"I am the Queen," Sadie said quickly, speaking over Eve.

It wasn't completely a lie since she and Jillybean were something of a package deal, and yet Wojdan rumbled in his throat, a sound that suggested he didn't believe her. "I take it that 'hmmm' is you thinking over the offer?" she asked.

"No," he said with a sad smile. "I reject it out of hand. All of it, including your offer to help. We will not be beholden to the likes of you. Our wounded would gladly give up their lives rather than be used as bargaining chips."

Sadie didn't know what to say. "But you will all die. I've seen it, your Excellency. I've seen how she...how you will die. You have to surrender,"

He shook his head, making his jowls swing. The sad smile assumed shades of grief, as if death was inevitable. "No, we do not have to. Your threats are meaningless, your Highness. Now, if you'll excuse me, we do have work to do." He bobbed his head and started to leave.

Tell them to stop! Eve raged in a voice that had grown from sinister and silky sweet to thunderous. It left Sadie swaying.

"Wait," Sadie said, her voice embarrassingly soft. The Bishop turned and blinked at her, expectantly.

Make them stay, damn it! You have guards, use them.

Sadie held up a finger to the Bishop and then turned around, hissing, "I can't. They have immunity. How will it look if we invite them here and then turn around and jail them?"

Who said anything about jailing them? Eve answered with a laugh. It was the laugh of crows haranguing each other over a field of dead bodies, and it rang in Sadie's head. It soon became deafening.

"Your Highness, we will not be abused," the Bishop said, his voice barely audible over the crowing laughter.

"Just a sec," Sadie said, weakly. "I just got to hold on. Eve can't keep it up forever. I just…"

As the room watched in dreadful fascination, the Queen's right hand lifted, hung suspended in the air for a moment and then went whistling in a vicious arc hitting her own cheek. The sound of the slap was so loud it was shocking.

"Jillybean!" Donna cried and jumped forward as the Queen collapsed. Donna tried to help her up, but the younger woman shoved her away.

"Don't ever call me that again," Eve snarled, getting to her feet. Her face was throbbing and her balance was a little off. Still, she wore a genuine grin. "Now, where were we? Yes, you were going to surrender."

Chapter 37

Gunner lifted the mealy apple up under the cloth hiding his face and took a bite. The others, especially Jenn, could barely stomach the apples, but he didn't mind them a bit. He was missing so many teeth, he liked his food mushy. *Like an old man*, he thought to himself.

This soured him on the apple and he pegged it at a tree. When it hit the trunk dead center, it exploded. "Enough sitting about. We gotta get. I don't have all day." They were a straggly trio, so battered that the girl was the strongest of the three and was the last to stand. She was squirreling her partridge bones in a small bag that she kept tied at her wrist.

"Rolling 'dem bones," he cackled. "I shoulda kept the beaks and the feet for you, like they do in the deep, deep south."

Jenn and Mike weren't exactly sure what he meant by that. She thought he meant Mexico and Mike thought it was South America, which stretched so far south that the summer became winter, or so he had heard.

Stu understood the reference. "Are you from the South? You don't have much of an accent."

Gunner laughed again in that strange wheezing mad cackle of his. "Not much of an accent! Ha-ha! That's rich. What kind of accent does a man with no lips have? I sound exactly as I am: ugly. There's no pretending otherwise. Now, let's cut the chitchat." The morning was still sharply cold and he wrapped his ugly cape of fur and crow feathers tighter about him before heading once more to the northeast.

Things were exactly as they had been the day before. In spite of his immense handicaps, Gunner marched tirelessly, while behind him Mike labored along in pain, Stu limped, and Jenn made sure to hold back even a hint of complaining. She was tired and ragged, but at least she was whole.

As the day progressed, the land gradually became less and less hilly and by afternoon they had reached a broad valley that had once been prime farmland but was now becoming a bramble-choked wilderness. At the far end of the valley was a deserted little town. Mostly deserted, that is. It had more than its share of the dead, most of them on the larger side since they had been grazing up the valley throughout the fall.

Jenn hoped they would try to creep past along the forested edge of the town where there was more cover. Gunner had a different idea and took them right down the heart of the town, slipping from house to house and from car to car. He had a knack for avoiding the dead, without which they would've been doomed.

As far as Jenn could tell, they were in the center of town when Gunner suddenly crawled beneath a jumble of wrecked cars. "What are you guys waiting for?" he asked in a whisper. "We're almost there."

"Almost where?" Mike wondered under his breath so that only Jenn could hear. "Almost to his trap?" It sure felt that way to Jenn. Things got even sketchier as she crawled through a narrow gap beneath the vehicles and emerged behind a crumbling fence.

Right on the other side of the loose boards was a pair of zombies. Jenn froze, afraid to move.

One of them had once been a black man; as a zombie it was many colored: strangely pale in spots, hugely scarred and grey in others and dusky brown everywhere else. Its hair was outrageously knotted and shaggy as an unshorn ram. The hulking thing next to it was faceless. Its features had been eaten completely away and now, after it pulled up a hunk of weeds along the aged fence, it shoved them down into an obscene hole where its cheeks and jaws had once been.

The sight was so horrific that Jenn feared she was going to vomit. Gunner seemed to like what he saw. "Proper watch dogs," he whispered before shuttling to his left where there were even more gaps in the rotted wood. He dug around in the overgrown weeds with his good hand until he found a stone which he heaved back and threw. It sailed over a rusting derelict van with broken windows and *thocked* loudly as it bounced off the front door of a house across the street from them.

The two barely humanoid beasts spun about and began to groan and shamble their way to the house.

When their backs were turned, Gunner darted in his crab-like manner through an opening in the fence and crept toward the house beyond. It was a long, low ranch with dirt-filmed windows and a gaping wound in front where a door had once been. A zombie had torn it and its frame right off the brick. The door sat, poking up from an out of control rhododendron that was slowly taking over the house. Already the bush was strangling the two back bedrooms and overflowing the driveway.

Gunner paused in the doorway to listen for a few seconds before heading further inside. Jenn followed right on his heels. She had seldom been in houses as gloomy as this one. The only light that made it inside had to fight tooth and nail to get through the overgrown trees and bushes and the thick dirt covering the windows.

They did not go deep into the house, stopping at an open bathroom door a few steps away from the kitchen. Gunner went in and came out with two stoppered bottles of what Jenn assumed was wine. It was actually fresh water. Gunner drank heavily from one bottle, finishing it in front of their eyes. He didn't hand over the second.

"I think now is a good time to talk payment," he told them, using the cloth covering the lower part of his face to wipe his ruined chin.

"Hold on," Stu said, coming to stand between Gunner and Jenn. "We told you our story, just like you asked. We don't owe you anything."

Gunner's dark eyes crinkled and Jenn could sense the evil smile radiating from beneath the veil. "You need to go back to school because you got a bad case of being an ignorant dumbass. You told me a story to get you outta that pipe and because I had saved you from those earlier zombies. But what about all my time and troubles before and after?"

Stu could only fumble out the truth: "We told you everything we know and we don't really have anything of value...except the boat." Mike sucked in his breath, looking as though Stu was going to hand over his first-born child.

"That's not even yours to give," Gunner told them. "You stole it. Kinda makes it fair game. 'Sides, I doubt you'll ever see it again. Do you plan on trying to make it back to that boat any time soon? If so, what are your chances that you'll make it past the Corsair's lair? No, sorry, you can't pay with other people's money."

"Then what do you suggest?" Jenn asked, crossing her arms in front of her. "You know we have nothing. You must be fishing for something." She was afraid that he would ask for *her*. She was even more afraid that if he did Mike and Stu would be dead in seconds.

It took Gunner a second to realize what she was asking. "Don't be stupid. I coulda had you whenever I wanted. No, I need more information. It's how I make my living. I'm the man who knows things. Sometimes it's big things, like how many ships the Corsairs have or how far the Portland radiation belt has drifted. Sometimes it's just local gossip. Who's dating who? Who's expecting a baby? Who's been messing around, or who's about to propose. You'd be surprised what people would pay good money for. Besides, I wasn't lying when I told you I was lonely. Knowing things helps me feel, I don't know, connected."

"I guess the only thing about us you'd like to know is that me and Mike are sorta an item," Jenn said. "Things have been so topsy-turvy that we really haven't gone on a real date. Unless you count that dinner." Mike shook his head; the dinner had been a complete fiasco.

"No," Gunner said, pointing the lip of the empty bottle at Jenn. "It doesn't count if you tell me stuff I already know. It's obvious you two are moony over each other. And it's not the past I want either. It's the future. I want to know more about Bainbridge."

Stu's dark eyes narrowed. "I don't think so. We hope to live there and we aren't going to go there as spies. No. It's out of the question. Name another price and we will pay it, obviously not right away, but over time we'll pay it."

Gunner didn't hesitate. "Ten-thousand rounds of ammunition." Mike's eyes shot wide, while Stu's narrowed even further until they were just slits. Gunner shrugged, making the hump on his back jerk up. "You said name my price and that's it. I'll take a thousand a year for ten years and I won't even charge interest, which is mighty fine of me."

"Be serious," Stu growled.

"I am serious. I've saved your lives more than you know. Remember that Corsair back at the pond? You ever wonder where he went? You ever wonder why all his buddies didn't show up and drag you out of that pipe? I'm the reason why, thank you very much. I've fed you, dressed you, kept you alive, and brought you all the way up here and this is the thanks I get? You can keep your stories. I'll take the money."

Jenn looked back and forth at Stu and Mike, hoping one would know what to say or do; however, both were just as lost as she was—Gunner had just admitted to murdering a Corsair for them. It made her feel dirty. "It's just a lot of money," she said, in a small voice. "I don't think we can do a thousand a year."

"You're going to have to figure it out because if I don't get paid I might go looking elsewhere for money and the Black Captain doesn't ever forgive and he doesn't forget. And not everything is as perfect as it seems on Bainbridge. One day you might wake up and it'll be just two of you. A few months go by and then it'll be one."

Stu pushed forward. "You evil son of a…"

In a black blur, Gunner dropped him with a punch to the chest. It was a quick, savage blow that felt like a kick from a mule. Stu's face went bright red as he struggled to breathe through lungs that were crumpled and convulsing. Gunner stood over him. "Don't ever walk up on me again, boy or I will break that pretty face of yours wide open." He turned his hard, horrible gaze on Mike and Jenn. "You've heard my offers. Pick one."

Jenn's shaking hand spidered down Mike's arm until she found his; it was clenched into a useless fist. He was furious, but also embarrassed that he had stood meekly by instead of going to Stu's defense. With his broken ribs, fighting was out of the question. If he had taken a punch like that, the bones in his chest would've crumbled like twigs.

"We won't tell you military secrets," Mike said, forcefully through clenched teeth. "We can tell you some gossip just like you said, but we won't be real spies."

Gunner's scowling eyes suddenly crinkled. "How tough was that? Huh? Here, have a drink." He handed Mike the other bottle and then reached down and heaved a still gasping Stu Currans to his feet. "Now we can be friends again. What I want to know first is about the Governor. Is she still popular? When is she due for reelection? Will she win? Who's her opponent? What are they like? Do they drink, cheat, gamble? Do they have kids? If so, what are their hobbies?"

"Hold on," Stu said, as evenly as he could with his diaphragm still hitching spastically. "All that seems a lot like spy-work to me. And what happens if maybe we start by giving you a little information and then you want more. Then what?"

"You can say no," Gunner said, sounding reasonable. "And don't get your panties in a bunch about the other stuff. I didn't ask about what sort of weapons they had or what their tactics are. What I'm asking for is all background information. None of it is exactly classified, you know what I mean?"

"It does sound a lot like gossip to me," Jenn volunteered. "I don't think anyone would really care if this is all we're telling Gunner." Even though it was the truth, she felt slimy saying this. No matter how this was coated, it was obvious he was a spy of some sort.

Gunner ducked back into the bathroom. He came back out with another bottle and a plastic bag bursting with walnuts. "Exactly. You'll see. Those guys on Bainbridge are talkers and so what if you become talkers, too. Now, eat up." Three of the fingers on his good hand were little more than scared-over stubs, the ends blackened like old cigars. Although he could grip his battleaxe without a problem, walnuts were another story. They spilled from his hand. Jenn bent quickly as Mike made a slow gesture to pick them up. She was about to sweep them into her hand when she saw that they had fallen in a ring.

Another circle, she thought. *But what did this one mean?* She didn't know. Seeing as it was in connection to Gunner, she figured that it meant something bad, and yet she felt a strange reassurance. The circle was another sign and it had come to her unbidden. It was something of a relief.

Absently, she ate the walnuts, picking lint from the handful. The group ate and drank for a few minutes in silence before Gunner suddenly said, "I have to go make sure our route is clear. There's a lot of unsavory people in the north these days. I think your friend's antics have attracted a lot of unwanted attention for Bainbridge. The Black Captain gets his revenge one way or the other. Remember that the next time you see her."

After he left, Mike asked, "Was he talking about Jillybean? I doubt we'll ever see her again. What do you guys think?"

Stu's rugged face clouded over. He didn't say anything, so it was hard to tell whether he wanted to see her or not. It seemed both ideas were painful to him. Jenn suddenly knew what the ring of walnuts meant. "We'll see her. I'm pretty sure of it." But would it be a good thing? She had barely been holding onto her sanity the last time they had seen her. The stress of war could have sent her over the edge completely.

If so, Jenn feared for the friends she had left behind.

No one said a word. They sat in the dark hall in a thoughtful silence until the thoughts faded into a drowsy, unthinking lethargy. Eventually, Mike stood and helped Jenn to her feet. "Let's find a couch or something more comfortable than this floor." The three wandered into the living room where they each found a spot to wait. Stu, alone on a heavy chair, Mike and Jenn on the couch facing him.

Jenn slept against Mike's shoulder and was out for a few hours before a distant crackle of gunfire woke her.

"That's at least two guns," Stu said. Chances were, it meant a fight.

Gunner showed up a while later, drying blood on his cloak and a snarl on his lips. "We can't wait until morning. We have to go now. Come on, kiddies. The tide waits for no man, right, Mike?"

"It doesn't. Are we taking a boat?"

"How else did you plan on getting to Bainbridge? It's still an island." Gunner didn't wait for them to wake fully, but was out the door in seconds. They crossed the yard, ducked through the fence and crept under the piled-up cars. Instead of popping up on the other side as expected, Gunner slithered down into an open pipe that Jenn had seen earlier. At the time she had feared what might come out of it. She had never expected to go inside.

The small pipe led to a larger one—a slightly larger one. Although she could walk hunched over, Mike had to move somewhere between a crawl and a scamper and poor Stu, who was even bigger, had to crawl on his hands and knees. Because of his hump and deformed back, Gunner seemed no taller than Jenn and yet he had the mass of a much larger man, and even though he filled the tunnel with his bulk, he moved with surprising speed.

It was difficult for Jenn to keep up, and Mike trailed far behind her. They were underground for half an hour and when they finally came up out into the cold night, even Gunner had to take a moment to stretch his twisted joints. But it was only a moment.

Stu was still wincing and cracking his back when Gunner forced them on again. They went due north until they ran into a black stretch of still water. Jenn asked if it was Puget Sound to which Gunner only grunted, "Around here it's all the same water."

He took them back up into the forests a little ways and then went on a course parallel to the stretch of water for another three miles. They were dog tired but he wouldn't let them rest. He was filled with an unnamed urgency that was bothersome right up until they heard gunfire off to their right.

It was very close. It was hard to judge at night, but Jenn guessed the shooter was no more than a hundred yards away.

Gunner had been soft on them compared to the grueling pace he set during the next hour. There was no let up. He forced them on, sometimes dragging Mike along as he wheezed and clutched his aching side. It seemed as though they were running for their lives, but what they were running from he wouldn't say. They barely had the breath to ask.

The chase ended when they finally reached the sound opposite Bainbridge's western-most point. The searchlights were dazzling even from half a mile away. Each traced a sparkling silver swath across the dark water as they swept slowly back and forth. Jenn had never seen anything so beautiful.

"Almost there," Gunner assured them. He cut through the brush heading along the beach for a few hundred yards until he came to a small house that had slid off its foundation and was mostly in the water. Reaching into a window, he slid out a long canoe. "I'm going to want this back, one of these days. In the meantime, you guys can use it to come back and forth. I want your first report in three days. We'll meet here at noon…"

A sudden splash stopped him. A shadow the size of a truck moved in the water, coming closer. Slowly, like some deep-dwelling leviathan it surfaced and came at them. The creature didn't look much like a zombie, it looked like something out of a horror story. It was covered in green slime; the stuff dribbled from its milky green eyes and from a huge gaping mouth. Entwined in its long black hair were living strands of seaweed which hung down its back like garland. Across its shockingly broad shoulders was an old fishing net, festooned with hooks and fish heads and unspeakable trash. It almost seemed to be wearing a shawl but then it struggled on shore and they could see that the net was huge. It dragged along behind the beast like the train of a demonic bridal gown, leaving behind small, scuttling marine animals and a long vile smear that consisted of a combination of green slime, evil-smelling bottom mud and what was more than likely feces.

"Be here at noon in three days and come alone," Gunner said. "I'll know if you try to pull some sort of funny business. Now, go on."

While they clambered into the rocking canoe, Gunner turned to face the eight-hundred pound monster. He was grinning beneath his mask.

Chapter 38

"Actually, we had no intention of ever surrendering," the Bishop replied to Eve. He was unmoved by her nasty smile and was completely unafraid, even though her mental state was deteriorating rapidly. "Your threats are useless. More than useless, in fact. If you make martyrs of us, our people will only fight harder."

She cackled, her eyes alight with fire. "Fight harder against what? Against who? Oh, you are a funny one, your Idiocy. Do I really have to demonstrate my power a third time? I tear down your wall and you pretend it doesn't matter. I send a few crumbs of my vast army at you last night and you barely survive. I have to wonder, is this biblical with you? Are you Peter denying Jesus three times before the cock crows? Are you the Pharaoh with the hard heart? Do I really need to bring down another plague before you let my people live?"

"Your people?" Commander Walker growled, stepping forward, his face twisted in anger. "Your people are thieves and murderers."

"Yes!" she cried, throwing a fist in the air. "Yes, exactly. Thieves and liars and murderers. I think you might even call them sinners. Those are my people. Wait! I have an idea, Bishop. Since you have such a problem with sinners, I'll take all of yours off your hands. You can keep your saints. Hmm? What do you say to that?"

The Bishop didn't say a word and Commander Walker looked suddenly uncomfortable.

"Come on," Eve said. "Here's your chance to purify your ranks. Who among you are completely without sin? Let him throw a stone at me if he dares. That's right, I listened when Jillybean read the good book. Our interpretations are not exactly the same on most things, but we both know that one's right. We're all sinners, so get off that high horse, Commander."

"Quoting the Bible is easy," the Bishop stated, flatly. "And using selective verses to your advantage is certainly nothing new. What would really impress me is if you tried understanding and living up to the tenets espoused in the Bible."

"Which ones? There are so, so many and sometimes they contradict each other or go off on some sort of prehistoric tangent. It can be very confusing."

The Bishop stuck his hands behind his back, thrusting his round belly out. "Since you asked, perhaps you could consider: *Thou Shalt not Murder*. It's a good start. Or maybe: *Love thy neighbor as yourself*." She scoffed at the suggestion, causing him to sigh. "As I thought, you're all talk. We're leaving now."

Eve snapped her fingers at the guards, who leveled their weapons. More guards appeared at the far end of the tent. "I don't think so. We tried to be nice about things, but you threw that in our face. I think it might be time to do things my way for a change." She nodded at Sticky

Jim, who elbowed his friend, Deaf Mick. They led an armed platoon toward the small group of Guardians.

Among the Corsair guards was a shadowy figure, who never looked up. He didn't seem to belong and yet no one said a word. He cast a wavering silhouette on the wall of the pavilion. It was so thin that it was as if a candle had created it. Thin shadow or not, seeing him brought a sneer to the Queen's face. She knew it was no guard; it was Ernest, sticking his nose in where it didn't belong.

Be smart, he whispered across to her as Troy Holt stepped boldly forward to challenge twenty men with his bare hands.

"I am being smart," she snarled. She hated him nearly as much as she hated Jillybean. The difference was that she and Ernest were sometimes on the same side. And, she reluctantly admitted that sometimes he did have some good ideas. She exerted what self-control she possessed and asked, in as off-hand a manner as she could manage, "What do you suggest?"

Show them our real army. It'll scare them into surrender and once they surrender peacefully, we can do what we want with them.

"What *I* want to do with them, you mean. And it's *my* army. Don't forget it." He said nothing to this and she grunted like an animal, baiting him, but he was still frail and didn't rise to the challenge. She turned from one weak enemy to another and stared intently at the Bishop, who had heard one half of the conversation.

He stared back, unblinkingly and she saw the sadness in his eyes had returned. "Don't get all weepy on my account," she said. "I'm perfectly fine." Even as she said this, her eyes flicked to the side to see Ernest hiding a smirk behind a hand. She had to resist the fantastic urge to pull out the little P238 she kept hidden in her coat and pop him a few times.

"If you're so fine, maybe you could tell me who you were talking to just now," the Bishop asked. He had never believed in dissociative identity disorder, what most people called multiple personality disorder. As far as he was concerned, it had been a fad diagnosis that had caused more harm than good. In a way, it was akin to a virus in that it self-replicated. One sensational diagnosis that found its way into the public domain would spawn a dozen counterfeits. This didn't mean he thought the Queen was acting in a fraudulent manner; no, there really was something wrong with her.

"Don't you dare question me when you're the one who's about to commit suicide," she snapped back at him. "It's death to defy me. And I suppose that's your choice, but you're going to drag all of your people down with you. Who are you like?"

Jim Jones, Ernest answered.

"Yes, Jim Jones. He was that crazy guy who made all his followers drink cyanide laced kool-aide. He was a cult leader. Is that what you are, Bishop? A cult leader? Have you brainwashed your followers so completely that they'll let themselves get torn to pieces?"

The Bishop raised an eyebrow. "I thought you said these were your people and yet you are the one threatening to kill them."

"My people kneel before me and if you really wish to save lives, you would be the first." His only response was to shake his head and stare steadily into her lamp-like eyes while all around them the Corsairs waited ready to start pummeling the old man.

The impasse lasted a full minute before she started hearing Sadie calling out: *Jillybean, where are you. Jillybean!* It sounded like Sadie was far, far away in a deep cave or buried beneath a building.

"Okay, that's enough. I will give you one more chance to prove you're not running a cult. I will show you the doom that awaits you if you don't surrender. I will show you what will destroy your town and everyone in it. Consider it a gift from me. It'll allow you to surrender with your dignity intact."

She turned to Donna with half-lidded eyes. "Send Yingling out with them and get an honor guard of a hundred men so they all remain safe and sound until they return."

"I can lead them, your Highness," Leney said, pushing forward. He had been ignored from the moment he had walked in and he didn't like it. He felt like he was being squeezed out. "Yingling is a Sacramento guy. Those types don't mix all that well with, you know, old Corsairs."

"They had better start mixing," she spat, her tone cold as ice. "Or I will assume their leaders are up to no good. Are they, Leney? Didn't you warn Jillybean about the possibility of traitors in your ranks?"

The cold evil coming off of her sunk deep into his bones and suddenly he regretted speaking up. "It was just a guess. I know the men and they can be fickle."

"Fickle," she deadpanned. "You get a possible assassination attempt from 'fickle.' No. Nope, that won't do. Find me the traitors now. This morning. I want three of them in chains before lunch. No excuses." Leney left in a hurry, wondering how he was going to get himself out of this trap. There was nothing worse in the Corsair world than a snitch; he'd have a target on his back the moment he snatched up the first man.

The Queen watched him leave with shrewd eyes. She wasn't as smart as Jillybean in most areas, however she had a sixth sense when it came to plots and intrigue; she could smell the evil coming off of Leney. It set her teeth on edge. When he had disappeared, she remembered the Guardians. "Donna, get these cultists out of my sight before I lose my temper."

The grim-faced guards began to close in and Donna was just hurrying the four Guardians away from the Queen when Denise Woodruff broke away. "Excuse me your Highness?" When Eve turned her hard blue eyes on her, Denise's courage failed her, and her knees buckled. She didn't try to stop herself and dropped to the floor. "I'm sorry. I can't go with them. I have to get back to the clinic. There are people who need me. Please," she added, subserviently dropping her gaze.

Eve liked what she saw. She liked the fear. She liked how the woman knew her place. She liked the begging quality in her voice. There was only one thing missing. She walked over and put her left hand out for the woman to kiss it.

"Denise," the Bishop warned, "don't do it. We only worship the Lord."

"I'm not demanding that you worship me, Denise. It would be a lie if you did. I'm asking that you demonstrate, what's the word Jillybean would use? Respect? No, fealty, that's it. Show me that. Show me some sort of devotion."

Denise closed her eyes and pretended she was kissing the feet of Jesus as her lips pressed against the Queen's knuckles. They were surprisingly hard and her hand shockingly quick as she reached out and grabbed a hunk of hair on the back of her head. A knife appeared like magic in Eve's other hand and was at her throat before she could blink.

The others were caught by surprise by the move. Troy made a futile gesture towards interceding but he was ten feet away with three ugly, tattooed guards between him and the Queen.

Eve gave him a wink as she pulled Denise's head further back. "Remember, Denise, now that you're on my side, never turn your back on your queen. And never say a wrong word, because I *will* hear it and the punishment for disloyalty is very severe. *Very* severe."

"Y-Yes, your Highness," Denise whispered, her eyes glued to the glittering knife.

A radiant smile broke across Eve's face. She released her grip and helped the quasi-doctor to her feet. "There you go. See how simple that was Mr. Bishop? Think about that when you see what awaits all those people my little Denise is going to go save."

"I will," Wojdan promised and he would, too. He would take into account her complete insanity and know that she could never be trusted.

Eve dismissed them all. She didn't trust her guards, except for Nathan Kittle and she trusted him only because he was such a coward that she knew he would never try anything. Unfortunately, he was also such a coward that he probably wouldn't fight for her. She needed someone both loyal and willing to fight.

Stu's handsome face jumped to the forefront of her mind, making her smirk. "He'd be the right guard dog, but he's gone. Who does that leave? You..." She gestured to Nathan.

"It's Nathan, your highness."

She waved a hand. "Sure, whatever. I need you to go get that stupid girl, the one with the messed up head."

"Do you mean Shaina Hale?"

The name sounded familiar. "Yeah. Get her and the kid with the one arm. I know they love me. And get the guy that got it in the chest a while back. And get that Islander. The Greek guy. Make sure they're armed. I need a little extra protection."

Nathan ran off leaving only her and Ernest in the tent. They stood with thirty feet separating them. It was as close as either wanted to get to the other. *You should get rid of the pills. If she keeps taking them, we'll…*

"I did something even better," she said and laughed, deliciously. "I switched out her 15-mg pills for 2.5-mg pills. They look exactly alike, but instead of her taking thirty milligrams, she's taking five. It's not enough. Not even close. Wow, to think dumb ol' Eve thought of that."

Wrong. She left you a giant brain to use and you're still an idiot How can you have missed how yellow your skin has become. Because of you, she's been taking more and more pills and now, not only does she have plenty of Zyprexa in her system, she also has all the other fillers and binders that go into the pills. You'll kill her and yourself uselessly.

"Oh yeah? If she has the meds in her why isn't she here? Why am I in charge? Why was Sadie? I say it's because she's starting to lose it for good."

And I say it's because she wants to be down there. I think she might have discovered something. Something long forgotten or something wonderful. You smelled the rolls. Don't lie.

She had smelled the cinnamon rolls. The wonderful aroma had filled the Queen's trailer just after Sadie locked herself in the bathroom. Eve's stomach immediately rumbled and her mouth had filled with saliva. These physical effects were nothing compared to the emotional ones. The scent had given Eve a wonderful inner warmth, an intimate sense of being protected, and the knowledge that she had been loved.

All of which had weakened Eve. She had been dwelling on that scent when Sadie came roaring back to take control.

"Jillybean can choke on the rolls for all I care. As long as I'm in charge, she can spend the rest of her life down…"

The tent flap whipped open and in hurried Shaina Hale holding a pistol by the barrel with both hands. She was wringing it, nervously. "Hi, your Highness. Nathan said you wanted me to guard you? I told him that I can try, but I'm not so good as a fighter."

She took a long breath and was clearly going to go on; however, Aaron Altman came in then, a huge revolver in an over-sized holster at his hip. It made him walk with an exaggerated step, something akin to a goose-step. He went right to one knee in front of Eve, who did her best not to look as disgusted as she felt. Aaron had something brown at the corner of his mouth. It might have been from his breakfast and it might have been from *something* else. She found boys to be disgusting at times.

In due time, she was surrounded by the catastrophically stupid Shaina Hale, the one-armed child, a limpy Gerry the Greek, a wheezy William Trafny and a nervous Nathan Kittle who jumped at every sound outside the tent, expecting an attack at any moment. As a fighting force they were ineptly frail and as an honor guard they were a joke. Still, they were better than nothing and better than having Corsairs at her back.

A few miles away, Commander Walker was thinking the same thing as he marched up through the hills east of Highton. The Corsairs were a dirty lot, so much so that a scraggy-faced man named Stinky Jim was the cleanest of them.

Their mouths were as foul as their unwashed bodies. For an hour, they made rude jokes at the Guardian's expense. These jokes were rarely funny, which did not stop them from laughing even if the laughter was forced most of the time. The Bishop appealed to Steven Yingling, the supposed leader of the little expedition, but he was a Sacramentan and the Corsairs refused to listen to him.

"Sorry," he said, offering a meaningless shrug to go along with his apology. "It's sort of expected. You are the enemy. It'll get better when you come over to our side."

Troy began to bristle, but stopped when Wojdan put a hand on his arm. "There is nothing you can show us that will make us change our mind. Death is preferable to a life of sin and debauchery."

"I guess," Steven answered. "We really don't do much sinning. I mean it's not the Queen's policy to do evil things, you know."

"I suppose we have a different point of view," the Bishop retorted blandly. "What are we going to see, by the way? More zombies? If so, we've wasted a trip. We saw plenty of zombies last night. We're not afraid of a few more."

Steven sighed. "We're almost there." They had been wending their way along the face of a steep, tree-covered hill. It had all of them except for Walker and Troy huffing. When they were just shy of the top, Steven paused and looked back the way they had come. The ocean stretched wide and blue, twinkling in the backdrop. Just in front of it was Highton, looking serene. Off to the north were hundreds of tents lined up in a grid pattern.

They all gazed back before going to the very crest of the hill. The view on the other side was terrifying. The hill dropped steeply away into something of a long gorge that ran away to the south for a mile or more. It was a third of that at its widest, though it was hard to tell exactly since it was completely filled with zombies.

There were enough to overflow a stadium.

Commander Walker was as tough as they came and yet he felt cold fear crawl right up his legs, cross his flat stomach and enter his heart. His Knights had slain less than a thousand of the beasts the night before. This was thirty times that number.

"They seen enough," Stinky Jim said in a whisper. None of the Corsairs had ventured to the crest. They knew what was on the other side. "Let's go."

The group was silent on the way back down. Even the Corsairs held their tongues. They only stared at the Guardians with knowing looks. It was a guarantee that they would cave and each of them was wondering how they were going to divide up the women. So far, the Queen had been downright prudish on the entire concept and they weren't happy about it.

But the Bishop shocked everyone by not caving. The group entered the pavilion—the surgical tables had been removed and in their place the Queen had set up a great chair to act as a throne. She lounged casually in it as if she were watching a movie in her family room at home.

"We saw your zombies," the Bishop said. "They were very scary."

"And?"

Wojdan gave her his sad smile. "Sorry, but they weren't that scary. We will not surrender."

Her eyes fairly gleamed with building excitement. She jumped up and went to stand directly in front of Wojdan; with her heels, they were roughly the same height. "You're calling me out?" she asked in the same gleeful manner an eight-year-old would when told she was getting a pony for Christmas. "Yes! That's what I'm talking about! You got guts, Bishop and I like that."

"Yea," he said, dryly.

"Damn right, yea! You just don't know what it's like to be me. Jillybean gets to do all sorts of things because everyone thinks she's bluffing, but me? I prep and prep until everything is perfect and then what do I get?" She hung her head, drooped her lips like licorice melting in hundred-degree heat and said in the voice of a faux moron: "*Sorry, but we give up.*"

She perked up in a flash and slapped her hands together in triumph. "But this is going to be epic. Like one of those plagues I was talking about. Ooh, you don't mind if we film it do you? I think Troy will look gooood wielding one of those spears, fighting for his life, surrounded by fifteen or twenty monsters. If you could manage to get your shirt ripped off during the fight that would be a big help. I will have to do something about the lighting." Eve broke off, wondering how she would handle the lighting.

Commander Walker stared at her in amazement. "A film crew in the middle of a battle? That's…" He bit back the word *insane*.

"No, I'll be using a drone. Just think of it as one of those old public service announcements. You know: *Don't do drugs,* or *It's ten o'clock, do you know where your child is?* We'll get some before and after shots and intersperse them with footage of the monsters eating everyone in your little village. And, and, brainstorm here…we'll get my fleet right up close and get some video of us shooting torpedoes into your little boats. We'll fill them with white phosphorus for a better effect. At night it will look wild!"

"I think we should talk to the other person, the one she calls Jillybean," Walker said to the Bishop under his breath.

"No," the Bishop said without lowering his voice. "This is the real queen. The other one is the bait and this one is the switch. Your Highness, we will be leaving now and I will pray for you."

Donna Polston was quick to say, "I'll lead them out." Eve didn't care. They were all extras in her world and she was onto the big picture. She wanted destruction on a level that would make everything Jillybean had ever done look like child's play—and she wanted it on film, so no one would ever second guess her again.

When the little group was out of earshot of the pavilion, Donna turned on them. "She's not kidding! That was Eve. She's an entirely different person than the Queen and she's evil. She'll sic that entire horde on you."

"Isn't that what the other Queen intended as well?" the Bishop asked. "Or did she summon those fiends just to scare us?"

"Probably. With her you can never tell what's going on because she's so smart, but with Eve…Your Excellency, you have to give up. She will destroy you."

The Bishop reached out and touched Donna's brown hair. "No, my child. We will not give up. Ever."

Chapter 39

Donna Polston crept back into the pavilion. She wasn't in a hurry to be anywhere near Eve. It was always frightening being within arm's reach of someone so bat-crap crazy. Thankfully the Queen had ordered the tent struck down so it could be moved back to the main camp. A few Santas were standing around scratching their heads, wondering how they were going to get the huge thing down without dirtying it. Donna didn't want to have to babysit them through the task and slipped out again.

Behind the tent, the zombies were being coaxed towards the trailers by Eve. She and Jillybean liked to play the part of "zombie tamer" perhaps because it enhanced the idea of their fearlessness. She held a long aluminum pole which she used to guide the blind and deaf creatures. With no other real stimuli to guide them, the beasts would lumber in the direction they were tapped. One to the face would set the beast moving forward; a tap on the right arm would turn it, and so on.

Even maimed, Donna hated being anywhere near the monsters and kept well back. As she was plodding up the hill after them. Gerry the Greek limped over. "So?" he asked. The one word was chalk-full of meaning.

"They're not giving up," Donna said, dolefully. "God, I wish Jenn and Stu were here. Stu could get Jillybean to come out like that." She snapped her fingers and sighed. "And if we had Jenn, I don't think we would be in this mess at all. I didn't really notice until she was gone, but I think Jillybean needed Jenn to be her conscience. You know what I mean? Her sense of right or wrong. And now without her, look where we are."

"Since we don't have either of them, maybe *you* should try to coax Jillybean out," Gerry suggested. "You know Jillybean and Eve pretty well, and both of those crazy chicks like you."

Donna smacked his arm. "What are you, an idiot? Never say anything like that out loud. If *she* hears you, she'll kill you, Gerry. God, how did we get stuck in this situation? In league with Corsairs? Using zombies to kill people. Having a..." she lowered her voice even further, "...a schizo for a queen? Everything used to be so simple."

It had been, and Gerry missed his old life as well, but Jillybean had been absolutely right about one thing, the happy little world they had been living in was never going to last. "We were living in a bubble, plain and simple. We have to forget it, because the past is the past. We have to worry about today. I don't know if I can be a part of unleashing those zombies on the Guardians. It'll be a massacre."

"I know, but what choice do we have? Unless we can get someone who's willing to risk Eve's anger, we're stuck." Donna didn't have the guts to try to outsmart Eve and she didn't think Gerry was up to the task. She had known him for too long. When it came to thinking, he was a bit of a plodder. He wasn't stupid, he just took his time coming to conclusions. Eve would see right through him if he tried to trick her into letting Jillybean out.

"Yingling's pretty smart," Gerry said. "He was a Sacramento guy, though. Damn, so is Rebecca Haigh. I was about to suggest her."

Donna didn't have Gerry's prejudice against Sacramentans. In his mind they were bottom feeders and only slightly better than the Santas. Still, she scratched Steven Yingling's name from her short list. She didn't know him very well and what they were contemplating was tantamount to treason in Eve's mind. If Donna was going to put her life in someone's hands, she wanted to be able to trust that person completely. She loved the idea of using Miss Rebecca; the girl had proven to be tough, smart and resourceful. The problem was that Rebecca had been left behind as acting governor of the bay area in the Queen's absence.

"What about Colleen White?" Gerry suggested.

"You really are an idiot. Colleen hates the Queen, both of them. And I'm sure Eve hates her, though it's hard to tell since she seems to hate a lot of people. Either way, I've had to assign hunting duties to Colleen just to keep her out of the camp. And you want to know what she's brought back so far? In three days, she's managed to kill a squirrel. That's singular. One squirrel and it took her seven bullets."

Gerry looked like he was going to be physically sick. "Seven bullets? That's the most ridiculous thing I…" A sudden splash of gunfire from the north shook the morning. It was a short burst with two or three weapons popping off shots. "Zombie, probably."

"Maybe," Donna replied. Her gut told her differently. The shooting had been closer than the other stray zombie kills. Out of force of habit she gazed around, looking for a sign in the trees, in the sky, in the particular way the clouds had arranged themselves. She saw nothing which only caused the nervous pit in her belly to grow. Once she had been the leader of the Coven. Once she could see signs from the way the leaves fell and interpret them anyway she wanted.

Jillybean had changed all that. Now if she said that she saw the destruction of the Guardians in the clouds, some jackass from Santa Clara would laugh and say: *All I see is a horsey*.

She sighed and said, "Colleen's out. Who else." They batted names back and forth, always finding fault somewhere. Charmel Gilbert was too sweet and Eve would eat her alive. Ashtyn Bishop was too unlucky, everything she touched became a fiasco. Claudia Stephens was still too skittish after her near death experience in the pounding surf off Alcatraz.

Everyone else was too ugly or too stupid. Eve could barely look at ugly people. Stupid people were almost as bad. Although she wasn't the genius that Jillybean was, Eve wouldn't let people with even a slightly lower than average IQ speak in her presence.

Another factor that ruled people out was bravery. Most everyone fell short in this category. Confronting Eve was very much like walking into a tiger's dens, naked and weaponless.

What they needed was someone strong, brave, handsome and smart. Donna immediately thought of Mike Gunter and Stu Currans—and sighed again. She had to shake her head to clear the image of their dead faces. The one that replaced them was surprising: Knights Sergeant Troy Holt. "What did Eve say about that Knight? The handsome one, Holt?"

Gerry ran a hand through his dark beard. "She said he was cute or something. You're not thinking of using him to get Jillybean back, are you? That's crazy. First off, he just left and second, whoever goes to get him might get shot by them or by us, and they will definitely get shot by the Queen. You know better than anyone that Eve holds grudges, and she won't be gone forever."

He was right. Whoever crossed the lines could never come back. "Unless they went in some sort of disguise and then snuck back after dark."

"Snuck back from where?" someone asked from behind them.

"Gah!" Gerry cried. Colleen White, dressed in form-fitting camo, had suddenly appeared at his side, causing him to jump. The three days of hard work involved in creating the river had worn down everyone except her. She looked as fresh as always, her black hair was still silky and her eyes as bright blue as ever.

"Nothing. I mean nowhere," he said, feeling foolish. "Where'd you come from?"

She pointed off toward the ocean. "Over by the beach." Donna frowned, creating tiny lines at the corners of her eyes and lips. "I was hunting," Colleen added, quickly.

"Because that's where all the deer like to hang out?" Donna asked.

The sarcasm was missed by Colleen who said, "They have to drink sometime. It must be at night. When everyone's sneaking around, right? Come on, I heard you guys talking about sneaking somewhere. What's going on for real?"

"Eve's back," Donna said and then proceeded to tell Colleen everything, hoping that she could come up with an idea. Colleen was quiet as they trudged along, heading, like everyone else, in the direction of where the shooting had taken place. It was only a few hundred yards from the main camp and already there was something of a crowd.

Donna, whose rank was somewhere between majordomo and serving girl, pushed her way to the front, where she saw Mark Leney talking with another of the ex-Corsair captains. They were standing over the bodies of three men. "What's going on?" she demanded. Leney began limping towards her; he was bleeding from a wound along the side of his thigh.

"We should talk in private," he whispered into her ear. "Can you clear these people out of here?"

"Of course." With Gerry and Colleen's help, they shooed the crowd away.

When it was just the four of them, Leney sat with a grimace, his back to the bodies. "You heard what the Queen wanted of me." Donna and Gerry both nodded; Colleen nodded as well a second after they did, though she had no idea. Leney motioned behind him. "It was them. I had heard some rumors a while back that someone was doing some talking. I had hoped it was just that, rumors, but when I confronted them…" He pointed at his leg as if that was all that needed to be said.

"They just started shooting?" Gerry asked.

"Not right off the bat. I was like, 'come on, guys, we know what's going on' and before I knew it, that guy, uh he reached for a gun. I was faster, but not fast enough and one of them nicked me."

"When you say you heard someone was talking, who were they talking to?" Colleen asked.

Leney looked startled by the question. "Uhh, just people. It's one of those things you hear sitting around the fire at night. People talk. You know. I heard from Bob, who heard from Jim that Ron was asking too many questions. That sort of thing."

"Are there more of these traitors?" Colleen asked. "Did they give you more names or…wait! That's Steve. Steve Yingling. He wasn't a traitor. He hated the Corsairs."

In a state of shock, Donna edged closer to the bodies. One was a Corsair she didn't know, one was a Santa named Runner, who did nothing but play cards all day, and one was Steven Yingling. He was covered in so much blood that it looked like he'd been shot by a machine gun. He had three holes in his chest, one through-and-through on his left wrist and was missing a finger on his right hand.

"Maybe he hated the Queen even more," Leney said. "I didn't get a chance to talk to him. Like I said, they just started shooting. That smacks of guilt in my mind."

"Yeah," Gerry said. He leaned in close to Donna and whispered, "We lucked out not using him."

Donna fixed him with a quick glare and pretended she hadn't heard. "The Queen is going to have a freaking conniption fit. She's already paranoid; Eve, I mean. If there's anyone else, she's going to resort to mass tortures, executions, the whole nine yards."

"There isn't," Leney said, speaking quickly. "None that I've heard at least. And I really don't know if these guys were for real. I just wanted to ask them some questions and the next thing I know they're pulling their guns." He looked eager to be believed.

"If only Jillybean was here," Colleen said, ignoring Donna's sudden twitch. "She's much more reasonable. She'd believe you, Captain Leney, just like I do."

Colleen was being so obvious, that Donna had to close her eyes so that Leney wouldn't see them roll back in her head.

Leney knew exactly what she was suggesting and she was absolutely, one-hundred percent wrong. Jillybean would take one look at the crime scene, for that's exactly what it was, and see that the three men had been murdered. After killing them, Leney barely had time to position the bodies and kick dirt over ill-placed blood spatters before the first person arrived.

It would be stupid to try to bring Jillybean back, but it would also be stupid to appear to fight it. "I can try to talk to her if you think it will help."

Donna tried not to look too excited. "It might," was all she was willing to commit to. The four of them left the bodies discarded in the high weeds and went to where the pavilion was being erected. Eve was nearby, listening to the Corsair Captain who had found Leney and the bodies. He was dismissed with evident annoyance and Leney was forced to go into the deprivation trailer with Eve.

When he came out ten minutes later, he was pale, looking as if he had kissed the wrong end of a baby. Donna caught his eye and he gave her a discreet shake of his head. Eve was still in charge.

Unexpectedly, Colleen said, "I'll go Highton. I'll leave as soon as it gets dark. I'll send that…what was his name? Troy? I'll send him back, but even if he's able to get Jillybean back, what's really going to change? Aren't we still going to attack? Don't we have to? The ex-Corsairs aren't going to go through all this work just to walk away when they could crush these guys."

"I don't know what Jillybean's plan was," Donna said. "She likes to play things close to the vest. Maybe she was hoping that the first attack would scare them enough for a bluff to work. They clearly aren't changing their minds. So, I'm worried that this is going to happen, Jillybean or no Jillybean."

"Me too," Colleen whispered, dropping her head.

She looked suddenly vulnerable. Donna gripped her arm. "Then maybe you shouldn't go. If you try and fail…"

"Eve will kill me. I know. I'm still going. I think I'm done with all this. And if I can do something to stop the slaughter, then I will." She started to walk away, then stopped and said over her shoulder, "If she wins this way, she'll be the new Black Captain. And someone will have to stop her."

Chapter 40

Eve was still in charge and growing crazier by the minute, when Colleen slipped out of camp just as the sun was going down. The Queen had spent the afternoon standing on the steep hill above her zombie army, gloating over it, breathing in the foul air that shimmered up. She wasn't fighting her inner demons, she was goading them and feeding them on raw hate.

Jillybean was becoming only a distant memory and Eve knew that when she marched triumphantly through the scorched streets of Highton the next day and saw the pools of red, the cast off hollowed-out skulls, and the litter of torn limbs scattered about in wonderful bloody glory, Jillybean would be crushed by the guilt. Even if this had never been her plan, she had set it all in motion and the horror of it would destroy her. To make sure, Eve would not just soak in the scene; she would wallow in it; she would literally bathe in it and, if she had to, she would drink it in.

A belly full of rancid, coppery blood was a small price to pay to finally cage Jillybean for good.

In the meantime, Eve's paranoia was growing along with her hate. There were spies all around her. Spies for the Guardians and spies for the Black Captain and, worse than all of them, spies for Jillybean. She didn't trust anyone and resorted to spying herself. Secretly, she had Gerry the Greek spy on Mark Leney, and she had Shaina Hale spy on Gerry the Greek, and had Deaf Mick spy on Shaina because maybe, just maybe the lumpy-headed girl was faking her intense stupidity.

Eventually, she had Mark Leney limping around spying on Shaina and Deaf Mick.

It wasn't enough just to stem her inner fears and the Queen clamped down on anyone leaving the camp. Guards were posted, facing inwards instead of out.

All of this was too much for Donna Polston, who chickened out and tried to dissuade Colleen from her mission, but the young woman wouldn't change her mind. Colleen held steady even when she heard the rumors that the Queen was going to kick off the attack as soon as it got dark.

She had planned to slip out of camp under the cover of darkness; now she would have to take a terrible risk and leave with the cool light of day on her.

With her rehearsed excuses in the forefront of her mind, she took a deep breath, squared her shoulders, stuck a smile on her perfectly made-up face and started heading north as if she had every right to stroll right out of camp. Within a minute, she was challenged by a swaggering Santa with the made-up name of Mordecai Monroe. It was no accident that it was he who stopped her.

For days on end, he had followed her around spouting inane sexual innuendos, letting fall gross hints about his prowess in bed and generally behaving like a pervert who was on the verge of becoming a rapist. Trusting her gut, she hadn't shot him down and now she was hoping to profit from her perseverance.

"Hold on," Mordecai demanded, moving to cut her off. He wore his hair greased back like he was part of a fifties doo-wop band; his sharply pointed widow's peak made him appear older than his thirty years. "Where do you think you're going?"

"Hunting," she answered, holding her pistol hidden in her coat pocket. The gun felt heavier than usual. Its grip growing slick as her sweaty palm oiled it. "You know, the usual."

"No one's supposed to leave the camp," he told her. "There are spies, you know. Spies slinking about ain't a good thing. You heard about those three guys today that got shot? They were the Black Captain's spies. I heard they were going to set the horde on us. Can you believe it?"

She could, very easily. She knew a great deal more about spies than even Donna knew.

"Yeah," she answered, shaking her head as if the idea was crazy. "I heard. I was there with Donna Polston and that Leney guy. You know I'm pretty tight with the Queen's inner circle, right? Me and the Queen go way back. If I had time, I'd tell you about how I saved her life. Trust me, the Queen is cool with me leaving. And I'm not gonna do any spying, it's just that my luck with hunting has been pretty bad and she's looking forward to some venison. You understand." She started to go on.

"I was told that no one can leave." He pushed in front of her. "Sorry. I'd let you take off if I could. But, you know what? This can work out for both of us. The big fight's about to go down and I can get you a front row seat. I got a primo spot picked out. I could get a blanket for us. Hmm? I got a good bottle of wine. Not hootch, baby, but a fine 2009 cab. Not a lot of people know this, but old wine is the best. What do you say?"

Colleen didn't want to say anything; she wanted to be left alone by this slobbering nitwit. A part of her envied Jillybean's insanity. She would never have put up with this guy. No, Jillybean would have pulled the pistol, sniffed the barrel with that hungry-to-kill look of hers and old Mordecai would've been out of there or on his knees begging. Jillybean did like to see them beg.

Yes, Colleen was very envious. There was power in insanity. It freed one from caring about the little things and the little people, and in the great scheme of things Mordecai was a little person with a little part to play. And yet he had a part. He was the perfect dupe, thinking with his penis instead of with his head. Only someone looking to get laid would ignore the fact that no sane person hunted at night. You were a thousand times more likely to run into a zombie than a deer.

She turned up the charm. "Well, I don't have plans for tonight," she told him, glancing up as if mulling over her options. "I'll think about it. Are you going to be here for a while?"

"Until ten, but you don't want to wait. Everyone's saying the fight's gonna happen as soon as it gets real dark. The Queen likes things dark when she gets her blood up."

"Don't we all," she said with an impish smile, even though every word out of his mouth set her teeth on edge. She let the smile fade into simulated despair. "Hey, can I tell you the real reason I have to leave camp?" After a glance back, she leaned in close. "This is embarrassing. I was sorta skinny dipping in the ocean this afternoon. I know, I was 'supposed' to be hunting, but I can never catch anything anyways. So, I decided to cool off and took a dip."

"Really? I bet that was cold."

She only just realized how silly her lie was—who in their right mind would try swimming in the ocean in deep November? Luckily for her, Mordecai seemed to be caught up on the skinny dipping portion of the story.

"Well, I get so hot from hunting and who wants to see a sweaty Colleen?"

"I do," he said, raising a hand and laughing.

Colleen was well-practiced at fake laughing along with men. "Ha-ha! You boys!" She put an intimate hand on his arm and gave him a gentle squeeze. "I bet you do, but I left my gun there and if I don't get it back, I won't be going anywhere. The Queen will have me digging latrines or something all night long."

Mordecai looked alarmed. "All night?"

"Maybe even tomorrow night, too." His alarm increased. She touched his arm again. "But if I can get that gun, it'll be okay. Look, I'll be back in a bit. Make sure you stay right here. I wouldn't want to run into someone else with a better offer; I don't want you to lose out."

He took a quick look around and then gave her a sly grin, showing her the gap in his teeth where a poor gambler from out of the hills had popped him one. "If you come right back…"

"I will, I promise. Bye, Mordecai." Her smile fell away the moment her back was to him. Her fear began to pile up. If she were caught now, Eve would string her up by the neck.

With her heart trembling, she walked slowly away. A guilty person would have hurried. She forced herself not to look back until she crested the first hill—the wind-blown land of rolling hills and dead grasses was wide open and she saw no one. Now she picked up the pace and half-jogged, half-walked another five minutes before she dropped down and hid behind the crest of another hill.

Slowly, she inched up, her pistol in her hand. Nothing moved. When she was sure she was alone, she slunk into a crouch and headed west where the sun was canted just above the ocean, turning the grey water to shining silver. It was a glorious golden sunset that was lost on her. Sunsets were for romantic ninnies and that wasn't Colleen White. She might have looked the part and she had certainly acted it at times, but she was no starry-eyed, dippy girl.

An angry part of her wished she could be around when Mordecai realized he had been used by a girl he had dismissed as just another conquest.

They had all dismissed her, even the Queen with her massive intellect. Yes, Jillybean had been so busy looking down her nose at her that she was as blind as the rest of them—and that knowledge, that true fact made Colleen blissfully warm inside even as the ocean breeze kicked up and blew back her long black hair.

Jillybean had dismissed her as just a backwards Hill-girl from the very start. They all had, and it was going to come back and bite them in the ass.

A white grin crept across her face. It was only part self-congratulatory. A large part was a stress response.

The night was going to be make or break for her. It could even be life or death, and as she came closer to the town, and the sun began to dip into the farthest part of the ocean, Colleen's heart began to beat faster and her breathing picked up.

"It'll be okay," she told herself as she laid her crossbow and pack in the tall grass and covered them over with shoots pulled up by the roots. "Think about it. What do you possibly have to fear from a bunch of Jesus-freaks? Nothing."

In the last few months, Colleen had known real fear. She'd come face-to-face with death a dozen times and she had certainly faced scarier people than the plump bishop she had seen walking around in a stylized bathrobe. The Queen, for instance, had gotten scarier every single day. She had started out a little nutty when Jenn Lockhart had brought her back from Bainbridge, but since then she had grown into something of a monster.

And there had been others who frightened her far more than the Bishop. Insidious men in black who made no bones about what they were after. One in particular still gave her a cold shiver whenever she thought about him—which was why she did her best to put her mental blinders on and do her job.

"You got this," she whispered before putting her hands up and marching straight towards the first barrier that the Guardians had erected in place of their wall. It was a frightfully disgusting mound of bloated zombie corpses that stretched in an arc from one section of the broken wall to the other. There was a narrow opening where the new river ran into the town. The river was no longer the swollen monster it had been. The reservoir was depleted and now the river was only a little larger than the average mountain stream.

As she approached the mound of bodies, crossbows and spears were leveled at her by bleary-eyed boys in men's costumes. They were part of the reserve force, keeping watch while the real Knights rested for the coming battle.

"Stop! Keep your hands where I can see them," one cried, in a high nervous voice.

They had rushed forward as she had tried to edge between the cold water and the corpses. "Give me a moment, will you?" Colleen's hands dipped as she nearly fell. "I'm not going to hurt anyone. I'm here on a diplomatic mission."

"What sort of mission?" another of them asked.
He stepped close and put his hand out to help her across the river. He was very gallant, despite appearing only to be in his early teens. The others around him were just as young. Their armor teetered precariously on them as if a strong wind would send it all crashing down around their feet.

The young Knight didn't even think about frisking her. Yes, she had little to fear from "men" such as these. "Thank you, sir. I'm trying to stop the Queen from attacking. I need the help of one of your men: Knights Sergeant Troy Holt."

"From what everyone says, he already talked to your queen," the young Knight replied, coldly. "He and the others were basically kidnapped. Is this going to be more of the same? Answer honestly now." He shot her what she supposed was his version of a hard, penetrating look; she had to fight to keep the smile from her face.

"Honestly? He might be shot on sight. That's the problem with the Queen. She's not herself and we need someone brave to bring her back. Either way, this isn't something I should be talking to you guys about. Who's in charge? How do I find Holt? I need to see him this instant if all of you want to live to see morning."

The teens conferred with silent looks of uncertainty until the gallant youth half bowed to her and led her into the little town. It was a busy place with people hurrying every which way, preparing for the fight. Some were loaded down with weapons, others had shovels and sandbags, still more carried food and water. In spite of the rush and the failing light, there wasn't the tang of panic in the air that Colleen had expected. The people went grimly about their business.

Although she patently didn't belong, the swarm of humanity was like bees, so focused that no one even noticed Colleen. It was a spy's dream and yet she was oddly put out. She was too pretty to be ignored, and besides, she was saving them, or at least trying to. Her mood only grew more foul when they came to a grey block of a building. In the lowering evening light, it was a gloomy, ugly place that she thought was a warehouse until the door was thrown back and light streamed out.

It was their church and it had been in constant use since the Queen's fleet had sailed into view days before. The pair surprised an ancient-looking priest who had been stringing a blackout curtain across the inner doorway. He was small and soft, his wispy, thinning hair was as white as snow. His wrinkles were many and deep. He was so very old that his eyes were rheumy and glazed with a light film.

"Eh?" he asked when the young Knight explained why he was there. "What's that?" The Knight repeated himself and the priest shrugged. "This queen business again. I'm getting too old to even think about kings and queens." He started shuffling away without asking either of them to follow. Colleen thought they had been rudely dismissed, however the priest kept talking as if they were right next to him. "Back in the old days we just had that one English queen and she had been hanging around for decades. You think this is the same one?"

"No, Father. This one's different. This one's younger. Is the Bishop in his office? I can show the young woman myself. There's no need to…"

"A new queen?" the priest asked, talking over the Knight. "Well, I guess it's about time. Not that we ever really cared one way or another over here across the pond. The Brits did their thing with their crumpets and what not, and we did ours. Nice enough people, the Brits. Not at all like these beastly Corsairs." He had been shuffling on again, but now he stopped and looked back at Colleen, squinting along his nose to catch a glimpse of her through the bottom half of his bifocals. "You don't look like much of a Corsair."

"That's because tonight I'm a Guardian," Colleen replied, loudly so as to be heard. She knew men and could flirt with the old and young alike.

The priest grinned and took her soft hand in his gnarled one. His knuckles were so swollen and pointed they looked and felt as though they were going to poke right out of his paper-thin flesh. "Quite right. We're all guardians of the faith in these times. Ah, here we are." He didn't bother knocking at the door. He bent and squinted down at the knob, looking at it as if it were a puzzle in need of deciphering. "Lefty loosey," he whispered, like he was reciting an incantation, before turning the knob.

Bishop Wojdan looked up from a map spread out on his desk. On his right was Commander Walker and on his left was an ashen-faced Virginia Keim, the new commander of the reserves. Three other men stood in front of the desk, their bodies contorted so as to see the map right side up. One of the three was Knights Sergeant Troy Holt.

Colleen was introduced and then forced to stand beneath the withering gaze of everyone present. *You can do this*, she told herself. "First off, the Queen did not send me. If I am caught I will likely be killed. That's how serious this is."

"We're surrounded by a vast zombie horde," Walker growled. "You don't have to tell us how serious anything is."

The Bishop put out a soft plump hand. "Now, now. The young lady has a right to be heard. Bravery, in all its forms, should be applauded in this dark hour. Go on." She explained what she needed in seconds and when she was done, even she thought the idea sounded not very well thought out and unlikely to succeed.

Troy looked confused. "I'm not sure what you want from me. You want me to talk to her. That's it? You think that just talking will coax this other Jillybean person out of her?"

Colleen opened her mouth but the old priest spoke first. "I knew a girl, way back, named Jillybean. Oh, that was ages ago and wasn't she the darlingest thing, with her..."

The young Knight put his hand on the old priest's arm and shook his head to shush him. Wojdan wore an embarrassed smile for the priest. "We can hear all about that when we're done, Father Amacker. Unless you wish to tell young David about it outside?"

"No, no. Go on, miss. This isn't the Jillybean I knew. She was a tiny girl, sweet but full of mischief."

Colleen cleared her throat, wishing the old coot would leave already. When he didn't leave, and no one showed him out, she sighed briefly and explained to Troy, "Yes, I know it sounds weird and it is a long shot, but all it takes to bring her back is to engage with her in the right way. Eve is nasty. You're going to have to put up with a lot of insults and even more threats. Just let them roll off you."

Troy's frown deepened. "We already had a taste of that and I don't see how being abused more will help anything. Chances are we'll make her even madder."

"On the bright side, she can't kill you more than once," Colleen said, trying to crack the hard exterior of the glaring men. It didn't work. "Your best bet is to steer the conversation towards things that Jillybean knows a lot about. Uh, like being a doctor. Or, like building things. She can weld and make things that Eve can't. You might even try talking about explosives, but it can be dangerous because Eve can't build them, but likes to use them."

"This sounds like a waste of time," Walker said. "And a waste of a good man. Troy is too noble of heart for trickery such as this. Lying and deceit take practice. She might be crazy, but your Queen is smart. She'll see right through anything that even smacks of dishonesty."

Troy sucked in a breath. "With permission, I still would like to try...not the lying part. Just the talking part. All day the congregation has prayed for a blessing and perhaps now one has come." He gestured to Colleen. "We have always been taught that the Lord works in mysterious ways."

Bishop Wojdan nodded thoughtfully, his lips pursed. Next to him, Walker scowled his face into dark crags. Father Amacker spoke into the silence with a voice as wavering as the candles in the room. "The Jillybean I knew had a sister. She was a turned around sort of girl. Why, I don't know, but she always dressed in black like a Satanist and yet she had the sweetest soul, always so protective of the little girl. It's too bad she died and poor Jillybean thought she was haunted. It was…"

"I think maybe you should get a little rest, Father," the Bishop said. "Perhaps you should take a nap or a…"

"Hold on," Colleen said, speaking right over him. "Was the sister's name, Sadie?"

Father Amacker smiled. "Yes, it was." Colleen felt a strange chill go through her as the old priest went on, "They came out of Colorado after all this started. That little girl was smart as a whip. She built a little tank out of a Honda…or was it a Toyota? The details, you know, they just slip the mind. Either way, she was a little firecracker that one. She could weld and work all that old technology. I remember when she escaped from three grown men. No, it was six of them. I forgot Sheriff Woods. She got away by using this tiny bomb…"

Colleen had heard enough. "Sorry, Troy. You're not going. He is."

Chapter 41

There was no way Knights Sergeant Troy Holt would allow the eighty-five-year old priest to go alone into an enemy camp. He wondered if the old man had the strength to even tackle the hill by himself; Father Amacker was frail and uncertain on his feet on the flattest of ground. During the processional at the start of mass he would go from person to person using each as a crutch and would always lag far behind the Bishop. On rainy days, he would arrive at the altar well after the opening hymn had ended and in the silence, he was sometimes heard whispering to himself: "Almost there. Not much further."

It didn't help that instead of wearing the simple black clergy outfit that priests frequently wore in day-to-day activities, he decided that night to go "all out" for the occasion of meeting with the Queen. He wore an ankle-length white alb with a white and gold stole that hung to his knees, and a wide, loosely tied belt of gold cloth. The array was striking, though hardly conducive to hiking.

In stark contrast, Troy wore his usual battle gear and was covered, neck to knees, in camouflaged tactical armor. He carried only his spear. With the dark descending on them like a veil, he hoped to get to the Queen's camp before she started lighting off her fireworks, knowing that if he failed to get there in time, his M4 wouldn't be enough to save him and the priest.

Unfortunately, time was not on their side. As he helped Father Amacker across the moat, a far-off horn blew. It was a deep brassy sound and was answered by a second horn which was much closer. It could only mean one thing: the Queen was preparing to unleash her horde of zombies.

"Did you hear that?" Father Amacker asked, sounding confused. "That wasn't me was it?"

"No, Father. It wasn't you," Troy said, taking him by the arm and guiding him toward a small opening that had been made in the ring of zombie corpses. "That was Jillybean. We're going to go talk to her, remember? We don't have a lot of time, so we're going to have to hurry."

"Oh, yes. Hurry, hurry. People always hurry these days. Time is one of those strange things that is beyond our understanding and so many people think they can control it. Back in the day, people would say: time is money, or time is precious. It's all poppycock. Life is precious! That's what I…used to…"

They were past the mound and the slope was already getting to the old man. He began wheezing.

Another horn sounded. It was a long, lugubrious note. An ominous note. If it was meant as a warning that the battle would soon be upon them, Troy took it to heart and tried to rush Father Amacker along even faster. It was a failed attempt as the priest did not have a fast speed or even a second gear. He was either at a complete standstill or plodding slowly forward.

The horn brought him to a halt. He stared up the hill. "Now, what is she up to? You can't go about blowing horns at night! It's a sure way to summon those awful demons. Tell me Troy, how sure are you that we're going to see Jillybean? The girl I knew would never blow horns at night. She was smart as a whip. Did I tell you that?"

This was the fifth time that he had. "Yes, Father. We're supposed to be going to talk some sense into her."

"Well, okay. It does sound like she's in trouble if she's blowing horns and making a big hullabaloo. But we can't be too rough on her. She's an orphan, the poor little thing. Did I tell you she had this sister? She was a turned around sort of girl that I was certain was a Satanist since she always went..."

Troy's hand clenched around his spear until his knuckles were white. Time was zipping by. Already the bright beacon of Venus was lost among the night stars crowding the dark sky. "You did indeed, Father. Now, we have to hurry. Please." He managed to get the priest going again and they went for quite a while, until, halfway up the first hill, Amacker broke into a coughing fit and had to rest again.

As they waited, they saw the first flare. It was a little golden light, small and innocent appearing and yet filled with such dreadful implications that Troy sucked in his breath at the sight of it. Desperation clawed at his insides and as the flare sunk behind the far hills, he whispered, urgently, "I could carry you, Father. On my back or in my arms. Please. It's important that we get to their camp as soon as possible."

Father Amacker gave him a reproachful look. "Oh, that wouldn't do. How would it look if we showed up like that? Me being carried like a baby! No, Troy, we must appear strong."

Troy didn't have time to explain to the priest that once ten-thousand zombies were set in motion there would be no stopping them. The horde would rampage and kill without mercy. He wondered if Amacker was beyond understanding even if he tried to explain. "Yes, Father," Troy replied, taking his arm again. "We should appear strong." The priest's skin had the consistency of parchment paper and his bones were like not particularly firm straws.

They made it to the top of the hill and saw another larger one ahead of them. They went down quickly enough, but at the bottom, Father Amacker needed another short rest. It was almost too much for Troy. He wanted to scream: *We don't have time!*

When the old man finally got going again, Troy placed a hand on the small of his back and propelled him up the hill without listening to the old man's excited squawks of: "Careful now. That's fast enough! Please, slow down." The Knight didn't dare slow. The horns were echoing and the flares were in the air nonstop. Worse than all of that was the soft rumbling coming from the east; it was the sound of an army of zombies on the move.

For a moment, Troy doubted. It was a strange feeling for him. His life choices, guided by the Bible, had always been so clear to him, and the dilemmas faced on the field of battle had always been cut and dried. Now, he stumbled spiritually. It was obvious he would never find the Queen in time to stop the horde, and yet to turn back would mean a valiant, but ultimately useless death.

It seemed that for the time, his trust in the Lord would end in failure and slaughter. He was at a loss and didn't know which way to turn. Normally, he would have gone to a priest for advice. Unfortunately, the nearest priest was doubled over, barely able to breathe.

I'll have to carry him, he decided. Though which way he would carry him Troy still didn't know. Forward to throw themselves on the mercy of an evil being or back to accept their death with what dignity they could manage. At least with the zombies it would be a quick death. The Queen would likely torture them first—nothing would ever change his mind about the Queen. She was a Corsair.

This thought made the decision for him and he was about to pick up the priest and go back, when he was startled by a new and completely unexpected sound. A frantic buzzing, like that of an enormous wasp came to them out of the night.

Troy had never heard anything like it. He swept his spear up, ready to kill, thinking it had to be some sort of monster transformed by the Queen. And it was in its way.

It was a strange, alien *thing* with four protruding arms and a red eye. It flew in the air! Troy made a jab at it with his spear as it came *whooshing* at them. He missed as the thing suddenly seemed to hop in the air and shot over them. With the spear again at the ready, Troy spun around to keep himself between the priest and the machine, for that was what it was, he decided.

Machine was one of those "old" words that had fallen out of use. He had been seven at the time of the apocalypse and could vaguely remember how televisions used to have movies in them in the same way that radios once held music. There had been many machines back then, but now they were all dusty relics—except for this thing.

"Do you think this is the drone she mentioned?" Troy asked.

"I dare say it is." The priest raised a withered hand. "Hello there. We would like to speak to your queen, if it's not too late."

Embarrassed, Troy gently pulled his hand down. "What are you doing? That thing can't talk to you."

"Actually, it can," the machine spouted in a staticky voice. Although it cut in and out, the voice was that of a growling Corsair and not that of the Queen. "Did you two want to be the first to die? Is that why you're here?"

"No. As I just said, we need to talk to the Queen," Amacker answered.

There was a quick burst of static, which was followed by laughter. "She can't come to the drone right now, she's doing her hair." This was spoken in a high falsetto and was followed by more laughter.

"This is not a joking situation," the priest snapped. "You do realize that if the zombies destroy us, you'll get nothing out of the deal. Nothing at all. Did you do all this work just to watch us die? I doubt it, so hop to!" Troy looked at the old man with surprise. This was how Father Amacker had once been: smart, wise, and tough when he needed to be.

He had also jolted the Corsairs. The laughter died and for a few moments there was only silence. Even the drone seemed to lose energy from the statement. It started to slide down and to the right. At the last moment, it jerked upwards to avoid crashing. It sat in the air about five feet from them and as more seconds ticked by, Troy felt the urge to jab it with his spear, stomp it into the earth and get out of there.

Just when he was getting fed up enough to give in to his desire, the drone whispered static at them and then said, "Follow the drone."

Troy hesitated; however, Father Amacker seemed to be flush with sudden energy. He took Troy's hand as if he were grasping the hand of a schoolboy afraid to cross a busy street. The priest's new-found energy didn't last and soon he began to cough again and his feet began to stumble. Troy threw Amacker's arm over his shoulder and then grabbed him around the waist, holding on to the wide gold belt. It felt somewhat like Troy was in a three-legged race. He carried almost all of Amacker's weight and still the priest sagged and coughed.

As the hill grew steeper, Troy began to tire. Then came more flares, closer flares, erupting in the sky. He had his head cocked to the side and was watching one drifting gently off to the south, carried by a stiff breeze, when the two were accosted by an actual person.

"Drop the spear! And get your hands up where I can see them." Shadows draped across the hill before them, making it impossible to see who had challenged them.

Troy did not drop his weapon. He straightened and set Father Amacker on his feet. "We're here to talk to your Queen. You may take my spear but you will be responsible for it."

A man with so many facial tattoos that he seemed part smurf hurried forward and took the spear from Troy's grip. Another ran his hands over their bodies, looking for more weapons. When they found none, the two Guardians were shown through a fence made of barbed wire that hadn't been there earlier that day. The fence stretched out further than they could see and was guarded by hundreds of people, including women, and men who were obviously not Corsairs.

One of them rushed forward. "I'll take them." It was Donna Polston looking frantic and sounding out of breath. She pushed one of the Corsairs away. "I got this. Please, get back to your positions."

Someone whispered, "What a bitch," just loud enough to be heard. A few men nearby snorted agreement.

Donna pretended not to hear. She marched up the hill, casting sidelong glances at the two of them, but mostly at the priest. "Maybe it should just be one of you who goes inside. Perhaps you'd like to wait in the Comm Tent, Father? It's warm inside it."

"Hmm? I think you might be mistaken, Miss. I'm the one she'll want to see. We go way back. She was just a little thing when I knew her, but still smart as a whip. There was this one time that she outsmarted…" Troy nudged the priest. "Hmm? Right, save it. Of course."

Donna's stomach turned over, afraid that she had heard him correctly. "We already had a priest talk to the Queen. She's, uh, not easily persuaded by faith and God and that sort of thing. So, if you could, you know, wait outside, it might be for the best."

Amacker tut-tutted her. "I have faith enough for both of us, don't you worry about that."

"That's not what I'm worried about." She was worried that she was staking her life and the lives of a thousand people on this tottering old man. It was going to be a disaster. The Queen would rip him apart. "If you both go in. Just remember to be very, very polite. Start by kneeling out of respect. That's how you should look at it. It's respect for a different culture…"

"We only kneel before God," Father Amacker stated, giving her the same friendly smile, he would if he were turning down an offered cup of coffee. "Oh my, is this her?"

Two enormous zombies were making their way along the side of the hill, pulling one of the modified campers along behind them. It was the same camper Troy had been in the day before.

"Whatever you do, be quick," Donna hissed. "If you can't change her mind in five minutes it won't matter whether it's Eve or Jillybean in charge, your town will be destroyed." She made a wide, fearful loop around the two zombies, went to the door and after wiping her sweating palms on her slacks, knocked twice. "Your Highness? There are two emissaries from the Guardians who wish to make a last-minute plea."

High laughter erupted from the camper. "Last second is more like it." The door flung open. As always, the Queen wore black from the collar of her leather coat to the heels of her knee-high boots. With red light pouring out from within the camper, Troy thought she looked like the devil. Her eyes passed right over the priest and settled on him. "Look who's singlehandedly bringing sexy back. Were you coming for a little fun in the sack or did you want an upfront view of the slaughter? Either way, come inside."

"No, thank you," Troy answered. "I'm only here to keep watch over Father Amacker. He says he knows you."

The Queen sneered, "Do I look like an altar boy? I don't know any priests. Unless you got some good sacramental wine under those robes, Father, you're not invited to the cool kid's party. Sorry. Maybe Donna is more your speed."

Donna tittered nervously while Father Amacker squinted up at the Queen, a smile spreading across his face. "It is you, Jillybean. I can tell by the eyes," he told Troy. "She always had the most marvelous eyes." He hobbled forward with his gnarled hands out. The Queen shrank back; her look somewhere between loathing and confusion. "It's me, Father Amacker. Don't you remember me?"

She shook her head, however there was doubt in her eyes and her right hand was fiercely gripping the doorknob of the camper.

"Yes, you do," he went on. "You came through Colton with that sweet sister of yours. Sadie. Her name was Sadie. It's funny, I can't remember what I had for lunch and sometimes I can't remember if I put on my socks in the morning, but I can remember the day I met you like it was yesterday. You were friends with little Corina Woods and Anita Nelson. They thought the world of you. When you left they both started trying to build a tank like the one you…"

Amacker went on in a long ramble with many exclamations and sighs, but the Queen wasn't listening. She stood in the doorway of the trailer with her mouth hanging open, her eyes vacant blue globes. She was somewhere else. She was deep, deep inside of herself in the middle of a tremendous, towering cave. It was a cave of her own making though she couldn't remember ever having made it.

Hanging over the cave was a piercing globe; it sat behind bulging, pale grey clouds, the kind that looked as though they could drop a blizzard at any moment.

The walls of the cave were painted with an endless mural that showed a town in suburban Philadelphia. It was always Christmas morning in that town and there was always fresh snow gilding the trees and frosting window ledges. It was an idyllic town, peaceful and picturesque, and in its center was a home that was as unreal as anything in the world had ever been.

The people who lived in it day and night lived a life of unchanging utter perfection. One was a mommy who loved to bake and wrap presents and cuddle, while the other was a daddy who read bedtimes stories, got into tickle fights and was strong and tough as iron.

There was also a little girl who dressed in pink, frequently drew outside the lines, and could never imagine ever leaving the perfect world she lived. It was certain she would never voluntarily do so. She was five and a half—a magical age for most children, though for her it was even more so. Every morning she woke to the sound of Christmas music and her mother's laughter, to the sweet smell of pine trees and the even sweeter smell of cinnamon rolls. She woke to bristling excitement filling, not just the air, but also her heart.

Who in their right mind would ever leave such a place?

Unfortunately, she wasn't in her right mind. She was broken and had been as far back as she could remember. Her one solace, in the few times of reflection that she allowed herself, was the knowledge that even normal people had minds that were only a sneeze away from coming unglued. They were filled with distortions, fragmented memories, and outright lies. Wishful thinking took the place of rational thought and subtle fears dominated life choices more than most people realized.

She only rarely thought about such things, however. These were all distant concepts that were, along with twelve years of her life, kept in a locked box buried beneath a pile of dirty clothes in her closet. She kept the closet locked at all times with a clunky lock of cold black iron. It was a lock that no little girl such as herself had business owning.

Since she had the only key to the lock, which she kept on a string around her neck, it was naturally a surprise that she saw the closet door was open when she woke on that particular Christmas morning, with her pillow-styled hair and one arm curled around Teddy-the-Bear, that.

A curl of disquiet squiggled in her belly. Warily, the little girl edged towards the door, ready to run screaming for her daddy. A child's laugh, high and happy from inside the closet, calmed her fear. She knew that laughter. It was from a long ago friend. A real friend.

"Corina!" the little girl cried and rushed to open the door wider. It was not the closet the door opened onto, however.

She found herself on a hill at night. The snow-clouds were gone, replaced by thousands of glittering stars. The smell of pine and cinnamon had been exchanged for the salty tang of the ocean. And the sounds of Christmas music and her mother's voice had disappeared. It was a hushed nervous night.

A few steps below the girl of five and a half was an old, old man. No, he was an old, old priest, and one she knew despite the extra wrinkles and the white, feathery hair. "Father Amacker," she said. He was not the only one who'd changed. Her voice had deepened and her hands were longer. She looked down at herself and saw a grown up. Jillybean almost bolted back inside the camper. "What's going on?"

"We need you to call off your army," Father Amacker said.

"Army?" Her eyes shifted around; there was a barbed-wire fence and people crouched low behind it. There were hills on either side and far down toward the ocean were the outlines of a town. "Highton," she said. Her memory started to come back and as it did her stomach churned as she swallowed the greasy rinds of shame. With every memory, the nausea built, and right when she was sure something horrible was about to come pouring out of her in a black fountain, she turned to run back inside.

It was late, and she needed to get home before her parents got too worried. The door did not lead to her bedroom, it opened onto a dim room lit by red lights. "What's going on?" she whispered to herself. The answer crawled out of her memory along with all the other horrors.

"It wasn't me, it was Eve. She did this." But was that true? Things were still hazy. She turned from the slightly befuddled priest and went inside to her monitors. The middle one showed the zombie army she had created marching relentlessly towards Highton. It was surprisingly close.

"It's not supposed to be happening like this," she said as the camper rocked. People were coming inside. They stood behind her and saw the grey wave; she was afraid to look back, afraid to see the hate. "And yesterday, too. Someone did something. They released them all. It was just supposed to be a few at a time."

Troy snapped his fingers in her face to focus her. "We'll deal with yesterday another time. We need to know how to stop these ones right there. Do you have more flares or anything like that?"

Donna shook her head. "They're firing off the last of them now… right at the town."

"Then we can't stop them," Jillybean said, in a whisper.

Chapter 42

The canoe had but the one paddle and with Mike still feeling the effects of being crushed by a half-ton zombie, Stu Currans gladly took it up. He stroked easily towards the lights of Bainbridge.

He was in no great hurry to reach the island since he knew his life wouldn't change much when he got there. He would still be in love with a crazy woman, who had almost killed him and forced him to leave his home. His people would still be in terrific danger. They were lost and defenseless. They were bleating sheep among wolves.

To top it all off, he would be a spy. Gunner had fooled Mike and Jenn; they could be as naive as children at times. They believed Gunner's lies because it was so much easier to swallow them whole rather than face the truth. Stu knew how things really stood. Gunner would start small with these innocent seeming reports to hook them and then gradually he would demand more and more.

But he wouldn't get anything of real value, not if Stu had anything to do with it. The next time he met Gunner, he would have bullets in his gun and he'd use them without hesitation and without warning.

Until then, he was still technically a spy. It made him sick to his stomach.

"Look!" Mike cried, pointing towards the little harbor. "The *Calypso*. Do you think they'll let us have her back? They should, right? She's not theirs. And it was Jillybean's idea to take that skiff. And you can't compare a dinky skiff to a real boat."

"They'll probably give her back," Jenn said, speaking softly. There were zombies floating in the Sound and the canoe was the least stable boat she had ever been in. Even a normal sized person could pull it over with little effort. "They seemed like good people."

Good people that they had agreed to spy on, Stu thought.

"Maybe they aren't so good," Mike said. "They were the ones who basically took her in the first place. If they had done just a quick patch job and given her back none of any of this would've happened. We would've never taken a Corsair boat and there wouldn't have been a war."

Right, Stu thought. *Jillybean had wanted the war, which meant she had probably talked her father into pulling the boat out of the water in the first place*. It seemed so obvious now. He was about to mention this when one of the searchlights swept across them. They watched as the light swung away and then slowly came back. Once more it passed over them and kept going, but not for long.

It suddenly stopped and then began groping in zigzags across the black water until it finally found them again. It blazed into their eyes and cast deep black shadows behind them. The light was so piercing that Stu got a queer chill. He felt naked and exposed, as if the glow was like some sort of X-ray that could expose his guilt.

Mike and Jenn shielded their eyes. Stu didn't have that option; he had to keep paddling forward, squinting at first, then as more lights swiveled in their direction, he closed his eyes entirely against the shrieking brightness. Eventually, they had a dozen lights roaming all around them, searching the empty waters of the Sound, hunting for more boats, in case the canoe was the first of hundreds in an all-out assault.

When they got close, someone on the wall challenged them. "That's close enough. We generally don't let people in after dark."

Jenn answered, "Could you make an exception for us? We were uh, chased by bandits." She had almost said that they had been chased by Corsairs, but changed her mind at the last second. It was possible they wouldn't be let on the island if they were dragging a Corsair army behind them.

"Were they Sons of Flame or North Benders?" the man shouted back.

"I don't know. We didn't see them. It was dark and they started shooting, so we ran and that's how we got here. We're looking for refuge. There's a guy named Neil Martin who can vouch for us."

From the top of the immense wall came a flurry of whispers. It went back and forth for some time until one of the guards told them, "Neil Martin is dead. Sorry. We're going to let you come in, but you'll have to give up your weapons. Also, we're gonna have to house you in the station 'til morning. I hope you understand."

"As long as it's warm and there's a bed," Stu said, sounding tired.

They came in through the water gate and were greeted by a sulking Danny McGuinness, the night harbormaster. He waddled out of his shack, wrapped in an immense blanket. He didn't make any move to help them from the canoe.

"It's you three," he said, recognizing them from the last time they had visited, weeks before. An unhappy sigh escaped him. "Come on. No sense standing out in the cold." The dock creaked under his weight as he went back to his heated shack. As he did, he cast a disappointed glance at the *Calypso*. It was scheduled for auction and he had planned on putting in a bid for the boat.

He was never going to sail it himself; instead he would rent it out on a daily basis, figuring that it would pay for itself in two years and after that was just gravy. Only here were the rightful owners, showing up just days before the auction, ruining everything.

"So," he said, after he had sat back in his leather recliner and arranged his blanket. Like a toad, he eyed them as they were frisked. They possessed almost nothing; a few of Jillybean's medical books and the last white and gold flag that had marked Jenn's brief time as queen. Danny thought it was a tablecloth and barely gave it a glance. "Once more you come to our island without anything except expectations to beg from our table."

"No," Jenn answered when Stu only glared, and Mike looked uncertain. "That's wrong. We plan on working. And we didn't come with nothing last time. We had the *Calypso,* which is worth a lot. It's better than all your dinky boats put together."

"Maybe. But the question I've always had is, where did you three kids get her? Did you steal her?"

His tone was aggressive to the point of being rude and had the question been any other, Jenn would have been properly angry. However, they had stolen the *Calypso*, at least initially and although they had replaced her with a bigger boat, it was still technically true. When she hesitated, Danny sensed weakness in her. His only chance at getting the boat was if he could find something illegal or unsavory about them.

"Is the real owner going to show up and demand her back?"

Before she could answer, one of the guards growled, "What the hell, Danny? They are the real owners." Todd Karraker was the oldest guard on duty. With forty closing in, he was somewhat soft in the belly and his camouflaged uniform was stretched tight. Still, he had a long-perfected scowl that caused Danny to shrink into his blanket.

One of the younger guards pushed forward. He had shaved the day before and wouldn't need to for another week. "Where did you guys go? You showed up all jacked up and then you just disappeared, like out of the blue, you know?"

"That's into the blue, Zoid," another said, shoving his friend. "I want to know what happened to Jillybean."

"Yeah, had you guys gotten back to San Francisco?"

"Dang, Zoid, it's *did* you guys *get* back? Where'd you learn English?" He gave his friend another push, hoping to catch Jenn's eye. "Did she fix up your friends?"

"Where is she now," Todd asked, quickly.

Stu turned away and refused to say a word about Jillybean. Jenn was afraid to say anything because she didn't know if they had done anything illegal in leaving the island the way they had. And then there was the possibility that they were semi-spies. How was she supposed to answer questions with that hanging over her head?

This left Mike, who stammered out: "We should talk to the Governor in the morning."

"I just want to know if she's still alive," Todd demanded. Many years before Jillybean had helped him and his brother escape a bandit chieftain; it was not something he would ever forget. People sometimes ridiculed her, but they never did so when Todd was around.

"Yes." Mike didn't think there was any danger in answering that question.

Relief washed over Todd. "Is she coming back?"

Mike looked to Jenn for help, but she only gave a weak shrug which Mike imitated as he answered, "I really don't know. She's not herself and, well, if she comes back it may not be good for you guys. You know what I mean?"

They all understood. The younger men elbowed each other, but straightened and assumed looks of innocence as Todd glared around at the small knot of people, daring one of them to say a word. When no one took him up on his silent challenge, he began to ask another question, but Stu cut him off. "No more. We already said we'd talk to the Governor in the morning and that's what we plan on doing. We've been on the run for days and I'm not going to say a word until I get some sleep."

Actually, he didn't plan on saying anything at all and if it was up to him he wouldn't even be in the same room with the Governor when Jillybean was being discussed. But it wasn't something he could leave on Jenn's shoulders. For a fifteen-year-old she was smart and capable and yet in many ways, she was still a kid.

Although Todd was frustrated by the answer, he escorted them to the island's only police station. While they walked through the cold night, he kept shooting looks their way, especially at Jenn. Finally, he said, "In the dark, you sorta look like her. Like Jillybean, I mean."

"Thanks" Jenn answered, honestly. Jillybean had an exotic and frequently dangerous beauty, while she had always thought of herself as something of a plain Jane. "Were you two close?"

"She was like a kid sister. That's how I tried to treat her, but she didn't really need or want a brother. Not after what happened to her real sister." He looked like he was about to go on, then his face clouded over and he remained troubled until they reached the police station.

Mike, Jenn and Stu had the exact opposite reaction. With every step, they felt their fears and worries recede. The island was wonderfully lit in preparation for the Fall Festival which was to begin the next day. Gold and orange lights gleamed like warm stars wherever they looked. Rivers of bunting swooshed and swirled like autumnal icing from the larger buildings and each house was positively plastered with autumnal decorations.

On every block was a decorated float—a trailer or long cart that was made up in some sort of theme. One was of a twenty-foot-tall turkey made of a mesh of stiff wire, leaves, and paper mache. Another was a gargantuan hollowed-out pumpkin complete with a six-foot tall candle. The most impressive was a smiling, straw-headed scarecrow that was three stories tall.

This was a happy place. It was a safe place.

The Hilltop had never been safe; it had been lucky for a time, but never safe. And Alcatraz had earned it nickname as "The Rock." It was cold and unforgiving. Bainbridge was the opposite; it felt like home to the three of them.

Jenn's hand found Mike's and the two strolled easily, pointing out their favorite decorations. They looked like they were coming home from a date. Stu was silently envious and, at the same time, was happy for them.

They even found the police station inviting. For one, it was warm. Jenn couldn't remember the last time she bedded down without wearing a hat and coat. It was also guarded by a pleasant woman with dark, Latin features; she had hair that was long, rippling, and black as the space between the stars.

The three slept soundly in consecutive cells and the night was marred only by its brevity. It was after three in the morning by the time they closed their eyes and the kickoff of the Fall Festival was not a quiet event. At sunrise the first of the three competitive marching bands began warming up.

Stu was out of his bunk at the *hhhroom* of the first tuba. Mike took a second longer because of his broken ribs. "Ow! Son of a...what is that?" People simply didn't play musical instruments on The Rock or the Hilltop.

"I think that's a tuba," Stu answered, grinning. He raised a fist and worked it up and down in time as the tuba began to *whomp, whomp, whomp!* This was answered by a brassy cry that rang across the island. It was taken up by others until Stu felt the demand of the music. "Let's go see what's going on."

The trio said a quick goodbye to the black-haired woman and went out into a new morning, smiles on their faces as a thousand bells began to ring. Hundreds of people were spilling onto their porches with bells in hand. Most were brass and the red bows on them gave them a Christmas feel. Some people clanked cow bells as if they were at a hootenanny. One family set up a stand for a heavy ship's bell that was green copper. The strangest of all was a large circle of shining gold that a man struck every few seconds with ceremonial slowness and a maniac's grin on his face. It was a Chinese gong and the shimmering sound it made was fascinating to the trio; none of them had ever heard a gong before.

It was a cacophony of merriment that was not universally appreciated. In the midst of everything, a flight of black birds winged angrily by cawing their contempt.

Jenn's smile dropped. Out of habit, she counted them. Five! It meant that sickness was coming. As bad as that was, at least there weren't six of the birds. Six meant death was coming. She had never in her life counted six birds and not had a death follow close after.

Even as a sigh of relief began to slip from her lips, another bird, just as black as coal kicked off from the gutter of a house and hurried after the first group. Before it could join the rest, she turned away, telling herself that it was five she had seen. They hadn't been altogether. It was a lie that she whispered.

"Are you okay?" Mike asked, smiling down at her.

She could barely look at him, afraid that she would see the birds—all six of them—cutting across the sky. "Yeah, I'm fine." Death was coming. Still, it didn't mean her death or Mike's or Stu's. It could be anyone. There were people everywhere; happy, smiling people.

"Yeah…it's just, what is all this? They act like…well, I don't know what. I've never seen anything like this at all."

"It's how you're supposed to ring in the Fall Festival," a grinning man said. He was red-faced and, in his excitement, his nostrils were flared as curvaceously as a dancer's hips. "Where you guys from? Agate Point? You coming to see who's got the best float this year? Wyatt Way East is getting the trophy back this year. You'll see!"

He slapped Stu on the back and left, laughing.

"Was he drunk?" Mike asked.

"He was something," Stu said, gazing around. If the man wasn't drinking, he was one of the few. Stands were being set up along the four-mile "inner circle" as the parade route was called. Some sold a drink called a Hot Toddy, which was apple-whisky, hot water, honey, herbs and spices. Another specialized in Irish coffee. Still another made hot chocolate with peppermint and vodka.

And there was every sort of pumpkin flavored drink imaginable, including something brutishly unpleasant called pumpkin wine.

Samples were given freely, and it wasn't long before Mike and Jenn were giggling drunk as much from the alcohol as the freedom and the sense of belonging that they felt. She had forgotten the crows after her third drink and soon after, Mike was too numb to feel the ache in his ribs. Stu tried to retain some sort of personal order since they had promised to give their story to the governor.

Still, he was pleasantly buzzed when the floats began to pass by. Although some were hauled along by donkeys, horses or in one case cows, most were pulled by teams of people who would often stop for refreshments along the way. When someone dropped out, another person gladly took their place.

It was closing on midmorning when the "real" floats began passing. These were the ones that were considered the front runners in the competition for best float. Some were staggering in their conception and brilliant in their color. The enormous scarecrow could be seen from half a mile away, while a fifteen-foot tall snowflake made from ten-thousand shards of mirror was like a beacon and people told each other that it could be seen from space.

Leading these front runners was the Fall Festival Queen. She rode on a white rose float that was hauled by a barrel-bellied grey mare. The actual rose was not overly large; little more than ten feet across. Where it lacked in size, it made up for in beauty. A thousand man-hours had been put in constructing it and other than the amazing gold trim on each petal, it was a perfect rendition of an actual rose.

In the center rode the Queen as voted on by children of the three schools on the island. She wore white and gold as well and would have been perfectly triumphant were she not perfectly sloshed. She was pasty grey when she appeared and by the time she came up to where Jenn stood waving, she couldn't keep the contents of her stomach in any longer. Heroically, she preserved both her dress and the float by holding back a mouthful of vomit until she staggered to the ground, knelt at Jenn's feet and vomited all over her in a great spray of orange, pumpkin flavored puke.

Chapter 43

"Then we can't stop them," Jillybean said, in a whisper, unable to look at the screen any longer. She had been pulled out of a perfect world for this? Just to watch her handiwork come undone, to see her people destroyed? No, she wouldn't watch. She would find somewhere to sleep and when she was unconscious, she would sneak away and head back down into the cave she had built and let Eve have this world.

Not only did Eve want it more, she deserved it, and the world deserved her. It was an evil, hateful place and no one was better suited to rule such a place than the Queen of Hate.

"There's nothing you can do?" Donna Polston asked.

Jillybean pointed without looking at the second screen. The picture wobbled and dipped as the drone fought the ocean breeze. It showed the Knights of the Cross preparing for battle. Most were readying weapons, but some were kneeling in prayer; they were going to make their final stand and it was going to be a sickening affair.

She shook her head. "They would need to listen to me as their queen and they won't. They'd rather fight and die, which is their choice. So, no. There's nothing I can do."

"You could make more flares!" Troy demanded, grabbing the Queen's arm and spinning her around. They were almost nose-to-nose, and he saw the change in her eyes as she became Eve. One moment he was looking into her sad, rather large blue eyes and the next they went dark, as an angry, vicious, sinfully joyful smile spread across her face. It was terrible to see such foul evil in one so young and pretty.

With Eve, her eyes were as truthful as she got. They were a window into her black soul that appalled people to such an extent that they couldn't look away; not even if their lives were in danger. As Troy stared, Eve acted. A five-inch knife appeared in her hand from nowhere; she slid it up under his chin.

She could've carved out his Adam's apple before he knew it. Instead, she only gave him a little nick, saying, "Never touch me, again. It's death to touch me without permission. Now beg for forgiveness. Throw yourself on *my* mercy."

Troy reacted with speed and precision. The flat of his left hand moved in a blur and knocked her knife hand away, while his right hand slammed forward. He could have punched her on the chin, the nose, or the throat; however, the code under which he lived would not permit him to hit a defenseless woman. Even though she had a knife, she was not a warrior and he was in no danger, especially since he was encased in armor from just below the cut under his chin down to his steel-tipped boots.

His hand slamming forward was open. It struck her high on the sternum and was more of a hard push than anything else.

It caught her by surprise and she fell back against a chair. Like a cat, she was up again, the knife held out toward him. "You'll pay for that," she hissed. "You'll pay and all your people will pay, as well."

"Get on your knees, Troy!" Donna cried. Her face had gone grey, except for the high red splotches on her cheeks. Troy was young, tall and strong, and in the peak of his physicality. He was a trained warrior who had slain zombies in single combat. He had Eve trapped in the corner of the trailer—Donna didn't think he had a chance. "Get down and beg for forgiveness, please."

Eve's eyes glittered. "Yes, beg that I let you keep one of your eyes. The other is mine. Your hands are mine, too. No one touches the Queen, EVER!"

"Stop the attack and you can have whatever you want," he replied, evenly.

She smiled that nasty smile of hers and took a step forward, the knife held low and away from her body. It was not a smart stance. It allowed for only a slashing attack which was all but useless because of his armor. As expected, she swung her arm in a short arc; missing him by a foot and a half. He knew she would reverse her strike and attack him backhanded. When she missed him again, he would step in while her momentum carried the knife away. Her arm would be extended and away from her. She'd be completely vulnerable.

Just as he foresaw, she swung the knife at him backhanded. He let it swish harmlessly by. His eyes were locked in on it and didn't see that she was bringing her left hand around right after. Instinctively, he threw an arm to block it, thinking she had to have a second knife. It was not a knife in her hand, but white powder which his arm did very little to block.

The powder plumed into a pale cloud that went into his eyes and was sucked into his lungs. It felt like burning, diamond-sharp grains of sand. The pain in his eyes was too much to bear and he could only clamp them shut. His lungs constricted on their own and the most he could draw in were tiny sips of air. He tried to cough, but only ended up choking.

"Pathetic," Eve drawled as she calmly turned away, picked up a water bottle and washed off her left hand. It was bright red.

Troy staggered at her, swinging a fist. He had heard the water splashing and assumed it was acid or venom, or something equally horrible. His fist hit the wall next to the TV screen with a loud *crack!* Eve laughed as she kicked the back of his leg. He dropped to his knees and as he hit the floor, Eve slammed his face into the wall. Blood poured from his nose; he barely felt it.

She had grabbed a short fistful of hair and hauled his head back, savagely. The knife was at his throat. "Any last words? Hmm? Sorry, I don't speak gruntanese very well. Did you say slash my throat or stab my throat? What do you guys think? Slash or stab?"

The young twenty-two year Donna Polston of twelve years before would have begged for Troy's life. That bright-eyed young woman had been replaced by the pragmatist, whose only thought was that dead men tell no tales. She was skating on the thinnest of ice with Eve and Troy was doomed, one way or another.

Father Amacker spoke up just as Donna was going to say *slash*. "Jillybean! What would your sister say if she saw you acting like this?"

"I never had a sister," Eve growled. "A pinky-swear doesn't make a person your sister. I'm sure your stinking bible would back me up."

Amacker wasn't one to give in so easily. "What would your father say?" Eve drew in a sharp breath and coughed from the residual toxin in the air. Blood began to drip down Troy's neck. "I think I know," Amacker went on, "Your father would tell you to put down that knife this instant."

"If I had a father, maybe," Eve allowed. "But I didn't have one. *She* did, and *She* let him die! The great Jillybean was the one who did that. *She* let him go out and *She* let him get bit. That's how this all started. I wouldn't be here today if *She* had any damned balls."

"How old were you when that happened?"

Eve hesitated, her eyes blinking and staring somewhat randomly. "I was six and it was night and it was cold. Like tonight. I told him not to go. I begged. I told him I wasn't hungry, but I was. I was hungry enough to eat my own hair and fingernails. And he went out because of that."

The strength went out of her and the knife thumped on the floor. She turned away from Troy and looked at Father Amacker with liquid diamond tears in her huge blue eyes. "I didn't mean it. I told him I was cutting my hair because of a game. That was a lie, Father. And he caught me." Eve had fled from the pain and it was Jillybean who touched her wild wreath of hair as if she wasn't quite sure it was still there. "I've never cut my hair since then."

"That is a sad story, Jillybean," Father Amacker said. "I'm not one for sad stories if I can help it, and we're going to have an entire host of them very soon." He raised a gnarled hand towards the monitors where the advancing army of zombies was nearing Highton. "How do we stop it? Do you have more flares or something like them?"

Her eyes slowly began to focus on the screens. "No. This is all wrong. Eve, Damn it!" She spun around and saw Troy struggling to breathe, Donna struggling to catch up with who was running Jillybean's body, and Father Amacker staring sadly back at her. "There's only way any of them will live and that is to obey me to the letter."

She went to a drawer, grabbed a bottle of water and rushed to Troy's side. "If you fight me in any way, that'll be it. Now, lay down," she ordered him. It spoke of his strength and courage that he obeyed. Quickly she washed away the residue of powder from his face; almost immediately his lungs opened up. She then shoved the bottle into his hands. "Rinse your hands and your eyes."

Jillybean was up a second later, heading for the one door leading out of the trailer. "Get the priest out of here," she commanded Donna, speaking over her shoulder as she jumped out. She had no time for stairs or anything else for that matter. The last of the flares were being shot over the town of Highton even then. The first of many thousands of zombies would be there in three minutes.

"Hitch them up, Will!" she yelled at the driver.

William Trafny knew better than to dawdle. Eve had twice threatened to feed his *parts* to the zombies that pulled the trailer. This was Jillybean; however and for her, he would hurry even if it killed him.

"You're going to stay here this time," she told him grabbing the long guide-stick. "I want you and Donna to guard the old priest with your lives until I get back. If I don't make it, find a way back to Alcatraz on foot. Don't go anywhere near those boats, understood?"

He understood perfectly. They all did. Jillybean had a hold of not just one tiger by the tail, it seemed she had four or five. Each of the different Corsair factions, as well as the Santas, were one mistake away from turning on her, and if she were to die, there'd be a civil war in a second.

They had the beasts hitched in thirty seconds and by then, Donna had managed to get Father Amacker out of the trailer, barely. He was just putting a questing foot down into the deep grass when Jillybean began poking the zombies into life. Inside, a dazed Troy Holt was knocked off his feet as the contraption jerked forward. He hurried to the door and looked out. They were already moving at a trot and the entire thing was bucking and bouncing.

He thought about getting out to run alongside Jillybean and would have if he wasn't still light-headed and wheezing. It would have been embarrassing, or rather *more* embarrassing. Not only had she beaten him, she could've killed him without effort and he had to wonder how many other tricks she had up her sleeves; literally in this case.

They began going uphill and the pace slowed enough for him to chance getting out. When he jogged to the front, he was surprised to find she wasn't even in sight. The zombies were simply blundering forward, heading toward the barbed-wire fence. He could hear her ahead of them, barking out orders.

She came rushing up, seconds later. "Back inside. I can't leave without you." He had no idea what she meant by that. It's not like he was going to run away. He climbed back in and just in time it seemed. The trailer began to pick up speed as if the zombies were flat-out running as fast as they could.

Jillybean suddenly appeared in the doorway, hanging on for dear life, trying to scramble inside. He reached out a hand and she clawed it like a cat as she climbed up him.

"Who's driving this thing?"

"No one. You better hold on."

Hold on to what? seemed like the perfect question, but again the feeling of embarrassment stole over him. In all likelihood, they were speeding to their deaths and he wasn't going to go out with even a hint of cowardice about him. He staggered to where the TV screens were and calmly sat in one of the soft, leather chairs. One TV showed Highton seconds from being enveloped by a great grey wave; a second showed an empty hill, and the third showed a runaway trailer, speeding straight down a very steep hill.

"Is that us?" He looked around and saw that he was alone; Jillybean had disappeared into the same small backroom she'd had the night before. It was just as well since the question hadn't been well thought out. Of course, it was them, only where were the zombies that had been hauling it? And who was steering the trailer? As far as he could tell, Jillybean was just trusting gravity to get them to Highton.

That didn't seem smart.

"And what in holy heck is that?" On the video feed, something was pouring from the back end of the trailer. "Lord bless us, that's smoke!" It had started as swirls of grey, but was growing quickly into a billowing cloud. And now there were flames, bright yellow fingers that seemed to be reaching higher and higher.

As he stared in shock, Jillybean burst out of the backroom in a cloud of black fumes. She rushed to the monitors and let out a wild cackle. "This is going to be crazy! Grab that chair." She pulled one of the chairs to the front of the trailer, sat down with her back to the wall and leaned the chair over herself. Troy sat down beside her. The trailer was bouncing now. He figured it was going to shake itself to pieces if it didn't burn up first.

Jillybean gave him a guilty look. "Sorry about the toxin and your nose and, you know, your neck. I wasn't myself. Sometimes I get…"

The trailer whammed over a log and she choked on whatever she was going to say next.

Her plan to ride the trailer to Highton took a detour at that point. The trailer began to curve away and as it did it took on a list that turned into a frightening lean. Seconds later, the entire thing pitched over and over and over. Up and down switched places so quickly that gravity couldn't keep up. Paper, glass, and jagged chunks of monitors seemed to float around them.

A moment later, brilliant, searing light erupted just as the back of the trailer exploded, and their out of control tumble ended with a jarring crash. Heat washed over them. It was so intense that Jillybean could only cringe against it. She pulled her leather coat across her face. Troy didn't have that luxury. He grabbed the chair he'd been hiding behind and held it up in front of his face.

"Come on!" he yelled.

Jillybean's head was still spinning and her legs were uncertain. When she got up, her hips went one direction while her shoulders went another; she fell heavily against the side of the trailer. Troy took a fistful of her leather coat and dragged her out into the night.

"Look what you did," he said, backing away from the trailer. The flames were gorging themselves on it and were forty feet high in seconds.

"A happy bit of luck, I agree. You'd better get down."

He turned and saw what seemed like the hill sweeping toward them in an undulating mass, almost like a wave. "What is tha…" It was the zombie horde turning towards the fire-engulfed camper. "We got to get out of here!" Troy tried to pull the Queen to her feet; she resisted but only for a second, only long enough for him to put his strength into the move. Then she let herself be lifted while at the same time she stuck a foot behind his back ankle. He went falling back into the dead grass with her on top of him.

She clamped a hand over his mouth and whispered, "Be still and don't say a word." The zombies were on top of them seconds later. Great hulking monsters that looked like giants to the two hiding in the grass. Now that they were close, they moved slowly, moaning, limping, swaying as if caught in a trance. In a sense, they were. Their simple minds could not comprehend the fire which amazed and attracted them in equal parts.

It wouldn't last. Jillybean knew that the fire which burned twice as bright burned half as long. She began creeping through the waist-high grass, moving far too slowly for Troy's tastes. The trailer had tipped over only a hundred yards from the mound of bodies ringing Highton. It was far too close, especially as the ring of zombies gaping at the inferno began to build. Sheer numbers would force some into contact with the defending Knights.

He tried to hurry and quickly discovered that she wouldn't allow it. She laid across his back, dragging him down. When he glared, she reached under his chest plate and twisted his nipple until the glare became a grimace.

She was weird. She was also naturally gifted at hiding from the monsters. She blended with shadows and the light rustle she made was swallowed up by the thrashing sound the zombies made as they waded through the grass. Quicker than he expected, they were outside the ring; then she was up and running for the safety of the town.

Troy was faster and went ahead, waving his arms, silently. "It's Holt," someone whispered when he was over the mound. Men started to crowd him and for some reason, it bothered him. He pushed them away.

"Yes, and I brought the Queen." He pointed. Jillybean had run up the side of the heap of stinking corpses and had stopped on its crest, one foot planted on a skull the size of a pumpkin. A gasp came from the doomed men.

"What can she do?" one asked.

"I can save your lives. Most of you, I should say. There is only one condition. You must obey me without any backtalk."

Troy stalked up to the mound. "We are not your servants or your subjects. We will not kneel."

For a second, her eyes were dark and filled with hate. It didn't last. She slumped, wearily. "A day will come when you will wish you were. A day will come when even I can't save you. But that is not this day. If you will just *listen* to me, you might have a chance."

A discontented murmur arose out of the group. Discontent wouldn't save them. Troy raised his hand to quiet the whispers. "I will listen. I will not dishonor myself before God, but I will listen." The crowd of Knights began to nod to this bit of wisdom. Troy turned to Jillybean. The camper was already becoming little more than a smoldering ruin and in the fading light, her white face was ghostly. "What would you have us do?"

"Simple. You have to hide."

Chapter 44

Knights Commander Christian Walker had been one of the last people to hurry over to see what all the hubbub was. Like everyone else, he had seen the flaming camper rolling at them and he had assumed that it was yet another way to entice the horde into the town. He had let out a silent prayer of thanks when it had crashed.

He was confused as everyone else at seeing the Queen. Was she leading her zombie army in person? That was a level of insanity that was beyond understanding. He was about to order her arrest when she explained her "plan."

"Ignore her," he said, in something just short of a bellow. He came stomping up. "Everyone back to your positions. We are Knights. We do not cower and we do not hide."

"Then you do not live," she stated, clear enough for everyone to hear. "And neither will your wives and children. So far, I have been thwarted at every turn by spies and my own personal demons. Now, I'm being balked by foolish bravery and asinine attempts at honor. Tomorrow when I walk these streets and smell your rotting carcasses, I will spit on your honor."

"Tonight, I'd spit on yours if you had any," Walker answered.

She lifted a hand and Walker was surprised to see a pistol in it. Her face was a mask of fury. Her teeth were bared and a snarl slipped from between them. *She's going to shoot me,* he thought to himself. He wasn't afraid, just surprised that she would kill him in cold blood like that when he was surrounded by his men.

"Don't do it, Jillybean," Troy warned. "You'll just bring the zombies on faster." Her eyes cut to him and the gun wavered. He went on, "You didn't come down here just to get ripped to pieces by the dead, did you?"

"No," she said, but sounded unsure. A second later, she shook her head and said again, "No," this time with more confidence. "I also didn't come down to watch you die. I can save this town if you'll just listen to me. And yes, it involves hiding. If you delay any longer Commander, you'll get your wish and nothing will keep you or your people alive. So, choose now, but know this, if you choose to fight it'll be the same thing as suicide. And that child of yours? It'll be murder when she dies."

His eyes blazed, and his face went cherry-red. "It'll be murder, alright, and it'll be on your head!"

"I'm the one trying to save them," she said with utmost calm. "And I will, if you'll just listen to me." There was a second of intense silence between them which was broken by the roar of a zombie. It echoed through the night. The beasts were coming. Some were now so close that hiding was fast becoming a non-option.

Walker felt a stab of fear in his chest. He wasn't afraid for himself. He had no fear of death, whatsoever. He feared for his daughter, Ryanne. "What do you suggest?"

Jillybean didn't answer right away. She stared out over the mass of Knights with their shining spears and their rugged armor. It was impossible to miss the church dominating the center of town. It was windowless, which made it perfect. "I need fifty men to hold this line until I give the signal. Ten to get me supplies and the rest need to fall back to that big building."

"The church?" Walker asked in surprise.

"That's your church?" Jillybean hoped no one saw the look of semi-disgust on her face. For a God-fearing people it was decidedly underwhelming. "If so, then all the better. Get in there and keep quiet no matter what. I don't want to hear a sound from it. Not a prayer, not a hymn; not even an amen. And no lights!"

Troy clapped his hands. "You heard the lady. Let's go! The ten fastest will remain with the Queen and do her bidding to the letter. The best fifty warriors know who you are. You'll remain with me. Borga, I'm going to need your spear."

"No spears!" Jillybean ordered. "You will use guns. Your kills will have to be precise and quick."

Some of the men hesitated until Troy started shoving them into compliance. Extra ammo was gathered and just in time, too. The camper had finally gone out as had a brief grass fire that was unintentionally stomped out by thousands of giant feet. The smell of burnt zombie flesh soured the men making them gag silently.

The mass of creatures started to wander and now gravity played a large role in drawing them towards the town. More than one of them fell on the hillside, starting a chain reaction of pushing and jostling and soon dozens were lumbering mindlessly towards Highton.

Troy watched them coming his way as he stood beside the gurgling stream in the exact center of their defensive line. He had said a final prayer and now he calmly checked his weapon and rolled his neck around on his broad shoulders. Without a nasty pile of corpses in front of him to slow the creatures down, it was the most dangerous spot to be and thus it was exactly where Bishop Wojdan expected him to be.

"This is not a scenario I could have ever expected," he said to Troy with a dry whispering sigh. "Most of us hiding meekly as she gives orders as if she's already our Queen. She must really be persuasive."

"I don't know if I was persuaded exactly, your Excellency," Troy admitted after a quick kiss of the man's ring. "She's just so…energetic? That's not the right word. *Certain*, maybe that's it. But she's also energetic. She just bowls you over and you find yourself going with it, whatever it may be."

Bishop Wojdan gave a noncommittal, *Hmmm*, before asking about Father Amacker. "He should still be alive," Troy said and then gave a very quick rundown of what had happened. As he spoke, his voice grew fainter. The hill was alive with movement and the moans of the dead were growing in volume. Not far away were seven or eight huge shadowy figures moving slowly towards the gap in the mound.

One paused at the stream, went down on all fours and began to drink noisily. The others bent as well giving Wojdan enough time to sigh again and quote: "*And they will go out and look on the dead bodies of those who rebelled against me; the worms that eat them will not die, the fire that burns them will not be quenched, and they will be loathsome to all mankind.*"

"Isaiah 65:24?" Troy asked.

"Close. It's Isaiah 66:24. Be well, Troy. Your people count on you to remain steadfast." He turned his portly body around and began to walk slowly away, his hands behind his back, seeming to thrust his belly further out than usual.

Troy breathed a sigh of relief now that he was gone. He couldn't fight with the Bishop looking over his shoulder. Fighting took a certain level of bestial savagery that he was loath to display in front of anyone, especially the Bishop. Sometimes when he fought the dead, he took a perverse joy in killing them.

It felt sinful.

At the same time, he knew it was right and proper to rid the world of evil, and the creatures were the very definition of evil.

Grimly, he stalked forward in a crouch, placing each foot with practiced care to keep from making any noise. Closer he came, and with each step the desire to kill grew in him until it became almost a hunger. He could satisfy that hunger very easily. As they drank, the undead were basically defenseless. He could kill four or five of them before they really knew what hit them.

With the M4 at his shoulder, he crept along the stream coming closer and closer, until he was so close that he could reach out and touch the closest of the creatures. It was hard to believe the thing had once been human. It was twisted and monstrous and the smell coming from it was that of rotting meat. It was the stench of evil.

Beyond was the army of the dead, looking as though they had just stormed the gates of Hell.

Unafraid, Knights Sergeant Troy Holt faced them. He felt completely alone, one man against the full might of the Devil. But he was not alone. A gunshot from off to his left proved that. One of the thousands of creatures had climbed the berm and was brought down with a perfect shot to the head. With that, the final battle had begun.

Instantly, the army of undead turned as one toward the sound of the gunshot and began to charge. The earth shook, the air trembled and the dark waters of the stream frothed. Whoever had taken that shot was only seconds from being overrun.

Troy wasn't going to let that happen.

As the nearest beast started to get up, he stepped forward and from a distance of two feet, blew a neat little hole in its head. The bullet drilled through its seldom-used brain, before ricocheting around the interior of its skull, turning its brain to soup. It fell, face-first into the stream. Troy was already moving on to the next, lining up another shot. He was so close that he couldn't miss.

The bullet hit dead center and the thing went over slowly like a chopped tree. The third closest zombie didn't bother to get to its feet. It scrambled at Troy on its hands and knees. Even so, it was huge, the size of a bull. It led with its face, opening a gaping mouth that was filled with jagged teeth. Troy didn't have time to aim; he fired right down the thing's gullet. A poor choice since blasted-out teeth didn't faze it a bit and nor did it slow it.

It crashed into Troy and as he went back, he fired twice. Both shots went home, piercing the frontal bone and destroying its brain. Although dead, the zombie's momentum continued on, slamming Troy down into the thick mud of the river. He was pinned beneath the enormous carcass, unable to breathe, unable to do more than squirm like a bug.

The only thing keeping his chest from being crushed was his tactical armor, but the steel plates across his torso weren't going to save him from having his face eaten off. Zombies were charging from all directions, screaming in fury. A foot the size of a snowshoe splashed down an inch from his face, covering him in a wave of black mud. It made him more or less invisible to the zombies.

They couldn't see him, but they could hear him as he began to choke. The sound drove the zombies into a wild frenzy. Some dug mindlessly at the river while one great beast bent down, and with the strength of an elephant, heaved the massive corpse off Troy and flung it as if were nothing. Like a hunk of gum stuck to someone's shoe, Troy was pulled up as well. He looked like a sloppy hunk of mud that dropped with a slapping sound back into the river.

He was dazed and battered, fighting to suck in a breath, but when one of the beasts peered down at him, he shot it in the eye. It almost fell on him. Just in time, he staggered out of the way, backing into another zombie which was just turning. Troy spun and shot upwards, the bullet blasting up through the soft flesh beneath the thing's chin and popping up out of the top of its head.

Black blood fountained for a brief moment before the creature's log-like legs buckled. It fell into another zombie as it turned on Troy. He shot that one as well and another and another after that.

Soon everything became a blur to him. He stood defiantly in the breach in the low mound and fired his weapon until he was half-night blind and more than half deaf. He built his own mound of corpses. It dammed the river which was just as well since the water was now black with blood. He gave ground slowly, killing as he went, mumbling over and over: "I will fear no evil. I will fear no evil."

Time lost meaning. The dead kept coming. Mud and sweat dripped from his brow and when it struck the barrel of his M4 it sizzled. For some reason, he could hear the sizzle with perfect clarity while the screams of the dead and the explosions of his gunshots seemed far off. They mixed with the sounds of fighting that were going on up and down the line.

Only there was no line. There had never been one. They had built the mound in an arc and now that arc was bending and bending. Some of the gunshots sounded almost like they were coming from behind him.

The defensive arc was crumbling from the sides!

A horn began to blow far to the rear a few seconds before Commander Walker's voice rang out, "Fall back! Fall back!"

When Troy turned, he was shocked to see fires burning in the town and for a moment his heart quailed. Had the city fallen already? It seemed like the fight had just begun and yet there were two houses in flames on either side of the main street into town. Standing between them was the Queen waving a burning torch.

"She's mad again," Troy said as he turned back to the undead pressing in from every direction. He fired in a long burst before running for the town.

"Form a line here!" the Queen shouted. "Come on! Stop your dawdling, Troy. Let me have the first…" She counted the survivors emerging from the dark. "Damn. Let me have the first twelve right here. The rest of you fall back with me."

Although Troy was not one of the first twelve, he got in line with them. With the fires burning on either side of them, he could see the men in line and they could see him. He looked thrashed and they weren't much better, except for tongueless Chris Baker. The right side of the mute's face was mostly torn off and torrents of bright blood glistened in the firelight.

The quick glances were all they had time for. The horde was bearing down on them. "Yea, though I walk in the valley of the shadow of death," Troy said, switching to a new magazine.

The ragged line took up the psalm: "I will fear no evil for You are with me; Your rod and Your staff, they comfort me…"

Their own guns drowned out the rest. They had light to shoot by and they opened fire at thirty yards. These were the best of the best. Their bullets wreaked havoc and the dead went down by the score—in vain. They faced an avalanche of zombies and the bullets did less to slow them down than did their own eagerness. Zombie battled zombie to be the first to kill.

Although Troy was the ranking man on the line, there was no reason for orders. The Knights fought bravely, but were thrown back at first contact. The sheer mass of the creatures attacking them meant they would fall back or be buried. They backed up, firing as they went. Amazingly they made it three blocks before the first man was lost.

All it took was a couple of missed shots for a zombie to be on them. The seven-footer was faster than the average and had a Knight by the head and was biting his face before anyone could do anything. Chris Baker ran up and put two holes in its temple. When the creature dropped, it fell on the Knight.

The other Knights made an attempt to save him but were driven back, each man engaging two or more of the beasts. Troy was fighting a trio of zombies. He managed to kill two of them, but the third seemed unfazed by the bullets blasting into its head. The creature grabbed Troy, pinning his arms to his sides and took a ferocious bite out of his shoulder. What sounded like fragments of glass shattering was its teeth breaking on the metal plates. It reared its head back to try a second time and as it did, Troy was able to bring his feet up. He thrust out with all his strength, putting enough room between him and it, that someone was able to stick a pistol up to its face and shoot it between the eyes.

"What did I say about dawdling?" It was the Queen, a wild smile on her face. She was firing nonstop. "Let's go. We're retreating." She didn't wait for him. She sprinted towards the next thin line of Knights who were standing a few blocks off between two more burning buildings.

Troy raced after her, noting there were only seven Knights running with them. They darted through the next line. Six went on. Troy did not. His place was on the line come hell or high water. Even if he was the last man left, he would not leave his town defenseless.

The Knights were firing even as Troy turned to face the next onslaught. Nothing seemed to have changed. Together they killed hundreds of the creatures and yet, it looked like the same horrible grey demons were screaming out of the dark. A few of the men were backing away as they fired, and that was okay with Troy. As long as they didn't run and as long as they kept firing.

It made sense to back away. There was no question that their pathetic defenses would be crushed if they stopped for more than a second. It was better to be elastic, to absorb the shock of the attack instead of being shattered by it.

When they came to an intersection, the men on the edges would turn and fire into the howling, screaming shadowy masses on either side. It was something to see as the river of undead collided at these intersections; the fights between the juggernauts were epic and more died in these bursts of violence than fell from the Knights' bullets.

After the fourth block, Troy chanced a concerned look back. They could not retreat forever. Awaiting them was the ocean and although some of them might be able to swim through the swells and breakers, they'd be leaving behind their loved ones to face the horrors of the horde. It wasn't something they would do.

Another fire and another very thin line of Knights awaited them. They were not far from the sharp drop into the ocean where the tide was coming in. He could hear the great, thrumming blasts as the waves beat against the cliff face, sending up explosions of foam.

"Is her plan suicide?" he asked in shock. He didn't want to believe that mass suicide was her end game, but nothing else seemed to make sense. If she had wanted access to the ocean, she should have cut to the north a half mile where the Guardian's small fleet lay sheltered in a tiny cove.

That way was now blocked. The zombie horde was outflanking their scant defense, coming from both north and south. He could see them teeming along the cliff face towards the fire.

It was beginning to dawn on him that, insane or not, she was succeeding in her goal of destroying the town. The dead were flooding down every street, moving like an irresistible tide. Not only that, the Guardian's fifty best fighters were being slain one by one, doing little besides using up the last of their ammo.

Come morning she could draw the horde away and pick up the pieces left behind without the least effort. She'd have a thousand new slaves to add to her growing empire.

In a spasm of uncontrollable fury, he spun and brought his M4 up, putting her directly in his sights. She saw the move and without the least bit of fear, she drew back her three-quarter length coat. It was almost as if she were daring him to shoot. Calmly, she folded it and set it aside. She then sat and drew off one of her long, leather boots.

A hand grabbed his shoulder. "What are you doing? Troy? We're falling back! Come on!"

Knights Commander Walker was yelling above the din of battle and waving them to the cliff's edge. Troy found himself running along with the others as bullets zipped past them to strike down the charging zombies. A few were not hit and Knights were pulled down from behind and dismembered in bloody chunks.

Troy put on a burst of speed and raced ahead of the others. He ran to the Queen and pointed his gun into her face. "I know what you've done!"

"I've saved you," she answered, softly.

"No. You haven't saved anything. You've declawed us. You've turned us into sheep, so we can be eaten by your wolves. I should kill you."

She smirked. "I don't mean to be rude, but you don't have the balls to kill me. Killing is hard. Harder than you can ever imagine. But killing the innocent in the name of the greater good is the hardest thing there is."

He loomed over her and growled, "You're not innocent."

The smirk became a tearful smile. "By the time I was seven I had killed five-hundred people," she said in a whisper. "I don't think I was ever innocent." She glanced back at the zombies boiling over each other to get to the little group. "Die if you wish, but if you do, who will protect your people from me?"

Troy's finger gripped the trigger and he was close to killing her. So very close. She only smiled and dove off the cliff, holding herself beautifully in a perfect swan dive. Troy's head dropped as all around him his men were shooting like mad. He had failed. The Guardians were beaten and Highton was lost.

Chapter 45

"A little vomit never hurt anyone," Jenn Lockhart said to the woozy Parade Queen. It sure had hurt her tennis shoes, however. The sickly-sweet, acid smell of pumpkin-spiced vomit was certainly one of those things that would out-live them all. "Besides, I've had worse on me."

"I'm sho shorry," the Parade Queen whispered, as she wiped away orange goo from her lips, using a handful of damp autumn leaves. She then croaked like a bullfrog and pawed uncertainly at the grass. Her tiara slipped from the top of her head to plop down onto the tip of her nose. She seemed confused, looking at the world through a crystalline lattice.

Gently, Jenn took the tiara. "You don't want to get any of that on your crown. Do you need help getting up?" Mike and Stu started to take her by the arms; however, she gagged again, making a deep hitching sound and they backed away as though she had a disease.

"Careful of the dress!" a woman coming off the back of the float cried. She could have been pretty if she weren't so stern. She wore a severe grey dress and had perfectly straight, brown hair. To go along with the perfectly straight hair, she had a perfectly straight and somewhat unsettling bar of eyebrow crossing her forehead from end to end. "Don't let her get any of that ick on it."

Jenn didn't know if the woman was speaking to her or to someone in the crowd around them that had sprung up, seemingly from out of nowhere. The gorgeous white-rose float had ground to a halt as the barrel-bellied mare stared to chew on the rope hooked to her harness. Everyone in the crowd was somewhere between tipsy and inebriated. One was nearly as sloppy drunk as the Parade Queen.

"Let's get hers back on to the flows…no, the froat," he tried to say. "The fa-rose froat. Someone get her ankles."

Stu stepped between him and the heaving Queen. "That's not how you treat a lady."

The drunk began to get his back up and a green glint crept into his eyes. He looked as though he were about to take a poorly thought-out swing at the rangy Hillman when the woman who'd been with the float squawked, "It is most certainly not how you treat a lady, Mister Graham. We are not grabbing anyone by the ankles. You two," she pointed at Stu and Mike, "*If* you're sober enough, help her inside."

They had been watching the parade, standing on the lawn of a little three-bedroom ranch. "This isn't our house," Jenn explained.

"No duh," the woman said. "Of course, it's not your house. You came in last night and everyone knows that Norris Barnes is always in bed by eight and nothing except an invasion would get him out of it until eight the next morning. The man's the human equivalent of a sloth. Come on. Don't be shy with her. She doesn't know which way is up."

Mike and Stu approached the girl slowly, in the same manner they'd approach a wounded animal. When she didn't attack or spray them with an orange fountain, they lifted her gently by the arms and helped her stumble inside, while behind them, Jenn snatched up her white shoes as they fell off, one by one. There wasn't much to the shoes; crystal-studded white straps and a spike of a heel, four inches long. She was both fascinated and mortified by them. *How could anyone walk in such shoes*? she wondered. This thought was followed up by, *Would anyone care if I tried them on?*

She was too nervous and set them aside as the two men laid the mumbling queen on a couch and simply stared at her, not knowing what else was expected.

The woman in grey hurried off to look for a bucket and some towels. "She's not done yet," she said over her shoulder as she rushed from the room. "Don't let her get anything on the carpet."

"How do we do that?" Mike whispered to Stu, who lifted a single shoulder in reply. It was not usual for any of them to see someone full-on puking drunk. On the Hilltop it was too dangerous to get this out of control, and while the people of Alcatraz were a little freer, they couldn't afford to be wasteful with anything.

They stood back, scarcely breathing, afraid that any movement would bring on another orange explosion. The Parade Queen held back until the bucket appeared and then out came another foul-smelling rush of fluid.

"Quick!" the lady cried. "Get her out of her dress." Mike and Stu backed away before fleeing the room altogether. The woman in grey snorted, "It's like they've never seen a girl in her underwear before."

"They probably haven't," Jenn told her. "This," she pointed at the girl, "is not a normal sort of thing where we're from."

"You're going to have to brace yourselves then, because it's going to be normal this week. Here we go." She had managed to slip the dress off in one piece. She held it up to the light to examine it for orange vomit and when she didn't see any, she held it up to Jenn. "You'll do just fine."

Jenn's blue eyes shot wide open. "Just fine for what?"

The woman arched an eyebrow. "To be queen, of course. Trust me, like I said, you'll be fine. You're a natural. All you have to do is wave and be pretty. It'll be perfect. You're new. What better way is there to get to know people?"

In a tornado of white silk, makeup and hairbrushes, Jenn was thrust into the dress and then thrust outside minutes later to be presented to a gaping crowd. One of the gapers was Mike Gunter who said, "Woooow."

She beamed at him. "Puked on one moment, a queen the next. You'd think that this would be a first for me."

"If you're going to be queen, you're going to need this." He held out the last flag that bore her symbol: a bold gold crown stitched on a pure white background. With Stu's help, they let it fly over the rose float. It got tongues wagging and Jenn took her place on the float to stares and whispers.

The moment dragged out until the woman in grey came hurrying from the house. "What are we waiting for? You people act like you've never seen a queen before. Let's get that float moving. We're creating a logjam, people."

In the dress and tiara, with her banner flying high, no woman on Bainbridge could have looked more the part of queen than Jenn Lockhart. It wasn't just the accoutrements and her physical beauty that created the image. Everyone saw that there was something deeper to her than just a girl who'd won a popularity contest. She carried herself differently than any previous winner; she stood taller and there was a touch of cold reserve about her. And her smile wasn't the usual toothy grin of a pageant winner. It was genuine and within it was a touch of melancholy.

Yes, on one level, she was only the queen of a meaningless parade of floats, and yet, on another subtle level, she was much more. If only for a short time, Jenn had been an actual queen, who had made life and death decisions, and these still haunted her. A day didn't go by without her thinking back and second-guessing herself. Her brief reign had been marked by one impossible decision after another, as well as one death after another.

Still, she could say, as queen, she had never faltered when given the choice between right and wrong—as a person and an unprepared surgeon, she could not make that same boast.

There was a final, very subtle aspect to her that made people look at her and see a real queen: for someone who lived by the signs that the universe provided, Jenn could not help but see the tiara as an omen. She didn't see it as a bad omen, however. In fact, it felt as though she were being given a little gift, as if the world was trying, in some small way, to make up for the hell it had put her through.

She took the gift and waved and smiled, and had a wonderful time, oblivious to the wild rumors that rippled along the parade route.

At first glance, most people actually mistook her for Jillybean and there was talk that she had spiked the real Parade Queen's drinks with one of her pseudo-magical potions. When it was discovered that Jenn was a complete stranger and one who had shown up the night before with her own royal flag, even wilder rumors raced around. Some said she was a real queen who lived in a stone castle somewhere on the coast. Others said that she was in hiding after the Corsairs had taken her lands. A few even suggested that she was "husband shopping" for the right man to be her king.

Soon, the streets became absolutely clogged with people and the Queen's float had no lack of volunteers to haul it along after the grey mare had wandered of to nibble on a discarded piece of pie. Despite being weak and wounded, Mike and Stu had been the first to grab the ropes. Now, there were always twenty men crowding on each rope, none of whom equated the two raggedy, bearded men with the beautiful young woman standing in the center of the white rose.

It was just as well. Neither wanted to spend the day repudiating all of the many rumors. They were content to enjoy the time drinking pumpkin beer and scarfing down slices of pie when they were offered.

Eventually, Jenn's day in the sun had to end, but it did in a most unexpected manner. They completed the circle around the parade route, which finished across from a brilliantly decorated park where there were booths and rides, and many little temporary theaters, all of which were little more than slapped-together wooden stages, draped by homemade curtains, and hand-painted backdrops.

A cheering, half-drunk crowd awaited the Queen's float. Front and center on one of the little wooden stages was Deanna Grey, Governor of Bainbridge, wearing a brilliant smile. When Jenn approached, walking through a narrow lane, Deanna didn't recognize her as the same filthy, worn girl who had brought in the sinking *Calypso* weeks before.

"Welcome to Bainbridge," she said, smoothly. "My name is Deanna Grey." She held a hand out.

Jenn hesitated, suddenly afraid to give her own name. If the Corsairs knew she was alive, it would spell trouble for everyone, Jillybean included and, despite everything, Jenn still had a soft spot for the real queen.

Stu had more than a soft spot. He was carrying a torch for her, one that could be seen from space. Still, he had his own honor to worry about. He would not be a spy even if he had to live his life looking over his shoulder day and night. When Jenn hesitated, Stu stepped in and said with utter sincerity, "Her name is Jenn Lockhart, Queen of the Hill People and all of San Francisco Bay from Sacramento to Alcatraz."

"Former Queen," Jenn said, quickly, standing as tall as she could, which was surprisingly tall with the four-inch heels propping her up. She shot Stu a quick glare that only confirmed to Deanna that neither of them were lying. And yet it was so unbelievable.

The Governor looked again at the flag and then back at the young woman. "You're not kidding, are you?"

"I was queen for a very short time," Jenn admitted.

It was such an unexpected thing to hear that Deanna was momentarily at a loss. She looked back at her advisers; every one of whom shrugged. Deanna forced her politician's smile back in place. "Being a queen must have been something. I have to hear all about it, but first diplomatic courtesies have to be followed, though I'm not sure what the proper protocol is."

Now it was Jenn's turn to be surprised as the Governor dipped into a deep curtsey, lowering her head. There was a moment of hesitation before the men and women around her did the same.

The kneeling spread as did the whispers of, "She is a real queen." Mike and Stu were the last to take a knee, each wearing confused expressions.

"No," Jenn said, taking Deanna's arm and gently lifting her. "I'm no longer queen. Jillybean is."

Deanna had knelt because her politician's instinct had told her it was the right move at the right time. Her instinct had not prepared her for Jenn's statement. Her eyes flew wide. "Jillybean? Our Jillybean? Wait, I know you." She pointed at her and then at Stu and at Mike. "I know all three of you. You came through a couple of months back and then disappeared…and you say Jillybean is a queen? A real queen?"

"Yes," Mike answered quickly. He was angry at Stu for having given up their identities so quickly and was worried that, in her naively honest way, Jenn would make it worse. "But we should talk about it someplace else."

"I agree," Deanna said after a pause in which more whispers spread throughout the crowd. "Joslyn can you see them to the mansion. I need to officially start the ceremonies and then I'll be right over."

Joslyn Reynolds, in an electric blue dress, couldn't stop staring at Jenn as she led them through the crowd and down a little, tree-lined side street to the Governor's mansion. She set them on a plump leather couch in the Deanna's office and then hurried off to fix tea. When she returned she stared some more before politely asking, "Were you good friends with Jillybean?"

It was a hard question to answer. Stu said nothing and only stared into his tea. Jenn wanted to answer "yes," but then hesitated. Sometimes…frequently, she thought she had never met the true Jillybean.

Mike, who had been the least friendly with her said, "I think so. She had her good points."

Jenn thought she deserved more praise than that. "I guess you could say I was her best friend. And she really is a good person down deep." That wasn't good enough, either. She was trying to think of something to say that would be more appropriate, when people started trickling in. This commenced a long painful silence that was made worse by the unabashed staring on the part of the Governor's staff. It was like they were having a contest in which the only loser was Jenn.

Deanna was the seventh and last person to enter the room. "Why don't you start at the beginning," she suggested from behind her desk. "How did you get off the island?"

The paranoid part of Jenn had hoped to keep the route a secret, just in case they had to escape, but the question couldn't be ignored and a lie right off the bat seemed like a terrible way to start their time on the island. "There's a secret tunnel in a building over by the cemetery," she admitted. "I think it's called a morg-tuary or something. The tunnel leads out under the wall and into the Sound."

"Go on," Deanna said. "You left the island and where did you go?"

Jenn did not liked the looks the Governor's staff were giving her. It was as though they were offended that they had snuck off the island. When she didn't go on right away, Stu, the quietest of the three, became their spokesman. He took his time and gave measured responses. He spoke in terse sentences, barren of all description, as he explained how they made their way to Grays Harbor, stole the Corsair boat and how it led to the first battle on the Hilltop. He maintained that an "incident" caused them to head to Sacramento where Jillybean first crowned herself queen.

"And people just bought it?" Joslyn asked in disbelief. "Hi, I'm queen and all of you have to do what I say. I don't see how that can possibly work."

"If you had seen the…the squalor and the filth they'd been living in, I think you would understand better. They were desperate people. Desperate for leadership and medical attention, and someone who could handle the Corsairs. Jillybean was all three. And there was something else about her." He broke off, momentarily, and gave Jenn a glance. "Something that made it seem right." *At first*, he didn't add.

Before he could begin again, Mike butted in to tell them about the *Floating Fortress*, which he described as a "miracle." He then went into too much detail explaining how they managed to wrestle the ungainly barge back to the Bay area in time to confront the Black Captain's armada.

"The fleet was immense," he told them. "The entire bay was filled with black sails and clouds of smoke…and bodies. They were floating everywhere."

He tapered off, allowing Stu to tell about the next series of battles, which he did in one sentence. "The Corsairs came again, more this time, and Jillybean was able to defeat them and ultimately turn many to her side." Twenty-one words to describe the tremendous clashes in which hundreds had died.

It took longer to tell how Jenn came to be queen and, as he spoke, he grew quieter until recounting Jillybean's treachery became too much to bear. His words faltered into nothing and Jenn had to take over. She told a much deeper story that had the seven on the edge of their seats. Just like Stu, she hit a point where she couldn't go on. For her, it was drinking the poison.

Her flesh was awash in a sea of goosebumps and she could feel her heartbeat throbbing in her temples as she remembered feeling the cold hand of death come over her.

Mike dutifully finished up and managed to restrain himself concerning their escape on *The Wind Ripper*. As much as he wanted to praise the ship's heroic lines and the way she handled in a crisis, he didn't want to bring up the death of Rob LeBar at Jenn's hands. The word *murder* kept creeping out of his subconscious and he was afraid he would accidentally say it.

He also didn't mention Gunner. Their harrowing flight from Grays Harbor became instead, a simple walk north where they "found" a canoe that brought them across the Sound.

When he had finished the tale, the room went silent as Deanna leaned back in her chair, her elbows propped up on the armrests, her fingers steepled beneath her chin.

"This is good news for us, right?" Norris Barnes asked after the silence had carried on for over a minute. He was a politician and he felt the need to fill any lull in a conversation with the sound of his own voice. "Kind of a two-birds-with-one-stone situation. Jillybean gave the Black Captain a good spanking, which is good, and now her dream, or whatever it is, of world conquest is over. She can't beat the Guardians."

"Yes," an older man agreed in a solemn tone. It was hard to take him seriously as he wore an orange tuxedo. "Their wall is said to be almost as big as our own. Torpedoes are impressive and she should be rightly commended for figuring them out. *But* they aren't much good on land. With the height of their walls, the Guardians should be able take out any catapult, or what have you that Jillybean might bring to play."

At this, Stu smirked and Mike rolled his eyes. Jenn sat up straighter, saying, "I don't think any of you know what Jillybean is really capable of. The woman I know will have destroyed that wall days ago."

"I agree with Miss Lockhart," Deanna said, as she got to her feet. "I was with Jillybean and helped her destroy the River King's bridge. And I was with her when the Azael were defeated. A wall will not stop her, not even our own. The question we should be asking ourselves is where will she strike next? If it's Jillybean who is queen, she'll destroy the Corsairs once and for all. If it's Eve, she may be coming here."

This cast a gloom over the room, while outside drums beat chipper cadences, and happy-sounding horns blared.

It all washed over Deanna. "I would like to talk to these three alone. The rest of you go and enjoy yourselves. Oh, except you, Perkins. I'm afraid I'm going to need you to do an inspection of the guards on the wall. We all know they've been drinking so don't be too hard on them. Just make sure they cut it out. I doubt Jillybean would come here, and if she did we'd have plenty of notice. It's just best to be on the safe side."

When her counselors were gone, Deanna drooped. Even her golden hair looked as though it sagged in spite of the great deal of product she had put in it. "Come with me." She led them through the empty mansion and down into the basement. For the most part, it was finished with plush carpets and pictures on the walls and rooms with silent televisions or empty fireplaces. In the very back; however, where the furnace roared and spiderwebs dominated, the floor was cold, grey concrete.

In the furthest corner, in a room that had once been used for storage, they found a version of Neil Martin, chained hand and foot to the wall. His eyes were blood red and his skin the color of old oatmeal. Emily was in the room reading to him. She looked as tired as her mother.

"What happened to him?" Jenn asked, stopping in the doorway.

Neil glared. "What's it look like? And what's with the get up? White was never your color, Jilly."

"This isn't Jillybean, Uncle Neil," Emily said, staring at Jenn in disbelief. "This is that girl that Jillybean ran off with. That's you, right?"

"It is her," Deanna told her daughter, "And I think she can explain why you were attacked, Neil."

"Why I was killed, you mean," Neil snarled, jumping up and straining at his chains. "That's what they did to me. I'm dead Deanna. Look at me. You and I both know what's going to happen. All the pills in the world won't to stop me from becoming one of them. I can feel it getting worse, Deanna. I can *feel it* in me."

Deanna almost touched him, but pulled her hand back. "I understand, Neil, but you need to pay attention. Focus. Jillybean has gone after the Captain and has defeated him in a number of land and sea battles. So, I think it's safe to say…"

What color there was in Neil's face drained away. "It was the Captain. I see it now. He's trying to get to her through me."

"Are you sure that's what happened to you?" Jenn asked. "Jillybean is days away. She probably doesn't know a thing about what's happened to you."

Neil made a growly noise in his throat. "You don't know him like we do. He's a hateful man. He's diabolical. Killing me is an insurance policy just in case she comes north. She'll send a boat for me and when she finds out I'm dead, there's no telling what will happen to her." Everyone in the room had a very good guess. The stress she was under already had her teetering. Neil's death might send her over for good.

"Then we better keep you alive," Deanna said. "One of Gina's pumpkin pies might do the trick. I'll go see if she has any left while these three tell you what's been going on."

Gina Sanders was always in the running for best pumpkin pie and, at this time of the year, she was sure to have seven or eight either on a rack cooling or waiting to get into her oven. They were Neil's favorite because she added just a touch of rhubarb.

As Deanna hurried up to the Sanders' home, she saw Eddie standing on his stoop, a cigarette in his hands. The cigarette was almost all ash and had singed the hair off his knuckles. He didn't notice. He was staring down at something tucked under the lip of his welcome mat.

When she got close, she saw that it was a picture of his son Bobby. The toddler was dressed as a scarecrow and sitting on one of the floats. His smile was wide and bright. The picture couldn't have been more than an hour old. Pinned to it was a one-word note that read: *Tonight!*

"What's going on tonight?" Deanna asked. He clearly hadn't seen or heard her coming, and yet, he didn't flinch. As if he were crawling out of a trance, Eddie slowly lifted his chin. He looked even worse than Neil. He was pasty white with drooping bags beneath his hollow eyes. Although Deanna had her hands full already, she asked, "Is something going on with Bobby?"

He nodded without looking her in the eye. "Y-yeah. W-we are in need of a babysitter. Do you think Emily could come over? Just for an hour or so." He might have looked doped up, but his heart was racing as she frowned and fumbled for an excuse.

"No, sorry. She's, um, um, grounded. T-That's why she's missing all the fun. Sorry. Really. She's going to be stuck at home tonight. Maybe her friend Bernice might be able to help."

"It has to be Emily," he said, the words spilled out of him fast and harsh. He was as desperate as he sounded. The picture, the second he'd received, was a stark, unvarnished threat to his son's life. "I-I just say that because Bobby loves her. You understand, right? The way kids can be. Maybe you could see your way clear to letting her out for a few hours."

"I wish I could," Deanna said, and meant it. She felt terrible that Emily was stuck with Neil so much. "I just can't. She needs to be alone to think about what she's done. I hope you understand."

Unexpectedly, Eddie brightened. "Of course. I understand completely." It had just dawned on him that this was better than he could have guessed. Emily would be alone while everyone on the island was out partying. It would be the perfect time to take her.

Chapter 46

Before Jenn peeled the white dress away, she stared at herself one last time in the mirror and wondered if she would ever be this pretty again. The moment the dress was hanging on the closet door, she looked like her old self—a somewhat cute and nice girl. And that was okay. She liked being that person. It was easy.

Being a queen, even a parade queen, was harder than it looked.

What was infinitely harder was being questioned by the being that had once been Neil Martin. Neil was no longer the kindly older uncle, trying to hide his middle-aged paunch beneath a sweater-vest. He was sharp and angry. He would rage one second and pick apart her words like a surgeon, the next.

Somehow, he could sense an equivocation or a half-truth and when he did, he would pounce, as if he were uncovering a great betrayal, when it was usually Jenn simply softening her words to make Jillybean look less psychotic.

The interrogation, for that was what it was, took two hours and by the time they were done, all three were exhausted. Lack of sleep over the last few days combined with too much pumpkin beer had them looking for a place to crash at three in the afternoon.

"You'll stay here," Emily determined, without asking her mother. Deanna had returned only briefly with a pie in one hand and a cake in the other; both orange. She was gone again in a flash, late for two different events. Emily was used to her schedule and took over the duties as lady of the house. "We have loads of room and you already know about Uncle Neil, so it just makes sense. Oh, hey, I forgot. He is supposed to be, like this big secret, so promise me you won't say anything to anyone."

They had mumbled promises and stumbled upstairs. Jenn was given the one spare guest room on the second floor while Stu and Mike were forced to climb to the third floor. Like old men, they sighed as they went up.

Emily ran around in a perfect state of happiness, making sure her guests had everything they could possibly need: all the proper toiletries, pajamas, towels for showering, hot cocoa, wine, extra slices of orange-frosted cake in case they got hungry, and so on.

Over the last week, she had been stuck in the house, dealing with Neil. It went without saying that she loved him, but that didn't make the minutes drag any less. Now, she had a real queen staying with her! One who had been on real adventures!

Jenn had singlehandedly fought giant zombies, she had battled pirates on the high seas, and had waged war against the fearsome Corsairs. She had faced death a hundred times and not only had she come away with barely a scratch, she seemed to have blossomed in the face of danger.

To top everything off, she had found a handsome mariner who loved her.

And Jenn wasn't all that much older than herself! After her guests were asleep, Emily wandered around the house, doing the chores that she had put off for the last week. She wanted everything to be perfect for when "The Queen" woke. As she worked, she daydreamed of being on an adventure, of slaying zombies by the dozen, of whisking sailing ships out from under the noses of the Corsairs, of finding a courageous man, who would risk everything for her.

She was just mentally describing the man—tall, of course, strong without being hulking, brave, a gentleman—when someone tapped on the front door. It wasn't a proper knock. It was more of a light, nervous tapping, and Emily guessed it was a child.

It was Eddie Sanders, looking strange...and frightened. He was pale and there was sweat in his thin red hair. His washed-out blue eyes kept shifting around, looking behind him and then to the sides and then behind her. "Oh, hi, Mister Sanders. Are you looking for my mom?" Emily checked her watch and was surprised to see it was seven and already fully dark. "I think she's at the high school for the potluck. Is there something wrong?"

Oddly, the question seemed to excite him. "Yes. Something is wrong down by the docks. Can you help me? It won't take long."

Emily frowned. "The docks? I-I don't know anything about boats. And besides, I can't leave, sorry. We have guests."

Once more Eddie looked past her and into the house. Other than a single light in the kitchen, the mansion was dark. He cocked his head, listening. Except for the steady tick of a grandfather clock, the place was silent. "Are they here?" He had heard about the new comers; everyone had. A hundred rumors were circulating about them, each sillier than the rest.

"They're upstairs sleeping. They had a hard time of it getting here."

"If they're sleeping it should be fine," Eddie insisted. "Like I said it should take two minutes tops. And it's not about boats it's, uh, it's fish. Danny won't help me unload them and everyone else has been drinking."

Her frown deepened and now there were three little lines marring the space between her large eyes. "Fish? You need help with fish? There's a wheelbarrow in the shed out back. You can use that. I'd help, only I can't leave."

Eddie Sanders was an average sort of man, not very tall or intimidating. He was also a nice guy, who no one ever had problems with. Emily had never felt even a smidgen of fear around him, until just then. Something was wrong about him. He leaned in close; she could smell sour sweat and gin. "It's important. Please."

The fear in her ticked upwards. Eddie might be average for a man, but he was still much bigger and stronger than her. And yet, this was Bainbridge. Nothing ever happened on Bainbridge. She summoned her courage and gave him one of her mother's fake politician smiles.

"I can't. Not right now, but when my mom gets home I might be able to." She began to shut the door when he unexpectedly stuck half his body in the doorway. Her fear began to peak and she felt a scream building in her throat. "Mr. Sanders, please. You're not supposed to be in the…" His hand, clammy and cold, snaked forward and clamped down on her wrist.

"You're coming with me," he snarled, yanking her out onto the porch.

Although caught by surprise, the eleven-year-old was not slow to react. She had her father's reflexes and her mother's instinct to fight when cornered. She went for the eyes.

Eddie had expected her to pull back or scream. The last thing he figured she would do was attack. Still, the eyes were difficult to claw out when the opponent was on his feet. Nails raked his face, digging groves and bringing up blood. It hurt but he could still see well enough to spin her around and slam her into the door.

"Settle down! Or so help me…"

There would be no settling down. Except for a vague notion of rape, which seemed so far-fetched she didn't really entertain the thought, Emily had no idea what Eddie wanted. In her mind, he had simply "gone crazy." She spun in his grasp and raked his face a second time. When he leaned back away from her clawing hands, she broke from his grip and darted inside. She tried to slam the door in his face, however, he charged and slammed his weight into the door, sending her falling back.

Nimble as a cat, she tucked into a ball, rolled and was back on her feet, racing for the stairs. He was closer to them and cut her off. As he did, he reached behind him and pulled a pistol on her. "Emily, settle down, please," he said. "I need you to come with me. If you do, no one will get hurt."

She didn't believe him, not for a second. Slowly, step by step, she began to back away. "You won't shoot," she said, pointing at the ceiling. "They have guns and they know how to use them. So, no, you won't shoot." It was a good lie and for a second, he glanced up. In that brief moment, she took off, running mindlessly for the back hall, inadvertently trapping herself.

When she realized this, she dashed for the basement stairs. Everything was dark, and she had to run by memory, dodging the little side table along the wall and narrowly missing the partially open door as she made the turn and went down.

Eddie clipped the table, slammed into the door, and then practically fell down the stairs. Still, he raced on, desperation feeding him speed. When she got to the bottom of the stairs, it sounded like he was right behind her and as she sprinted down the basement hall, she wailed in a terrified voice, "Neeeeeil!"

Right before she made it to the very back room, she dug the keys to Neil's handcuffs from her pocket. He was on his feet when she threw herself inside. "It's Eddie!" is all she had time to say as she tossed the keys at him. She then turned and launched herself at the door. It was an inch from shutting when Eddie crashed into it from the other side. The door smashed into the side of her head and shoulder, knocking her down.

"Get back!" Neil seethed, momentarily forgetting the keys in his hands. In his sudden rage, he felt strong enough to break the metal with his bare hands. He strained against the cuffs, his veins bulging and his eyes strangely alight with fever. The flesh on his wrist began to part and dark blood trickled down his hand.

At the sight of him, Eddie actually took a wobbling step back. "N-Neil…you're alive. How are you still alive?"

"Someone messed up, that's how," Neil said, giving the cuffs one last furious tug before realizing that he would pull his hand off before he broke free. He went back to trying to use the tiny key, glaring at Eddie as he did. "What the hell, Eddie? What's with the gun? Why are you scaring Emily?"

"*They* want her."

"They?" Neil asked. He had just slipped the key into the lock but the word was so ominous sounding that for a moment he forgot it existed. "Who is they?"

"The Corsairs."

Neil began blinking, rapidly. In stark contrast, his mind moved with agonizing slowness towards the obvious. "The Corsairs? How would you know what the Corsairs want…" He sucked in his breath in shock. "It was you! You poisoned me. Son of a bitch! If I get these damned chains off, I'll kill you." He tried to twist the key in the lock, but in his fury, he couldn't get his fumbling, numb fingers to work like they used to.

"I had to do it," Eddie whispered. "They were threatening my family. They said…" From high above them came a rumble of feet; Stu and Mike were hurrying down stairs to find out what all the ruckus was. Eddie went as grey as Neil. His Adam's Apple started bobbing up and down. "If they find out that you're still alive, they'll kill Gina and Bobby. I have to kill you."

"And what about Emily? Huh? Go ahead and shoot me, I don't really care. Someone's gonna have to do it, eventually, but don't you dare touch her. Promise me, Eddie."

The pistol was shaking in Eddie's hand. "I'm not supposed to kill her. I'm supposed to deliver her alive."

"To where?" Neil demanded.

"You know where."

Emily didn't need to be told where: Grays Harbor. She had heard the horrible rumors of the place. They were so sick that she knew Mr. Sanders couldn't be thinking of taking her there. It had to be a joke, or a prank, or she was in a dream. It certainly felt like she was drowning in a nightmare.

Her life had been swimming along just fine two minutes before and now it was crumbling.

Neil started scrabbling at the lock again, his rage filling his throat with bile. "If you touch her, Eddie, I swear to God I will rip out your throat."

Eddie had let the gun fall; now, as Stu came down the basement stairs at a run and Neil finally got the key turned, Eddie pointed it again. "I'm sorry, Neil."

"Don't!" Emily screamed. "Don't do it!" She started to get up but was too slow. Eddie pulled the trigger. There was a flash of light and what sounded like an explosion. Blood splashed on the wall behind Neil and then her uncle was down, a hole almost dead center in his chest.

The sound of the gunshot was so shockingly loud that not only was Emily deafened, it felt as though she was concussed as well. Her mind felt like jelly. She stood and teetered in place, the room spinning around her in slow motion. A hand grabbed her before she could go to Neil's side. She was spun until she was facing the door and then something stinging hot touched her temple. The smell of burnt hair crept into her nostrils.

Nothing made sense; the smell, the ringing in her ears, the blood on the wall. She thought she was going to faint.

One of the newcomers—Stu—appeared in the doorway. He took in the room, a rock-hard scowl etched onto his youthful features made him look thirty-one instead of twenty-one.

"Get in here," Eddie demanded in a strangled voice. "All of you. Get in or I'll kill her."

The hot barrel pressed harder, but Emily didn't care. She twisted in his grip, though not to escape; she needed to see Neil. She needed him to be alright. He wasn't. Around him was a ring of blood that was spreading further and further outward. It was so much blood and he was such a small man.

Roughly, she was yanked around again as Eddie yelled, "All of you get in here, now! I won't ask again."

Stu eased in with his hands up followed by Mike. Jenn was nowhere to be seen. Eddie started licking his lips rapidly like some sort of snake. "Ok, look, nobody wants you guys. All they want is her. So just be cool and get down on the floor and no one's gonna get hurt."

Mike knelt with a grimace; he had tweaked his ribs jumping out of bed. Stu didn't budge. He stared at Eddie with flinty eyes. "You work for the Corsairs? Listen to me. They want me way more that they want her. Trust me, you'll come out ahead if you let me take her place."

"Get down!" Eddie thundered, pointing the gun.

"Down there?" Stu asked, pointing at the bare cement next to Mike.

Eddie was almost purple with rage. "Yes! Get your ass down. I'll shoot you just like I shot Neil. Don't tempt me."

"But it's so dusty," Stu drawled.

"You think I'm playing, don't you?" Eddie said, thumbing back the hammer on the pistol. "Try me one more time. I'm going to count to three. One…two…"

Stu's eyes went to squints. "Could you count to four, instead. That guy's taking forever to get up." He gestured with his chin behind Eddie.

Eddie refused to look back. He knew what Stu was trying to pull. "I'm not going to play your game. Three." Eddie didn't know if he was going to pull the trigger or not, but Stu sure thought he was. The rangy Hillman dropped like a grenade was about to go off and just as he did, Neil slammed into Eddie from behind.

The gun went off, punching through the wall right where Stu had been standing. Emily was thrown forward, landing on Stu, while Eddie landed on her with a rabid Neil Martin at the very top of the pile. It was a wild tangle of arms and legs and wriggling bodies. Blood was everywhere; Neil's was rich and dark, while Eddie's was bright red, shooting from an artery that Neil had torn open.

Seconds into the melee, Eddie's gun went off again. There was a guttural scream of rage and before Emily could squirm out from the entire thing, a knee dug into her back. Her breath was crushed out of her as she was pinned against Stu. She felt as though she was suffocating and for a few moments all she cared about was drawing her next breath. In desperation, she twisted sideways. The knee slipped off her and now pinned Stu.

Even though her diaphragm was still partially paralyzed, she knew she needed to help Neil. He was a small, middle-aged man, who had been weak and somewhat frail even before a bullet had torn a gaping hole in his chest. He wouldn't be able to last, or so she thought. As she twisted, she saw that Neil had changed. He was blood-maddened. His eyes were red as a demon's and his normally ugly, scarred face had been transformed into that of a monster.

With a roar, his fingers dug into soft flesh as he finally found the leverage he was looking for. Emily was shocked to the core as her little uncle picked up Eddie Sanders by the crotch and the throat and threw him across the room.

Eddie landed in a crumpled heap; his eyes going in different directions. It was a good bet that he was too stunned to put up a fight; that didn't matter to Neil. Emily's kindly uncle had become a fiend. He

rushed on Eddie and made good on his promise by tearing out his throat
—with his teeth.

Emily backed away as Neil did more than just kill the man. He fed
on him, the sounds; the slurping, the crunching, and the grunting, were
so repellent that she thought she was going to puke. Next to her, Stu
was the color of old cheese as he too backed away.

It took Stu a second to gather his wits. "Where's the gun?" Eddie
was no longer the problem. The gun was nowhere to be seen, which
meant it was still with or near Eddie's corpse. No one wanted to get
close enough to Neil to find out.

"We should leave him be," Mike suggested and was just pointing
at the door when they heard steps on the floor above.

"Is that Jenn?" Emily asked.

"No, I'm right here," Jenn said from the hallway. The room had
been so crowded and the fight so quick and sharp that she hadn't had
any time to do a thing.

"Mom?" Emily yelled, her voice shrill with fear. "We're
downstairs. Th-there's been an accident." The room looked like the
scene of a multi-murder, not an accident. The four of them decided to
get out of there before Neil turned completely. They gently shut the
door and were hurrying for the basement stairs when the person
walking about above them decided to come down. The four were
unarmed and they held their collective breaths until they saw that it was
just Joslyn Reynolds, now wearing jeans, boots and a heavy fleece coat
that was two sizes too large for her. She had her hood up against the
cold.

"What the hell happened?" she cried when she saw the blood on
Stu and Emily. "Were you attacked?"

Stu felt as though they had stumbled into something that really
shouldn't have been their business. He didn't know who knew what, or
what the dynamics of the situation were. He left it up to Emily to
explain. She was getting the shakes. It made her voice tremble as she
gave an explanation that was both stilted and rambling. It also didn't
make any sense. She cut out Neil's presence entirely, which left gaping
holes in the story and made it sound implausible.

"And you're sure Eddie's dead?" Joslyn asked. "I guess I don't get
how he cut his throat."

"He just did. And that's not the point, anyways. He was a Corsair
spy! He wanted to kidnap me. We have to tell my mom."

Emily started up the stairs; however Joslyn stepped in front of her.
"Slow down. Your mom is speaking at the potluck right now. She's also
one of the judges for the pie contest."

"Don't you think this is more important than pies?" Jenn asked.

"Yeah," Emily said, and once more tried to push past Joslyn.

Joslyn stopped her again. "Hold on! Give me time to think, will you? We can't just run off half-cocked. We need a plan. Eddie is dead. I just can't believe it."

"A plan for what?" Jenn asked. She had the feeling that something wasn't right with Joslyn. She was upset, sure, but she wasn't afraid or even bewildered. She seemed angry. An odd reaction. "Who needs a plan to tell the Governor that her daughter was attacked and almost kidnapped?"

"I agree," Mike said, gently pushing Jenn behind him. "Tell me what's in your pocket."

The older woman had come down the stairs with her right hand in her pocket and her left trailing along the banister. Her right was still unseen. She pulled it out now and there was a flash of silver. It was a tiny 380 Ruger LPC. "You should be careful about what you ask for, boy, you just might get it."

Chapter 47

Stu Currans felt like the forgotten man. On an island of thousands of people, he stood alone, unspoken to, and unwanted. Normally, this wouldn't bother him. He had always been both self-sufficient and self-contained. This night was different. He wanted to be heard, but no one would listen; he wanted to be part of the group but no one wanted him near them.

Deanna had nearly come apart at the seams when Stu told her that her only child had been kidnapped. During his story she looked scattered and lost, as great crystal tears brimmed over and dropped onto her cheek—then Stu came to the part Joslyn Reynolds had to play.

Grief turned to rage in an instant and where before she had been pale, she now went crimson. "Tell me one more time," she demanded. "Start at the beginning. I want every detail."

It hadn't been easy to tell the story the first time and as Stu rehashed it once more, his voice cracked. It wasn't just Emily who had been kidnapped, Joslyn had taken Mike and Jenn as well.

"Sorry, but I have to," Joslyn had said. She hadn't looked sorry at all. She had looked hungry. "The Captain doesn't allow for mistakes and Eddie was a mistake. The girl will make up for it. Jillybean's best friend. Yes, you'll do just fine."

"I *was* Jillybean's best friend," Jenn insisted in something of an uncharacteristically high whine. She no longer looked the part of queen to Stu. For once in her life, she looked like a girl, soft and vulnerable. She had been given just a taste of what a real home could be. For one day, she'd had everything. She'd been safe and loved. She'd been popular. She had a full belly and a soft bed. The people around her had been friendly and generous and amazing. This was what real life was supposed to be and she didn't want to lose it. Not so quickly, not after everything she had suffered.

It was a desperate, tearful fifteen-year-old girl that Stu barely recognized, who begged, "We already told you that she tried to kill us. Please. Please. You don't want me."

Joslyn hadn't been convinced and the gun did not waver even slightly. "I'm sorry, but it's either I take you or I kill you. I really don't see any other option."

"You could kill yourself," Stu suggested. "It would make the world a better place, believe me."

"Better for who?" Joslyn sneered. "If I kill myself, it won't be better for you guys, or for Bainbridge, or for anyone. The Black Captain is too strong and Jillybean is a nutcase. She's not going to last and when she falls, her little empire is going to crumble."

"I'll take my chances with her," Stu said. "She's a little off, but deep down…"

Joslyn's laugher interrupted him. "Deep down she's even crazier! And no, she won't last. The Captain has spies and assassins everywhere. There's probably twenty on Bainbridge, alone. He hooks you when you're weak. That's all it takes, one moment of weakness and then he has you and he won't let go."

"You could take me instead," Mike said. "I promise I won't try to run away. I'll even help you get off the island."

"There's no instead," Joslyn told him. "There's no either or. I'm taking you too, since I need someone to pilot the *Calypso*. And, get this through your thick heads, I won't hesitate to shoot anyone who tries to run away. We all know what happens to spies if they're caught. So, if my life is on the line, so is yours."

She kept the gun leveled as she dug in her back pocket for a pair of handcuffs. "Cuff the girls together," she told Stu. "And then go into one of those back rooms and plant yourself."

Stu was surprised. "You're not taking me?"

"No. You'll end up getting us all killed by doing something stupid. Don't pretend that you don't know what I'm talking about. I can see your little mind working, mister hero." She wasn't wrong. He had remained tense, ready to spring at her the second her attention wandered.

Now, he wouldn't get the chance. He went to a back room, but he didn't sit. Instead, he stood at the door, listening to the thumping sounds coming from somewhere on the floor above him. When the house grew quiet a minute later, he raced for the stairs only to discover that the one door out of the basement had been barricaded. He heaved at the door, straining with all his might. When that didn't move it, he threw himself at it in desperation.

His shoulder was bruised to the bone when Neil Martin came sauntering from the back room. He didn't seem to notice the hole in his chest.

"Whatcha doing?" he asked, sucking his teeth.

"That woman…Roslyn, took Emily and my friends."

Neil squinted back the way he had come. "No. That was Eddie who tried to do that. And who is Roslyn? Do you mean Joslyn? Joslyn Reynolds? You must have the wrong person."

"No, it was her. She was with the Governor this afternoon. Five-foot-three, brown hair, pretty, probably around thirty-five or so."

The sleepy, contented look on Neil's blood-reddened face fell away. "And she took Emily? That bitch! Look out." He stomped up to the door and hurled his small frame against it, leaving a ghastly red smear behind. The door held against his strength, which was appalling to Stu; however, it did not hold against their combined strength. Gradually they pried it forward. When they had a ten-inch gap, they squirmed through and then raced through the house to the front door. It was only then that Stu saw Neil was carrying Eddie's pistol.

"I better take that," he told Neil. "I don't think people will understand seeing a guy who's part zombie carrying a gun." Stu was surprised when Neil handed it over without a thought. The two then limped and gimped down to the docks which were strangely dark and eerily silent. The twenty-three foot *Calypso* was just pulling through the water gate, heeling far over with all her sails set.

"Shoot it!" Neil hissed. "Shoot the boat." Stu wouldn't. He could see Mike at the helm, his blond hair streaming, but he couldn't tell Joslyn from Emily or Jenn, and couldn't take the risk. "Are you always this useless?" Neil growled, as he pushed Stu aside, nearly knocking him into the water. Neil had been limping and now it became more pronounced as he stumped to the little shack that the harbormasters used to keep out of the cold. Inside they discovered three contorted bodies in a ghastly heap.

Although their faces were swollen and purple, Stu knew Danny McGuinness by his sheer size. Neil bent down and heaved him away as if he were filled with air instead of lard. He then picked up the next corpse by his jacket. "That's got to be Todd Karraker. Damn it! Todd was a good guy. And crap! That's Steve Gordon."

"Perhaps you shouldn't touch them," Stu cautioned, leaning back from the doorway. "They were probably poisoned. It could still be in the air."

"Maybe if I'm lucky, it'll kill me," Neil growled. He stepped over the bodies and began ringing the brass harbor bell for all he was worth.

He was hoping to gather a posse together to go after Joslyn. Instead, the two were arrested on the spot and it was thirty minutes before Deberha Perkins, the island's lone sheriff, was able to inspect the evidence at both crime scenes. Her official report to the Governor was, "They may be telling the truth."

By then, the entire island was in an uproar. A posse was indeed formed and every boat on the island was launched. Those with sails went north, chasing the *Calypso,* which could still be seen at the far end of the island, beating heavily against a seven-knot headwind. The dingies, rowboats, and skiffs were thrown on the now forgotten Fall Festival floats and hauled to the very tip of the island where they were launched with every available rower.

All but Stu and Neil Martin, that is. Stu was invariably shunned, while Neil had to suffer the humiliation of having his old friends shoo their children indoors when he walked by. He didn't suffer it in silence. "Jeeze Carl, I'm not going to eat your kids. I'd eat your wife first. I'm just saying that someone should." Carl Tamsen pointed a rifle. "It was a joke, Carl. Jeeze! I'm not a cannibal."

"You ate Eddie," Stu reminded him in a whisper.

"He had it coming," Neil snapped. After a moment's reflection he added, "I wish he had shaved. I don't think men really appreciate how prickly they can get."

"I guess no one gets that zombies have their problems, too."

For a few seconds, Neil glared, fury in his blood-red eyes. Then he burst into laughter that was shockingly alien sounding. Neil's laugh was similar to a saw trying to cut rock, and Stu got a case of the goosebumps from it.

"That was a funny one, Stu. I like you and, who knows, maybe I won't eat you. You're too skinny anyway."

There was nothing funny about Neil Martin. He had been shot through the chest and also through the thigh, but other than a phlegmy cough and a dragging limp he seemed...well he hadn't seemed fine even before getting shot, he was still alive-ish; and that wasn't right.

"Neil, you can't talk about eating people or they'll kick you off the island." *Even faster,* he didn't add.

"Ooh, I'm shaking in my crocs." Stu looked down and noticed for the first time that he was wearing odd rubber shoes. They were purple. Neil, scratched some of the flaking blood from the side of his face and told Stu, "I'm not staying either way and neither are you. That girl that came with you, was going on and on about that Mike guy as if he was the second coming of, I don't know, Noah or something. I'm just saying that if that was Eddie, he would've been caught by now. If your friend is as good as you guys say, no one's going to catch that boat and they're going to get away. So, where does that leave us?"

They had gone north to watch the chase, but when it ran beyond the range of the searchlights, they had wandered back to the Governor's mansion. Neil climbed up onto the rock wall separating Deanna's property from a neighbor's yard. To Stu, he looked like a wretched and gnarled gargoyle as he sat with his feet tucked up to his chin.

"Is there an *us* that I should know about?" Stu asked. "It's not like we know each other. And you are going to turn into one of them, or are you going to pretend you weren't enjoying yourself earlier when you ate Eddie."

"I'm not turning any time soon and so what if I liked it? It's not like I'm hungry for brains or that sort of thing. It just happened and I sort of went with it. I'd prefer we don't make a big deal about it."

Since he had saved Stu's life, Stu gave him a quick promise and Neil slapped him on the back. "Good. Thank you. Now about us. I'm going to get Emily back one way or the other."

Stu nodded. "And I'm going to get Mike and Jenn back. I guess an 'us' makes sense. The question is, do you have a boat?"

"Not one that will out-sail the *Calypso*. But we don't need to out-sail her. We both know a short cut."

Again, Stu nodded. The overland route was close to sixty miles, but if they could take one of the smaller boats and use the same water route that Jillybean had shown them weeks before, they could cut that in half. "It's a short cut but not that short of one. We're looking at thirty hours and that's if we leave right now and don't stop for nothing." He licked a finger and held it up. The wind was out of the north, and although the *Calypso* was being slowed going in that direction, they would fairly fly down the coast. "The wind is with them. Joslyn could be in Grays Harbor in a day, well ahead of us."

A scowl darkened Neil's features, and with the scars and the blood and his grey skin, there was no getting around it, he was a zombie. It was strange to see one think. "I thought you said your man was good. It seems to me that a good sailor could slow down his boat if he wanted to."

Having this pointed out by a zombie made Stu feel especially stupid. There was no way Mike was going to race to a torturous death at the hands of the Corsairs. He would spill his wind, or drag a sea anchor, or do something to slow them down.

Neil grinned, his teeth black in the moonlight. "You see it now. If we play our cards right, we might be able to cut off the *Calypso* right after she enters the harbor. Joslyn may not even see us coming until it's too late. Even then, she'll probably just think we're Corsairs."

It was a good plan, with one major flaw: Neil was a zombie. Sure, he could walk and talk but that didn't make him any less dangerous. Stu needed someone on his side he could trust. "We need back-up, just in case. Also, we need permission to take one of the boats."

"We don't have time," Neil shot back.

"Don't you think we should make time to do this right?" Neil didn't think so, but had his vote nullified as Stu simply walked away. He slipped through the now crowded mansion to Deanna and explained their plans to the distraught governor.

She grasped at the straw. "Yes. Take any boat you want. And, and, and we'll get volunteers. Everyone loved Emily." Unfortunately, a dozen years of safety and comfort had made the people of Bainbridge weak—just as Jillybean had known. Everyone who loved Emily had an excuse: Norris Barnes had a bad hip; Sheriff Deberha Perkins was too old; and so on.

There were almost a hundred people in and around the mansion, and not one volunteered, and Deanna lacked the authority to force anyone to go with them. "Then I'll go," she stated, getting to her feet, and staring boldly around. Those who caught her eye, looked away, quickly. "The Corsairs do not frighten me any more than the Azael did. I may be a woman but I can fight. Tell them, Neil."

"You were a golden Valkyrie," Neil said from the far corner of the room. "Nothing could stop you then and nothing can stop you now. You have five minutes. Pack light but smart. It's going to be cold. Oh, and make sure you get a gun with plenty of ammo."

Stu could not believe his ears and the second Deanna stormed out of the room, he turned on Neil. "You want to take her? Are you kidding me? She's too old for one and…"

"We'll talk outside," Neil stated, cutting him off. Afraid to be touched, the crowd in the room parted as he swept through them. Once outside, he didn't slow and Stu had to almost jog to keep up with the much shorter man.

"What are you doing? Neil? Where are you going?"

Neil glanced up, a sneer on his lips. "We're going to the docks. Duh. Do you think I want Deanna tagging along? She was a Valkyrie once, and if the Valkyrie was coming along, I'd welcome her. But she isn't. Deanna's coming as a mother, a frightened, emotional mother. That won't help us get Emily back."

It made sense and yet, Stu was still uneasy about traveling with a zombie. Neil wasn't without his good points. Not only had he become completely fearless, he also didn't care one wit about offending anyone. He marched straight down to the docks to the harbormaster's shack where a gaggle of people were just then moving the bodies. With the dark they didn't see Neil and Stu until the pair were right on them.

"Poor Todd won't be needing this," Neil said, and picked up Todd's M4. He handed it to Stu and then snatched up Steve Gordon's rifle.

"What are you doing, Neil?" one of the men asked in a hoarse whisper. The rumor was that Neil had come back from the dead. As far as rumors went, it seemed very believable.

Neil charged the weapon, making everyone take a step back. "We're going to save Emily. Any of you boys want to come along?" In answer, he received only excuses or silence. "That's what I thought. You're all a bunch of pansies. When the Black Captain comes you'll deserve everything he does to you."

He left them white-faced and roiling in an impotent fury. It was a sad realization for Stu. These were young men who had cowered for so long behind their wall that they had become actual cowards. They could have easily stopped the two from taking one of the flat-bottomed skiffs, yet they did nothing except raise the water gate when Neil barked at them.

They paddled out onto Puget Sound where the cold wind helped push them south. They needed all the help they could get. It was a long way to Olympia and this time they didn't have the benefit of Jillybean's electric motor. The two men paddled endlessly, stroke after stroke.

Neil seemed to sleep even as he kept up the rhythm. His head dropped to the V in his sweater vest as he went on relentlessly. After two hours, Stu was envious. His back ached and his hands were blistered. His wounded arm screamed with pain and his bullet torn muscles were the first to cramp. Even his ass hurt.

Despite all this, he did not complain, knowing that Emily, Mike, and Jenn would endure far worse if the Black Captain ever got a hold of them.

Five hours of the most intense torture passed before the vague outlines of Olympia appeared before them. "Neil. Neil! Wake up. I think we're here." The winter sunrise was still forty minutes away and in the dark Stu wasn't a hundred percent certain he was even in the right city. The last time he had come through, he had been only a day removed from major surgery and under the effect of powerful pain meds.

Neil coughed up something black that was the size of a mouse. It made a little splash when he spat it out. "Great," he rumbled. "Now for the hard part."

"Yeah," Stu agreed with a disgusted sigh. They wouldn't have a zombie slave to help them haul their boat. They'd have to do it themselves. He angled them towards the shore where the high tide made it easy to clamber up among the ruins of a harbor-side restaurant. The first thing Stu did when they were on dry land was dig his knuckles into his back and bow his belly outward. He was rewarded by a string of cracks.

Next, he began massaging his dead arms. He could barely lift them and yet, he was supposed to help carry the skiff. "I don't see how that's going to happen." He turned back towards Neil and was startled to see a shadow move away from the side of the building. It seemed to float in the darkness as if it was made of nothing at all.

It was made of flesh and blood, however. It was a hulking man that yanked Neil's head back and brought a black knife to his throat.

"Don't move or I'll cut the girl's throat."

Stu was shocked to realize he knew the voice. "Gunner?" No one else sounded so bestial.

"You're not Eddie," Gunner growled.

"And I'm not a girl," Neal said and took a ferocious bite out of Gunner's arm.

Chapter 48

The dive from the cliff took Jillybean deep into the cold black water of the pacific. She went so deep that for just a moment, she wondered if she would have the breath to make it back up to the surface and if she did, would she come back as herself?

She did, though it was close. Eve wanted to drown Jillybean even if it meant killing herself in the process. And it wasn't easy to maintain herself when she broke the surface. The night was utter chaos. Men and zombies were leaping into the water so that it seemed like it was raining bodies.

Troy Holt was in the water calling out, "Fight the surf! Get away from the cliff!" It was easier said than done and two men were turned to pulp by the crashing waves. Two more drowned; one because he jumped in fully armored, and the other because he couldn't swim.

"You can't blame either of those on me," Jillybean said, when Troy glared at her. "Who jumps into the ocean with fifty pounds of armor on?"

"It's *all* your fault," he growled.

"Even that?" She pointed as a fantastic white sailing ship with lights blazing slid into view. Troy looked at it as if it were a miracle until she added, "You can thank me later for saving your life." She had ordered four of the Guardians to bring the ship around, not just to save them, but to destroy her own zombie army.

Seeing the boat with its torches lit and hearing the horn that began to sound was enough to get the stupid beasts to lemming right off the cliff. Most of them didn't die—killing zombies wasn't *that* easy—but the tide and current slowly swept them south. Where they went from there didn't concern Jillybean; they were someone else's problem.

The few remaining Knights were pulled on board, where they helped to keep the boat on station and blew the horn until their lips were numb. Jillybean went below deck, took the largest cabin for herself, and changed into dry clothes. She slept until the first light of morning woke her. Feeling refreshed, she went on deck and saw that they were being towed back into the tricky little cove that protected their small fleet.

A glance toward the town showed that it was zombie-free, except for the many corpses that is. They looked awful. *That was you. You did that. Youuuu diiiid thaaaat!* Eve sang.

Jillybean ignored her. Imperiously, she ordered a group of men in one of the rowboats to fetch her boots and coat from the cliff. Troy rolled his eyes and then nodded for them to do as she asked. She changed into her damp clothes and when her boots and coat arrived, she allowed herself to be rowed ashore.

She started walking towards the center of town and with her came her bedraggled escort of Knights. "Isn't she our prisoner?" one asked.

This caused Jillybean to laugh. "Look at the hill and tell me what you see?" Her army was marching towards the town. "You can either deal with them or with me. They will kill all the men, rape the women and children for the next week straight, then sell them into slavery. I am only asking that you accept me as your queen."

A pallid, drooping Bishop Wojdan appeared with Commander Walker, who looked as though he could barely contain his loathing for her. They had both heard the Queen.

"I've already told you, we won't kneel," the Bishop said. "We are not your subjects or your servants. We will not obey a single command of yours."

Sudden hot anger coursed through her. It came from the fury deep within, where the hatred was volcanic. Her hands balled into fists as she fought to hold onto her sanity. Somehow, she held herself together. "Your Excellency, you do not understand what's going on. You do not understand the danger you're putting your people in. I'm the only one who can save you. Look at them." She pointed at her army.

They were marching without orders from her. It was a bad sign, as was the fact that they had already broken into factions. The Coos Bay Clan marched as a unit under their red and black flag on the right, while the Magnum Killers were on the left. In the middle was Leney with most of the ex-Corsairs. Lagging behind were the Santas.

"They won't take no for an answer," she said. "They'll drag your children out into the street and you don't want to know what they'll do to them."

The Bishop didn't even blink. "If you think that will force us to comply, you are mistaken. Besides, you're still their queen, aren't you? I don't think you would allow that sort of thing."

She was very near to tearing her hair out in frustration, because he was right. She didn't have it in her to do more than threaten. Furiously, she snapped her fingers and demanded, "Come with me, Bishop. We need to talk. Alone." Although it was technically an order, he followed her into the nearest house. The moment he shut the door, she rounded on him.

"I don't need to kill anyone. I can burn down this town. Is that what you want? I can take everything from you. Your food, your boats, everything."

"You would like a boat? Stealing isn't needed. I would much rather give you one than cause you to fall into sin." He was calling her bluff again! "I would suggest *The Star of David*. She's our finest ship."

Jillybean folded in the face of his unrelenting pleasantness. With a loud sigh, she threw herself down on a couch and thumped both boots onto the coffee table in a less than lady-like manner. "Fine. You win, at least for the moment."

Bishop Wojdan seated himself across from her, perched just on the front edge of a patched leather chair that seemed decades older than the couch. Wojdan's ponderous belly hung between his knees. It was his turn to sigh. "What more do you think you can threaten us with except straight-up annihilation?"

"Oh, I won't be doing anything to you…or for you. You have made your bed and soon you will roast in it. You and pretty much everyone else."

"Unless we kneel before her Royal Highness, of course."

She didn't bother even commenting on his tone, which was borderline rude. "Exactly. My army is, and was, and will always be on the verge of mutiny. For the most part they are ex-Corsairs and, for the most part, they would like to go back to being, at least in some fundamental ways, Corsairs. They don't want discipline. They don't want moral absolutes. They want to rape and pillage just like they've been doing for the last dozen years."

"And you won't let them?" He shrugged. "I suppose that's a good start. Attacking innocent people; not so much."

She ignored him completely, unsure whether that had been him talking or someone inside her. Either way, it was just talk. "The only thing stopping them is me. They don't know what to make of me. There are a hundred rumors about me and I let them all go unchallenged. The more they fester, the more nervous they are. I even use my…*imbalance* to my benefit. All to keep them second guessing."

The Bishop sat back in the old chair. It's worn springs and decrepit foam could not bear his weight and tried to swallow him. He struggled to extricate himself, saying, "Because if they ever realize that you are just one woman they'll turn on you." He blew out through puffed cheeks as he got back to the edge of the seat. "You've managed to put yourself in a no-win situation. Eventually, they will realize that you are not infallible or omnipotent."

"I'm in a difficult position, not an impossible one, your Excellency. A victory against the Black Captain would go a long way to cementing my hold and bringing lasting peace to everyone. Forget the spies in my ranks and the people hatching plots, my biggest problem is that I'll be bringing Corsairs into battle against a man they fear beyond almost anything. Can I depend on the Coos Bay Clan? Will the Magnum Killers turn on me? Will the Santas actually fight? I need the Guardians to give some moral clarity, as well as a backbone to my army."

"It sounds like you need someone to do the actual fighting," the Bishop said, looking pained, a grimace on his face. "Perhaps it's cannon fodder you want."

Eve flared up, wanting to smash his teeth in. *Let's give him a reason for that pained look!*

"Stop it, Eve," Jillybean warned.

"And there's the problem," the Bishop said. "You think you are controlling this imbalance of yours, but it's the other way around. You are dangerously insane, and in the moments you have your wits about you, you're an insatiable megalomaniac. Your Highness, if you could look at things from my point of view, you'd see that you're unstable. You speak to people who aren't real and spend half your time in a fantasy world."

Her fists were now like rocks, her fingernails digging tiny crescent moons into her palms. "So, because of my imbal…insanity, you think you're in no danger from the Corsairs? Is that why you haven't sent trading ships north of San Francisco in the last year?"

"The Corsairs are marauders, not conquerors."

"They *were* marauders." She stood and glared down on him. "I may be dangerously insane, but you are dangerously insulated. You do not live in a static world, Wojdan. Things change and if you don't adapt, you'll get swallowed up. May I suggest that before you rebuild your wall and hide yourselves away again, that you find out who it is you're hiding from."

By all rights, Jillybean should have been crowned Queen of the Guardians, only the Bishop wouldn't kneel, not even with a thousand guns staring him in the face. No matter what she said, he would only smile placidly with that knowing look in his eyes. It was as if he were egging on the darkness inside of her so he'd have an excuse not to comply.

Her frustration mounted until he almost had his wish, which would have ended with his lifeless body nailed to the doors of his church.

In disgust, she left the town with her disgruntled and very confused army following slowly after. Although they hadn't been promised a share of the town's wealth in the form of weapons and slaves, it had been implied. What other reason was there to come all this way and work so hard?

The only thing they got out of the deal was *The Star of David*, which the Queen promptly renamed *Queen's Revenge*. It was a paltry and disappointing revenge, which did little to quell the whispers that had sprung up. There was talk that the Queen was going soft; that she was losing "it."

The moment they made it back to camp, she could feel the stares and hear the whispers that followed her. They were carried on a cold, corpse-stinking wind.

She was just wrapping her coat around her when Leney cleared his throat. "Your Highness, I hate to be the bearer of bad news, but while you were out running around last night, we sorta lost three ships. From what Captain McCartt says they just ghosted out of formation without anyone seeing. Supposedly. McCartt says they're not his and Steinmeyer's saying the same thing. They could be some of the boats the Santas were driving."

This was the last thing she needed. It was one thing to desert while on guard duty, to slink away when no one was watching, it was another thing altogether to take three boats. It was a public embarrassment that would further undermine her. "Find out who they are."

I know who they are, Eve laughed. *They are all spies. Tinker, tailor, soldier, sailor! They are all spies. Or worse! Every one of them could be your assassin. You screwed up, Jilly. If you had just let me destroy the Guardians, we wouldn't be in this situation. But nooooo, you wanted it all. You tried to rule as Queen of the Dead and Queen of the Corsairs and Queen of the Cross-groveling Guardians and look where it got you.*

Jillybean kept her expression blank until Leney gave a stiff half-bow and left. Then she spun around and snarled, "I'm doing fine, thank you very much!" Except, it wasn't close to being true. She was barely holding on and Eve knew it.

If you're so fine, why are you talking to me? Or didn't you notice? And if you're so fine, why do you want to burn the Queen's Revenge down to the waterline? I know that's what you really want to do to her. Is it because she is a consolation prize? You always hated participation trophies, but there you are staring at the biggest one I've ever seen. The Queen's Revenge: a great white loser's trophy.

"I didn't lose!"

Did you win, Jillybean?

"No," she admitted. She hadn't lost, but she hadn't won either, which, in a very real way, was as good as a loss. Her momentum had been checked and her authority flagrantly dismissed by people with no ability to defend themselves. Her soldiers were deserting and the talk against her was heating up. She knew that soon the ex-Corsairs would realize that she didn't have an army, she had a slapped-together force that was just one step up from a mob of criminals.

The mob was staring again. She ducked inside her tent and pulled the flap closed behind her; she did not step in, however. Paranoia reared up inside her and she gazed around trying to see if any of her belongings had been touched. Quickly, she went through her books, her notes, her surgical equipment, her meds…

It was only then she saw that her Zyprexa had been changed to a lower dose. "That doesn't make any sense. Who would…Eve!" Eve tittered, laughing in Jillybean's head. "No wonder they weren't working. You could have killed us, Eve. You know our liver problems. And now I have to take six of these damned pills."

She grabbed a canteen and was about to swallow the hated pills when the diffused light coming through the thin tent showed a slight oily sheen on the lip of the canteen. A shock of fear raised fields of goosebumps on her arms. She took a hesitant sniff. As it always did, the canteen smelled mostly of old plastic. There was also a strange hint of something beneath it.

"Tobacco," she whispered. She knew her poisons and either someone had tried to dose her with concentrated nicotine or they had cooked down insecticide—neither of which was something most of her ex-Corsairs could figure out on their own.

There were actual assassins in the camp.

They know you're weak, Eve whispered softly in her ear, *and you know better than anyone they despise the weak. You should've let them rape and pillage. You should've let them feast on the Guardians. That's the only way this would've worked.*

"And let them worship *you* as their new Black Queen?" Jillybean was feeling guilty enough over the hundred and fifty Guardians who had died in the last few days. She kept telling herself that it was for the greater good and yet, Eve's growing presence was an indicator of her immense guilt. If she had let the ex-Corsairs raze the town, the guilt would have sunk her—and Eve knew it. "Go back into your dank little hole, Eve. I don't need your help to figure this out."

There was very little to figure out. She had to limit her exposure to any would-be assassins and the easiest way to do that was to get aboard a ship, something she needed to do regardless. The longer they sat lurking over the Guardians, the more the resentment would build up and the more problems would develop.

Besides, she knew the Black Captain was certainly preparing his defenses for her arrival and the less time she gave him the better.

She knew that she could not spare a second and yet she hesitated, held in check by uncharacteristic doubt. The canteen beckoned. The poison would be a quick death, but would the next attempt on her life be so easy? She wasn't one to dwell on negative thinking. It did little for the individual except make every decision that much more difficult.

In this case, she had to concede there was a better than even chance that an assassin would take her down. If that happened, she knew things would be much worse than before. Her ex-Corsairs would revert back to being actual Corsairs and once the Black Captain had gathered his "lost children" he would head south to wreak vengeance. She had to take precautions to prevent that from happening.

Jillybean hopped up and went to the flap of her tent. Peering out, she saw William Trafny. "William," she called. He knelt as he entered the tent. For once, she didn't ask him to stand right away. "You've always been loyal. Even back on the Hilltop."

"I owe you my life, your Highness. Without you, I'd be dead right now."

This was exactly what she had thought he would say. "Are you willing to lay down your life for me?" she asked. He didn't hesitate and nodded right away. "What about for your people?"

Now there was hesitation. He thought he'd been dealing in the rhetorical. "Yeah, I guess I would. Why? What's going on?"

"Perhaps nothing." She went to a chest that she not only kept double locked, she also sealed with a tiny amount of wax so she'd know if anyone had opened it. Inside were all manner of odd things: her own poisons, weapons, her most secret documents, and a few small radio-controlled bombs. She handed one to William.

"You will be traveling with Captain Steinmeyer. If anything happens to me, kill him. I would suggest hiding it in his cabin. Can you do that?" His voice deserted him and he nodded. "Good, can you find Lexi May for me?" Another nod. He left, white-faced and sweating, and Jillybean picked up another bomb. There were five more in the chest and she figured she would need them all.

Chapter 49

Neil's diseased teeth bit through the fur of Gunner's strange leather and crow-feather coat but were turned aside by the metal cap he wore over the stump of his left hand.

Gunner swatted him aside as if he were swatting a gnat. As Neil stumbled away into the night shadows, Gunner dropped his knife and drew his gun before Stu could even move. "What's going on, Stu? Where's Eddie Sanders? He was supposed to be here an hour ago."

"Eddie's dead," Stu said, as calmly as he could with a gun staring him in the face. "I-I, we, I mean, were coming to tell you."

"We were not," Neil snarled, scrambling awkwardly to his feet. He looked like an angry drunk who'd fallen off his barstool. "Who is this guy? What's with the mask? Huh? Who wears a mask, huh? Felons, that's who."

Gunner threw back his head as far as his hump would allow, and roared laughter. "A felon? I've been called a lot of things but never a felon. Stu, who is this guy? And what's with him? He looks messed up." Gunner peered around his pistol; even in the dark he knew there was something wrong with Neil.

Stu was floundering, stuck between two creatures who were both nearer to being monsters than men. He would be more than happy if they would kill each other and let him go on. "He got bit by a zombie but hasn't turned all the way into one. He's kinda stuck in the middle. It's why he's so cranky."

"I'm not cranky!" Neil snapped. "I'm, uh, I'm upset. I always get upset around Corsairs. And I wasn't bitten, I was *assassinated*." He said the word as if he were a carnival barker trying to rook a crowd into a tent where stitched together remains of pigs sat in glass jars and were being passed off as aliens.

"Stuck in the middle?" Gunner said in his usual growling rasp. He stepped closer to Neil and inspected him in the growing predawn light. Because of Gunner's gnarled and twisted body, the two men were much of the same height. Their masses were far different; however, and Gunner looked as though he were three times Neil's weight. "How the hell does someone get stuck in the middle?"

Neil folded his arms across his thin chest. "If you must know, I was given *the* vaccine a long time ago. Apparently, its effectiveness has diminished over time. What's your excuse? You look as though you were stuck in the middle of a trash compactor. You smell like it, too."

Gunner wrapped his hideous fur and feather cloak around him tighter. "My business is my own. And I'm the one asking the questions here and we're going to start with Eddie. What happened to him?"

"Well, like I said, Eddie died," Stu said, trying to stall as he tried to figure out how not to get killed by Gunner, who was clearly part of the conspiracy to kidnap Emily. Stu had to keep him calm and talking until he let his guard down. Then, three seconds was all he would need to get his M4 off his back.

Neil didn't seem to understand the concept of stalling or even treading carefully. "He didn't just die like he had a stroke or something. I ate him. Not all of him. I ate parts of him. His throat and, and, other parts. Some were not so good."

"*Some* were not so good?" Gunner asked, incredulously. "Jeeeeze."

"Jeeze yourself," Neil spat. "Don't sound so disgusted, Corsair. I can't help the way I am. What's your excuse? You're filth. Kidnapping innocent girls and raping them, is that how you get off? Is it?" In his mounting fury, Neil stomped right up to Gunner, who kicked him in the chest and sent him flying back.

Stu jumped between them, his hands up, palms out. "Look, Gunner, it's the virus. He doesn't mean it."

"Gunner?" Neil hissed. "Did you say, Gunner?"

"You know him?"

Neil got to his feet and advanced again, his head twisting back and forth, trying to see past the square of black cloth Gunner wore over his disfigured face. "Oh, I knew him from ages ago. The Piggly Wiggly back in Alabama, right Gunner? You were into kidnapping little girls even back then. You sick, sick bastard. What happened to you?" Neil reached up and plucked away the cloth.

Stu cringed at the sight. He had never seen Gunner's face fully exposed. His nose had been torn away or cut off with a ragged instrument; only two wet black holes remained in its place. His lips were gone, as well, as was a good deal of flesh around his jaw. Stu could see right to the bone. His exposed gums were black. His ears were mere stumps of charred flesh.

While Neil stared, Gunner stuffed his pistol back into its holster before grabbing the mask back. "I ran into the wrong crowd. You could say it changed me."

This caused Neil to snort. "That's something of an understatement."

Gunner let out a slow hissing breath before turning suddenly and clamping his huge hand on Stu's shoulder. "Finish telling the story. What happened to the girl?"

As always, Stu was able to condense a long story into a few short sentences. When he got to the part that Joslyn Reynolds played, Gunner turned furious. "That two-timing bitch!" He stalked away. Quickly, Stu grabbed for his M4 and had it half off his back when Gunner spun. "Put the gun away, boy. I don't want to have to kill you. Besides, you need me."

"How on earth does he need a Corsair?" Neil cried in a high voice. He too was trying to get his gun off his back. Unfortunately, he had become tangled in the strap. The more he pulled, the more it choked him.

"It's not just him, grey-meat. You both do, if you're going to have any chance at even making it to *The Wind Ripper*, let alone getting her through the harbor."

Neil looked confused, uncertain when anyone had told Gunner of their plans. Stu was equally confused, but twice as nervous. He was about to make a general denial when Gunner waved his stump of an arm in irritation. "Stop trying to think up a lie. I know your type, Stu. You'll risk life and limb for your friends. And you, 'Uncle' Neil, were an idiot twelve years ago and not much has changed. So, instead of wasting everyone's time, just say: 'Thank you, Gunner,' and let's go."

"No," Stu answered and resumed pulling the rifle around.

"Don't be an idiot, Stu. I told you I'm not a Corsair. Do you want proof? Come on, follow me."

Stu had his gun ready as Gunner walked off, heading toward the same ramshackle docks Jillybean had used weeks before when they came that way. Stu and Neil glanced at each other; they both shrugged and then followed after. It wasn't far and yet the sun was up over the horizon by the time they got to the docks. In the water beneath one was a dead body in black. It was a Corsair and one who'd been mutilated badly before death.

"It was our good friend here who told me what the plan was for taking Emily. I was all set to free her but you guys messed that up pretty damn good."

"And what were you going to do with her?" Neil demanded, jabbing his rifle at Gunner as if it were a spear.

Gunner shook his head at him. Stu guessed that he probably had a look of sad disgust on what features he had left. "You haven't changed a bit, except for being a zombie and all. Do me a favor and get your booger hooker off the bang switch, will you? I wasn't going to hurt the girl."

"Were you going to sell her to the highest bidder?" Neil shot back. "Or were you going to keep her for yourself?"

The wrinkles around Gunner's eyes deepened. "Zombie-Neil is much feistier than the old Neil. And that's okay."

"Answer the question, Gunner!"

"I don't have need for a woman. No woman can stomach the sight of me and when one starts to gag or scream at the sight of me, well, it just kills the moment. And I don't need money. I have all the bullets a man can use. I told Stu that I deal in knowledge, but I also deal in favors. If I had the Governor's daughter, I could have *anything* from her, and you as well, if my informers are right."

The fire died in Neil and now his head felt thick as though filled with wet wool. He glanced at Stu who was studying Gunner. "And we're just supposed to trust you?" Stu asked.

"You don't have a choice," Gunner told him. "Between here and Grays Harbor are about a thousand bandits who've come down out of the mountains. They were just starting to trickle in the other day when we came through. Now they're everywhere." He pointed at the body in the water. "That guy told me war is coming. He said that the Queen has thrown down the Guardian's wall and has her boot on their neck. She's getting stronger, while the Black Captain is getting weaker. That's why he's been making big promises to the bandit chiefs."

"Like what sort of promises?" Neil asked, hollow-voiced. "Will he give them Bainbridge?"

Gunner laughed. "Hell no. He intends to keep that plum for himself. My poor unfortunate informant didn't know. He thought maybe it would be some of those southern lands; Alcatraz and that weird place the Santas have. Either way, the one thing the Black Captain fears is that Bainbridge will march overland as the Queen attacks by sea. To stop that, he's using the bandits. If you don't believe me, you can go on without me and find out the hard way."

Stu and Neil shared another look. Neither were much good at bluffing and Gunner knew they were about to give in. "Besides, do either of you really think you can pilot *The Wind Ripper* through a harbor stacked with Corsair ships?"

The look came again between them. Neil knew next to nothing about boats and had become irritatingly clumsy to boot. Stu, who had much more experience, didn't think he could out-sail any Corsair captain, especially with a half-zombie as his only help. It seemed Gunner was right, they were doomed without his help. But would he really help them, or was it all a ruse? Was he going to turn them in to the Corsairs to make up for the fact that Joslyn was going to deliver the real goods?

Reluctantly, Stu said, "Maybe you can come with us. I want to know what the catch is. What do you want in return? You aren't going to risk life and limb for nothing."

Gunner tried to make a snort of derision; however a man without a nose couldn't exactly snort. It came out as an unsettlingly wet "gushy" noise that made Stu grit his teeth. "I'm risking life and limb just standing here." He gestured with his stump at a hippo-sized zombie struggling in the water ten feet away. It had been in the water so long it seemed to have forgotten how to use its legs properly and was making little headway in its effort to get at them.

"I'm not afraid of death," Gunner told them. "But as to what I want, hmmm, I haven't decided yet. I'm thinking Christmas dinner. You know, with all the fixings. And not just one, either. I want it to be yearly. Maybe I'll ride up to the mansion on one of them floats. And I want the dinners cooked by the Governor. She can cook, right?"

Stu had been envisioning the same thing, only sitting across from him was Jillybean. He glanced over at Neil, who was staring at the zombie with dread fascination. The queer little man jerked as if coming awake. "Yeah, she can cook. But I think we should get this on the table. If you double-cross us, I will kill you, pure and simple."

This made Gunner laugh which only sounded marginally better than his snorting. "You could try. I don't think you have much of a chance, but stranger things have happened. Come on, we got to get moving. If the bandits catch us here yapping, everyone loses."

"What about the boat?" Stu asked as Gunner walked right past it.

"We're leaving it," Gunner said. "The river is gonna be guarded just like the roads. If you want to get safely through we're gonna have to take to the woods. You gonna be okay with that, Neil? Back when I knew you, you were a little squeamish about getting your Crocs dirty."

Neil looked up at Gunner and promptly stumbled over a root. "That was then. I've changed a good deal since you knew me."

The snot-sounding snort came from beneath Gunner's mask again. "Besides being a zombie and a few scars, I'm not seeing it."

It took Neil a moment to figure out what had changed about him. "These are hiking Crocs for starters and this sweater vest is new." He held it by the lower hem and pulled it out away from his body. "I guess that hole is new, too. I should think about sewing that up. I'm not so good at sewing. But I'm okay at pottery. That's new, too. I took it up last spring. It didn't last, but I made some bowls."

"Yeah, you're completely different," Gunner scoffed.

In the growing light, Neil looked to be getting grayer by the second. He began to mumble. "Everything I ate from those bowls tasted earthy. I used to think it was bad for me, like I was eating some of the clay and it would build up in my bowel and that I would pass a brick eventually. I'm not worried about that anymore."

Gunner glanced back. "Okay, new and improved Neil, why don't you quiet down?" They were passing through suburban Olympia, angling southwest. Like a disease, nature was swallowing the city, encroaching from all sides including from below. The streets were buckled as much from the weather as from the trees shooting right up through the asphalt.

Everything was overgrown, which made travel dangerous. And it wasn't just the zombies that seemed to lurk in every shadow, eating the dying grasses or pulling down branches to their faces, there were bandit scouts as well. These were far more dangerous and trouble came quickly.

It started with a shot from an out of sight sniper. The bullet kicked off the broken cement a few feet from Neil. He turned slowly from where the bullet had gouged the street to where the echoing gunshot had come from. Then he blinked into action, bringing his gun up.

"Don't," Gunner warned him. He had slunk behind a tree and now gestured across the street to an apartment complex where four zombies were gazing blankly to the south. All four were grey, haggard females with pendulous breasts that hung past their swollen bellies. The beasts weren't huge, probably not much more than five hundred pounds. "Just get down."

Stu hauled Neil behind a bush as the sniper shot again, hitting almost the same spot. "He's not much of a shot," Stu remarked.

"I think he's better than he's letting on," Gunner whispered. "He's two blocks up in that brown apartment building. If he wanted to kill us, he would indeed be a terrible shot, but if he wanted us to return fire and have those four beauties come after us, then he shot well enough."

Neil was slowly piecing things together. "If we fired, then those four will come after us…"

"And maybe more," Gunner added.

"Yes, and maybe more. We'd run of course. Where?" He looked to his right at a narrow street that seemed more like an alley due to all the trees growing up along it. A perfect spot for an ambush.

Stu had no idea if any of this was true. Normal people didn't think like this. Then again, bandits weren't normal people. Slaves had to be taken alive and unharmed if they were to have any value, which meant ambushes had to be set up.

"So, which way do we go?" he asked. Back and far around seemed like the only logical direction.

Gunner formed a knife with his good hand and pointed it at the four zombies to their front left. "Keep quiet and trust me. They won't even see us." He had his battle axe slung on his back next to his hump; he pulled it off. "Come on," he said, then ran hunched over towards the zombies. They were gazing south, trying to figure out where the gunshots had come from and didn't see the three humans slipping behind them, edging against a row of parked cars that looked as though they belonged in a junkyard.

"Simple as pie," Gunner murmured as they took a turn around the nearest apartment building where they ran into another zombie. This one was also female, only she was eight-feet in height and strangely lean, which made her look even taller. With a harsh grunt, Gunner jumped high and came down, embedding his axe in its forehead before it could even growl.

As Gunner was working his axe out of the thing's head, Neil was gazing placidly up at the top of the building across from them. "Look. Green smoke. It might be a signal, right?"

"Yeah," Gunner agreed. He handed Neil his bloody axe. "I think you might need this. I'll take the gun."

"Sure," Neil said, grinning. Stu thought the axe looked way too large for such a small man. Then again, he wasn't completely a man anymore. He gave it a practice swing and nearly fell over.

Gunner laughed his harsh laugh, clapped Neil on the back and then took off, heading around the side of the building emitting the smoke. "Watch my back, Stu," he ordered, before walking backwards away from the building, his rifle trained upward. They were in a courtyard that had a rusting playground square in the middle. One of the swings gave a mournful squeak in time with the soft wind.

Stu had his own rifle trained on the building in front of them. There were so many windows he didn't know which one to point at. Like Gunner, he chose to aim at the upper floor windows and thus missed the zombie that came charging out of a first floor apartment. All he saw was Neil, rushing past him, the black axe raised.

He turned the rifle on an arc, aiming to kill the roaring monster, only Neil was directly in his line of sight. Even the axe blade got in the way of a head shot. Stu hesitated, hoping that Neil's zombie strength would do the trick. Neil swung a ferocious stroke at the monster and buried the axe in its chest...uselessly. The zombie wasn't even slowed. It slammed into the small man and only the axe handle that Neil smashed into its mouth kept his face from being bitten off in one bite.

Just as a shot rang out behind him, Stu rushed up and shot the zombie with the bore of his M4 pressed against the thing's head. A rain of black blood sprayed out in all directions coating Neil, who was still grinning as he licked his lips.

"I used to hate this stuff," he laughed.

"Oh, Neil," Gunner groaned at the sight. "Just stop. We'll get you some fresh blood later, okay? Now we gotta hightail it out of here."

Zombies and bandits were pouring into the area. Although the bandits wore grey camo and moved with more stealth than the average survivor, a few small battles broke out between them and the zombies. Gunner aimed for one of these, slinking from building to building until he saw an opening where *only* three huge males squatted over a dead bandit eating strings of intestines like it was hot mozzarella.

Gunner hurled a rock across a parking and into the windshield of a Dodge Ram. Immediately, the three beasts charged at the truck and tore it to pieces. The doors were ripped off, as was the hood and the front passenger seat. While they were at it, Gunner led Neil and Stu away.

"Jillybean used to do things like that," Neil said, staring back at the dead bandit with something like longing on his face.

"Distracting the dead?" Gunner shrugged. "Anyone with any sense knows to do that. Hey, stop looking at that guy, Neil." He slung the rifle and grabbed Neil's arm. "There'll be plenty to eat further on."

There wasn't more food further on, however. There were only more bandits and more zombies.

Chapter 50

Gerry "the Greek" Xydis was the last to leave with a bomb tucked up under his shirt. He was pale and twitchy. Jillybean didn't think it was possible for anyone to look as guilty as he did.

The second he was gone, she thundered, "Leney!" in a voice heard from one end of the camp to the other. He had been two tents down, limp on a cot, his snores loud and steady. Blearily, he poked his head out, and the moment he did, she ordered. "Break down the camp. It's time to destroy the Black Captain."

"Huh?" he asked, squinting down at the ocean where only the Queen's fleet could be seen. "He's here?"

"No. He's hiding in his little rat's nest. We're going to have to smoke him out." This reminded her that she would need a metric ton worth of smoke bombs for her next attack. "Let's get these lazy slobs out of bed."

Even if they wanted to sleep, few could have as she began issuing orders in her usual manner. It was something akin to a verbal barrage of artillery. If anything, she was louder that morning, and her words came faster. Few could keep up with her. "Shaina, get my belongings on board the *Queen's Revenge*. Yes, the new white ship. Donna, head down to see the Bishop. I'd like to borrow two of his ships with a skeleton crew for each. Steinmeyer! You're taking over as Commander of the Fleet and if you lose three ships, you'll be losing three fingers."

And so on, and so on.

No one could match her energy, which she aided with amphetamines and black coffee. In a feat that probably had no rival in history, she loaded an army of two-thousand soldiers, along with all their stores and belongings on board a hundred and thirty ships in under six hours.

Her men, who had been up all night, were too tired to grumble and it was an eerily silent fleet that was about to set sail when Knights Sergeant Troy Holt came walking along the beach, a pack on his back, his rifle slung on one shoulder and a new spear in hand. Amazingly, he knelt in the sand in front of the Queen.

"Bishop Wojdan has asked me to act as ambassador for the Guardians," he told her in a flat voice. "I am to ascertain the truth behind the Corsair threat and assess her Highness's mental stability. I am also to protect her Highness and fight for her as long as the fight is deemed just." He wouldn't look up.

"Try not to sound so excited about the idea," she replied. "I wouldn't want you to strain anything."

Donna chuckled, while Leney only sneered. "I don't like it," he said of Troy. "He's basically saying he's a spy."

"But an honest one," Jillybean replied. "I doubt he'd tell a lie if his life depended on it. Watch. Troy, what do you think of me? Do you like me?"

Troy didn't hesitate for a second. "No. Not in the least. A hundred and fifty people are dead because of your ego. You are an evil, evil person. There's nothing about you that I like."

"Not even my new boat?" She pointed behind her at the *Queen's Revenge;* Troy only ground his teeth. Jillybean turned to Leney. "See? He's painfully honest. Luckily for him, Eve thinks he's cute. She *might* not kill him."

Leney still looked like something was curdling in his gut. "That's disappointing. After all their hard work, the boys would love to see one of these holier-than-thou types swinging from the masthead. Just a thought, your Highness. It might be good to, you know, throw the dogs a bone once in a while."

"Treat them like dogs and they'll behave like dogs," Jillybean sniffed. "Treat them as men and they'll behave like men. Leney, I want you to take Knights Sergeant Holt under your protection. If something happens to him, I'll hold you responsible in a reciprocal manner."

"Reciprocal? What's that?" He had a guess and he didn't like it.

She stared out at her fleet laying at anchor and answered without looking back at him. "An eye for an eye. That's how I do things, Leney. You'd be wise to remember that."

Leney's eyes shifted away at the threat.

Oblivious to what was really being said, Troy tried to explain that he didn't need anyone's protection. "I'm a Knight and equal to any five of you." He wasted his breath. The only person in need of protecting more than him was the Queen herself. She came on board the *Queen's Revenge* and found very few friendly faces.

She stalked right up to the least friendly of them, a tattooed gorilla of a man named Greg Bennet. "Why aren't you on your knees?" Despite what the Bishop thought, her insanity was an effective shield. Her men might have respected her skill in battle and her immense intellectual capabilities, but they were afraid of Eve. And rightly so.

Because they know that I'll do what it takes to...

"Shut the hell up," Jillybean growled without taking her eyes off Bennet. She had her hand in her coat pocket where she carried a small frame .357 Taurus. She stared him down to his knees. Without taking her eyes from his she said, "Leney, tell me everyone on this damned boat is kneeling."

There was a quick rustle of cloth and quite a few thumps. "All but your pet Guardian."

She turned and Troy dropped to one knee. "Please excuse me, your Highness," he said with some difficulty as his jaw was almost completely clenched shut. "I was told to give you every courtesy due your rank, but I'm new to, uh, royalty."

"Learn quickly," she answered. "As for the rest of you…" She took the gun out of her pocket. "When I come on board, you kneel. When the captain comes on board, you come to attention. You did neither. If it happens again I will make an example of at least one of you."

Her anger, which was explosive one second, disappeared entirely in the next. "Everyone up. I want to see what this baby can do." She slapped her hand on the rail of the *Queen's Revenge*. Her excitement over the ship was all an act designed to turn the crew's focus from her to something they enjoyed.

It was a new crew on a new boat and as the sails were raised, the shrouds tied off and the booms adjusted it was obvious that its pecking order had not yet worked itself out. There were a number of scuffles and near fights.

As captain, it was up to Leney to divide his sailors into three watches and assign duties to each. Having judged them as they got underway, he made his decisions. The third watch was sent below, while the second found places to wrap themselves against the cold and keep out of the way of the first, which led the fleet out to sea.

Jillybean stood on the soft teak deck of the *Queen's Revenge* her hair spinning and whipping like flame in the gusting wind. She gazed up at the mountains of snow-white sail. They reminded her of the winter peaks of Colorado and, for a time, melancholy struck her, overshadowing the great dissatisfaction she had with the ship.

There was nothing in particular about it that she could point at and say: "There. That's the problem." In many ways it was a perfect ship. Certainly it was the finest she had ever sailed on.

The *Queen's Revenge* was a double-masted thoroughbred. She was sleek and trim. Her hull was so clean that she seemed to skate across the top of the water instead of pushing through it. She was so fast that Mark Leney allowed her sails to sag just a touch. Had they been drum-tight, she would have raced away from the rest of the fleet as if they were nothing but garbage scows.

From the top of her seventy-foot-tall masts to the bottom of her keel, she was brilliantly, magnificently white. Everything about her spotless and beautiful. And yet the Queen was not happy with her. Nor was she exactly happy with Knights Sergeant Troy Holt, who always stood at the bow, staring straight back across the deck at her. She liked to stand at the bow on occasion and watch the keel knife through the low waves. But now she couldn't. The judgment coming off him was colder than the wind.

Tell Leney to push him over, Eve suggested when they were miles from Highton. *It'll be quick and relatively painless. With his armor, he'll sink like a stone. No fuss, no muss, no rotting carcass.* She tittered at her joke.

"Shut up, for God's sake," Jillybean whispered, sticking a pinky in her ear, and giving it a wiggle. Eve often felt like an itch in her brain that she couldn't quite reach with her nail and, every once in a while, she considered jamming a pencil in there to end the irritation once and for all.

What do you know of God? You can read all the bibles you want, we both know the Pearly Gates will be shut tight when you finally…

"Leney!" Jillybean snapped, cutting Eve off. To drown out her hated twin, she had been unnecessarily loud, or so it seemed to the superstitious sailors crowding the decks. The ocean was being gentle that day and they didn't see the need to get her riled up. "Do a turn around the fleet. I want to see how they're bearing up." In truth, she wanted her ex-Corsairs to see her, to know that she was always watching. She also wanted to be doubly sure that no one tried to skate out of formation.

"What the hell is Beggar Tim doing?" Leney snapped, watching the *Night Arrow* creeping up a line of ships. "Tell him to get back in formation," he snapped to his signalman. Flags were sent up the main mast and the *Night Arrow* drifted back into position.

Jillybean, who was not interested in the moment-to moment running of the ship, decided to head to her cabin to check on her belongings, and to set a few strategic traps. The incident with the canteen made her realize that she had been too sloppy by half. She had not expected an actual assassin to infiltrate her troops, and the shock of her near miss had left her edgy and paranoid.

Only a soft, grey light managed to filter down below deck, which was teaming with men. Everyone except the Queen was hot-bunking it. Even on a sixty-foot ship there was precious little space. There were only seven actual bunks, so most of her crew slept on a thin layer of blankets strewn on the floor. A few of the lighter hands were able to string hammocks in strategic locations and swayed gently as the ship nudged over small waves.

She tip-toed through the men, only because she didn't want to step on any of them. There was no sense trying to keep quiet; most of the men were snoring with such exuberance, it was as if they were in competition with each other. Worse than the snoring was the unexpected stench; already the stagnant air stank like a hog pen. It wrinkled her nose.

None of that really compared to the idea that there was an assassin among them. It made sense that he was somewhere on board. Anyone with a modicum of intelligence would have realized that she would almost have to take the *Queen's Revenge* as her flagship. Every few steps she would pause and gaze around, expecting someone to be staring at her, and there was.

The gun was halfway out of her pocket before she realized it was only Troy Holt. She didn't bother to hide it, letting the bore track across his belly as she turned. He didn't flinch and even that was disappointing in its way. "Are you following me?"

"I was told to protect you," he said.

"I'm going to the bathroom. I think I'll be okay."

He gestured to the gun and she shrugged. "I heard that sometimes big boats like this have rats. Bilge rats they're called. I'm not a fan." He didn't believe her lie, since it was an especially poor one. Thankfully, he didn't give her a sermon on the perils of sinning and, even better, he didn't leave. He crept along behind her until she came to her cabin where he waited outside her door.

Although a true assassin would make short work of him, she was glad that Troy was there.

As far as she could tell, her things were untouched. "Now to make sure they stay that way," she whispered. She had neurotoxin and needles; the two would make a lethal combination when placed strategically. "Eve, how would you do it?" Death was her area of expertise, after all.

As if only partially summoned from hell, Eve was a mere shadow on the wall. She stretched her arm out until it was seven feet long, her flat black fingers pointing at Jillybean's trunk. *Clip a needle and glue it here in the trunk's release.* The long arm twisted and spread across the far wall, aiming for the bed. *Use three or four razor blades under the seam of the mattress, here and here where someone would most likely lift.* The shadow then fell along the floor to a small closet where it snaked inside. *I'd use a needle on a spring in your med box. Smaller needles along the handle of your dresser and...*

Jillybean cut her off. "That should be enough. I have to live here, you know." The shadowy arm retreated back until it was once more a thin, wavering thing behind Jillybean.

She went to her stock of poisons, thinking she would have to come back down every four hours to reapply the toxin. It tended to dry quickly and lose most of its effectiveness. She had meant to experiment using different oils to make the potency last longer, but things kept getting in the way.

"Like world conquest," she muttered as she worked, boobytrapping her own cabin. "No one appreciates how much time it takes to conquer over the world."

It's a very involved process, Ernest agreed. He too was a shadow, whispering from the darkness in the closet. *I would also think about roughing up the edges of those needles. It'll give something for the fluid to adhere to.*

"Smart." She used a whet stone and was happy with the result. She was just stepping out of her cabin after placing her traps, when she realized that she had forgotten something. "Hold on," she told Troy. "I really do have to use the bathroom."

Troy had heard the whispering and although he knew about the Queen's mental illness, he still glanced past her into the cramped room, half-expecting to see someone else. "Take your time," he told her. She didn't take her time. She felt trapped in the cramped spaces below deck. There was nowhere to run and nowhere to hide. She felt hemmed in with only a very thin door between her and two dozen men who would like nothing more than to rape her to death.

Being on deck was a slight improvement. The ocean didn't scare her and the light gave her comfort. She could see into the faces of the people around her. In the light, it was hard to hide guilt. But it was not impossible.

Troy gave her comfort, as well. He trusted no one without being burdened by paranoia. There were scant few people he trusted on board and from his vantage point at the bow, he was able to watch everyone. They were all vermin in his eyes with the exception of Donna Polston and Gerry the Greek. He was told by the Queen that he could trust Nathan Kittle; however Troy didn't like his nervous laugh and his quick eyes when it came to Jillybean.

That night, after an unappealing dinner of dried fish, Troy discovered that he had been correct about Nathan. They found his stiff, contorted body on the floor of the Queen's cabin.

As always when she went below deck, Jillybean had her gun in hand. She whipped it out and dropped into a crouch as Troy searched the room. It was empty. "Leave us," she said, "and don't say anything about this to anyone. Though I don't suppose you will. You're quiet. I like that in a man." He reminded her a lot of Stu Currans. They were both long and rangy; they were both quiet, and they both hated her.

She was wrong about Troy being quiet. Normally on board a boat he was fond of singing, despite having only an average voice. And he was quick to laugh and make jokes. Surrounded by enemies, he would do neither.

He left to stand outside her door. Inside the cabin, she was alone with the dead and the croaking shadows. Kneeling, she inspected the body, whispering, "Nathan, damn it. What were you doing in here? Please tell me you were a thief and not an assassin?"

I know which I was, only I'm ain't tellin' nothing," Nathan whispered through unmoving lips. *Y'all gonna die here soon enough. One of us is gonna get you and make y'all scream…*

Jillybean punched him savagely in the mouth. "Shut up," she hissed and then punched him again.

Nathan growled through slack lips as she went through his pockets, hoping to find something that would let her know one way or another. She wanted him to be an assassin, that way she could relax. What were the chances there were two assassins on board?

There might could be a dozen of us comin' after y'all, the body said. It was as if the sound was coming from something croaky and wet within him.

"Trust me, Nathan, I'll get you all. Make no bones about that." She stood, pulled out her .357 and shot the corpse twice in the chest, making it jump. At the thundering gunshots, Troy burst into the room, the entire boat came awake while all around them. She shook her head at Troy's confusion, warning him not to say a word.

"Any more assassins among you?" she demanded, stepping over the twice-dead body and stalking into the narrow galley. Her heart was racing and she had the copper taste of fear in her mouth. But she couldn't let them see that she was afraid. All that kept them from rising up and doing unspeakable things to her was her mystique.

"Deke?" she asked, pointing the gun at a thick-lipped Samoan. "Do you want to try me? You want to try your luck?" At the sound of the gunshots, he had instinctively reached for the Beretta next to his blanket. He glanced at it with a flick of his eyes. Jillybean smiled. "You want to, I can tell." Slowly, she tucked the .357 into the waist of her black pants. It was within easy reach.

"How about now?" she purred, her blue eyes daring him to make a try for his gun. She knew the ex-Corsairs. They did not love her, not yet at least. However, they did fear her and she had to keep that fear ramped up if she was going to get them to face the Black Captain.

"No, your Highness," Deke answered, dropping his eyes, and pulling his hands well away from the gun.

"Anyone else?" Her eyes roved among the sailors. None would look up. "Excellent," she said, suddenly all smiles. "I knew I could count on you men. Together we'll…"

"Sail ho!"

The shout came from almost above her head. Jillybean forgot the assassin for a moment as she charged for the stairs. "Where?" she asked in a high voice. Ten hands pointed northward. "Glasses!" Binoculars were thrust into her hands. At the edge of her sight, something perfectly black was framed against the distant stars.

"Give chase, Leney," she ordered. "Who's running the flags? Wet-neck? Signal Steinmeyer to keep the fleet in position and prepare for battle. Gerry, where are you? Give Troy a hand and dump the body overboard. And everyone else not on watch, clear the deck!"

Chapter 51

When the world was as empty as there's was, a thousand bandits and half that many zombies felt like an immense army. Everywhere Stu, Neil, and Gunner went in the city of Olympia they ran into one or the other.

Frantic to get away, Gunner used every trick in his arsenal: false trails, fire, smoke, sound traps—anything to confuse his pursuers. Against him were bandits who made a living hunting humans. They had seen it all and gradually the cordon they threw around the trio grew tighter.

Since he couldn't outsmart the bandits, Gunner had to wear them down. He detoured, swinging far out of his way, hoping to circle the bandits entirely. More zombies in their way changed the plan and they found themselves going deeper into the city than they wanted. When they ran up against an arm of Puget Sound, they were forced to double back at a run. Because of his twisted body, Gunner was a shambling spectacle who looked more like a zombie than Neil.

By luck, the three found a seam through their pursuers and escaped —heading in the wrong direction.

Wasted hours and long miles passed before Gunner tried again to find a way through, only to run into more bullets and smoke. The sound brought the undead down on them like a grey wave, forcing the three to crawl through gutters and sewers to escape. For an entire day they zigzagged back and forth, hounded by bandits with forked beards or shaved heads or symbols burned into their faces. And, of course, what seemed like endless numbers of zombies.

The little group was stumbling away from a new dawn when Gunner finally allowed them to stop. This was only for Stu's sake. Gunner seemed able to subsist without rest and Neil had a zombie's ability to go on forever.

Stu piled onto an unknown bed in an unknown house in an unknown part of the city. He was asleep as soon as his head hit the dusty pillow. Three hours felt like three seconds and he was red-eyed and dull of mind when Gunner shook him awake. The only thing to eat was a handful of pain pills and water scooped from a hot tub. It had a yellow tinge and tasted like leaf soup.

Their abbreviated rest proved useful in more than one way. The bandits and the zombies had washed over the neighborhood they were in and were now searching for them a few miles away. The men were able to slink out of the city and soon they were lost in the rolling hills where food became plentiful. They ate old brown apples and old soft cherries and old squash they hacked out of the frozen ground.

Although not the most appealing fare, it kept them going for another marathon stretch. They had lost a day and all three were afraid they would be too late by the time they reached Grays Harbor.

On the march north it had taken three days to cover the distance; now Gunner wanted to cut that in half, and he set such a grueling pace that even the rangy Hillman found himself barely able to keep up. He even began to find himself jealous of Neil, who walked in a trance. When someone called his name, he would look around as if just waking from a deep sleep.

Their one saving grace was that the land seemed to have emptied of enemies. It was just them, a few squirrels and hill after hill, and mile after mile.

Twenty hours passed before Gunner allowed another stop. Stu didn't remember lying down, but he woke in a bed with pink sheets and a unicorn blanket. Gunner gave him another handful of pills and more brackish water. The sun rising made it seem to Stu that had gotten a full night's sleep when it was really only another short three-hour pause in their journey.

"Almost there," Gunner lied.

Four hours of marching passed before Stu caught his first whiff of the sea. It was another two before they crested a hill and saw a grey haze on the horizon. An hour after that, a gull flew past, cocking a curious black eye at them. Things went quicker then. The land sloped down and gravity pulled them along to their fate.

"She's still here," Gunner said.

"She?" Stu had been close to sleepwalking in a perfect imitation of Neil and was only just realizing they had stopped. In front of them was a hidden pond and there was *The Wind Ripper*, laying half on her side, covered in limbs and branches.

Stu was staring blankly at the ship when Gunner said, "I'm going to go scout the harbor. You two get her ready to sail."

He was gone before Stu could whisper, "Yeah, we can do that." Stu was so tired he didn't know if he actually could. Bleary-eyed, he waded into the icy water only to stumble over a submerged log that lay half-buried on the muddy bottom of the pond. His road-weary legs lost a feeble fight for balance and he went right under.

Gagging and spluttering, Stu splashed to the surface. "Great. This is just great." Now, he was freezing as well as exhausted, but at least he was awake. The water was strangely refreshing. It was like taking a shot of caffeine.

The water worked to bring Neil back to life, as well. In his mindless stupor, he fell over the same logStu had, and when he came up, he asked, "Is that the boat?"

"It is."

"Good. I was tired of walking." The two waded and half-swam to the back end of the boat. They got their shoulders up under it and heaved it into the center of the pond where the water was deeper. Free of the muck, *The Wind Ripper* righted herself and bobbed back and forth, shedding most of the branches herself.

Neil climbed up first. He was like a toddler who had never seen a ladder before. Stu had to guide his hands and feet for him. Then, when he got to the deck of the boat, which rocked gently beneath him, he fell over, cutting his forehead. "I'm just a bit wobbly. Once I get my sea-legs under me I'll be right as rain." He looked like a newborn giraffe trying to stand for the first time. His legs shook and he held tightly to the wheel, which wasn't the smartest thing to hold. When it spun, he went with it and crashed once more on deck. More blood sprinkled the deck.

The third time was the charm. He finally struggled to his feet and by the time he did, Stu had cleared the deck and was about to pull the boat out into the river. "Do you need help?" Neil asked.

And watch you fall into the river? Stu thought. He wasn't about to perform mouth-to-mouth on a zombie. "No, I got this. You, uh work on getting your sea-legs back."

At thirty-three feet, *The Wind Ripper* wasn't large and Stu was able to manhandle her into the river by himself. He tied her off and then climbed slowly aboard. Neil was standing with his feet splayed and his hands out for balance.

"Do zombies get seasick," he asked, his face grayer than it had been.

Stu didn't hesitate. "No. It's impossible." It was bad enough Neil's infected blood was everywhere, he didn't want his vomit as well. He had no idea if zombies could get seasick, but he didn't think so. Then again he was certain they wouldn't be affected by the power of suggestion, either. "Let me get you a change of clothes. Just stay right there. Don't move."

Mike would kill Neil…again if he messed up his beloved deck any more than he had.

There were plenty of clothes to be found in the cabins below. Stu wasn't the easiest to fit, while Neil could make do by rolling up his sleeves and pinning his cuffs. When it came to color, their choices were black or camo. Since they were now in the land of the Corsairs, Stu chose black for both of them.

Neil changed right out in the open and Stu found himself staring. For such a soft, mild little man, Neil had many old scars. His lifeless grey flesh was crisscrossed with them. He'd soon have more. The bullet wounds he'd suffered were already sealing themselves in what looked like a black crust.

"Where's Gunner?" Neil asked.

"Scouting," Stu answered, though he did so with a touch of fear. Gunner had helped them just as he had said he would. The question Stu had, was Gunner now helping himself? Was he off telling the Corsairs exactly where they could pick up the Queen's adopted father and her ex-lover?

A muttered curse escaped him. If the Corsairs were coming they'd be caught without any trouble. Stu was in no shape for another chase and *The Wind Ripper* was in no shape to put to sea. Her mainsail was hanging in two pieces and Stu just wasn't a good enough seaman to get her safely away with just a jib.

"Can you sew?" he asked Neil. Their one hope was for Stu to find some sort of repair kit. He figured that a sea-going ship had to have one, and he was right. Even better, there was an entire mainsail folded neat as you please stored in the engine compartment. It even had instructions.

He hauled it out into the fading daylight. "Neil. Help me. We have to cut down the old sail. Just don't cut the lines."

"Lines? What are the lines? Like the hem?"

Before Stu could answer, Neil fell off the ship. He hadn't tripped as far Stu saw. He just lost his balance and over he went. Stu only shook his head and went to work, cutting away the remains of the old sail. Neil was back on board, once again soaking wet, by the time Stu was ready to string the new sail. With the instructions laid out in front of him, Stu was able to get the sail in place in only an hour. He ran it up and down to make sure there weren't any snags.

"Looks like I'm just in time," Gunner said as he slipped from the bushes on the side of the river. Stu looked past him, trying to pierce the heavy underbrush. "You act like you don't trust me, Stu. I'm much wounded."

"Sorry, but when something looks too good to be true it probably isn't."

Gunner leaned over and grabbed the single mooring line tied to a tree. With a single pull of his strong right arm, *The Wind Ripper* slid over to him. He only had to wade in up to his waist. "I swear it sounded to me like you just called me good-looking." He found this hilarious and was still laughing as he came up the ladder. "Man, I haven't been called good looking for ages. Remember back when I was studly, Neil?"

"I remember when you kidnapped me and Sadie. And I remember when you wanted me to fight to the death in one of your arenas."

"Ah, the good 'ol days. I wish we could reminisce all evening but it's getting late. And we're in luck. The Black Captain has hidden his fleet up one fork of the Hoquiam River." Gunner laughed and slapped his thigh. "He's put a dam right on the fork. Ha! He's trapped his own fleet! What an idiot. He's so afraid to lose it that he makes it worthless. It's always better to go down fighting."

Stu ran a hand through his beard. It hadn't been stubble for days; it had gone full beard at some point when he'd been fighting for his life. "Are you saying the harbor is clear?"

He was grinning again behind his mask. "Yup. There are a few barges laying down anti-landing obstacles, but they could never catch us. So, let's get going."

Once more Stu felt that he was in the realm of "too good to be true." And once more he felt he had no choice but to hope that it was true. "Alright," he said and gestured to Gunner.

"Alright what?"

"Alright, let's get going."

The smile was gone. "Then let's. What? Do you think I can pilot this thing? I'm sorry if I gave you that impression. I just meant I could help. I knew Neil wouldn't be able to do anything. Please, tell me you can pilot this thing."

Stu nodded without any enthusiasm. He was far from an expert. It had always been Mike Gunter who had taken command, especially when they were close to shore. "I can. I can do this," he said, looking around, trying to take stock of the boat. "Mast, sail, wheel…" The only thing he was missing was the wind. The black Corsair flag hung limp, stirred every once in a while as a stray gust found its way down from the hills. "Ok, since you're wet, Gunner, why don't you shove us off. Not too hard. We want the center of the river."

The river was not fast, wide, or deep, which made it perfect for Stu to get a feel for the wheel and rudder. Still, the two miles went quick. He ran up the main and set her neutral so that the boom pointed directly at him. From there, he could turn it quickly in one direction or the other.

Just before Grays Harbor itself, was the tired-looking town of Aberdeen. Although it might've had its pretty parts, the area around the river was decidedly ugly with its rusting warehouses and expanses of broken cement lots. Making it more unsighting were hundreds of milling zombies.

"Did I mention that the Captain is pulling out all the stops?" Gunner remarked. "He's securing one flank with the undead. And look, you can just see the east fork of the Hoquiam River." The boundary between Hoquiam and Aberdeen was a two-hundred-foot wide river, or at least it had been a river. Now it was two-hundred feet of bog, greasy black pools, and mud deep enough to trap a zombie. Already there were a few dozen forlorn-looking zombies stuck up to their hips in the sucking quagmire.

Nothing was going to make it across.

Stu was caught staring when a north wind heeled the front of *The Wind Ripper* to the left. He fought her back, ordering Gunner to swing the boom around. When he did, the wind leaned the boat over, tilting the deck and sending Neil rolling. He would've gone into the water again if Gunner hadn't snagged him by the back of his shirt.

Neil watched glumly as one of his purple Crocs slid into the water. "You're better off without them," Gunner told him. "What kind of Corsair wears purple crocs?"

"The comfortable kind of Corsair," Neil said.

"Can you even feel your feet anymore?" Gunner asked. Neil looked down and tried to wiggle his toes; they only twitched. "It's a bitch, but I think you have bigger things to worry about." He helped Neil to the stairs and told him to sit on them and not to move.

Stu was glad that Neil listened. He was having more trouble than he expected trying to keep the boat aimed straight down the center of the harbor. She wanted to pull southward which he supposed was better than pulling to the right toward the Corsair hideout in the town of Hoquiam.

There were six long barges along the waterfront of the town. "What are they doing? Are they pushing cars into the water?"

Gunner sniffed loudly. "Yes, sir. The harbor isn't very deep. The Captain is cutting off another avenue of attack. On the other side of the town is the west fork of the Hoquiam River, which is now double in size. The Queen is going to have to come down from the north. And that's also bounded by the Hoquiam River. The Captain is going to make her attack on a very narrow front and that spells trouble. She can't afford too many casualties, not with her soldiers."

"I wonder if they'll fight at all," Stu said.

"If I know her, she'll get them to fight and I'm sure she has her own tricks up her sleeve. And…what's with the boat? You see the shore is getting closer, don't you?"

For every hundred yards forward, they were sliding thirty to the south. "I see it. There's a current that's running in that direction. I can't seem to break out of it and I really don't want to have to come about." The current ran southwest, while the wind was coming straight south— nature was doing its best to send them right onto the muddy shores.

"You're going to have to do something," Gunner warned. He leaned over the rail. "I can see the bottom. We're going to hit and soon."

Stu cursed and then swung *The Wind Ripper* into the wind. They tacked sluggishly northeast and gained only fifty yards. When they came back around, they shot like an arrow but again angled toward shore.

"Do it again," Gunner said, again leaning over.

Stu was about to when Neil suddenly stood up. "I think I see a boat. Is that a boat or a cloud?" He was pointing west where the clouds had become violently dark. Framed against them was a little triangle of white. It was so small that it could only be one boat, captained by one man. No one but Mike Gunter would ever consider taking a dinky boat like the *Calypso* out in a storm like that.

Chapter 52

Fears of assassins fell away as Jillybean gazed with hungry eagerness towards the distant ship. It was a black ship with black sails, and it had once belonged to her. The hunger was so great that it defied her usual cerebral inquisitiveness. All she knew was that she *wanted* that ship badly. She felt like a lioness eyeing a tender newborn gazelle. Had she analyzed her feelings, she would have realized that she was feeling the hunter's instinct coming alive inside her for the first time in her life.

The same hunger seemed to have infected the entire crew and was strong enough to meld them into one body, one force. The *Queen's Revenge* fairly flew across the water as her sailors worked in a building harmony.

At first, the Corsair ship made few moves and seemed content to slip along with just her black mainsail flying and a white feather of foam at her bow. Even in the dark, there was no way she could miss the great white ship bearing down on her and yet, for a time she seemed unconcerned. Just long enough for Jillybean to grow uneasy, fearing a trap.

Then, like magic, out popped her genoa and, a minute later, what looked like a third sail in front. The boat leapt ahead, moving unexpectedly fast.

"Yep, that's the *Skater*," Leney said, binoculars stuck to his face. He sounded disappointed. "It's hard to see in the dark, but I think Noonan just put out his flying jib. She's going to be tough to catch and Noonan knows it."

Skater was one of the three boats that had stolen away the night before. If it had wanted to put a hundred miles between it and Jillybean's fleet it could have. Instead, it had been lurking in the dark. "He's keeping tabs on us," Jillybean said. "We need to sink her."

"We have to catch her first," Leney replied. "She's the fastest ship in the fleet."

"She was the fastest ship," Troy Holt interjected. "The *Star of*…I mean the *Queen's Revenge* is faster. If you ease her a point over to port we'll pick up at least a knot." Silence greeted this and no one moved a muscle to do as he suggested. He waved a calloused hand. "Do what you will. I only did my training on board her is all. Her keel is deeper than you'd think and at this angle, it's causing some drag."

Jillybean said, "Do it."

Leney sighed and carried out the order. The *Queen's Revenge* didn't exactly spring forward. However, she did slowly gather speed until it felt like she was running downhill. In response, Noonan turned the *Skater* slightly away; she was sailing her fastest and still the white ship was closing. He began to hoist a series of colored lights from her main.

"What do they mean?" Jillybean asked Wet-neck the signal man. He had a book of laminated cards set on his lap and a hooded lantern in his hand.

"I don't know, your Highness. I don't recognize this pattern. You see, the initial light tells you which code is going to be used. But look. He started with purple." He showed her the page marked with a purple tab. "Yellow, green, red, yellow would mean: starboard, retreat, starboard, come about. You may not know sailing lingo, but let me tell you, that's gibberish."

"It could mean we're running into an ambush," a nearby sailor warned.

He was roundly shushed. It was like suggesting that water was wet. The idea had crossed all their minds long before and every pair of binoculars on board was being trained outward.

The only person who hadn't shushed him was Jillybean who had thought it was Ernest speaking.

"I think they're telling their friends to run," she said. "And I think he was trying to draw us away earlier. It's what I would've done. How soon will we be in range?"

"At this rate, five minutes maybe," Leney told her.

She had a squad of riflemen brought up and just as they began to settle into firing position, the *Skater* made a sharp turn, putting the wind on their port beam and doubling back. It was a Hail Mary move made by a desperate captain who knew his ship was overmatched. The *Queen's Revenge* spun faster and Jillybean enjoyed that lioness sensation again as they ate up the distance with amazing speed. She was about to order her men to start shooting when bright flames suddenly lit up the night.

The *Skater* was on fire, her sails turning from black to brilliant orange in seconds. By the light of the flames they could see that her deck was empty when it should have been crowded with men rushing around fighting the inferno. Next, a popping sound drifted softly across the night water.

"What is that?" Leney asked.

"Gunfire," Jillybean said, as the cold November wind suddenly stole to her heart and froze it. The sound of the guns were muffled and, oddly, weren't accompanied by the hissing sound of bullets whizzing by. It could only mean that the Corsairs were killing themselves.

Do something! Eve raged. *Shoot, damn it! Fire a torpedo. What are you waiting for? This is our kill.* The chase had got her blood flowing hot and now no death would be satisfying unless it was her own hand that directed it.

"No, Eve. It would be a waste of ammo," Jillybean told her, oblivious to the sailors around her nudging each other. "We'll get our chance to kill. Trust me." The next few minutes passed in silence as the guns gradually stopped. Soon there was only the crackle of flame and even that died away to nothing as the boat burned down to the waterline and sank. It went fast.

Leney ghosted the *Queen's Revenge* around the spot where the boat went down. All that was left of the *Skater* was a reeking grey smoke that hung just over the water. Men drew back from it as if it were cursed or poisonous.

Although her sailors had been hell-bent on killing everyone on board the *Skater,* the mass suicide cast a strange pall over them that could be described as unexpected despair wrapped in doubt. The pall was felt deepest by the Queen who understood better than anyone what had just happened.

Although he was hundreds of miles away, the Black Captain had once again demonstrated his power. His men had been ordered to kill themselves rather than face her and, unbelievably, they had. What would they have revealed under torture? That her army was riddled with spies and assassins? That Nathan Kittle hadn't been acting alone? That more attacks were being planned?

"He's getting desperate," she told her silent crew. "The Black Captain knows his time is about up. He knows he can't win, and so do his people. When we sweep away the remains of his fleet and set his lair on fire, we can expect a lot more of this."

Leney swallowed, loudly. "Yeah," was all he said.

She had hoped for a better response.

What do you expect? You're a monster, a child-like voice said. Jillybean jerked around; the words had come from the stairs leading down into the galley. Gun in hand, she leaned to the side, but the stairs were empty.

You know who that was, right? Ernest asked in that softly sinister way of his.

She knew. It had been her own voice. Her own little kid voice from many years ago. "I am not the monster," Jillybean whispered. The men were staring at her. She hated their judging eyes. *Who are Corsairs to judge me!* she thought in rage. It took an effort to hold her gun hand in check. Eve wanted to pull the trigger and put out those hated eyes once and for all.

"Not yet," Jillybean said under her breath. Louder, she ordered Leney to take the *Queen's Revenge* north again in search of the other two ships. It was a wasted hour; they were nowhere to be seen.

With that pall of doubt just as thick, they returned to the fleet. Jillybean was dreadfully afraid she'd find more of her ships missing, certain that the loss of even a single ship would infect the entire fleet with the same sense of doom hanging over the *Queen's Revenge.* Thankfully, all her ships were in position and the cold, bony, outstretched fingers of death retreated from her. "Back on our previous course, Leney. Wake me when we get to San Fran."

As much as she wished she could sleep all the way to Grays Harbor, she had the fleet make a stop into San Francisco. She woke to the familiar sounds of screeching gulls, the clanking of buoys and the deep groan of the Golden Gate swaying in the wind. For just a moment, snuggled warm in her covers, she smiled. The sounds reminded her of sweet Jenn Lockhart, simple and easy-going Mike Gunter, and rugged Stu Currans—they were the only friends she had ever known.

The smile did not last. The stress on her was immense and only getting worse as she heard the muttering of her crew through the thin walls of the boat. No one wanted to go on to Grays Harbor.

"It's too cold and everyone knows the weather could turn on us at any moment."

"I'm worried that the Black Captain is still too strong. They say he gots floating mines now. They say he gots the harbor chock full of them."

"An' how the hell are we supposed to get at his fleet? You know he'll bottle them up in the damned river. With them big anchor chains there'll be no touching them."

"I gotta know if the Queen thinks this is all a game? We had the bible-thumpers right where we wanted them and she just let them go without even asking!"

"You know what I heard. I heard old McCartt ain't gonna fight. And if he don't fight, you know Steinmeyer won't. And we all know them Santas are pussies through and through. It'll be all on us."

Everything Jillybean heard reinforced the urgent need to get moving as fast as she dared. Without giving a thought to the catastrophe that was her hair, she jumped up, stepped over Troy Holt, who'd been sleeping just on the other side of her door, and went on deck. There she took charge of resupplying her fleet with great stores of food, ammunition, and extra torpedoes. As an excuse to reduce the cramped conditions, she also sent nearly all of her Bay Area people ashore.

In reality, the Queen was hedging her bets. With the mounting possibility of assassination, her men growing weak in the knees, and spies whispering mutiny in every ear, she put her chance of beating the Black Captain at fifty-fifty. Normally, she was an optimist, but with Ernest slipping images of dead children floating in the bay, she began to fear losing more than she desired to win.

You should fear losing, he said, his voice growing stronger. *Think of the children. Think of little Lindy Smith and Ryanne Walker. You know what will happen to them if you lose*. He sent a horrifying picture into her head and their screams were so real in her ears that she turned away with a gasp. She spied Donna Polston about to board one of the launches.

"Donna!" She heard the desperation in her own voice and could only hope no one else had.

Donna was pale as milk as she knelt, afraid that the queen was changing her mind about sending her ashore. The older woman was deathly afraid of the Black Captain and she didn't want to get within a hundred miles of Grays Harbor.

"No more kneeling," Jillybean said, helping Donna to her feet. "At least for now. I think a hug might be more appropriate." Donna had never been hugged by the Queen before and her return hug was so wooden it was like hugging a manikin. "Tell Rebecca to string the chains beneath the bridge again," Jillybean whispered into her ear. "Also fortify the approaches to it on both ends. And post lookouts up the coast. You have to be ready."

Jillybean's words were so soft they tickled Donna's ear, but she understood the need. She had heard the rumors as well and knew that sound carried. "Ready for what?" she asked through a plastic smile, her lips barely moving.

"In case I lose."

Donna went so stiff that she was almost in full rigor mortis. "You can't lose!" she hissed. "Don't even think that. We don't have enough men to defend ourselves."

There were only a couple of hundred people left of fighting age in the bay area and most were women who had rarely been called on before all this started to kill anything greater than sea bass in a bucket. But that didn't matter. Jillybean knew that if she lost, someone would have to make a stand somewhere.

"Rachel has learned my lessons," Jillybean said, quickly. "And we still have the Guardians. I want you to go to them. Do whatever it takes but get them here. It's the only way." She kissed Donna fiercely on the cheek and then broke away. "I'm going to miss you," she said, loudly with a bright smile on her face. "Be well."

Donna looked dazed as she made her way to the back of the boat where a small dinghy was bouncing up and down in time with the choppy water.

Behind Jillybean's smile, her teeth were clenched so hard she feared they might shatter. With a final wave, she turned from Donna and was immediately the cold queen again. She had to be cold as ice. She couldn't let the cracks show. The very act of admitting there was a chance she could lose had thinned the wall between herself and Eve. The dark girl inside her seemed huge, as if she were wearing Jillybean as an ill-fitting suit.

Without looking anyone in the eye, she went to her cabin, checked her traps quickly and then, without thinking about the consequences, swallowed a dozen Zyprexa.

You're going to kill us! Eve screamed. *Puke that up, damn it. Puke it all up, right now!*

Jillybean actually started to gag. She gripped the side of her dresser with both hands and clamped her mouth shut, thinking she would swallow her own puke if she had...

"Are you okay?" Troy asked. He was standing in the doorway, disgust turning his full lips ugly.

The need to vomit blinked away as Eve retreated. Jillybean took a moment to work a smile into place. "Just a little sea-sickness. Nothing to worry about."

"I just saw you take half that bottle of pills. I don't know a lot about medicine, but I'm pretty sure that's bad."

As she deftly pocketed the bottle, she saw how yellow her skin was; it would only get worse. "Don't be worried. They're half-strength and I just need them until we reach Grays Harbor, something we'll never do by standing around." She hated being seen as weak as much as she hated being weak. She thrust her chin out and stormed past him. In seconds, she was back on deck barking commands over the wind and the hum of the rigging. Under her supervision, everything moved like clockwork and by mid-afternoon the resupply was complete.

The Queen, salt wind tugging at her black coat, watched Alcatraz dwindle as her fleet hove out to sea. "We go to win an empire," she said, speaking to no one in particular. Louder she said to her crew, "If any of you have any doubts that we will win, jump into the ocean and swim back to Alcatraz."

She waited, knowing that none of her crew was brave enough to display that much cowardice. As she waited, she gazed down at a zombie struggling against the side of the ship. It looked ancient and alien. The seawater was dissolving its flesh, turning it slightly pale white in some spots and translucent in others.

"I mean it," she said. "Now is the time to back out. I want only real men with me. I want only warriors. So run now because if you fail in the face of the enemy, I will kill you. I will shoot you down and give your bodies to the likes of them to feast on." She nodded to the struggling zombie. No one said a word and no one budged. "Good. We will soon be feasting in Grays Harbor and the world will be ours."

Don't you mean it'll be mine? Eve asked. Even with the pills turning her blood toxic, she was there, quieter than before, but still there.

Jillybean went below to check her traps and as usual Troy came with her, stopping outside her door even though she had left it open. "It's unseemly for a man to enter the room of a woman un-chaperoned," he explained.

"Don't worry about that, I have the entire fleet watching me." She smiled, her teeth looking extra white compared to her yellowing skin. "Trust me, the open door wasn't an invitation. I am committed to another." He raised an eyebrow as if he couldn't tell if she were lying or not. She wasn't. She still loved Stu Currans, though sometimes she had to wonder why. It had been an impossible relationship to begin with and now it was even more so. She loved him as much he hated her.

She sighed. "I'm committed to the Black Captain. We will dance and play our parts, and one of us will die."

Troy's uncertain look did not waver. He did not know what to make of her and the more he got to know her, the less he understood. "I'll pray that it isn't you."

"Good, that'll save me the trouble," she said, without meaning any disrespect. Her plate was already full and on top of Eve and mutinies and assassinations, she had to make her plans to deal with the Black Captain and his army.

"But not his navy," she said to herself, already so immersed in thought that she didn't notice Troy shut her door. "No, he won't risk the remains of his navy, at least not at first, not unless he can spring a trap." She sat back on her bed and pictured Grays Harbor with its odd bulges and its flat sandy islands.

The mouth of the harbor was narrow, only a mile or so across and there was a chance her fleet could come under fire by soldiers on either side. A withering crossfire would tear her ships apart. What was left would be easy pickings from converging Corsair fleets lurking to the north and south, just inside the harbor.

"But I have drones and thermal scopes," she murmured. These would give her advanced warning if the Black Captain tried something so obvious. She wished he would. It would be simple to land troops further up shore and bottle her enemies on flat, open ground. "And how would he respond?" Her mind worked over the problems seeing point—counterpoint. Thrust—parry—riposte—feint—lunge.

Jillybean saw the battle laid out before her. Or rather, she saw a hundred battles laid out, each one slightly different depending on the variables introduced. Did the Corsairs have mines? Torpedoes? Had they figured out how to make smoke generators? If so, would they float them? Or would they deliver them in the form of aerial bombardment? Speaking of bombardment, did they have actual artillery? Did they have allies, such as the mountain bandits? Or would they use the dead? Would they leave a skeleton crew to defend their lair and operate a second force outside their lines, able to attack wherever and whenever they wanted? Would they use their slaves as human shields? Would his assassins wait until the heat of battle to shoot her in the back? Or would she drink from the wrong cup and fall over dead in minutes?

The Black Captain was the toughest adversary she had ever faced. The Azael had relied almost completely on numbers and a willingness to use the undead; the Believers had been slaves to their false religion and their false prophet. They had been willing to do atrocious things in his name. The River King had his fantastic wealth and all the hired guns money could buy. They all had lacked imagination.

On the other hand, the Captain had been methodical in his accumulation of power. He had out-thought all his opponents except for Jillybean and she was sure he was going to use every trick at his disposal to stop her. She feared his ability to adapt and manipulate the most. It opened up so many possibilities that she could not commit to any one exact plan of attack. When asked by Leney how they should form for battle, she always answered, "It depends," and didn't bother explaining any of her hundreds of: "If he does this then we do that" scenarios.

She told him that the situation was fluid while in truth it was far more than simply fluid. It was a mental maze, woven in deceit, trickery, and a thousand dead ends, each one ending with her bleeding body at his feet and the annihilation of her people.

The stress on her was terrific and it only got worse when they found Wet-neck dead the next afternoon. He was cold and stiff sitting in his usual spot near the wheel. He'd been there since noon and no one knew when he had gone from being a man to a corpse. He'd been poisoned, drinking from a canteen that matched the Queen's new one.

Eve was close to bursting through her drug-induced haze at that point until Jillybean took another small handful of pills. Her liver damage was becoming more pronounced every second and her eyes were so yellow they were almost green by then. She barely managed to hold on mentally and physically by reminding herself that she *had* to win.

And she knew she could win. She had an immense advantage over the Black Captain; she was on the offensive. She had the initiative and could strike wherever and whenever she pleased.

That was the plan at least, as she drew up to Grays Harbor and turned her fleet due east. It was growing late in the afternoon and the sky was building black in the west, blotting out the sunset and giving everything a queer yellow tinge. Above, gulls wheeled endlessly, screeching with piercing voices. Jillybean wanted to shoot them.

"Hold on, you're almost done," she said, forgetting to whisper. "Okay, Leney send up the drones." Leney gave the okay and three drones buzzed away from the fleet. He was personally operating the center drone and at first flew by line of sight. When it became too small to see, he looked down at his screen.

It took ten minutes for them to fly to shore. Everyone on deck crowded around the drone pilots eager to see, and that included the lookouts.

"Nothing on the north peninsula," one of the pilots said. "Not even like a guard or nothing."

"Same here on the south. We could waltz right in."

"If there ain't no mines," Leney reminded them. "Which I don't see." He had his drone hovering over the mouth of the harbor, going back and forth, looking for any shadow that might indicate a mine was anchored just under the surface. "Nope noth…what the hell?" His head popped up and he stared east. "That's a sail. There's a boat right there."

Everyone turned to stare east where, sure enough, a small white sail could be seen just slipping into the harbor mouth. "Leney, find out whose ship that is," Jillybean ordered. "Everyone else get to your battle stations."

There was a mad scramble as the men stumbled over each other. Although half the crew belonged below deck, no one wanted to miss what was happening, which resulted in a throng of men choking the stairs down to the galley.

"She's not ours," Leney said. "I mean she's not a Corsair boat. It's got to be from up the coast. Maybe a Vancouver boat or a…"

"It's the *Calypso*," Jillybean said, feeling a wave of nausea strike her. She knew the boat just like she knew the handsome golden-haired captain steering right into danger. "Make all sail! We have to stop her."

This was not in any plan she had foreseen. It was reckless and stupid, and she had absolutely no choice.

"What about the rest of the fleet?" Leney asked. "Are we just going to go charging in blind?"

"No. Have them move to within half a mile of the harbor." She grabbed a set of binoculars from the forward lookout and stared into the harbor. From what she could see, it was empty. "Leney get your drones up high. We need to see where the Corsair fleet is."

The drone whipped upwards, while the *Queen's Revenge* sprinted madly towards the harbor. With the wind on her beam, she was a cheetah and soon she was racing down on the *Calypso* which putzed along small and pokey.

"I don't see the fleet anywhere," Leney said. "Wait, wait, wait. Hold on, I see one ship it's breaking from the Markham shoal. She's black alright. Anyone know her?"

No one knew. The light was failing quickly and the boat was still too far away. But it wouldn't be for long.

The *Queen's Revenge* was gaining quickly on the *Calypso* which was cutting southwest towards the Corsair ship, something that didn't make a lick of sense. "Mike, what are you doing?" Jillybean whispered. Louder, she ordered, "Get between them, Leney. I don't care if you have to ram both of them. And get me a rifle squad up here."

"What about a torpedo?" Leney asked.

"Yes," Jillybean said. "Get one ready. We're going to blow that boat out of the water."

Chapter 53

"You shouldn't make yourself such a target," Troy Holt murmured in Jillybean's ear. He got a mouthful of her swirling hair for his trouble as she spun. It was good advice. She was a perfect target, standing boldly at the bow of the *Queen's Revenge* as it knifed into the Black Captain's harbor. Death could come from any direction. Spitting out the hair, he whispered, "At least move to the back of the boat where it's safer."

"Marginally safer," she replied. She knew the dangers she faced: snipers lurking along the shore surrounding them, at least one assassin hiding among her crew, someone on the Corsair boat could take a shot at her. None of that seemed to matter.

Her entire focus was on the *Calypso*. The presence of the little sailboat was completely baffling. Why here? Why now? Why was she angling *towards* the Corsair ship? These were not insignificant questions. The fate of the invasion and the lives of thousands of people rested on the answers.

And for once, Jillybean didn't have the answers.

Logic no longer seemed to be the determining factor in anyone's actions. The Corsairs should have been running away, the *Calypso* should have been coming about, and the *Queen's Revenge* should never have gone blundering into the harbor in the first place.

The sailors around her had their guess: "*It's a trap. Don't she sees it's a trap? They got mines and flying bombs and...*"

Although she was able to ignore her whispering crew, it was harder to ignore the whispers growing in her head. Eve wanted to send the torpedo off as fast as possible. Ernest wanted to gut crew members one at a time until they found the assassin. Ipes wanted her to turn around and get out of there before something bad happened. And Sadie wanted to rescue her friends on the *Calypso* no matter what the consequences were. These were the loudest whispers, but there were more.

"Shut up, all of you!" Jillybean snapped, causing her whispering crew to glance back and forth at each other. For a few moments there was only the sound of the wind singing along the lines and the wash of water along the hull, then the little girl who kept to the shadows giggled, making Jillybean's skin crawl. "She's not real," she told herself, only to hear the giggle again, louder, and more clearly as if it was coming from right behind her. She refused to look back.

Angrily, she jammed the binoculars against her eyes. The lone Corsair ship jumped into blurry view. Fiddling with the magnification didn't help. The day was dying and the sun's light was quickly fading. It was a smallish boat with rakish lines. On board were three shadowy figures.

"Only three?" The low number made as little sense as anything else. She swung the glasses toward the *Calypso* which, because of its white sails and hull, came easily into focus. There were four people on the small deck. Mike, with his broad shoulders and golden hair streaming in the wind, was easily recognized. She could only guess at the other three. One was almost certainly Jenn, but which one, Jillybean couldn't tell. The other two were mere figures, though she guessed that they were women by their size.

The sound of grunting and cursing from behind caused Jillybean to turn, her hand reaching for her pistol. It was a trio of men bringing a torpedo to the front. It weighed no more than eighty pounds and yet the men were sweating in fear.

"You can relax," she told them. "It won't explode and I think you may want to hold on for a moment anyway. In case you haven't noticed, we're doing roughly twelve knots." Their blank faces suggested they didn't understand the significance of this. "That's just about the same speed as the torpedo, soooo..."

"We'd get there at the same time?" one asked.

Jillybean touched her pert nose with her pointer finger. "Bingo. And that would be bad. Let's have the riflemen instead. I'd like the ship intact, if possible." In her mind she pictured a quick thunder of rifle fire and a few screams before she snatched up both boats. Reality was far different. Her riflemen had to contend with the failing light, the wind picking up, and the water growing choppy; they missed with remarkable consistency.

Almost as if they want to miss, Ernest suggested. *Almost as if they don't want to kill some of their own.*

Eve agreed. *They're spies, Jillybean. Kill one and make an example of him. It's the only way to make them respect us.*

"No," Jillybean said, hitting the side of her head with the heel of her hand. She hurried up to them, her boots thudding on the deck. "What the hell? Shoot straight for goodness..." She jerked as blood blasted from the head of one her men. One moment he was fine, and the next, his head just exploded. A second man spasmed and spun, showing off a gapping hole where his right eye had been. A third suddenly began to gag as a burning hunk of lead tore through his throat.

The next thing Jillybean knew something slammed into her and threw her down onto the bloody deck. She couldn't breathe or move as more bullets flashed over and around her, slapping with meaty thumps or making popping sounds as they punched through the hull.

"Are you hit?" Knights Sergeant Troy Holt cried almost directly in her ear.

Only then did she realize that she hadn't been shot, she had been tackled by the Knight. "I don't think so."

"We can't stay here. We're too exposed." He started to get up when a fast rustle of cloth rushed towards him. Troy dropped, crushing her beneath him again as one of the booms swung past, out of control.

"Get off!" Jillybean demanded, furiously. In spite of the danger, she struggled out from under the Knight and saw that the deck of the *Queen's Revenge* was deserted. At first it appeared as if there were only corpses left to man the ship. Then she spied men crawling like worms down the stairs and others cringing, hugging the chewed-up teak deck. "Leney! Get these cowards up and get this boat pointed in the right damn direction, this instant." The ship was spinning sideways to the wind and was taking on an unpleasant lean causing the corpses to slide over the side.

There were still two riflemen left, each trying to hide behind the other. She kicked the closest, saying, "The Corsairs have stopped firing, morons." The reason they had, was just as infuriating as everything else. Mike had pulled the *Calypso* between the *Queen's Revenge* and the Corsair ship.

"We'll port around them," Leney was telling his unwilling crew. "Come on! Everyone up."

The *Queen's Revenge* slowly got back up to speed and would have been too late to intercept the *Calypso* if the Corsair boat wasn't being sailed so poorly. It tried to tack away from shore, losing headway and only managed to get some speed under her by heading west. She then turned unexpectedly east just as the *Calypso* turned west. The two boats almost collided and blew past each other with almost no room to spare.

"Now" Jillybean shouted to her crew. "Get between them before they can come together." Leney shot through the gap only to have the two other boats make the most unexpected moves possible. The *Calypso* turned and headed straight north, aiming for the Black Captain's lair, and the Corsair ship turned and sped directly at the *Queen's Revenge* as if it wanted to ram the much bigger ship.

"Turn! Turn! Turn!" someone on the Corsair boat screamed, while at the exact same time someone was screaming the same thing at Leney. The two boats turned, but not fast enough. They came together, beam to beam, amid a blast of gunfire and a scream of wood. Jillybean's two riflemen had screwed up their courage and leaped up at the last moment to fire over the side.

They almost couldn't miss. Almost. One of the Corsairs tumbled down below deck, while the other two threw themselves into the harbor.

"Cease fire!" Jillybean ordered as the other boat…*The Wind Ripper*, she now saw, scraped white paint off the side of the *Queen's Revenge* as it slowly began to spin away out of control. It didn't spin far. Its boom was at the perfect height to catch the anchor chain of the *Revenge* and before anyone could stop it, the two ships were tangled.

Jillybean stared in disbelief as both ships began to slowly turn together like the hands of a clock. She couldn't understand how *The*

Wind Ripper of all ships had been caught up in this strange chase. "What am I missing?"

Everything, Ernest said, his voice rustling along the edges of the wind. *Your men failed you. They let the Calypso get away on purpose. They're all in this together. Tell Gerry the Greek to light off his bomb. You remember he has a bomb, don't you?*

She looked north. The Black Captain's lair was two miles away and already the *Calypso* had a half mile head start. They would never catch her. "I remember the bomb."

Use it now, Eve urged. *The Captain is going to get Mike and Jenn, and you know what he's going to do with them*. A horrible bloody image struck her mind like a hammer blow, causing her to reel back into Troy. She tried to blink away the image, but with each blink the blood got redder and the terror on her friend's ripped-up faces became more real.

Troy asked if she was okay, but she didn't hear him, her head was filled with Jenn's screams. They were so piercing that her eardrums stung and her teeth hurt. She clamped her hands over her ears and crushed inward, wishing she could crack her own head like an egg and let the screams fly out to infest the world. She was even looking around for a hammer when she saw a creature slink up from the galley stairs of *The Wind Ripper*.

It was a small zombie wearing Neil Martin's face. It couldn't be Neil, she told herself, but all the same, her mind began to swirl grey horrors into the bloody mix. Next, she saw one of the Corsairs in the water and he was pretending to be Stu Currans. "No," she whispered. Now she knew she was on the verge of falling to pieces and there'd be no putting them all back together. She would crumble like sand and Jillybean would be gone forever; and maybe that would be good.

She wanted that bliss, but her eyes were still her own and they showed her a monster, a real, honest-to-God beast pull itself out of the harbor. It had no face. It was beyond hideous.

Without a word, she turned and went down to her cabin where she sat with her hands clamped over her ears, trying to mute the screams. What she had seen in the water and on the boat hadn't been real. She knew that. And the screams weren't real, probably. But the fact that Mike and Jenn were going to die was very real. And it was her fault. She had started the war without realizing that she would come to love her pawns.

She had told herself over and over: *It's for the greater good; it's for the greater good*, but now only truly good people were going to die. Nothing could change that… "Unless I trade myself for them," she said. For a moment this idea cut through the violence in her head. It was the perfect idea. She would die and Jenn would live. It was a perfect idea. Jillybean would have her evil raped and stabbed and tortured right out of her—and innocent Jenn Lockhart would live.

NOOOOOOO! Eve thundered. The screams suddenly grew into a hurricane of sound until she couldn't think. Then in the midst of the noise she heard a door slam above her head and the patter of little running feet, followed by a wild screeching giggle.

"That's not possible. There is no door on deck," she whispered. "It's wide open and…"

The floor is hot lava, Daddy! Quick, jump on the bed. Jillybean knew that voice. It was her own.

Not lava again, her Daddy said, laughing and clapping a hand on his forehead. *We really should consider relocating. Dear? Can you grab a mop? We have hot lava again.*

Jillybean could hear her mother's light step in the hall, and with a rush of excitement, she ran to the door and flung it open. It wasn't her mother on the other side. It was Knights Sergeant Troy Holt. Her mouth popped open. "What?" she barked as she looked past him, hoping to catch a glimpse of her mother. Just the hem of her skirt would do. Or just her shadow. Anything.

"The prisoners would like to see you, your Highness. They say they know you."

"Don't listen to them. They aren't real." She gave him a quick smile to show him that she was still *normal.* "Hey, you're smart, aren't you Troy? You could fight the Corsairs for me, right? I mean for Jenn. She should be queen and you would be her commander. I bet you could win. I'm thinking of leaving. Trading myself, really and I'm going to need someone to win this war for me. What do you say?"

Her eyes were rolling in her head and her hands shook as they clutched his uniform. He gently pried them away, saying, "Huh? Lead? Are you asking…? Do you want me to lead your Corsairs into battle against the other Corsairs?" He laughed and shook his head. "No. They would never listen to me. And you can't trade yourself for anyone. This operation is already hanging by a thread."

And so am I, Jillybean thought. It was a tiny filament holding her shrieking mind together and it wouldn't last. She knew what would happen when the Black Captain started sending bloody pieces of her friends to her: she would break and the whole house of cards would fall. It was better to get out in front of it. She would allow herself to be tortured to death in Jenn's place.

Jenn would be queen and Troy would lead the army. Hearing it in her head caused a burst of laughter that cascaded and spread so that it sounded like a pack of hyenas were loose in her skull. She wiggled a finger in her ear, but the laughter kept going on and on. "He'll be fine," she lied to herself as she pushed past him and headed for the stairs. She had to hurry before the screams came again. The laughter was one thing but the screams would tear her apart. "We have a few minutes to go over some of the more obvious scenarios. The situation will be fluid, but as long as you keep the momentum going, you'll have the advan…"

She had reached the deck where she saw the three Corsairs, kneeling, guns to their heads. They weren't real. They couldn't be real. Her mind was playing the sickest of cruel jokes on her. Averting her eyes, she turned to run back down.

"Jillybean," Neil Martin said softly, stopping her.

"Stop talking to me. You aren't real."

"I am real. Turn around." The voice was still Neil's and it alone had the power to turn her. She wouldn't look up, however, she stared at a bullet hole in the deck. "They tried to kill me, Jillybean, but they only changed my appearance. It's still me. Look at me."

Jillybean looked at his sagging grey face. He was more than half zombie by then. She glanced at Troy and asked, "Do you see that?"

"I see something. I just don't know what, exactly."

"And are the other two real?" He nodded. The fact that he and everyone else on deck were fish-belly white, told Jillybean that they were all seeing the same thing. "A zombie, a ghost and a monster," she said, looking at each in turn, still uncertain, her mind teetering on the edge of inescapable madness.

"It sounds like the beginning of a joke," Neil said. "A zombie, a ghost, and a monster walk into a bar." He grinned hideously. "Can I get up now? I can't feel my knees." He didn't wait for an answer and when he stood, she saw that he wore a single purple croc on his right foot.

Only Neil Martin would wear purple Crocs into battle.

Sudden laughter blared up from out of her and she threw herself into the arms of the zombie, crying, "It is you! Neil, I can't believe it. And Stu!" Her heart swelled. She wanted to respect his wishes, whatever they were, but she couldn't stop herself and she hugged him as well, whispering, "I'm sorry," into his ear. When they parted, there were tears in his eyes and she wanted to hug him again and kiss them away.

She refrained, not knowing exactly what they meant. Instead, she turned to the "monster." He had lost his mask and his face was revolting to look on. She didn't care and hugged him, too.

"Jillybean!" Neil said, quickly. "Hold on. You don't know who that is. That's Gunner. You remember, from that little town in Alabama."

Her laughter this time was pure and sweet and so loud that it drowned out the last of the screams, the whispers, and the giggles in her head until it was just her laughter that she could hear. Everything now was so wonderfully quiet in her mind that she touched her wild hair to see if she had been clubbed on the back of her head.

"Neil, your poor eyes must be playing tricks on you. This isn't Gunner, this is your old friend, Captain Grey."

No one had ever seen a stunned zombie before and it was so comical that once more Jillybean broke into peels of laughter that could be heard for miles. As much as Neil looked surprised, Grey looked angry, if a hideous, faceless being could look angry that is.

"I'm sorry, Mister Captain Grey, sir, but it's time he knew the truth."

"What truth?" Neil asked. "We…I thought you were dead. Deanna thought you were dead. Your daughter thinks it, too. Why would you hide like this?"

Captain Grey took a quick look around at the staring ex-Corsairs. He wasn't used to being on display like this. "Not here."

Jillybean escorted them below. They were followed by Troy, Leney and half the crew. She stopped Troy at the door. "Make sure we're not disturbed. Leney, bring the fleet into the harbor, and send up the drones again. The rest of you. Find something to do. Get *The Wind Ripper* manned and fix whatever damage we've sustained." She shut the door in their faces. She then turned back to the three men.

Although, for the moment, her mind was clear, her emotions were all over the board. Having Captain Grey with her was an immeasurable relief. Stu made her heart race out of love for him and fear that he still hated her. And Neil's presence as a zombie made her both heart-breakingly sad and ragingly angry.

Neil grinned, an especially odd look for a zombie. "I never thought I'd have to bow to my own daughter," Neil said, and then bowed, going so far forward that he fell.

Stu caught him. "She likes it better when you kneel." He did so and she let him kiss her hand. Neil went down groaning, his knees popping. He too kissed her hand.

Grey would have none of it. He stood as tall as his warped body would allow with his tremendous arms folded across his massive chest. "It was supposed to be our secret, Jillybean."

"It was, but now things have changed and *she* is going to need you and she would never trust anyone posing as Gunner of all people."

"Then I'll call myself something else. Deanna can't know about me. It wouldn't be right. I would…I would just ruin her life. Promise me you won't tell her, Jillybean. And you too, Neil."

He looked like he would take their heads off if they didn't. Neil was still trying to wrap his mind around the idea that this beast of a man had been his friend. "I think you owe me an explanation first. After the explosion, we all thought you were dead." Ten years before, the three of them had been instrumental in clearing the last of the bandits from around Bainbridge. Jillybean had created a cataclysmic explosion that had killed the great majority of the bandits, as well as Captain Grey, or so it had been believed by everyone but her.

"And I nearly was killed," he rumbled, "and I would've been without Jillybean. She stitched what remained of me back together and every day for a year we both figured that each sunset would be my last. I had blood clots and infections and everything you could think of and yet, I never died. Jillybean said I was too pissed off to die and I think she was right. By the time we realized that I wouldn't die, I knew that I had waited too long and that if I emerged as this freak, I would forever put Deanna's life on hold. She would be stuck with this." He pointed at what was left of his face.

Neil didn't think it got any better to look upon no matter how much time passed and he had a green tint to his grey flesh. "I suppose I understand. Maybe better than anyone now. We're once again two peas in a very ugly pod."

Now that she knew they were real, Jillybean didn't seem to find any of their faces difficult to look upon. She was smiling from ear to ear. Her eyes clear for the first time in months. "I'd like to promise I won't tell, but things have a way of coming out under torture."

"What torture?" Stu asked, a strange unpleasant sensation creeping in his guts. "What are you talking about?"

"The Black Captain will undoubtedly do things to me once we make the exchange. I'm going to trade myself for Jenn and Mike, but it will be okay. I see it now. I see how it will all unfold, perfectly."

Epilogue

The Black Captain made his expected offer to meet with the Queen three hours after sunset. The message came by way of a rowboat, oared by two shifty-eyed Corsairs. "His lordship, the Black Captain would like to meet in two hours." They gave the place: a muddy, half-submerged island along the north shore of the harbor. They then sat back with an air of superiority as they looked down their noses at the men who had once been their comrades.

Jillybean gave an answer that made their eyes go wide: "I will trade myself for your new captives. *All* of them. That will be the only deal I'll accept." In minutes, the two were paddling back to the Captain as fast as they could. She watched them go with perfect satisfaction. Beside her, Stu was both apoplectic and too stunned to move. He was desperate to come up with some solution that would save her and the others. It seemed impossible and was made more so because he was the only one trying.

Captain Grey had only demanded that the trade include his daughter, Emily. When Jillybean heard that she had been kidnapped as well, she had blithely said, "Of course, she'll be part of the trade. As much as I love Jenn and Mike, exchanging me for those two was going to be ridiculously uneven. This will make things fairer for both sides."

"Is fairness really what we're looking for here?" Stu demanded, speaking to the wall apparently. No one paid the comment any notice.

Neil, who loved both Jillybean and Emily equally, astonished Stu by winking a blood-red eye at Jillybean and saying, "Would you like a little scratch? Being a zombie takes the edge off of torture."

"Take the edge off?" Stu growled. "Do you guys hear yourselves? Why do we have to trade anyone? If we win, we can get them back then."

"That's a big if," Grey said. "I know for a fact that the Black Captain has some heavy-duty armaments. It's safe to say he's not going to go down easily. He's going to turn this battle into a slog so that it takes days and days. And every day, he'll make sure we know he has Jenn and Emily and Mike. He'll torture them and record their screams and play them over loudspeakers, because he knows that it'll drive Jillybean mad."

Stu was being torn into pieces. He found that his love for Jillybean had not cooled in the slightest; he would kill for her or die for her. "Maybe they'll take me."

Grey shook his head while Neil gave him a sad smile and said, "I've been there, Stu. You're just going to have to ride it out." Stu was serious and began to splutter his sincerity. Neil faced him, taking his shoulders in both hands. "Stu, the fact is, the Captain doesn't want you. He may not even want Jillybean. He might come back with an entirely different offer. We don't know."

"We do know," Jillybean said. "He wants me. If he has me he thinks he might get everything back, and more. He doesn't think anyone will follow Jenn and even if they did, he doesn't think she's the commander that I am."

"That's because she's not," Stu replied. "I love Jenn like a kid sister and I know better than anyone that she's not ready to lead this fight. It's why this whole idea is crazy."

Jillybean touched his arm for just a fleeting moment. "She won't be leading my armies. Captain Grey will be. He was a captain of rangers for the U. S. Army before any of this started. No one left alive knows more about tactics and strategy than he does."

Grey dipped his head at the compliment. "My only question is why do you want Jenn to lead? Why not Stu? Or better yet, why not the Guardian? No offense Stu, but Holt has leadership experience and, if he were king, he could get the Guardians on our side easy as pie."

"First," Jillybean said, cocking a thumb, "Troy would not take the position. Second, the Corsairs are even less likely to follow him than they will Jenn. In their eyes, he's way too goody-goody. Third, they think of Jenn as a worthy opponent. It was her white and gold flag that flew when they were suffering defeat after defeat in San Francisco. Fourth, they saw her die, and they'll see her escape from the Black Captain, unharmed. Do not underestimate the power that the mystical has on some people."

A pained look swept her features as she stuck out her pinky. "And finally, unlike me, Jenn will be a *good* queen. Her heart is always in the right place. You will never have to question her, Stu."

Just then Stu was embarrassed that he had ever questioned Jillybean in the first place. She had taken it on herself to fight the greatest evil in their little part of the world when no one else would. She had been willing to die from the very start, while he had been petty and immature, refusing to see the bigger picture even when she laid it out plain as day. Embarrassed, he couldn't look her in the eye.

She laughed suddenly. It was a free, happy laugh as if she were sitting in front of a fire on Christmas Eve, gazing at a stack of presents taller than herself. "Don't be sad, Stu. This is a good thing."

"How?"

"Because I'm free. My head is completely empty." With everyone watching, she pulled him down and kissed him on the lips. "It's good to be queen sometimes," she said, and then left, breezing out the door. Within two steps, she was barking orders. She called for the sailor who was best with a needle and thread. She yelled for Gerry the Greek, who was the acting quartermaster of the fleet. She bellowed Leney's name.

He came at a run as she ordered him to, "Get McCartt, Steinmeyer, and Lexi May over here. We have a lot to discuss and not much time."

Signals were run up the mast and forty minutes later, ten people were crowded into the Queen's cabin. Troy had been added at the last minute. Everyone cast nervous eyes at Captain Grey and Neil. The one was clearly a zombie and the other looked like he was a second from tearing someone's arm off. Jillybean made quick introductions and then dropped the bomb on the group concerning the change in leadership.

"You will listen to the new queen in all things," she ordered. "And, if you want to win this war, you'll listen to Captain Grey. He will lay out the plan of attack. Captain Grey."

"Hold on," Leney said, quickly, holding out his hands. "Let me get this straight. We're getting a new queen and she's going to have a zombie as an adviser and this *thing*," he gestured at Captain Grey, "is going to be second in charge? After all I've done for you, this is how things are going to be?"

Jillybean took his tattooed hands in her own and her smile for him was genuine. "Your part in this will not be forgotten. From the start, you were my staunchest supporter. I want you to have your choice of roles. The army will be divided into three battalions and the…"

"I want to be in command of the fleet," he said, before she could finish.

"I don't think the fleet will play as big a role in the coming action as our ground forces. It will be almost all resupply. It will be vital, just not sexy. Still if you want the position I'm fine with it. I only ask that you transfer your command to a different ship." She glanced at Stu. "I think Mike would love the *Queen's Revenge*."

Stu mumbled something that might have been a "yes." All he had heard were the words: *love her* and these spun in his head. It seemed everything was spinning and everything was moving way too fast for him. In no time, McCartt and Steinmeyer were assigned battalion commands, while Captain Grey kept control of the third.

"We'll be attacking as soon as humanly possible," Jillybean told them. "The Captain has got to be reeling in shock seeing his own fleet turned against him. He and his men will be demoralized, and when we land our troops so close to them, it'll add a great deal of fear to the mix." There was a second reason she wanted to hurry, she couldn't allow any mutinous elements within her ranks time to hatch their plots. Speed was vital.

Captain Grey had agreed. He wanted to land his forces west of Hoquiam under the cover of darkness and move them up as fast as possible. McCartt would engage directly from the west, Steinmeyer would hit them from the northwest, while Grey would swing around and come down from the northeast an hour later in the hope of catching their flank lightly defended as the Corsairs ran to defend the first two attacks.

Grey was supremely confident. "We'll hammer them with blows before they know what hit them, and crack their defense. The landing should commence as soon as we're done here."

This was a bit of a surprise to Jillybean. "You're going to begin this while I'm meeting with the Black Captain? Don't you think that's a little underhanded?"

"I guarantee that he's not waiting for you," Grey retorted. "He's maneuvering and so should we. Right now, minutes count more than men." When she still hesitated, he said, "Trust me, I won't attack until I know Emily is safe."

More than anyone, she knew the necessity of speed. Orders were given, more drones were sent up and in no time the entire fleet disappeared into the dark, leaving a quiet *Queen's Revenge* alone in the harbor. There were only seven people on board with Gerry acting as captain until Mike arrived.

Jillybean was the quietest of all. She stood at the bow, delving into every possible reaction the Black Captain could make. Stu wanted to go to her, to kiss her and hold her before it was too late, but he held back, really afraid for the first time in his life. His courage failed him and by the time he was able to take the first step toward her, Neil came stumbling up. "It's time," he said, pointing at the glittering watch on his grey-skinned wrist. He hugged her and whispered something into her ear. She nodded and went to the launch that waited.

Troy nudged Stu. "Are you coming? She asked for you." The dark hid his face as it went white. She wanted him to see her taken by the Black Captain? It felt horribly cruel to him. "She needs you to be strong," Troy said, before heading for the launch

Stu followed, his head held high. It was a small boat and his knees pressed against hers. His shook while hers were steady, making him wonder if he was actually there for her to calm him.

"It'll be okay," she whispered, catching his eye.

"I screwed up," he told her, his voice cracking.

"Maybe there'll be a time when you can make it up to me." She nudged his knee and smiled.

That time, if it ever came, would be far in the future. Already they were nearing the island. He wanted to stop. He wanted to paddle backwards. He wanted to come up with something to say that would make everything alright. Instead he stroked the oar until they ran up on the sand.

At least he could be a gentleman. He was out first and held his hand to her. She shook her head. "I don't want my boots to get wet. You're going to have to carry me." She was light and yet his heart thumped heavily.

Her smile disappeared when he set her down. "I'm a queen no longer. Troy, the flag." She held out her hand and the Guardian gave her the one she'd had put together: white with a gold crown. Troy then jogged forward to do his job, making sure that the Black Captain and his two men were unarmed.

She and Stu were frisked as well. "Whenever you're ready," the Corsair said, holding a lantern in her face. "Unless you want to back out that is. If you do, I get to rape the young one right on the beach."

"Take your childish threats somewhere else," Jillybean answered, coldly. Turning her head slightly, she whispered to Stu, "I will see you again." She squeezed his hand once and began walking to her fate. Despite claiming to no longer be a queen, she was more regal than ever. Stu didn't want to blink as the darkness surrounded her, held back only by the pale light of the lantern.

Shadows moved toward them. The light paused as the two groups came together. Jillybean knelt and gave the flag to the ghostly figure of Jenn Lockhart. There was no time for words. Almost as if the flag was the essence of her royalty and that giving it up made her once again a mere mortal, the Corsair grabbed Jillybean by the arm and dragged her roughly to her feet.

She was pulled away as Mike and Troy made empty threats. They could do nothing. Jillybean was now the property of the Black Captain.

Jenn came to Stu, holding the flag as if she were holding the still warm corpse of a beloved family pet. "She made me queen again. I-I don't want to be queen. Ever." Her eyes were haunted, as were Emily's. They clung to each other.

"You don't have a choice," Stu told her in his usual growl. "She may not be the only one who dies for your crown, so you better wear it."

Her young shoulders sagged as if the metaphorical crown had very real weight. "I'll be queen if we just get out of here," she said, looking back over her shoulder. "The signs, Stu. I know you don't believe in them, but they're filled with death. They are another thing I don't want."

This was even more alarming than their frightened faces. "Is it Jillybean who's in trouble?" Stu demanded.

"It's all of us."

Stu had no fear for himself; he could only think of Jillybean and was three steps in her direction when Mike Gunter grabbed him. "Don't! They warned us not to go back. He said they had snipers. I don't know if I believe it, but we can't take the chance."

The Captain did indeed have snipers. He whistled for them to return from their hiding places as Jillybean approached. He bowed from the shoulders. "Your Highness." The Captain was so velvety black that the light from the lantern seemed to slide right off him. All she really saw of him were his mocking eyes.

"I'm a queen no longer," Jillybean replied, as she had earlier.

"It's true," one of his men said. "There was a little ceremony, and some kneeling. I'm not going to lie, I shed a tear." He laughed a little too loudly, as did some of the snipers.

Jillybean gazed around her at the men. "You missed your chance, you could've taken all of us. Unlike you, Corsair, we actually came unarmed, like we had decided."

He shrugged as if he didn't care. "I'm not too worried," the Captain said, smoothly. "That boat will never get out of the harbor, and even if it does," he flicked a hand, "That idiot girl queen would likely be more valuable to me out there where their mistake will multiply and cascade, until in the end, they will die from the very avalanche they started. But I do wish I could see their faces when I spring my first surprise. If we hurry, we might get a front row seat."

Icy fingers gripped Jillybean's heart as they entered a small, short-masted skiff. The cold grip grew painful when the Captain's men began to paddle further out into the harbor, heading in the direction where Grey's battalions were being off-loaded. By her calculation, they should have been close to being done.

"If you'd sown mines they would've..."

The Captain laughed at her. "Don't bother trying to guess what I've planned. If you could have, you would never have come."

As the Corsairs steered toward her fleet, Jillybean couldn't help herself and ran through every possible military situation that could have the Captain so confident. He certainly didn't have soldiers hidden along the empty hills; her drones would have picked up their heat signatures. The same was true of zombies. And there wasn't any scarring of the land that suggested there were hidden defensive works in Grey's rear. And there wasn't...

A radio crackled to life. "The boats are light. We are in the clear. Say again, the boats are light. We are in the clear." She knew the voice —it was Leney. Her mouth popped open in surprise.

The Black Captain had been watching for exactly that look. He threw back his head and let out a booming laugh. "You should see yourself! It's so precious. I don't know if I have ever seen anyone look so surprised. You know what, though? There are going to be a whole mess of people wearing that same look in about ten seconds."

He picked up the radio. "Light 'em up Leney."

Jillybean expected gunfire, instead a hundred boats were suddenly lit by lanterns, and in the flickering light she could see her silver crown slide down from as many masts. In its place was the Corsair standard, a square patch of black flapping in the wind.

"Your friends, McCartt and Steinmeyer and all those stupid Santas, have just been left high and dry. There'll be no resupply, no more ammo, no more food, no more nothing. And you want to know what's worse than being stranded behind enemy lines?" Jillybean refused to answer even though she knew a few things that were worse.

The Captain didn't wait long to answer his own question. "It's being stranded behind enemy lines and surrounded by zombies. And they'll have you to thank for that. It was a neat trick when you pulled it on me and I've been waiting for just the right time to return the favor."

He clicked the radio. "Let's get those flares going, Sticky Jim. Make 'em go real high. We don't want any of our zombie friends to miss out on the banquet."

A second later a shrill scream ripped through the night as a flare raced high into the sky. In its light, the Black Captain looked like a demon. His eyes were golden and terrifying. "I believe that's checkmate, Jillybean."

***

The End

Author's Note:

Before you ask, yes the Generation Z story continues! Luckily, there is a way for you to read Book 5, chapter by chapter, before anyone else! All you have to do is go to my Patreon page (**Here**) and support my writing. The tier levels are exceedingly generous with freebies running from autographed books, video podcasts, free Audible books, signed T-shirts, and swag of all sorts. At a high enough tier you will even get to meet me in person as I take you and three friends out to dinner.

Patreon a great way to help support me so I don't have to go back into the coal mines…back into the dark.

Another way is to write a review of this book on Amazon and/or on your own Facebook page. The review is the most practical and inexpensive form of advertisement an independent author has available to get his work known. I would greatly appreciate it.

Now, that you've gone to my Patreon page and left your review— thank you very much—I would love for you to take a look at another series of mine: **The Apocalypse Crusade**:

Forget what you think you know about zombies…

Forget the poorly acted movies and the comic books. Forget the endless debates over fast and slow walkers. From this day on, all that crap will fade away to nothing. America is on the precipice of hell and not for a moment do you believe it. You have your cable and your smartphone and your take-out twice a week and your vacation to Disney Land all planned, and you tell yourself you'll drop those ten pounds before you go.

But you aren't going anywhere.

In one horrible day your world collapses into nothing but a spitting, cursing, bleeding fight for survival. For some the descent into hell is a long, slow, painful process of going at it tooth and nail, while for others it's over in a scream that's choked off when the blood pours down their windpipe. Those are the lucky ones.

But you will live, somehow, and you'll remember day one of the apocalypse where there was a chance, in fact there were plenty of chances for someone to stop it in its tracks and you'll wonder why the hell nobody did anything.

At first light on that first morning, Dr. Lee steps into the Walton facility on the initial day of human trials for the cure she's devoted her life to; she can barely contain her excitement. The labs are brand spanking new and everything is sharp and clean. They've been built to her specifications and are, without a doubt, a scientist's dream. Yet even better than the gleaming instruments is the fact that Walton is where cancer is going to be cured once and for all. It's where Dr. Lee is going to become world famous...only she doesn't realize what she's going to be famous for.

By midnight of that first day, Walton is a place of fire, of blood and of death, a death that, like the Apocalypse, is just the beginning.

What readers say about The Apocalypse Crusades:
"DO NOT pick this up until you are ready to commit to an all-night sleep-defying read!"
"WAY OUT WICKED"
"...full of suspense and intrigue, love, both innocent and romantic, hate, both blinding and unnatural, non-stop action, and a very real gripping and palpable fear." Peter Meredith

PS If you are interested in autographed copies of my books, souvenir posters of the covers, Apocalypse T-shirts and other awesome Swag, please visit my website at **https://www.petemeredith1.com**

PPS: PS If you are interested in autographed copies of my books, souvenir posters of the covers, Apocalypse T-shirts and other awesome Swag, please visit my website at https://www.petemeredith1.com

PPS: I need to thank a number of people for their help in bringing you this book. My beta readers Greg Bennett, Joanna Niederer, Eric Gothier, Paul Clay, Jeanette McGaha, Connie Nealy, Ezben Gerardo, Jenn Lockhart, Nancy Spedding, Fi Findlater, Kariann Morgan, Roy Bost, Kari-Lyn Rakestraw, Doni Battenburg, Marinda Grindstaff, Brenda Nord, Monica Turner, S.D. Buhl, Michelle Heeder, Charles McClure, Cathie Mantell, Corrina Troost, Michelle Stewart, Brenda Rummer, William McClean, Cody Mann, Carla Keller Walker, Gemma Louise, Jo Kappel, Virginia Keim —Thanks so much!

Fictional works by Peter Meredith:

A Perfect America
Infinite Reality: Daggerland Online Novel 1
Infinite Assassins: Daggerland Online Novel 2
Generation Z
Generation Z: The Queen of the Dead
Generation Z: The Queen of War
Generation Z: The Queen Unthroned
The Sacrificial Daughter
The Apocalypse Crusade War of the Undead: Day One
The Apocalypse Crusade War of the Undead: Day Two
The Apocalypse Crusade War of the Undead Day Three
The Apocalypse Crusade War of the Undead Day Four
The Horror of the Shade: Trilogy of the Void 1
An Illusion of Hell: Trilogy of the Void 2
Hell Blade: Trilogy of the Void 3
The Punished
Sprite
The Blood Lure The Hidden Land Novel 1
The King's Trap The Hidden Land Novel 2
To Ensnare a Queen The Hidden Land Novel 3
The Apocalypse: The Undead World Novel 1
The Apocalypse Survivors: The Undead World Novel 2
The Apocalypse Outcasts: The Undead World Novel 3
The Apocalypse Fugitives: The Undead World Novel 4
The Apocalypse Renegades: The Undead World Novel 5
The Apocalypse Exile: The Undead World Novel 6
The Apocalypse War: The Undead World Novel 7
The Apocalypse Executioner: The Undead World Novel 8
The Apocalypse Revenge: The Undead World Novel 9
The Apocalypse Sacrifice: The Undead World 10
The Edge of Hell: Gods of the Undead Book One
The Edge of Temptation: Gods of the Undead Book Two
The Witch: Jillybean in the Undead World
Jillybean's First Adventure: An Undead World Expansion
Tales from the Butcher's Block

Printed in Great Britain
by Amazon